Controlling COSETTE

My Beautiful Suicide
Book Two

ATTY EVE

CONTROLLING COSETTE: My Beautiful Suicide, Book Two

Copyright © 2014 by Atty Eve

All rights reserved. No part of this book may be reproduced in any form or by any electronic or mechanical means, including information storage and retrieval systems, without permission from the publisher, except by a reviewer, who may quote passages in the review. Please purchase only authorized electronic editions through authorized dealers. Do not participate in electronic piracy of copyrighted material at any time. Your support of the author's rights is truly appreciated.

ISBN-10: 1942366000

ISBN-13: 978-1-942366-00-3

eISBN-13: 978-1-942366-01-0

Cover design by LLPix Designs.

Cover Photograph © Mike Metzing at Pictured Events

Spikenard Publishing
Jeffersonville, IN 47130

This book is dedicated to Mike,
my husband and best friend.
Thank you for putting up with me.

Controlling COSETTE

AT WHAT POINT does true fear begin?

Is it that moment when a little voice in your head whispers, "Run away?"

Is it the moment you realize you should have listened to that voice?

Or is it the moment you know it doesn't matter, that you're dead either way?

For me, I thought my fear was Hilda, my bully. Every time she came around, my stomach turned. When I accidentally killed her rapist, my fear turned from her to not getting caught.

I didn't discover true fear until I saw who I had become after my eighth murder, when the prospect of a ninth and tenth became exciting to me. My true fear happened the moment I knew I was off; I felt no remorse, but only pleasure from creating a victim. I didn't want to be like this, but I knew it was a part of me. I let this monster inside take over. I let her get carried away.

My best friend Mattie doesn't know. I don't know what scares me more: her finding out, or me not being able to control myself around her. She is pure and perfect.

I didn't want to look her in the eyes. My shame and guilt were too much for me. I couldn't live with it, nor could I numb myself to it. With each death, the darkness grew.

WHEN DID MATTIE'S fear start? She is so scared now.

Was she scared after my first murder when she felt something was wrong with me? Or just now, when she found me in the alley shot by the Poser?

Her hands are shaking. I wish I could comfort her. She shouldn't be afraid for me.

I'm not afraid. I know where I'm going. I know it will be horrible, but I'm too afraid to stay.

I hate seeing Mattie cry like this. She's trying to be strong as we ride to the hospital. The EMTs keep asking her to let go so they can work on me.

It feels good to me, the pain. I want to let go, but Mattie won't let me. She's been praying hard and crying and babbling something. I'm a little foggy at what's going on.

I'm mad at Chris, my boyfriend, the Poser. Not for shooting me but for not finishing the job. He didn't aim right.

"PLEASE, COSETTE! STAY with me. I can't lose you. Don't you leave me! You fight!" Mattie is crying, fumbling with my hands.

I don't want to fight, Mattie. Why should I? There is no reason the earth should want me to stay.

There are only three people that want me here: Mattie, Mom, and Chris. But they'd be better off without me. They just don't realize it yet. If after I'm gone Mattie and my mom find out about the eight people I killed, they'll realize that my death was a good thing, for everyone.

THE AMBULANCE STOPS, and they lug me out. My mom comes out of the hospital screaming for me.

I know it hurts now, Mom, but it will be better in a little while. You'll see.

"Ma'am, you have to stay back!" The EMTs push her aside.

"Come on, we'll wait out here." Mattie calms my mother. I'm glad they're not allowing Mom to work on me. She would do everything she could to keep me here.

They wheel me into a room and start to cut me open. I feel the drugs kicking in which is a shame. If I have to go through this, I would like to feel every cut. I hope they can't reach the bullet. I would hate for them to trace it back to Chris.

I wonder what he's doing now. It's hard to think about him with all this commotion. I hope he's careful with Hilda.

Poor girl. She should have kept her mouth shut. I wonder how long he will keep her alive.

I wonder when her fear began.

Chapter ONE

"...OPERATION WENT WELL. It was a clean shot, but we still need to exercise some caution. She's stable for now, but as you know, the next twenty-four hours are crucial. I expect she'll be out if it for a while."

My doctor's voice is soft and calming. I recognize it as belonging to a woman I've met at several hospital events. Unfortunately, she's a woman whose intellect is overshadowed by her cuteness.

"Thank you, Dr. Wigham. Thank you." My mom's quivering voice is muffled, probably in a hug.

A puff of cool air enters with the squeak of a door. "Did they say she'll be okay?" Mattie's cold hands wrap around mine.

"Ask me in twenty-four hours," Mom says.

"COSETTE," A DEEP voice with a Haitian accent calls to me. I'm tired. I'm drugged. And I think I'm hallucinating.

"Cosette come walk with me." A thin, dark-skinned hand reaches over and lifts me out of bed. The Haitian is warm and small framed. He's dressed in a linen white shirt and linen white pants. Crisp, clean.

I hold hands with him as he guides me out of my hospital room. I turn back to watch my mom stroke my hair while Mattie squeezes my hand, praying. Can't they feel I've left? How come the monitors aren't flatlining?

"They aren't flatlining because you're not dead." He stops and turns to me. "Cosette, I don't need you here, yet. There is more work for you to do there."

"I don't know who you are, but there is nothing left on Earth that I want to do."

"You know who I am. I am the one keeping them away from you." He shifts to the side so I can see my victims trying to claw their way out of a fiery pit to get to me.

"They want to hurt you, Cosette. The pain they will inflict on you will make them feel better. But pain doesn't bother you, does it? Where is your fear, Cosette?"

"If I had any, I don't think I would be here with you." I know who he is. He's not as ugly as I expected. I'm surprised. He's kind of a weasely little guy, and there's no pitchfork or horns or anything.

"Down here, I can hear your thoughts, Cosette."

"Sorry. I didn't mean to be rude. What do you want with me? Why can't I stay?"

"It's not up to me. You aren't going to die from this. Even if you were close to dying, with her around there's nothing I can do." He points to Mattie. "And her help is coming. I can't go against them. When you wake up, I want you to continue being yourself. Don't hold back. If you do what you want there, I will protect you when you get here."

The flames behind him crackle. He clears his throat and thick bars slam down, caging my victims in the pit. Chris's Uncle Pen and cousin Dickey, the husband and wife drug-addicted child abusers, two pimps, and one left-handed pedophile — all growl and stretch through the bars toward me.

I stare at them for a moment. I put them here. To see them again stirs up something in me, but it isn't fear.

Mattie is frantically praying as her pastor walks in. He's a confident man. He touches her shoulder and tells her and my mom not to say a word. Then he places his hand on my gunshot wound.

My dark host cringes and disappears. I think he's scared of Mattie's pastor. I don't blame him. I am too.

As the cage and flames fade into the hospital hallway, I feel myself being pulled back to the bed.

"No, please leave." I try to talk to the pastor, but no sound is coming out. I can't open my eyes or feel my body. I just have to lay there and listen to them.

Mattie's cell phone rings. "Chris! Thank God! I'll be right down to get you."

"I'll go get him, Mattie. You stay with Pastor Sam." My mom leaves believing the pastor and Mattie are doing some good by praying over me. I guess it's working. I am alive. I will live, for now.

Pastor Sam leans in to whisper in my ear. "I know who you think you are, but that's not you. You have been lied to. You need to come back. God has given you a second chance. We are here for you, Cosette. Just come on back. We will help you. We are here for you."

I'm back. I'm not happy about it, but yes, I am here.

I won't stop. The second I feel better I will find a way to have an accident.

I will end it, again.

Chapter TWO

"COZY, COZY, IT'S me, Chris. Please wake up. I'm so sorry. I couldn't do it. I couldn't let you go. Please, baby, please wake up for me. If it will make you feel better, I didn't hurt her. I still have Hilda. She's waiting for you. I'm keeping her as a gift for you."

We must be alone. There is no way he would say that with anyone else in earshot.

"It's been two days. The doctors say there is no reason why you shouldn't be awake. But I know. I know why you won't wake up. Please, baby. I promise we will stop. I promise I will help you, and you can help me be good. Just come back to me. I will do anything you ask. I will deny you nothing. Please, just come back to me." His voice is shaky. He's been crying.

I've been crying too. I don't want to look him in the eyes. I have so much shame and guilt. No one knows what I feel like nor do they have a clue. Chris doesn't feel remorse like I do, or does he?

Is that why he's saving Hilda? Could he not kill her? Or is he saving her so we can do it together? I can't go there.

I know my Haitian host said I should do what I want when I get back here. But the second Mattie's pastor came, he had to leave. He also said that Mattie had control, not him. How can he keep my victims from getting to me if he doesn't even have control? If Mattie has control, then why should I listen to him? I know who I want to be, and Bonnie is not it!

If Chris doesn't agree to that then I can't be with him.

My heart is breaking.

My eyes are opening.

"Cosette! Cosette!" Chris frantically kisses me. It's good to feel his lips. I guess they took the tubes out. I seal my lips, can't imagine what my breath smells like.

"Water." Is that all I can say? I guess I'm so thirsty my instincts are taking over.

"Water. Yes, honey. Here." He quickly spoon-feeds me some crushed ice to suck on. "I love you so much, please don't hate me. I couldn't do it. I couldn't lose you. You are my whole world, and I have been here waiting for you. Please don't be mad."

He sounds so desperate. How can I be mad? If it were the other way around, I would've done the same.

I hold his hand and pull him towards my whisper. "Hilda?"

"She's alive and well. I have her locked up though. I'm keeping her warm and fed. She thinks it's her third attacker that has her captive. Which it is, but she doesn't know it's me."

I twitch my nose. He stinks.

"I am so sorry, Cozy. I had to take up smoking, just for a few days for Hilda's sake."

I don't understand.

"With her super sense of smell, I couldn't take a chance. Do you want me to call your mom or Mattie? Your mom had to go home to shower, and Mattie's bringing you food in case you wake up. They have been here nonstop. So have John and Decker and Rosy and the sisters. They have been rotating watching you. Then they help search for Hilda. There's a huge manhunt for her."

"And?"

"I'm still working on it. I haven't done anything. I couldn't hurt her. I couldn't do anything without you."

I start crying. "No. I can't be her. No Bonnie."

"Okay, honey. I know." He strokes my hair. "I'll figure out how we can get out of this. It'll come, but for now, Hilda's safe. I couldn't touch her. All I could think about was you. I won't ask Bonnie back if it means you'll want to leave me again."

"No Bonnie."

"Okay, honey. No Bonnie." He kisses me softly on the forehead. It's the most wonderful, loving kiss he has given me. Maybe we can be a normal couple.

"Excuse me." Sierra and Shelby's dad, the chief of police, knocks on my door. He's accompanied by some stiff in a suit.

Chris leans in and whispers, "They have no leads. You don't remember anything."

"May we come in? I just want to ask a few questions." Chief Rickert stands at the foot of my bed. The stiff pulls up a chair then sits and crosses his legs.

"I'll go call your mom." Chris kisses my cheek and leaves.

"Hi. I can't talk." I tell them.

"I understand. When they put those tubes in, they can do a number on you afterwards. First of all, how are you feeling?" The chief is kind.

"I'm okay. I don't feel anything actually."

"I think it's the drugs. And from what the doctors have told us, you were shot in the best place possible. The bullet didn't hit any major organs."

I smile. Mad. But I smile.

"Do you remember anything from that night?"

"No. I don't even remember leaving school. What's today?"

"It's Sunday. The doctors think the shock put you in a comatose type of state for about two days. Your physical wounds are not that bad, but they think that whatever you saw made you shut down. We need to find out what you saw, but we don't want to scare you. I can have someone talk you through this if you're too scared to remember," Chief says.

"I don't think I can remember."

"I don't want to push you, but we have a girl missing, and we think the guy who shot you took her," the stiff says.

I look at him, confused. I have to play this off, at least until my mom shows up.

"This is Agent White from the FBI here to investigate the Poser murders." Chief introduces the stiff. "The missing girl is Hilda. She called your friend Mattie and said she wanted to meet her at Three J's Café, but she never showed up. When Matilda heard the gunshot, she came running out and found you bleeding in an alley. A few strands of Hilda's hair were found in that same alley. Did you see something? Did you catch someone attacking her? And that's why they shot you?"

I start crying. I can't help it. Both nights are running together; the first night when I killed Hilda's rapist and the last time when he killed me. Or faked killing me. All the emotion is coming out. I can't stop it. I can't stop crying. How do I hold this in? How can I protect Chris?

"It's okay. Just tell us everything you remember. Any little detail counts."

"I can't remember. All I know is I was scared. I am so scared!" Those are the only words I can choke out. My throat is dry and swelling up, and I'm sobbing. I can't breathe. The nurses run in and ask him to leave. They quickly put a mask on me, and I'm out.

THERE'S A FUNNY smell in my room. It's a mix between latex, rice croquettes, and Mike's mac-n-cheese. I think this is heaven.

"She's smiling!" Lucy yells.

"I knew this smell would get her. Wake up! It's Mattie and Lucy. We come bearing gifts."

Mattie's sitting next to my bed, holding under my nose a bowl of barbeque, bacon-wrapped shrimp, layered on a bowl of mac-n-cheese. Her mom, Lucy, is on the other side of my bed with the rice croquettes. Rose and Decker are holding a huge bouquet of balloons.

"Your mom said you should be getting out of here tomorrow. We scheduled shifts for watching you at home. I asked my boss, and she said it was okay. Here, ya hungry?" Mattie shoves a forkful of shrimp in my face.

"Starving." I didn't realize how hungry I was until I smelled that. I gladly accept the gift. Not sure what I've been eating these last few days since all of them seem to blur together. "Am I okay to eat this?" I mumble with a mouthful.

Lucy holds my hand. "The doctors think you were okay a while ago. So, yes, go ahead and eat it. They think the trauma has been preventing you from staying awake. We've been here visiting you, and you would start talking to us then just pass out."

"You do tell some wild tales." Decker bats a balloon out of his way. "I'm not sure your mind knew what was dream and what was real."

My blood runs colds. What did I say? What was I talking about when I was half dreaming, and who heard what?

"Just ask Chris." Mattie spoon-feeds me. "He heard it all. He's been here almost 24/7."

That's a relief. He can tell me and make an excuse if I said anything too revealing.

"We said he needed to take a break. He had to go home to tie up some loose ends." Decker gives me a sly smirk.

Chris must've told Decker about Hilda, and Decker is covering. Shit, I can't breathe again. My heart is racing.

"Whoa, Cozy. Settle down. Breathe in through your nose. Relax. We just came in to check on you." Lucy pats my hand.

Is this what happens? I get lightheaded when the guilt comes, and I just pass out?

She adjusts the tubes under my nose. I sniff in the oxygen, blink my eyes, and try to sit up.

"Here, let me help you." Rose comes and fluffs my pillows.

"Thanks, Rose. I think I stink. I haven't taken a bath in a few days, huh? Do I stink?"

"That's what you are worried about? How you smell?" Rose giggles.

"I think you are offending no one here. We can handle any odor you give off." Mattie shakes her head as she spoons me another bite.

Decker blurts out while reading his phone, "They're tweeting about you but not giving out your name or anything. I guess in case the killer comes back."

"Decker!" Rose slaps him.

"What? It's true. He might find her." Decker grabs the TV remote and turns on the news.

"...CAFÉ OWNERS AND other downtown businesses have opened their doors to help the search party. The second shift of..." The news reporter Cheryl Lockerby stands in a crowd of police and civilians in Three J's parking lot, the headquarters for the search.

"Turn it off!" Rose pulls the TV plug. "She doesn't need to see that. Don't worry about her, Cozy. You take care of yourself." She comes and rests next to me and strokes my hair, keeping me calm.

"It's okay, Rose. I'm safe in here." I know the killer won't hurt me. He didn't do it right the first time. "Mattie, you all are hosting the search party?"

"Yes, we have the room and had to do something," Lucy answers.

"I think it's great." I can feel my eyes growing puffy, and I know I'm about to break down and cry.

"Cozy needs her rest." Mattie places the mac-n-cheese on the tray in front of me. "We'll check up on you in the morning. Let's get out of here."

"Don't forget we're praying for you. God brought you back to us for a reason. We just have to find out what that reason is. So gather around. Let's pray before we leave so Cozy can get her rest." Lucy stands and grabs Mattie's and Rose's hands.

They all surround me and I feel strangely warm. Lucy says a wonderful prayer, though I don't understand any of it. I say goodnight and they all leave. Hopefully, tomorrow I can leave too.

Chapter THREE

"HERE, HONEY, LET'S put you here." My mom has the living room arranged for me to watch TV all day. "I have a lap desk for you for when Mattie brings home Friday's and today's homework. And here are all the TV remotes, and I have a basket with snacks, and there's a basket in the bathroom for when we have to change your bandages and..." she stops to catch her breath but breaks down and sobs. "I am so happy to have you home. I couldn't survive without you! You are my life! I love you so much."

"Mom, it's okay. I'm safe." I lie down.

"I have never felt so scared, so alone, than when you were in the hospital. Do you realize you could have died? Mattie and Lucy and Mike were praying hard for you. You are proof prayer works. I am so glad to have you. I will always keep you safe. I will do whatever it takes to protect you." She hugs me tight, almost choking me, but I say nothing. I don't want to ruin the moment.

"I'll be okay, Mom. I'm safe." How could I leave her? How selfish! How sickening and selfish. "I'm sorry I scared you."

That makes her cry more. We are a mess. Our long stringy hair mats to our face because of the tears. Her makeup is running and her eyes are bloodshot. "Mom, don't cry. You have to go back to work, don't you? Don't worry. I will be right here waiting for you when you get back. Chris is supposed to come by after school, right?"

"No, Mattie's first on the schedule." She sniffles and wipes her eyes. "And Chief Rickert is gonna be here in a few minutes to ask you some questions. And I told Monty to keep an eye out for you while I'm gone."

"I have no idea who Monty is."

"Our next door neighbor, the guy who works at Target. Red shirt? Yappy dog? Anyway, he'll keep his eyes open, but we have your care planned out for the rest of the week. I called the school, and they're not expecting you in till next Monday. And even then we have help for you."

"Is that what it takes? I need to get shot to skip school? Why didn't I think of this before?" I snicker.

"Don't joke like that."

"Mom, I'm fine. Go to work."

She wipes her face and tries to clean up her mascara.

I shake my head. "Don't bother. You'll cry it all off by the time you get to work."

She nods. "Do you want anything else? Water? Coffee?"

"No, thanks. I should be getting this stuff myself though, right?"

"Yes, but not without someone here. I don't want you falling or hurting yourself." A rumble in the driveway cues my mom to open the front door. "The chief is here."

He takes off his hat as he crosses the threshold.

"Hi, Chief. Welcome to my cave." I pull the coffee table close for him to sit.

He wags his finger at me for doing any manual labor. "You look like you're doing much better." He sits. "Nice comfortable setup you have going on here. I might have to kick off my shoes and join you." He chuckles deep. It's fitting for his height. "If you don't mind me sitting here with you, I'd like to ask a few questions."

"Shoot."

He and my mom look at me crooked. "Sorry, just a little gun humor. Go ahead and ask."

"At least you can be happy. That's great to see." He leans in a bit closer. "Now, when Mattie found you, you had a knife."

And with that, the happiness leaves. I start stammering. "I, uh. I go jogging a lot, every day."

My mom finishes answering for me. "Chris told me he gave it to her for protection. I guess it didn't help in this case."

"Actually, I think it did," chief Rickert assures her. "I think this might have been worse had Cosette not been ready. I also heard that you attended the self-defense class with Shelby and Sierra?"

"Yes, sir." I look down.

"You have nothing to be ashamed about." He scoots forward and grabs my hand. "Cosette, you survived an attack by one of the worst predators we have ever had in this area. You should be proud."

"I can't, sir. Hilda didn't survive."

"We don't know that yet. Please tell me what you remember. And here, I think you will need this back." He hands me Blue. It feels so good to hold my knife again.

I put it on the lap desk and adjust my couch pillows. Mom dives in to help.

"I was going on a run. I was training for the Kentucky Derby Marathon when I heard a noise. It was a muffled, whimper? I think. I don't remember too much. I took my knife out and ran into the alley. It was hard to see."

I lean forward and squint at my mom, who has over-adjusted my pillows. She understands and apologetically flattens them back down.

"Just tell me what you can," Chief asks.

"He was standing on her hair. I think I surprised him when he saw me. I held out the knife and I just remember a pain in my stomach. There are a few more images, but they're blurry. Then I woke up in the hospital." I clench my blanket, scared that I'm not believable. "It's just too foggy right now."

"I'm sure you will remember more later. I want to let you know how lucky you are. If you feel like you need protection, we can have a car watch you."

"No, please keep them looking for Hilda. I'm fine." I readjust my demeanor, remembering that I'm a shooting victim. I pretend to be scared. "Why the protection? Do you think he knows who I am?"

"No, I think you will be safe. No information has gone public." He stands up. "If you remember anything, even if it's at three in the morning, then please let me know." He gives me his card. My mom takes one too, thanks him, and escorts him out.

"Okay, honey, I'm going to get to work." She pulls out her phone. I hear it vibrating in her hand. "It's Chris texting me. He said he'll be here about an hour after Mattie leaves. He said he has to feed his pet. What's that about? Why are you laughing?"

It shouldn't be funny, but it is. I hope he feeds Hilda well. She's already going through hell.

"Chris's uncle left him some animals to care for. I'll be fine, but, Mom, can you hand me that notebook? I want it ready to write down stuff if I remember."

She hands me a notebook and a pen and kisses my head.

"Ewwww, Mom, don't kiss my nappy hair. I need a real bath."

"I will bathe you when I get home," she says as she puts on her coat.

"Mmmm, my mom bathing me. That sounds appealing."

"I'll wash your hair in the sink, and the rest will be up to you. I already trained Mattie and Chris to dress your wound. It needs to drain, and you need to stay on your antibiotics. I'll text you when it's time."

"Thanks, Mom!" I yell as she walks out the front door.

She pops the door back open. "Wait until someone comes before you move too much. You need to keep walking to build up your strength, but you need someone here."

"I'll be fine, Mom. Love you!" I yell as she closes the door and locks the deadbolt.

SILENCE ENGULFS ME and I suddenly feel empty and alone. "I'm sorry, Victor." I look up. "I tried to see you, but I didn't make it. From what my dark host said though, it looks like I'll be on Dad's end. I should have known that Heaven was not going to welcome me with open arms."

I pause a few seconds waiting for Victor to disagree. He doesn't.

"There's got to be a way to get there for me. I don't want to leave Mom or Chris or Mattie. I won't let them hurt like that. But if I change, like really change, do I have a chance to get in? Isn't God supposed to forgive and forget? Does He even care?"

My phone buzzes, startling me. It's Mattie texting with the answer to my question. So creepy when she does that.

Hey, Coz. Just praying for you. I hope you're doing well. I'll be there this afternoon with Bible in hand. We're going to help you through this. Remember, you'll never be alone. God loves you and will take care of you. Get some rest.

I text back.

I was resting until someone buzzed me. JK. Love ya. See you soon.

I turn on the TV and find the religious channel. It makes me feel closer to Mattie, and I need her. Most of this stuff I don't get. It seems so unnatural to me, but maybe I just don't understand them. Mattie I understand. She's driven to make the world a better place. She knows what she wants and she works hard for it. Her whole life's mapped out on how she's gonna make a change, a difference. Her life is going to be significant. It's enthralling and I want that. I want to make a change. So far, the only change I've made is...

I'm not gonna think about it. I turn up the volume on some sweaty, yelling preacher. He's passionate and so is his congregation. Wish I could feel what they're feeling but I can't, just like they can't feel the hunger I'm suppressing. My evil side, Bonnie, is prepared to fight. I shoo her deep inside and keep on watching the TV. Fake it till you make it, right?

Chapter FOUR

"HEY, COZY, I'M home!" Mattie startles me awake with her best *I-Love-Lucy* accent.

"Cute." I slowly sit up. "I'm glad you're here. I need help getting to the bathroom. The drugs are kicking in, and I'm dizzy. I hate this feeling."

Mattie escorts me to the bathroom. She takes a step then pauses, takes another step then pauses. She starts humming the wedding march and waits for me to get it.

"I'm grateful for you taking it slow, but you're an idiot."

"Yeah, but I'm fun to be with. Now you may be my best friend and all, but please don't ask me to clean you up. I will if I have to, but I do have limits."

"Gross. I'm not that dizzy. I think I'll be fine. I do need to brush my teeth though. No kissing this yuck mouth."

"I wasn't planning on it, but okay. Thanks."

"Aww, sorry." I grab her face and peck her lips. "These kisses are saved for Chris. But if you want a bigger one, I'm sure Shelby's dad can schedule a jailhouse visit with your favorite assistant principal, Mr. Jarvis."

"Funny. But true. I would make out with him anywhere. Be

careful in there. Scream if you need me."

"If I'm not out in ten minutes come in and rescue me." I close the door.

"Cosette, are you watching the religious channel?" Mattie yells.

I can't answer with a mouth full of minty foam, so I grunt 'yes'.

"I have a few shows I watch all the time. I'm setting your DVR to record them. If you have questions, you know I'll be thrilled to help!"

I swing open the bathroom door and suck in through my teeth. "Fresh!"

"You couldn't have kissed me after your teeth were brushed?" Mattie helps walk me back to the couch.

"No, sorry. I said they were saved for Chris."

She carefully lays me on the couch. There's an uncomfortable silence between us. Her eyes are starting to water, and her nose is turning red.

"Mattie, don't cry. Why are you crying?" I turn off the TV.

"I lost you. I lost you, Cosette. You were gone. I didn't think I would ever get you back." She's shaking and looks so scared.

How could I leave? This is like visiting your own funeral. You never know how much people love you until you're gone.

I am so selfish. Even trying to spare my mom and Mattie grief by becoming a victim was still a selfish way to go. I need to suck it up and grow up. I need to stop feeling sorry for myself and just deal with the consequences if I'm ever found out.

"I'm here, Mattie. I won't leave you. You brought me back."

"No. God brought you back. I just begged Him to." She has the box of tissues between us, and we're going through them fast. "I'm not going to the Air Force Academy. I can't. I can't leave you knowing the guy who almost killed you is still out there."

"What? No! You can't!" I sit up fast and grab her. "You've worked so hard for that. That's not fair to you. I'm so proud of you. You're my bragging point."

"I can't leave you. I'm too scared. I just want to hold you and never let you out of my sight. When I heard the gunshot in the alley, I knew. My soul felt like it was being ripped out of me. I just knew it was you. Something told me to run out to meet Hilda and walk her back to the café. I thought it was for her protection. Then when I heard the shot, I knew who I was running to save." I hold her in my arms as we cry on each other's shoulder. It hurts crying this hard, but the release is needed. "I can't ever lose you, Cozy. I can't ever lose you."

"Mattie, help." I pull back, lift my shirt, and look at my bandage. It isn't bleeding, but it isn't dry.

"Oh, I am so sorry. I didn't mean to..." She frantically looks for something to clean me up.

"I'm fine. It's just a little pus. I know it's gross, but help me change it."

"Alright, lift your shirt." She gingerly tugs on the bandage. "Am I hurting you? I'm so sorry."

"Can I confess something to you?"

"Sure, confess away."

"I like the pain," I tell her. It doesn't register. I just let it simmer for a while. She blots the wound dry then tapes me up.

"Almost done, and there. Good as new. Now, uh, what?"

I pull my shirt down and sit back.

"Did you just say you liked the pain? Did I hear that right? You know that's not normal. Normal people don't get shot and say they liked it. Is that why you smiled in the ambulance? That's not normal, Cosette."

"You think I'm a freak, don't you?"

"There are other reasons I think you're a freak. This is just the icing on the cake."

"You think I'm a freak."

"I think you have issues. No, I know you have issues. I was expecting to hear a confession today, but I didn't think this was it."

"Confession? What confession?"

She holds my hand. "Do you trust me?"

"With my life," I answer quickly.

"Do you trust that I can keep a secret?"

"Why are you asking me this, Mattie?"

Her eyes dart back and forth across the floor. She's calculating her words. "Cosette, I know."

I stare at her for a second. She stares into my eyes, not letting me go. What is it that she knows?

I don't know what to do. Do I play dumb and lie to her again? I trust her only because she is so perfect. But perfect people do the right thing. And the right thing in this case would be to turn me over to the police.

I AM TIRED of not breathing.

I am tired of feeling like my freedom is constantly being threatened. Do I confess and pray that she will go against everything she believes in? How can I put her in that position? How can I expect her to choose to protect a friend, or to do what is right? This is where I never wanted to be.

I blink my tears out. "For the sake of our friendship, I am going to act like you didn't say anything. You can do what you want with the information you have. I won't blame you for anything. I cannot... I will not, say anything."

She bites her lip and thinks. Her eyes dart to the floor again. She squeezes my hand and looks at me. "Do you remember a few months ago I had an aunt who cheated on her boyfriend?"

"Yeah?"

"I was the only one who saw it. I didn't tell her boyfriend. I helped her and talked to her until she felt strong enough to confess to him. She was so sorry, and he forgave her because *she* confessed. It would have turned out horrible if I was a tattletale. Do you remember? Do you understand?"

I understand.

My eyes are gushing and my swelling throat keeps me from saying a word.

"Coz, I know you're going through a horrible time. Maybe not physically since you seem to enjoy that," she jokes, "but emotionally. I'm here for you. And it might help you feel better if you tell someone what's going on. I wasn't going to go anywhere with the information I have."

I'm shaking so hard I feel like I'm going to fall off this couch. My voice squeaks, "Tell me what you know, and I will fill in the blanks, but you cannot tell anyone. Wait. No, Mattie. That's unfair to you. I can't do that to you. I won't say anything because if I did you would either betray me or betray your faith. You can't have it both ways. You have a moral obligation, and it's not fair for me to ask you to..."

"You killed Hilda's attacker."

HOLY SHIT! I roll off the couch and crawl away.

Excruciating pain comes from my wound, but I can't sit there.

What do you say to that? I never wanted her to know. At what point do you decide, yes, this is the person I want to drag into my living hell?

She knows and there is no unknowing. I stop at the edge of the kitchen and turn around. "Yes, I killed him. Can we drop it now?"

"Do you trust me?"

"Shouldn't I be asking you that? Because your answer should be no. No, you shouldn't trust me! I'm a murderer, and I would do it again! I don't have a problem with it. I enjoy pain, and I have no guilt or shame for the things I've done." I wish I did though. Maybe I wouldn't be such a monster if the guilt from my first kill was enough.

"Do you trust me?"

I huff. "Yes, Mattie, I trust you."

"I know it was an accident. You kept crying and apologizing to Chris. Don't worry. Chris was asleep, and no one else was in the room when you were in one of your dream confessionals. I also know you attacked Hilda."

A wave of disgust moves me to the kitchen.

"Cosette, don't you hide from me!" She comes in and sits on the floor next to me. "I know your idea of a good Christian would be for me to run to the police." She turns my head to face her. "But I won't go to them. What's done is done. I have an obligation to *you*, to show you the right way to go. *You* have the obligation to confess. It's not my place to do that. I'm taking the side of a Catholic priest or a psychiatrist. It's between us only. I think of it like if you were an alcoholic. I could turn you in for underage drinking, or I could help you get better."

I collapse on the floor bawling. I can't take this.

She hugs me and pulls me to my knees. "There is, however, a

verse in the Bible that says *nothing in all creation is hidden from God's sight.*

"God saw everything you did, Cosette. And He *still* listened to my prayer and brought you back. You will have to stand in front of Him to be judged, but then again, so will I. I could just turn you in, but then where would that leave you? I'm here to walk you through this and help you get better.

"Your job is to listen, pay attention, and grow strong. You are weak right now, and you are listening to the wrong voices. I was warned, remember? I told you my dreams. God gave you a second chance. Don't screw it up."

She almost didn't sound like my Mattie. She's much stronger, more sure of herself. She has no problem sparing my feelings for the sake of teaching me a lesson. I need to wake up and listen to her.

She's right. I don't want to be like this. I don't want to wallow in darkness. It's so cold and lonely here. That vacuuming feeling is so strong. But now with Mattie around, it's weak. It's weak like my dark host. He had to back down when she was praying for me. How stupid of me. I need to straighten up.

"It was an accident. I didn't mean to," I confess, drying my eyes.

"I know, but you still ran. You're supposed to face your problems. Running solves nothing." She sits me up. "Why apologize to Chris?"

I don't want her making any connections until I talk to Chris. I know I need to open up to her, but I won't betray him to do so. "I apologized to Chris because I kissed Hilda. When I attacked her, I just, it was overwhelming, and she just looked so scared, and it just took over... Do you think I'm a freak?" I'm still worried.

"Uh, yeah! You're worse than I thought. You kissed your enemy, killed someone, and you like pain! Of course I think you're a freak! But you're my freak. And I love you. And I'm here to walk you down a better path. Even if I have to tie you up and drag you by the hair, you're going down the right path with me."

I laugh, picturing it in my head. She laughs too. But then my wound reminds me I'm supposed to stay calm. I cringe.

"Is there a limit to your pain? How much can you handle before it hurts?" she asks.

"I'm there. This hurts." I roll to my side and she checks my dressing. I didn't do any damage.

"It's good to know you're still human."

"I'm still human. I'm ashamed. I'm sorry. I couldn't tell you because..."

"I know. I can see why. I wish you would tell the police though. They might be able to help you remember details about the other attackers so we can find Hilda. No wonder she called me. She sounded so worried about you. Do you remember anything?"

"I'm still working on it. We'll find her."

I don't want to go into a deep conversation about that, so I change the subject. "Chris knows."

"About what? All of it?" She lifts me off the kitchen floor and we go back to the sofa.

"He pulled me off Hilda. He also stopped me from doing a lot of stupid things."

"Then I will have to give him a big kiss and thank him for protecting you."

"You should, Mattie. He's a good kisser. Do you want to try? He'll be here later."

"You are a freak. You want me to kiss your boyfriend?"

"I know it's odd, but I like the way he kisses, and I guess I just wanted to share."

"No offense, Cosette, but you don't have a lot of guys to compare him with to judge whether he is good or not. Jeremy Olsen was a dare. I don't think he counts."

"I know what a good kisser is like. Come here. I'll show you." I pucker up while making loud, obnoxious kissing sounds.

She laughs and holds me at arm's length. "I don't think so. I don't want to put your kissing to shame. Besides, I only go one way. I love you, but not that much."

"Your loss. You should kiss Chris though. He is good."

"Who are you, and what have you done with my innocent, insecure, perfect little Cosette?"

"Forget I said anything."

"Oh no, no, no, you offered. I'm taking you up on it! It'll shock the heck out of him, won't it?" Her eyes open wide.

"He might hurt you. You better not." My stomach tingles thinking about how rough he can get. I love it, but she might not.

"You two are so odd. Yet fit together so well."

"You have no idea. Well, speaking of the devil." I hear Chris's truck pull up.

"We do not speak of the devil, Cosette. Right path, remember?"

"Got it. Go ahead, Mattie. Get him when he walks in. See what he does."

She stands by the front door. The second he steps in, she presses him to the wall and kisses him. He flips her around fast and kisses her back, pressing his whole body against hers.

"See, Mattie? I told you!" I watch them for a minute. He did well.

"Ugh. Chris, you may be a good kisser, but you taste like cigarettes. That's disgusting. When did you start smoking?"

"Why are you kissing me?"

I clap, giddy at his performance.

"Cosette?" He glares at me in shock. "You put her up to this?"

"Are you mad?" I try to hold in my giggling. "I told her you were a good kisser. I kind of pushed her on you."

"I'm not mad, but I wish I'd known. I wouldn't have had that last cigarette." Chris winks at Mattie.

She wipes her lips. "Please tell me, Chris, that you didn't start smoking. That is the most disgusting habit."

"I didn't. I have a white trash family. We're too poor to celebrate with cigars. My cousin's girlfriend is knocked up. That's all."

I'm impressed. That's a good lie and quick too.

"Mattie, you're a good kisser yourself. I'm surprised at you. I always thought you were a prude. When Cozy gets better, maybe the three of us can..." He twirls her hair.

"I don't think so. I've had enough of this freak show for tonight. Cozy," she says as she pushes him away, comes back, and hugs me. "I love you, and I'll be praying for you. God brought you back for a reason. Don't blow it!" She kisses my forehead. "I'll bring you back some food."

"Ugh, don't kiss my nappy hair. I need a shampooing."

"Your hair's fine. I think I am done kissing for a while anyway now that Chris has spoiled it for me!" She laughs as she walks out the door.

"Smart ass!" Chris yells after her then shuts the door. "So, Cozy, what was that all about?"

"I liked watching you kiss her. It makes me want you."

"What? You didn't want me before? Keep calm, Cosette." He strokes my cheek, but I don't want to keep calm. I want to rush him. All of my trying to be good and watching the religious shows washes out of my mind the second I see him. But I do need to take it easy so I can physically get back to normal soon.

"How are you feeling?" he asks.

"She knows."

"What?"

"Mattie knows. Just about my first murder, which I never really apologized to you for. Chris, I am so sorry. If I had known... I guess I should have just walked away. I am so sorry to have taken your uncle Pen away from you."

"It wasn't your fault." He props me up and slides in behind me. I rest on his chest. "I know my uncle deserved it. We all do. I know it was an accident. Do you want to tell me what happened to Dickie though?"

"I was at Ice Cream Willies when I heard a dog whimpering behind Dickie's meth house. I went to go help the pup. Dickie came to attack me. I hit the ground, and he was kicking me. I jumped up and hit his chin with my head, and he fell back. Then he threw a brick at me. I got mad when it cut open my cheek, so I kicked him. He was still alive when I left. I guess I kicked him too many times. Chris, I am so sorry. I am so sorry."

"It's okay. You were only defending yourself; he was on his way out. He was out of control anyway. When we'd kidnap a girl and... I'm sorry. Does it bother you for me to talk about what I've done?"

"I was so focused on me that I hadn't thought about it. But I don't think it would bother me. Unfortunately, maybe the opposite. You probably shouldn't for my own sanity. I want to be good. I need to be a good person."

"You don't have to change. Please don't change for me. I love you either way. I want you either way, and I'll do whatever you want.

You just let me know."

"You are so perfect."

"Yeah, yeah, yeah. So, it's okay about Dickie. Don't think I'm upset. I think I'm kind of relieved."

"Uh, what?"

"I would rather him go out like that then a drug deal gone wrong or an overdose."

"I'm so sorry. If I had known... If I had known, none of this would have happened. I dig myself deeper and deeper. I don't want my life to be this rollercoaster ride. We need to fix what we started and be done with it. I want us to enjoy each other like typical teenagers do. Maybe go out on a normal date, go to a party, something normal."

"You know you can never drink," he says as he strokes my hair down my chest.

"What? Why?"

"After your hospital confessionals and me blowing it off like you were having a bad dream, the last thing you need is to get drunk and spill your guts. Think about it.

"Or what happens when you're drinking and you start to loosen up and some guy approaches you and you feel threatened? You've already crossed that line without being tipsy. What do you think you'll do when you're uninhibited? You cannot drink unless you're in certain company."

"Like Decker?" I cock my head to look up at him.

"Did he say something?"

"He mentioned that you were out tying up loose ends. Did you tell him you have Hilda?"

"No. I only tell him what I think he can handle. He's a coward. That's why he has submissive Rose. I let him in on a few secrets and let his imagination run wild. He and Rose are gonna be here tomorrow after school. Then I'll be back after I take care of our guest."

"How is our guest?" My mind races, but my body doesn't as I stand to make my way to the bathroom.

"In what capacity are you asking?" He stands to hold me steady as I walk.

"That's an odd question. Do you want to know what I think you should do with her? I don't know yet. Hilda knows everything about me killing her attacker. She doesn't know about Dickie or that they're related to you. Who does she think took her?"

"She doesn't know. I assume she thinks it's the Poser. I've been smoking around her to throw her scent off. And I stole a bunch of drugs from Aunt April and my soon-to-be Uncle Ben, you know, Tear-Tattooed Ben? The poser gang's new recruit. I'll spike Hilda's food to keep her drugged up. But I don't know how long I can do that. What do you want me to do with her? Do you think you will be strong enough to help me?" He turns on the bathroom light. I unfortunately can see what I look like. I need a shower.

"We're walking a fine line with her, Chris. Don't get me excited about having her. I can't do that anymore. No more Bonnie. If I get close to Hilda with that frame of mind, she will most likely not survive."

"Would that be so bad?"

"No. And yes. I can't go through that low again. Especially with Hilda, I don't know that I would recover at all. I can't bring Bonnie out. I won't make it. You've done it before, Chris. Of course you aimed better with your other victims than with me." I start to get undressed.

"Your last low was nothing. You had fun and slept it off. Like a long night of drinking. I think you'll get over it. Besides, I saved her for you. She's my gift to you. We could have so much fun." He pulls my top off and kisses me. My heart flutters.

How sick that his gesture brings me happiness. But we can't be that couple. I'm supposed to be walking down the right path, or Mattie will drag me.

"And, Cozy, you know my aim is excellent. I didn't hit any organs or bone or anything bad."

"Don't get me started on that. You left me like this. Come help me. I want to shower. I feel gross."

"You can't get it wet, can you?"

"It's bandaged well enough. I'll get in and out fast. I just need to wash my hair and rinse off completely. I smell like dirty alley."

"I don't think you smell. If you do, then I must say I like the dirty alley perfume you have on." He pulls off his shirt.

"Eau de alley?" I step out of my pajama bottoms. "What are you doing?"

"I need to make sure you're safe in there. I'm taking a shower with you. I'll wash your hair. I'll wash the eau de alley perfume off. I'll take care of my girl, protect her. I will never let anyone hurt you. Other than me of course."

I am so in love with him. How can I refuse? "We can't be long. And I'll be keeping my unmentionables on until you step out. And you need to keep yours on too. We can't tempt each other. I need to heal."

"You're frustrating, but I agree. I'm just glad to be this close to you again." He kneels in his boxer briefs and takes off my fuzzy socks. He runs his hands up my calves and thighs to my bandaged back.

"Oh, honey. I am so sorry. Have you seen this bruise? I don't think I've ever seen a bruise that bad. I thought your last ones were bad. Baby, I am so sorry I had to do this to you, but you gave me no choice."

"I know. I haven't seen it, but I feel it. I like to lay on it, but the wound needs to breathe. And I need to shower."

I turn the hot water all the way up, then we step in.

"Holy crap that's hot!" He jumps out.

"Wimp! Do you need to take your sensitive sissiness out? I can do this myself." I laugh at him.

"No. I'll be fine, if this is what you need."

It is what I need. The scalding pain refocuses me, but the look on his face is controlled pain. "I'll turn it down. I don't want you to go." I turn to face him, to let the water soak my hair. He grabs the shampoo and massages it in. "It feels so good to be clean." Physically clean that is.

Slowly and gently he caresses me as the water spray tickles over us. He runs his hands over my body and back through my hair, letting the water rinse the shampoo out. His fingers get stuck in a tangle, yanking my locks. I like it, and he knows it. He reaches up underneath, grabs two handfuls of hair, and tightens his grip.

Pleasure is added to the sting. I kiss him hard as he pulls harder.

It's romantic. It's frustrating. I want more. I'll risk the damage to my healing wound.

"Stop! Cosette we have to stop." He leans away.

"Why do you take me to where I want to be, just to drop me off a mile before? You're a tease!" I push him against the shower wall.

"I want it just as much if not more than you do. Let's get you healed then we can have our fun." He pulls me in and kisses my forehead. "Until then, it's cold showers for us."

"Well not for you. Just for me."

"Do you want to explain that, Cosette?"

"You have Hilda. Until we figure out a plan, she's yours."

"No. I have her saved for you. I haven't touched her."

"You have to."

"Uh, what?" He gives me a look of astonishment.

"You have to sleep with her, Chris. She was kidnapped by the Poser. The rapist, Poser? She should be expecting it. Besides, you said she's drugged up. She won't know it's you. So when she gets free from being kidnapped by the Poser, it will make sense. Or you could just kill......" What the hell am I saying? I don't care so much that he is with her, but I can't let him kill her. If I do, is it just as bad as me doing it? Yes, it is. And I really want to do it.

But I was brought back for a reason. I doubt that killing Hilda is what Mattie was praying for.

No, I can't be that person. I have to protect Hilda, like I did the first time. I can't have her killed, but she knows too much. How can I let her live?

"Cosette? Bonnie? Who is at the helm of your head? What do you want me to do with Hilda?" Chris tilts my head up, drawing my focus.

"Let's get moving." I slam off the shower.

"THERE, COZY, YOU'RE all dry. Ointment?"

I hand him the Neosporin. He gets to work on my front wound, agitated that I haven't answered him. "Now, what do I do with

Hilda?"

"Who does she think took her?" I tell more than ask.

"The Poser."

"Exactly, then you have to treat her like the Poser."

"But I don't want to sleep with her."

"You're in a gang of rapists! Do your job! You're the Poser. Act like it!"

Chris looks up at me, a little stunned at my demand. "But I've been holding back for you." He pops up from bandaging my wound and stands away from me at the edge of the bathroom. "I love you, Cosette, and I don't want anyone else."

"That's good to know, but this isn't about want. You have a part to play, and until I figure out how to bring her back alive, you have to be the Poser. Please, Chris." I stroll over to him and run my fingers through his hair. I pull him close and kiss his neck. "When she gets back, how's it gonna sound that she was kidnapped by a rapist and wasn't touched the whole time? Have your fun, but don't touch her face. She's so pretty. Just keep her alive and drugged until I figure out what to do."

"Are you sure you're okay with this?"

"No, I'm not. I wanna be there. I wanna watch, but I can't. I want you to keep her alive. We can't kill anymore. I don't want to kill. I don't want to be Bonnie."

He clenches his jaw, not happy about what I'm asking him to do, not happy about losing Bonnie.

"Think of Hilda as my token. If I can keep her alive, then I know I'm not a monster. Then I know the darkness won't overtake me. If I can protect Hilda, then Bonnie will stay locked away inside, and Cozy can stay out here. Do you get it?"

"I get it. No killing Hilda. If Hilda dies, you die."

"That's a good way of putting it. I'll have to find an alternative to satisfy Bonnie. I think I hear a car. Get dressed."

"What about you?" he asks.

"I still have to cover the exit wound. Who is it?"

He hops to the door while putting his pants on. "Mattie's back. She brought food."

"Just let her in. I don't care if she sees me like this."

"Okay."

He buttons his pants then opens the door. She darts past him to put the takeout bags on the kitchen table.

"Hi, guys. I come bearing gifts. I thought you all would be hungry... Holy crap! You are so hot! Oh my gosh, Cozy. He is hot!" Mattie says, just now noticing my shirtless, sexy boyfriend.

"I know, huh? Perfect body? Too bad I'm wounded and can't do anything with him. You can if you want."

"No, thank you. And you need to get dressed, Miss Embarrassing. Hey, first can I take a picture of your wound? Everyone should see this. The exit wound bruise on your back is amazing."

"I can't see it very well, so yeah, take a good picture before we have to cover it."

She takes out her phone, ready to snap some pictures. "Chris, can you get her some clothes? I don't want to get caught with this on my phone and get in trouble for sexting."

"I won't tell anyone you sext dirty pictures, Mattie." Chris brushes against her as he goes to my room. "I'm really getting to know you." As he returns with a matching bra and panties set, he stops in front of her. He puts both arms against the wall, trapping her. "First you kiss your best friend's boyfriend, then you take naked pictures of her, and now you want to text them? Cozy's underage, Mattie. In this state, that's child porn."

"Funny, Chris," she ducks under his arm and walks away. "Behave or I'll tell everyone you're a bad kisser."

"I can prove them wrong. Do you want another shot? I'm shirtless over here. When will you get an opportunity like this again?" He holds out his arms, waiting.

"You are too arrogant. Cozy, control your man."

I give him a wink. I don't want to control him at all. I like him flirting. She helps me step into my panties. "Okay, now take the picture. Maybe we'll post it for a day by day healing progress."

Chris hands her my bra. "We'll have to post it under a fake name. We don't want the shooter coming to find you to finish the job."

"Chris!" Mattie's appalled.

"He's right, Mattie. We can't give any clues to where I am. It's bad enough that the news reported me released from the hospital. I'm just glad I'm a minor, and they don't know where I live."

"Alright, I got it. I'll post the pics later," Mattie says. "When Rosey and Deck come tomorrow, you might want to keep your clothes on. You know how insecure Rose is. And she thinks you're beautiful and wouldn't want Decker to see. Not everyone is as free with their mates as you two freaks."

"Who are these freaks you speak of?" Chris teases.

"Get her dressed. I can't stay for dinner, so you're on your own. Do you need anything before I go?" Mattie asks as she sets up the takeout dinner for us.

"No, I'm doing alright, and I can get around fine. I'm just a bit slow." I get my big fuzzy robe and elephant slippers on.

"I'm on call and only a spit away if she needs me, Mattie," Chris says.

"Okay, but before I go, I want to pray with you guys." She grabs our hands and bows her head. We follow suit.

"Dear Lord, thank You for giving us back Cosette. Thank You for the grace You have shown her. Give her wisdom and guidance. Give her strength and heal her." Mattie touches my wound. Her hand radiates heat. It's comforting. "Heal her physically, but Lord, heal her emotionally also. I know You love her, so I ask that You put a hedge of protection around her. Thank You for Chris. Help him guide her the right way. Thank you, Lord. Amen."

"Amen," I repeat.

"I don't think I've ever prayed like that. That was cool. Thanks, Mattie." Chris looks as if he's discovered a new concept.

"You should pray more often. You both could use it. Here, Coz, take your antibiotics and painkillers. Yes, take the painkillers. Your body needs to relax to heal. Love ya, guys. Enjoy dinner." She kisses my forehead and leaves.

Chris closes the door then helps me to the dinner table. "I'm gonna go to the farmhouse to turn on the heat for Hilda."

"Thank you. You need to be nice, but not too nice. The Poser wouldn't be."

Chris holds up a piece of sweet and sour chicken. "Meat. That's all she is to me. I'd just as soon kill her as to look at her. I'm only doing this for you, but I know if Hilda dies, you die."

Chapter FIVE

"IT'S HEALING NICELY. Very fast." Mom softly presses the bandage tape. "Keep drinking water. You won't need to change the dressing until this afternoon when Rosy and Decker get here."

"Thanks, Mom. I'm doing okay. I don't need the world to come babysit me. They should be out looking for Hilda." I want to sound like I'm scared for her. Truth is, I want to see Rose and hear what Shelby's dad, the chief of police, has found out.

"There are plenty of people looking for Hilda. This week you can be selfish. Get all the rest you can because come Monday, it's back to school. Did Mattie bring your homework?"

"Yeah, I got it. I'll do it later. When can I go for a walk? I feel cooped up here."

"Maybe Thursday or Friday I'll take you to Perrin Park. You are doing better than I expected, and I don't see any signs of infection." Mom gets her coat on.

"Can I walk the circle? Maybe to the mailbox and back?"

"Fine, but wait until Rosy gets here."

"Thanks, Mom. Have fun at work. I love you."

"Love you too." She closes the door, but then opens it again to come kiss me bye. "I love you. You're all I have."

"You're all I have too, Mom. Hey, how's John doing? I know he's busy looking for Hilda, but how's he doing?"

"Not good. That's a situation no parent wants to face. I haven't seen him much. I think the fact that you survived and his daughter is missing is hard to deal with. There're so many questions still unanswered."

"I'll try to remember more. I'm sorry, Mom."

"Oh, honey. It's not your fault. No one is blaming you. We'll find her. You remember what you can, and let the police do the rest. I love you."

"I love you too, Mom," I whisper as she slams the door. "I'm gonna get her back. She'll be happy to be home, and I can be a normal teenager. Did you hear that, Victor?" I ask my brother in Heaven. "When I get Hilda back, I'll be fine. When I'm healed, I can start running and focus on the marathons instead of this, this, empty anxiousness I have. I mean, what is that? Bonnie? Is that you? Because you are dead to me. I'll do anything to get rid of you."

I wiggle myself into the couch, frustrated at the crap that's on daytime TV, frustrated that I can't run. Mad that I have to sit here with my thoughts.

I think the whole death thing has changed my attitude. I want a normal life. I probably won't get it, but I do want a life. I want to live. I have people who need me. My mom would be lost without me. Mattie would give up her dreams, and Chris? I think he'd go off the deep end.

Speaking of Chris, my phone buzzes with his text.

I open up the picture and try to figure out what part of the body that is. It looks painful.

"What is this?" I text.

"I'll show you, I'll b right over."

"I am going to kill him!" he yells. Thee door slams behind him.

"Chris, what happened? Who did this to you?" I jump up and walk as quickly as I can to the freezer.

"My Uncle Ben did this. Aunt April's tear-tattooed asshole fiancée! He thought April stole his drugs and started beating on her, but I stepped in. We went at it, and I got a few good shots in, but then April pulled me off him. She was scared for *him*! He went to beat her up, and she pulled me off him! They are fucked up! My dad and stepmom came downstairs and told me to stay out of it. So I came here."

I hold out the icepack. He takes it and sits at the kitchen table. "It's my fault. I stole the drugs for Hilda, and he took it out on April. But fuck her! Stupid bitch, I tried to protect her!" He presses the ice pack to his jaw. "Even after I got Ben to replace Dickie! Fuck!" I get two more ice packs for his lip and cut-up knuckles. He starts to calm down.

"Cozy, I'm sorry to go off like that. I know that's not what you want to hear. I need to stay calm for you. I'm sorry."

"Don't apologize to me. Where's your aunt?"

"At home with Ben and my dad and stepmom. I'm going to kill him. I don't know how, but he can't do that to her. And even though she's stupid, she's blood; he is not. I protect my family. I'm going to take him out."

My heart is pounding, excited at the thought. "How much did you steal?"

"Enough for Hilda for at least another two weeks. I didn't know how long you would be out."

"What were you planning on doing after two weeks?"

He didn't answer.

"I guess you weren't expecting her to live that long, huh?"

He nods with a smile.

"I'm not changing my mind, Chris. I won't kill again. She's now my token. My symbol that I'm better and I won't kill again. If I kill her it will..." My mind stops me from finishing. I stare at the floor.

"What? It will what?" He waves his hand in front of my face, regaining my attention.

I look up at his cut-up face and smile. The devious plan formed so fast. I quickly jump into action.

"When you go home, I need you to get a few things." I take out a notepad and start scribbling. "You need to go to Horner Novelty."

"What is your brain doing?"

"When you sleep with Hilda, is she blindfolded?"

"I haven't touch..."

"Damn it, Chris! You have to!" I get up and reach for my purse.

Chris grabs it for me so I don't have to move. "Thank you. Here. Get closer to me. I don't want you to go to school today." I pull out my mascara and try to put it on him.

"I don't think so."

I grab his hair and pull him close. "Just deal with it. I want you to go to Horner's and get dark brown contacts. When you get to Hilda, make sure she's drugged, make sure you smell like smoke, and put on your ski-mask."

"But..."

"No buts. You have to be rough with her. Your uncle Pen was cruel, and you have to be too. But don't hurt her. Wait until she's so drugged up that she can't feel you hitting her. You have to bruise her to make it look real. And in her drugged-up state, let her see your eyes, after you put in the brown contacts though." I sit back and look at him. "You are so hot. Go to the drawer beside the fridge please. There's a green dry-erase marker."

He retrieves it for me. "I think I will never, ever, go against you. Ever."

"When you're done with Hilda, bring me those things on that list."

His eyebrows wrinkle in worry as he hands me the marker.

"Thank you. When does he work?" I ask as I draw two tears on his face.

"When does who work?"

"Don't be naïve, Chris. Ben, Tear Tattoo. We're going to frame him. When does he work?"

"Off and on. He gets paid cash for repairing lawn mowers. It's hard for a convict to find a real job."

"That's so perfect! There's no time clock. He can't defend against eleven other murders without having a regular job to clock in at."

"Seventeen."

"Seventeen what?"

"Seventeen murders."

"You killed seventeen people?" I start to smile and a wave of heat floods my body. "I'm sorry, I shouldn't hear about this." I want to. My god, Bonnie wants to. But I shouldn't. "How's your jaw?"

"Good enough for a kiss, or a little more."

I give him a small peck. "You need to behave." I want to attack him, especially after that huge turn on, but I can't. "Now, do you have enough drugs for Hilda until we execute our little plan?"

"Plenty. But I wish you would change your mind. We could have so much fun with her. Then we'll stop."

"Nope. You're just mad that I'm making you wear mascara."

"That's it, Cozy. That right there is the only reason."

"I have problems, Chris. I have this anxiousness I can't get rid of."

"It's an addicti..."

"No! It's not. I won't let it be. That's a horrible thing to be addicted to. We need to get Hilda back, so I can stop thinking about it. Framing Ben for the Poser murders will be a giant step towards me getting back to normal. So take care of Hilda while I try to focus on something else."

"You can focus on me." He gives me puppy dog eyes.

"That's all I want to do. I miss you. I want us to go on a normal date and do normal things. I want us to..."

"Be normal? We can't, Cozy. We're not." Chris softly strokes my cheek.

"We are! We have to be. Now let's finish this, or I'll have to take on a new addiction."

"Daytime soaps won't satisfy?"

"If only. Nothing on TV will satisfy this hunger."

"Okay, Cosette. Well, while you're immersing yourself in daytime drama, I'll be working on your little plan to cure our drama. Decker and Rose are coming to help you after school. I'll take care of your token again when they're here, then I'll be over."

"Good. When you sleep with Hilda, let her take a bath or something. I know how disgusting I felt in the hospital. I would hate to be dirty in some barn somewhere."

"I have her in a cellar. It's not too cold or too warm. I'll give her a bucket with warm soapy water."

"Thanks. I need her in good condition. Feed her well. Can you give me some insight on Decker? I know he knows something. Do you want to tell me what?"

"I would let him know everything if I could, but he can't handle the pressure or guilt."

"Oh, yeah, cause I've done great at that." I overexaggerate my sarcasm. "What does Deck know?" I ask.

"Not a lot. He knows how wild you are though."

"You better explain that one," I threaten.

"If he asks to kiss you, then it's okay with me. I told him you were a good kisser."

I push him over. "I guess I should brush my teeth before he comes then, huh? What about Rose? That would leave her out."

"I'm sure he'll let you kiss her too."

"Smart ass. I just might. But I couldn't do that to her. Decker might think it's a great idea, and she's so submissive she'd do it just to please him. How long have you been friends?"

"A while. Decker is like my best friend. He's an odd one. He likes the idea of doing bad things, but when it comes down to it, he has his limits. He'll do me favors because it's almost like living vicariously through me. He has the fun without the consequences."

"We have to protect them. All of them, from us. We have to protect our friends from knowing any of the things we were involved in. If I hadn't walked into that alley that night, my life would be perfect right now. We can't let them experience any of this. We never know what monsters we would create."

"Well, I am happy with this monster." He leans over to kiss me again. "I have to go. I have a lot to do, and I have a test this afternoon. It seems trivial."

"If you don't graduate with good grades, you can't get into college. So you better do well on the test today. I don't want a loser for a boyfriend."

"Funny."

I give him a kiss as I unlock the door. "Be sure to wash your makeup off before you get back to school."

"Ugh, the messes you put me in, Cosette." He snarks, rolling his eyes, then leaves.

Chapter SIX

ALONE IN MY thoughts, I wander back to the sofa. Funny that a few weeks ago this moment would have spent crying, wallowing in my misery. Then a few days later, wallowing in my guilt, and then a few days later wallowing in blood.

"Damn it, Cosette! Stop it!" I scream to myself, slamming my fists into the couch. "I can't do this, Victor. I can't stop thinking about it. There's no other feeling in the world like it, but it's sick and unsustainable. I need that feeling. A synthetic way to feel it is what I need. Yes. That's what I need, a replacement high, a drug-free replacement high."

"You are my sunshine, my only sunshine," my phone sings, halting my cravings.

"Hi, Mattie."

"Are you watching the news? They're at the school. Turn it on. Carla and Sarah are on."

"Okay, hold on." I snap on the TV. "Got it. Wow, TV does add ten pounds. Carla looks normal, not her boney little 'I'm only eating five almonds a day' dieting self."

"That's funny. Poor girl has issues."

"Maybe you can counsel her," I tease Mattie.

"Shut up, watch the show."

"I'm recording it. I'll analyze every word later. Maybe when they rescue Hilda I'll show how her best friends basked in her fame."

"That was cruel, Cozy."

"No, it wasn't. They'll find Hilda, and then her cheerleaders will bask some more."

"They don't care about her."

"They do now. They appreciate her absence."

"You're mean, Coz. I gotta go. The news people are eyeing me. I think they recognize me from the search headquarters at our café."

"So humble. That's why I love you. Have a good day, Mattie."

"You too. Behave. Take your medicine. Watch those shows I recorded for you."

I'll watch religion later. Instead, I rewind the TV interview of Sarah as I down the horse pills.

"And you know Hilda personally?" The young female reporter looks like she isn't buying Sarah's act.

"Yes, but she's a fighter. She'll get through this. We'll find her. My brother's law firm is volunteering and I'll be searching with them." Sarah wrinkles her eyebrows to show concern.

I feel sorry for Hilda. What does she have to come back to? Sarah and Carla? They aren't worth it. But she does have her dad and... me, I guess. I'll be her friend. We share a bond no one would understand. I know what she's going through.

I know because I'm orchestrating it.

"Police are looking for any leads in the case. Please call the tip line at ......"

I turn it off and dial the tip line.

"Chief Rickert speaking."

"Hi, it's Cosette Hugo." I speak softly, I want him to think I'm still a naïve, frightened little girl.

"How are you? How are you feeling? Do you need help? Do you want me to send someone over to you?"

"No, please. I don't want to see anyone."

"I understand," he says. "What can I do for you?"

"I remembered something. He stunk."

"What?"

"He stunk, not like alley stunk, but like, uh. You know when someone smokes for a long time and they don't wash their jackets? That's what it smelled like. Stale old cigarette smoke. And his face was dark with a ski mask. But his eyes were dark. Like I could see a black head, with I guess lighter skin around the eyes. But the eyes themselves were really dark. I don't know if it was a shadow or what, but when I woke up this morning, I remembered dark eyes, with like a mole or birthmark by one of them. Does that make sense?"

"That helps. Thank you so much, Cosette."

"It's not a lot, but at least it's..." I pause.

"Cosette? Are you there? Cosette?"

"Shhh. I think I hear..."

"I'm sending someone over!" His voice, unsteady, frightened for me.

"I thought I saw something out back. It must just be a cat or something. I'm fine. I'm just jumpy. Please don't send anyone. Just find Hilda."

"I'll send a patrol to check it out anyway. They'll see you in a few."

"Thanks, Chief." I hang up satisfied.

A FEW MINUTES later, a patrol car pulls in.

"Hold on. It'll take me a few minutes," I yell as I creep to the door.

"I'll wait," the officer says.

I open the door. "Hello?"

"Hi, remember me? I'm officer Crance."

"How could I forget? You dragged me out of school in handcuffs." She has chin length brown wavy hair, and her eyes are brown and average. With some makeup, she might actually be attractive. But if it weren't for the handcuff incident, no, I wouldn't remember her.

"Those handcuffs were for your protection. And by the way, I'm sorry about your dad and stepmom." She pauses uncomfortably.

"Thank you. I'm fine."

"I was just looking around out here. I was told you had a scare?"

"The chief didn't have to send you. I just thought I saw

something moving in the back. Do you want to come in? I'm sorry, it's a little stuffy in here." I open the door wide and breathe in the cold winter. "I'll leave the door open." I wedge the welcome mat into the door holding it open. The fresh air begs me to run.

"It's fine in here." She looks around, taking in every detail of my apartment. "Do you mind if I look around?"

"Please do. I don't mean to be so jumpy. He didn't have to send you." I back up and let her in.

"You're fine. I completely understand. I'm jumpy about this too."

That's an odd thing to hear a police officer say. Not very comforting.

"Where did you say you saw movement?" She looks in our bedrooms.

"It was just a rustling in the bushes out back. I told him it might be a cat. I was on the phone with him when I saw it. I wouldn't have called it in because it's no big deal."

"When it comes to a situation like this, everything is a big deal." I guide her through my kitchen to the back patio. She scans the yard, moves a few branches, and inspects the path to the neighborhood behind mine. She walks back towards the apartment. Opening the lid of the grill she asks, "What were you cooking? It doesn't look like food."

Shit! What would make her want to open that? I suck at lying. How am I gonna fib this one? "Please don't tell my mom. I was burning some clothes." So much for lying.

She touches my hand to stop me from pinching my arm. "Okay. Why?"

"My dad gave them to me, and I was mad at him. But now I wish I didn't." I close the lid of the grill thankful that the bloodstained clothes had burned almost to nothing.

"I understand. I'm so sorry. There are so many stupid things we do that we wish we could take back. Then our loved ones die, and we lose the moment forever."

She speaks like it's recent.

"What happened?"

"I'm sorry." She stands straight, gathering her emotions. "I just need to check a few more things." She walks out the front door and around the front of the duplex apartment. She's thorough.

"Is everything okay?" I ask when she comes back to me. Her face is filled with sorrow.

"It was my sister."

"What?"

"The Poser, he killed my little sister. She was his second victim. She was only seventeen. I joined the police academy the next day. I know how scared you must be, but we'll do everything to find him. We will protect you. I will protect you. I promise."

She comes over and gives me a small hug. It feels like she needs it more than me. It feels like she's remembering what it was like to hug her little sister.

"If there is anything else you remember, I will be here for you. You look a lot like her, my sister, except for the dark hair of course. She was blonde. I guess you got lucky there. Here's my number again, if you don't feel comfortable calling the chief."

"Thanks, Officer Crance. Thanks. And I'm sorry. I really am."

She smiles and walks out my door.

So many people affected. So many lives ruined, for what? For a brief moment of pleasure? The faces are real. Their pain is real. I have to be better. Chris has to be better.

My heart is breaking.

We are monsters.

Chapter SEVEN

"HI, COZY, SORRY we're late." Rose cheerfully bounces in, ready for her babysitting session.

"I brought you coffee. Mattie had us swing by the café to pick up some food." Decker walks in with a bag from Three J's. "Let's see, we have fried cauliflower cakes. Those would be for Rosy. A hamburger and fries for me, and two mac-n-cheeses for you and Chris?" Decker empties the contents out on my coffee table.

"I'll get the forks and stuff. What do you want to drink?" Rose yells from the kitchen.

"I'll just have water. There are sodas in the fridge." I grab my food from Decker.

"No beer?" he asks. "What kind of party is this?"

"My mom doesn't drink. She says stupid people do stupid things and wind up in stupid situations when they drink." That was my mom's don't drink lesson for me. No other explanations came with it, but I have my own reason not to drink.

"That sucks. I'll just take a soda, Ros." Deck opens the front door. "You're late, Chris. We already ate without you."

"I was busy at my uncle's farm." Chris comes and gives me a kiss hello. "So, interesting thing happened at the farm today. Wanna hear?"

Butterflies in my stomach start moving. I'm mad at them.

"Wait for me!" Rose yells while bringing in a tray of drinks and silverware. She sets it down and serves us. "Okay, go ahead. What farm are we talking about?"

"My uncle Pen passed away, but he wrote me into his will with the rest of his kids. Turns out, I own a part of that farm."

"Yee haw!" Decker slaps his knee. "We's got ourselves a farm boy."

"Decker, you're an ass."

"Well aware, Cozy."

"Anyway," Chris snaps his fingers to refocus Decker. "My cousins are out spending their inheritance, and I need to keep the farm up, so I have to go there every day after school to feed the animals."

I almost choked on my food.

"Are you okay?" Rose hands me my drink.

"I'm fine. I'm almost seventeen. You'd think I'd be used to eating by now."

"Some things take longer to perfect. So Chris, what kind of animals do you have?" Rose asks.

"A few cows, chickens, and a kid." Chris smiles at me. I'm not appreciating the teasing.

"A kid?"

"A goat, Decker. But we're selling them all and concentrating on the crops. I have happy memories there. My cousins? Not so much. My aunt was psycho. She died last October. My uncle went off the deep end after that.

Anyway, now I'm responsible for some animals until I can sell them."

"I wanna pet a goat!" Rose puts her empty plate down and sits next to me. She then swings my legs onto her lap. "Just lie back and eat and relax. I'll take care of you. I hope you don't mind, but a good foot massage always helps me no matter where I'm hurting."

"Uh, okay, thanks." I wiggle my toes, wishing I had a pedicure. "It's winter so my nail stylist is on vacation, somewhere warm, I'm sure. At least I shaved my toes for you."

"That's funny." Rose laughs loud. I never heard her laugh like that. "So, Chris, when are you gonna show us the farm? I want to see the goats."

"Sorry, Rose. They will be dinner for someone next week. I can't stand them. They freak me out. When they bleat, it sounds like screaming."

"You're lying," Decker mumbles with his mouth full.

"Nope, hold on." Chris pulls out his cell phone and shows us a few videos of screaming goats. If they're screaming while Hilda is screaming, no one would give it a second thought.

"That's creepy. They would freak me out." Rose rubs my ankles and calves. I'm melting in her hands and can't concentrate. "I think I would sell them too, but not for dinner meat. That's awful." Rose switches to popping my toes.

"Oww, that feels weird." I sit up sharply, but the motion pulls on my staples. I cringe as pain shoots up my back.

"Oh, I am so sorry, Cozy." Rose takes my bowl of food away from me and stands there with her hands out, oblivious to what she should do next.

"I'm fine."

"She's tough, Rosy." Chris helps me stand. "But we should make sure nothing's torn." He scoops me up and takes me to the bathroom.

After locking the door, he gives me a kiss. "Sorry I smell like smoke."

"I'm glad you do. How is Hilda?"

He smirks. "She's fine." He raises a flirting eyebrow. "Do you want details?" He knows me too well.

I do want details. I want to know everything, not because I'm jealous, but because I crave. It's horrible that he knows this. "No, I don't want to know. I want to be good, Chris. Don't do that to me."

"I will give you anything you ask. Don't try to be someone you're not to please me. I will deny you nothing. I'll give you Hilda. Hell, I'll give you Rose. Do you want Rose?"

"Stop it. You're not playing fair. I'm not trying to be good for you. I'm doing it for me. Stop leading me into temptation." I pull my sweats down and my shirt up to check on my gunshot wound. "Here, help me out."

Chris kneels down and gently pulls off my bandage. "You're the one leading me into temptation."

Rose knocks on the door. "Cozy, I'm so sorry. Are you okay? Can I help you please?"

Chris opens the door wide giving Decker a great view. If I was inhibited in any way, I'd be mad, but I think he's testing me.

He should not test me.

I tuck the rim of my shirt in my bra exposing my entire midsection. "Here, Rose. You can help me. Apparently Chris thinks any skin exposure is an invitation."

"Then I'll be your nurse." Rose pushes him out of the bathroom. "Out with you, Chris. Go eat." She closes the door.

"If this bugs you, Rose, I can do it. I just get dizzy standing for too long."

"I'll be fine. I can do it. Here, lift up your shirt more."

"I'll just take it off." I take off my shirt and sweats and lock the door.

"That's gonna drive Deck nuts, not knowing what's going on behind locked doors." She giggles. When she turns back to me, she stops and stares at me half-naked. I like her looking at me. "Those are pretty. I guess now that Chris is here, we'll leave."

I look down at my lacy bra and panty set. "I didn't wear them for Chris. I wore these because they're comfortable. Right now, that's all I care about."

"Well, they are pretty," she sheepishly replies. She pulls her deep red hair back into a loose ponytail and starts to inspect the wound.

"Rose, is Decker bossy to you? Does it bother you? I hope I'm not being too forward, but I never get to talk this close to you."

Her Irish eyes smile at me. "It may seem like he is, but I like it. I have almost no responsibility. If I really wanted something, then I'd demand it and he'd give it. But for everyday things, I don't care. Let him make the decisions. If he makes the wrong one, then it's all on him."

I'm impressed with her logic. I guess she's not as weak as I thought she was. "Wow, your relationship is interesting."

"So is yours. Did you really let Mattie kiss Chris?"

"He's a great kisser. I wanted to share."

She smiles, dreaming. I know she likes Chris. Everyone does. My boyfriend's hot. "You guys are so perfect," she sighs.

"Obviously not." I look down.

She gets on her knees to change the bandage in the back. "You have a perfect body and so does Chris. You're not jealous or insecure."

"I am plenty insecure."

"You're standing here looking like a Victoria's Secret model." She looks up to me, gently pulls off the old patch, and softly runs her hands up my side. It tickles. "I'm sorry I hurt you."

"You would have to do a lot more than that for me to be affected by pain. Besides, my whole body is relaxed after that foot massage. I should have you over more often."

"You should. I'd be good for you."

"Sorry, Rose, you can't. I wouldn't be good for you. I'm not a very good person. At least I wasn't, but after being shot, I'm taking that as a sign. I wanna be better. I'm just not."

"I think you're good. And I don't blame you. After everything that's happened in your life, I think you have a few 'Get out of jail free' cards owed to you."

"I wish it were that easy. I have issues." Issues which are stirring deep inside at the moment.

"Everyone has issues. So does Decker. The sisters have issues for sure, but we all fit together. We're all miserable in our own way."

She takes a washcloth and runs warm water over it. After squeezing out the water, she gently presses it against the wound. She has a soft touch. A perfect touch. She makes me feel good, not in the way Bonnie feels, but a new way. I like it. If I could replace the feeling that Bonnie brings with this feeling, I think I'll be able to make it.

I need to keep Rose around. Maybe with Rose here, Bonnie won't be a factor. "Do you know why I call you Rose instead of Rosy?"

"Why?" She looks up at me with her dark green eyes.

"Because, I think more of you. A rose is perfect and soft and beautiful. Your dark red hair and milky white skin are beautiful. It's my own way of complimenting you."

"Thanks, Cozy. I needed that." She hugs my legs then runs her fingers over my large bruise. "Does it hurt? It looks like it would hurt."

"No. I'm okay with it." I push in the yellow and blue skin. "You're making me feel so much better. Thank you."

"That's what I'm here for." Rose's response is quiet and unsure.

I softly brush her bangs to the side as she gets closer to me. Her hands gently skim over the discoloration of the bruise.

"You're so pretty, Rose. You look like a forties pin-up girl."

She humbly sighs. I can feel her warm breath against my leg. I pull my panties down off my cheek just to see what her reaction will be. "Look, the bruise goes down all the way to here."

She touches it. I'm glad. Her one hand holds onto my thigh, the other softly moves across my panty line. She bites her lip, holding in a smile.

A knock on the door startles us, and we both giggle.

"You okay in there?" Decker asks.

"I told you, locked doors drive him nuts," Rose whispers.

"Then open it. I don't mind."

"Really?" Rose is intrigued. I can see her thoughts spinning.

"I'm sorry, no. If it bothers you I…"

Rose opens the door wide to a stunned Decker. He stands there like a deer in headlights.

"We're almost done, Deck. Hand me the ointment," Rose demands. She gives me a sneaky smile accompanied with a wink.

Decker fumbles with the tube and with his eyes fixed on me, he hands it to her.

"Hey, Deck!" Chris joins us in the bathroom. "Now's your chance to kiss her. I won't offer again."

"Real funny, Chris." I glare at him. Chris is beaming. He's playing with Decker, watching him squirm. "I'd kiss Rose before I'd kiss Deck."

An insulted Decker stands back and crosses his arms, "Go ahead."

"I'm just kidding. I won't do that to you, Rose."

Chris laughs loud and puts his arm around Decker. "Cosette

won't do that because then Rose will leave you for her."

"More like she won't do that because she's a coward." Decker raises one eyebrow challenging me.

"Don't test her, Deck," Chris says, knowing it will push him.

"Cosette will always be our wet noodle," Decker taunts me. His cockiness pisses me off.

I grab Rose, push her against the bathroom wall, and kiss her. Stunned, she doesn't kiss back.

"Wet noodle, huh?" Chris taunts.

Decker pulls me off his girlfriend. "What the hell!"

"Oh my god, Rose. I am so sorry. I'm so sorry, Rose." I back away, cover myself up, and push everyone out of the room.

"THEY'RE GONE, COSETTE. You can come out of hiding." Chris knocks on the bathroom door.

I yank it open. "How could you do that to me? How could you do that to Rose?" I storm as fast as I can to the front door and open it, inviting him to leave before I kick him out.

He closes it and scoops me up, then carries me to the couch. "What is your problem, Cosette? Stop hitting me! Do you really want me to drop you?"

He puts me on the couch and covers my legs. "Decker was asking for it."

"But Rose wasn't."

"What's the big deal?"

"The big deal, Chris, is that you can't, I mean you shouldn't, it's just that, ugh! I'm so frustrated I can't even talk."

"You're frustrated because you liked it, and you don't want to like it. Don't you like her? You like her, right?"

"Of course I do. She's gorgeous. But I'm trying to be good here. Don't you remember? Chris, I'm a horrible person, and me kissing someone else's girlfriend is a horrible thing to do."

"Decker was shocked. He shouldn't have called you a wet

noodle. He'll figure out soon enough what you can do."

"I don't want him to! I don't want to be a criminal."

"And kissing Rose makes you a criminal?"

"No, but..."

"Stop with this guilt crap!" He stands. "In case you don't realize it, every person you killed attacked you first. It was complete self-defense..."

"Yeah, but I..."

"You gave them what they deserved. Just because you enjoyed it doesn't make you a criminal."

"But I'm a..."

"You're denying who you are."

"No. I'm denying who I want to be for who I should be!" I'm so mad that he doesn't get it, or he doesn't care.

He steps away from me. "Did you ever stop to think that maybe *Bonnie* is who you should be?" Mad, he grabs his coat and heads for the door. "I have to go. I have a pet to feed. A pet I'm taking care of so *you* can feel good about yourself. I'm framing a family member and sending them to the electric chair so you can keep your pet as a symbol, a token of your new fake personality!" He slams the door as he leaves.

Chapter EIGHT

"SHELBY, SIERRA, YOU girls don't have to stay." I sit up on the couch. "I know it's late. I thought Chris would be here by now. I guess he's not coming." I feel bad for the sisters having to come over, but Mattie has to work, Chris is mad at me, and I doubt Rose will ever talk to me again. I'm such a shit.

"It's only five. Are we so boring that you want us to leave?" Sierra asks. "Cause I can think of tons of things to talk about to keep you entertained."

"Stop it, Sierra." Shelby whispers to her embarrassing sister.

"Don't worry about it, Shelby. I know I screwed up. I guess I was the talk of the lunch table today." I'm trying not to cry.

Sierra crawls up on the couch next to me. She grabs a lock of my hair and starts weaving tiny braids. "Yeah, you were the main subject. So you really let Mattie kiss Chris?"

"Is that all you heard?" I'm relieved.

"We heard that, among other things." Sierra hints. Shit! They do know about Rose.

"I'm a horrible person. You all should leave." I pull my hair away from Sierra. She pouts.

"We're staying until Chris gets here," Shelby assures me. "And I don't think you're a horrible person."

"You're sweet, Shelby, but you don't know me that well."

"I do, and I think you're perfect," Sierra says.

"You poor girl, you must have serious issues if I'm your idea of perfection."

"She has issues alright." Shelby pulls her younger sister off the couch. "Give Cozy some room."

"I'm fine, Shell. Sierra reminds me of my friend from my grandma's old neighborhood. Her name is Melodious. We called her M&M. She had to run away though. I haven't seen her in almost a year."

"Why'd she run away?" Shelby asks.

"Her mom tried to get her hooked on crack. She wanted M&M to start hooking so she could have more money for drugs." How sad that it just rolled off my tongue like an everyday happening. I certainly can't tell the rest of the story.

"Wow, and you think I have issues, huh?" Sierra laughs. "I'm sorry about your friend though. I can't imagine being used like that."

"She wasn't much older than you either. Poor girl. Anyways, her mom's in jail for killing her drug dealers, so hopefully she'll come back now that it's safe."

"She'll never be safe," Shelby whispers to herself.

That's very telling. Now, I'm curious.

"Sorry, I don't want to bring you all down. Melodious is very blunt and petite and funny like you, Sierra."

"So does that mean I can sit next to you again?"

"Sure, come on up." I open my arms wide.

Sierra crawls up next to me and takes my arm and wraps it around her like a mother would hold a child. It's odd but comforting. "You're like a little teddy bear."

"Shelby doesn't think so. She won't hug me like this."

"Maybe because you're too old?" I laugh.

"You're never too old to hug." She pulls my arm tighter around her. "So, I hear you kissed Rose."

"Sierra!" Shelby stands.

I try to pull my arm away, but Sierra tightens her grip and won't let me unhug her. "Nope, you can't leave until you answer my question."

"I, uh, it's just that, uh, I was, and Decker and..."

"It's okay, Cozy," Shelby tries to comfort me. "Chris told the table all about it."

"Well, I feel like shit about it, so let's not bring it up again."

"Why? I like that you're a lesbian." Sierra intertwines my fingers with hers and suddenly this whole cuddle-me-like-a-teddy-bear scenario is becoming very clear.

I try to pull away, but she won't let me. "I'm not a, I just, I'm with Chris and ..."

"Stop it, Sierra!" Shelby tries to control her sister.

"And what are you going to do about it, Shel-by?" Sierra taunts, emphasizing the syllables. "Don't worry, Cozy. If Rose doesn't want you, we'll take you."

"Sierra!"

"I'm not. I'm just... can we change the subject?" I pull my hand out of Sierra's.

"Fine." Sierra flips over to face me. "But just to let you know I'm uh..." She pauses and I see Shelby slightly shake her head no. "I'm uh... I'm sure Rose is not mad. I think the one who is really mad is Decker. You called his bluff, and he's pissed that you did. I thought it was awesome. Right, Shelby? Rose isn't mad, right?"

"No, she's not mad." Shelby pats my feet in assurance.

"Oh, thank you." My eyes start watering. I can't help it. All this pressure to be good, and I'm screwing it up so bad. It's overwhelming. "Then how come Rose isn't returning my texts? I've been trying to apologize forever."

"Her mom restricted her cell phone. She can only have it during school for emergencies and even then, it's turned off. She got a 'C' on a test. Can't be a famous hand surgeon like dear old dad with a 'C' ruining your perfect GPA." Shelby's chin wrinkles as she frowns. She feels sorry for Rose.

I had no idea Rose's parents put that kind of pressure on her. To be so beautiful and smart must be hard when everyone expects it of you. And then to have an ass for a boyfriend? I feel even more sorry for Rose than I did after I kissed her. Poor girl needs a release.

"If you talk to her, tell her I'm so sorry. It was wrong."

"She'll talk to you soon enough. Tomorrow is her day here with you. But don't worry. Decker won't be with her. His uncle's funeral home is getting a new client. It was a suicide. Some girl killed herself after she was attacked by the Highway Rapist. Decker has to help. Her funeral is Friday."

"I heard about that. How sad." It makes my reason for my attempted suicide seem even more pathetic.

"It reminds me of Hilda," Shelby says. "I can't imagine what she's going through. Sierra and I have been searching the woods up near Borden with Telly's team."

"I have no idea who Telly is." I hate being out of the loop, especially when it comes to Hilda.

"Telly and his dad head up one of the search teams out of Three J's café. I don't know why they have us looking up near Borden, but that's where they think she's been taken," Sierra says.

"Yeah, they found some plant or insect or something in the alley that led them there. Who knows? But when the FBI gets involved, they put the smart people on the case. We'll find her."

"The FBI is still here?" My stomach feels like it's imploding.

"Yeah, my dad is pissed. They haven't come by here?" Shelby is surprised. I'm terrified.

"No. And I'm glad. I saw Agent Stiff in the hospital room. I guess I didn't have anything good for him. I don't want anyone here. I don't trust anyone but your dad. He did send a new officer to check on me though. Her name is Officer Crance."

"Don't know her," Shelby says. "But he must trust her. I bet she's new and that's why he sent her." Shelby's eyes widen at Sierra.

"The FBI would think nothing of him sending a rookie on a routine call." Sierra sits up. She and Shelby get excited thinking their dad had one up on the FBI.

"What did she ask? Did she find anything?" Sierra practically crawls into my lap. Shelby pulls her back, and they both kneel by the couch.

"There's nothing here to find. I thought I saw something in the bushes, but it was nothing."

"If you see anything, please call me or Sierra or my dad." Shelby is practically begging. "Just us."

"I promise I'll keep you in the loop only if you keep me in the loop."

"Deal!" Sierra bounces with excitement. "So, what did you see?"

This is beginning to look like an advantageous scenario. Now I don't have to hear everything through five interpretations. I can get the information straight from the sisters. I'm glad they came over, especially since I have no idea how I'm going to face Rose.

Chapter NINE

"ARE YOU SURE you want to come in?" I peek through the eyehole.

"Yes! I'm freezing," Rose yells.

I open the door and she hugs me, pressing her cold cheek to mine. "See? Freezing."

She takes off her gloves and coat and sits on my couch. I turn off the religious programs Mattie has me watching.

After a long silence Rose asks, "You ever get this feeling deep inside that makes you want to do the stupidest things, and you know you shouldn't, but you do anyway?"

I sit on the loveseat, far away from her. "Yeah, I get that. Mine's a hunger. I call her Bonnie."

She laughs. "You named it? You're too funny." She comes and sits next to me. "There's something different about you. It's deep, or dark, or I don't know."

"I'm different alright. I'm a bad person, Rose."

"Because you kissed me? I'm fine with it. Never kissed a girl before. It was kinda fun."

"But you didn't kiss back."

"I was in shock. So was Decker. You should have heard him at lunch. 'I'm a good kisser right, Rosy? I can't believe she did that. And you, Chris, you just stood there. You didn't stop her.'" Rose laughs at her Decker voice.

"That was a perfect impression. What did Chris say?"

"He told Decker not to challenge you because you have bigger balls than Deck does," she says.

"That's funny. But my big balls get me into trouble."

"I like trouble." Curious, Rose scoots closer.

My whole body is flaring up.

Exploiting her curiosity, how much fun would that be? I have this drive to just take her. I bet I could.

I know I could.

And after I take Rose, I know I could take Decker too.

The thought burns inside, and with that, Bonnie is awake. I try to calm her, knowing I'm supposed to be good.

"I am trying to protect you, Rose. I like you, a lot. But you have Decker, and I have Chris, and I don't want you to lose Decker because you don't know what you're getting into with me."

"See? Dark and mysterious."

"Stop it. I'm serious. I'm trouble." I grab her hand. She flinches slightly, but Bonnie won't let go. "But don't worry, Rose. I'm trying to be good."

She squeezes my hand back. She's drawn to me only because I'm different. I'm drawn to her but not in the same way. She's beautiful, yes, but she's also manipulatable. She's someone I think I can control, and that's the most attractive thing about her. "What does Decker think about you coming here?"

"He likes you though he won't admit it."

"And that doesn't bother you?" I ask.

She shifts back. "Did it bother you seeing Mattie kiss Chris?"

"Unfortunately, it had the opposite effect on me."

"I love that you're so honest. I guess... I don't know. I guess it would bother me." She tilts her head, and her insecure eyes look up at me, scared of what I might do. I want her. I want to make her mine. It would be so easy. And Bonnie wants to do it. But this is not who I should be. I stroke her hair off her face. "You're so beautiful. But I can't. I've been to hell, and I don't wanna go back."

"What do you mean by that?" She sits up, intrigued.

"When I was in the hospital, I had a visitor. He told me he would protect me down there if I continued to do all the things I've done up here."

"Oh, you meant like literally? I thought you meant getting shot and stuck in the hospital was hell. Why? Why would he say that? What have you done up here?" Her worried eyes tell all. She's afraid of me and yet wants more. She's mine for the taking.

I stand up. "I've done nothing that you need to worry about. I'm starting a new life. The old one died in that hospital room. The new one will be better. I want to be better."

"So, then what? What are you planning on doing?" Rose asks.

"For one I should stop kissing other people's girlfriends. I don't want to ruin your relationship with Decker."

She laughs. "Thanks. I guess it would get kinda sticky."

"Unless Decker was on board with it, yes, it would be."

"What about Chris? Wouldn't he be mad?"

"What's mine is Chris's. I share everything with him. That would include you, so no, he would not be mad. And speaking of which, here he is." I opened up the curtain to the sound of Chris's truck coming up my drive. I'm relieved and scared. I'm glad he came back, but I'm afraid he's still mad at me.

"I better get going now that he's here." She stands up.

I pull her close. "Rose, I want to, but you need to stay away from me." I softly touch her face. She closes her eyes, enjoying my caress but her body is shaking. She's terrified. That's just how I like them. I make her crave while pushing her away. She'll want what she thinks she can't have.

I love this. Little satisfactions without committing any sins. I give her a kiss on the cheek and brush my lips across hers. I can't help it. This hunger inside is so strong.

Chris walks in. I hug her tight then let her go. "Thanks for checking in on me, Rose."

Trembling and not saying a word, she stares at the ground as she walks by Chris. He shuts the door behind her.

"WHAT HAVE YOU done, Cosette?" Chris asks.

I sit on the couch and don't look at him. I try to act innocent, but really I'm ashamed that I couldn't stay good for even a few days. "What do you mean?"

"You know exactly what I mean." He drops a grocery bag on the kitchen table then comes back to me.

"Are you mad?"

"I don't think so. Should I be?"

I pause and think about it. I am who I am, and maybe Chris is right. Maybe this is the real me. I'm not killing anyone, so as long as I have everyone's permission then it's acceptable, right?

"I've done nothing. I'm being good."

He leans over and kisses me, ignoring our argument from earlier. "I'm proud of you. I want you to be yourself." He holds the back of my hair and pulls me up until I'm looking him in the eye. "I like to study other people. The way they act, the way they treat strangers, and the way they treat their so-called loved ones. I have come to realize that most problems in relationships come from people not being honest with each other or themselves. Sometimes people don't understand who they really are, and they're lost..." He stops, not finishing his thought. He gives me a kiss and walks toward the kitchen. "Tomorrow's the big day. Are you ready?"

"Are you? Is Hilda? Has she seen you?" I follow him.

"Hilda's seen what we need her to see. She will make an excellent police witness. And when this is done I won't have to wear those contacts or mascara anymore. Although I don't mind the smoking."

"I mind the smoking." I insist.

"Fine. I have a few strands of her hair and some blood for Ben's van. The evidence won't lie." From the grocery bag, Chris hands me a pair of Tear Tattoo's shoes and a baggie of cigarette butts. "Do you want me to put them out?" he asks.

"No, I don't want you to be identified. There has to be no doubt that it was only your uncle that was hiding in the bushes watching me. I'll put them out tonight." I pull him close. "Chris, I'm scared."

"Why? We planned it out great," he says.

"I just hate doing this to him."

"Would it make you feel any better if I told you one of the people he killed was a witness to his first murder that happened to be your stepmom? The witness was a woman with two sons."

"Really?"

"No, I just wanted to make you okay with the whole thing."

I slap him. "Not nice."

"I know you're trying to be good, but sacrifices have to be made. It's either Ben or Hilda. You choose."

"I know. I'm just. I know."

"I hope you do. I can't be there to help you. After Ben and I kidnap you and take you to the farm, I'll have to turn around and leave. I need to be home in time to find you're not there for our date. Are you strong enough for this?" He looks concerned, but we have gone over this plan enough. No stone is left unturned. I hope.

"What's there to be strong about? You left the bat in the van, right? So when he gets me out of the van to put me with Hilda, I'll jump out and bash him in the head. Just make sure you wrap my wrists loose enough that I can get free. After I knock him out, I might have problems dragging him to tie him up somewhere, but it has to look real, so I'll struggle. I won't call the police until ten. That should give you time get home and notice that I stood you up for our nine o'clock date. Then you start calling Mattie and Rose and Shelby looking for me. Make sure you call Shelby last."

"Don't worry, Cozy. It's perfect. We'll kidnap you and take you to the farm at eight o'clock sharp. I'll get Hilda ready for your rescue."

Chapter TEN

"YOU'RE DOING WELL, honey. No dizziness?" Mom hands me bobby pins as I braid her hair for work.

"Thanks, Mom. No dizziness. I'm fine. See? I'm good enough to go out. Mattie wants to take me on a date. Pizza."

"Yum. Is Chris not invited?"

"No, he's not invited for pizza. His dad has him doing a few side jobs. But he'll be picking me up for a movie around nine."

"That sounds like a lot for one night."

"It's just dinner and a movie. Only it happens to be with two different people. Don't worry, Mattie will drop me off early enough for me to rest before I sit in a theater with Chris for two hours. Not like we're going ice skating or bowling or anything."

"Okay. Here's a twenty. Be careful what you eat. And don't move too fast. And make sure you change your bandage when you get home from pizza. And..."

"I'll be fine, Mom. I'm just tired of being cooped up." I hear a car door slam. "I think that's Mattie."

"Go get the door." Mom pulls out the hairspray. I leave and shut the bathroom door as the cloud forms.

My next-door neighbor, the Target guy, is walking his dog. He smiles and waves at Mattie. I think he watches until someone interesting pulls into the circle before he lets the dog out.

I open the door for her. The fresh air feels good. I can't wait to get out of here.

"I come bearing gifts." She holds up my homework.

"Awwww, that is so sweet of you. Just for that, would you like to come in?"

"Sure." She steps into the foyer and stops. Her expression turns sour. "Cosette, what have you done in here?"

"Why? What's wrong? Mom is hairspraying in the bathroom. Does it smell bad?"

"What have you been doing? It's not right in here."

It's odd, but it's Mattie. She does things like this. I think it's her oversensitive God sense. Maybe she feels leftovers from Rose. Maybe she feels like something bad is going to happen. Like me getting fake kidnapped to frame Tear Tattoo.

"I just need to brush my teeth. Where are we going?"

"Somewhere public, away from alleys." Mattie puts her hand on my shoulder in a sarcastic effort to console.

"Funny girl. Give me a second. I'll be right out." I go to the bathroom to brush my teeth as Mom exits.

"Hi, Mattie." She models her hair for Mattie, who applauds. "Thank you. I'm outta here. Be careful with Cosette. Watch what she eats. Don't let her move too much."

"Don't worry. I'll be boring tonight and will have her home early." Mattie holds out my mom's jacket and purse. Mom gives Mattie and me hugs and darts out the door.

"I feel cleaner, at least my mouth does." I smile and suck minty air in through my teeth.

"Good, let's get out of here!" She walks me to the car and opens the door for me.

"You cleaned little 'P'?" I ask. Her Pacer is polished and smells like Armor All.

"I did clean him, but not for you."

I frown.

"I'm taking you to a restaurant to see someone. His name is Ken Telford, but everyone calls him Telly."

"Okay, why?"

"Because his last name is Telford. Duh." She rolls her eyes at me, knowing that's not the question I asked. "I need an excuse, so I'm using you. Is that okay?"

"I thought you looked good today. Hair is pulled back. Makeup is perfect. You smell pretty, and your car is clean. I'm glad I look like a slob."

"Me too. Thank you." She folds her hands in a thankful prayer.

Mattie is a perfect catch. She could walk in wearing a floor mat and would still look good. It's nice to see her like someone. No one at school is remotely close to her league. At least not in my opinion. No one is good enough.

"So tell me about this mystery man," I ask while buckling up.

"He's been into the coffee shop to help with the hunt for Hilda."

"That's great." I readjust the seatbelt. It's a bit uncomfortable. I'm still sore.

Mattie is giddy talking about Telly. "So he's from Louisville and he's been over every day with his father. His dad is on some special police team that's helping with the search. Anyway, he works at a pizza joint downtown. So I thought a little garlic bread would be good for you."

"And here I thought you were taking me for pizza because you loved me. Does he know we're coming, or are you just stalking him?" I braid my hair on the way over.

"I am just stalking him. I haven't got the courage to say anything more than 'Would you like a refill on your coffee?'" She mocks her own voice.

"Cute, does that work for him?"

"I think so. He's hocked up on caffeine by the time the search starts. Anyway, I think I like him, and I just wanted to see him work."

I know Mattie. She invests her time before she makes any move. She wants to see this guy's work ethic and how he's treated by his co-workers. I hope he passes her test. Even though she may not realize it, she's testing.

Mattie parks the car, and she digs out a handful of quarters for the meter.

"Are we planning to stay overnight?" I tease her. I don't want to stay too long. Chris is supposed to be picking me up at eight.

"I don't want a parking ticket. Don't worry. We'll eat, then stare, then leave."

"Sounds good."

"Do you hurt? I mean, more than how you like?"

"Ha ha. I feel fine. Not a lot of pain, just a bit sore. Not enough to keep me from watching you flirt."

"I will not be flirting, at least I don't think so. If I am and I act like an idiot, please tell me."

"No, no. I'm going to sit back and watch."

"And I thought I could trust you!" She fake cries, blinking her eyes and frowning deep. I laugh. "By the way, Coz, he doesn't know that you were the girl that got shot. No one knows. I'm going to tell him you're just my best friend. I don't want to put you in any danger."

"You don't want the guy to finish me off?" Her disposition drops. "It's okay, Mattie. I know my reality. But I can't stay cooped up and scared forever. That's what Hilda did to me, and I couldn't handle it. I refuse to stay scared."

She stops to hug me. "I'm proud of you."

"Don't be," I whisper to myself.

WE GET IN and the hostess seats us in Telly's section. It's dimly lit, and the old dark wooden booths give it a comfy atmosphere.

Telly comes to our table. "Well, hello there. I'm glad to see you on this side of the river. Did you cross just to see me?"

"No, the pizza. You were a bonus." Mattie's coy.

"A bonus? Okay. I can work with that. And you are?" Telly addresses me. He's about six feet tall with short dark brown hair. He has dark eyes and deep dimples. He's decently built. Athletic but not extreme.

"This is my best friend, Cosette."

"Nice to meet you." I hand him my menu.

"Good to meet you too. What can I get you all to drink?"

He takes our drink and food order, and we watch him work. Correction, Mattie watches him work. I watch her stare at him.

He brings our food out, smiles a flirty smile at Mattie, and whisks off to serve the other tables.

"It's good to see you happy," I tell her. "It's nice to see you focused on something other than the Academy or softball or church."

"I don't have time for a boyfriend." She sighs.

"You have to make the time. Before Hilda was taken, John came to see my mom any time he could. Even if it was for only five minutes, to him it was worth it. Of course, now he's busy and worried. I haven't seen him since I got out of the hospital."

"I talked to Shelby. I know you did too. Have you remembered anything?"

I remember everything. I can't let her fish for answers. She'll see right through me. "I can remember why we are here, and it's not for me. It's getting crowded. How many tables does he have?"

"Looks like six. He's handling them well." She stares at him. He writes nothing down. In her eyes that means he's smart and pays attention.

As Telly passes through another server's section, he pulls out a chair for an elderly lady. Respectful. Mattie hides her smile.

"How are my two most beautiful customers doing?" Telly comes over to check on us.

"I'm not sure how they're doing, but we're doing great." Mattie's eyes light up.

"My shift is about over. I don't like to stay for the drinking crowd. Would you ladies mind if I take you out?"

"I think that would be nice. We'll wait."

"Great. I'll finish up. Sorry, but I do have to leave you this." He plops the bill on our table and turns to finish his shift.

"Thank you. We'll take it. Cozy, do you mind if he takes us out?"

"That's fine, although I should get home soon. Make sure he doesn't mind driving to Jeff to drop me off. Then you two can have a good night without me being a third wheel."

"You're not a third wheel. You're a buffer."

"I'm a third wheel, and unless you want to start doing threesomes, you will need to drop me off at home."

"Gross. I'm not into threesomes."

"I am, but we just met him," I joke with her. I want to see her reaction. It's exactly what I expected. She doesn't notice for a second and then...

"What? What did you just say?"

"Nothing, Mattie. You don't need to hear talk like that."

"Cosette, you're supposed to be good. Please, try to be good. Please tell me you haven't done anything like that. Please tell me it's just you and Chris. Stay on the right path."

"I am not hurting anyone." I sit back in protest.

"Everything is permissible, but not everything is beneficial." A Bible verse. This is her final authority. This is her rule book, and whether or not I follow it, she does. She's the one who prayed to bring me back. She's the reason I am here. I need to have respect.

"I'm just kidding, Mattie. I was just testing you. Besides, who would volunteer?"

"Be careful, Cozy. You are walking and crossing fine lines that will cause a ripple effect. You may not see it now, but it will bite you in the butt later. If not for you, then protect others. Your decisions affect many others."

This hits me hard. I remember officer Crance. How the brief moment of pleasure killed her little sister.

"No threesomes. Got it."

"Try to be moral. God gave you a second chance. Don't screw it up."

"Okay, Mattie. I'll try."

Telly comes over and sits next to her. He changed his shirt and fixed his hair. Nice to see he cares enough to not subject us to pizza smell all night.

"Are you ladies ready?" He holds out his hand to escort her. Chivalrous. Score one more for Telly. "Would you like to take my car?"

"No, I need to drop off Cosette. She has a time limit," Mattie informs him. "I'm parked over here."

We walk over to her car and his face lights up. "Please tell me that the blue Pacer is yours."

She nods.

"I love this car! I saw it where you work. I didn't know if it was a volunteer's. I'm glad you're driving." He opens the driver's door for her then opens mine. "I'll get in the back."

"No, you get in the front. You need the leg room." I crawl into the cramped back seat.

Mattie smiles a "thanks" to me.

As we cross the bridge into Louisville, Telly looks out the window. "So, Cosette, huh? Where's your castle?"

Mattie laughs. "She's never seen the show. She's never read the book or heard the music. Have you seen *Les Miserables*?"

I'm not happy to be referenced to that musical, especially since I have no idea what he's talking about. Especially since one of the last things my dad told me was that he named me properly; he made my life miserable.

Telly shifts to face Mattie. "I love *Les Miz*." He turns to me, and I shake my head no. "You've never heard it? Your song, "Castle on a cloud"? It's a fantastic musical."

"Her last name is Hugo. Her brother's name is Victor."

Great. Thanks, Mattie.

"Ahh, no wonder you've stayed away. I understand. It's like your life was prewritten for you."

"I like this guy, Mattie. I approve."

"I was being judged?" He laughs. "There's only one judge for me. Sorry, Cosette. You are not Him."

This God reference makes Mattie happy. I can tell. She squirms in her seat. How, out of all the people she comes in contact with, does she happen to pick out the Christian?

"Believe me, Telly, I am in no way, shape, or form, fit to judge anyone."

"None of us are," Telly says. "So, Matilda, tell me more about yourself." He shifts to face her, his happy eyes taking in all they can.

"I can tell you. Mattie would never brag about herself, so I'm gonna have to. She's perfect. She's going to the Air Force Academy, she's the captain of the softball team, she helps run a food pantry from her church, and she is a straight-A student. She's going to change the world."

"Wow. I am impressed." He turns to a red-faced Mattie.

"I'm so sorry, Telly. That was embarrassing," she tells him.

"That was embarrassing, Cozy!" She scolds me through the

rearview mirror.

"Just getting it out in the open. He needs to know the high standard of perfection he will be dealing with this evening. Otherwise, it would be unfair to him if he wasn't even in your league."

"I hope I qualify." He turns to me. "I guess since I don't have my best friend here to give you my credentials, I'll have to do it myself. I'm first baseman of our baseball team. I love to swim and read. I play bass for the praise and worship team at my church, and I will be going to seminary in the fall."

"To study what?" she asks.

"I want to be a youth pastor. These are the best days of our lives, but so many kids screw it up by making stupid decisions. I just want to let them know there's a better way."

"He's perfect for you Mattie. Absolutely perfect. You both are perfect. I think I need to get out of this car. It's getting hot in here."

"You're fine, Cozy. Relax. And thank you for embarrassing me yet again," she says in the mirror.

"You shouldn't be embarrassed. She's right." His eyes sparkle at her. It's so obvious even I feel it.

She smiles back at him. They're hooked on each other.

I need to get home.

My phone buzzes. "Sorry, guys. It's Chris."

"Her boyfriend," Mattie whispers to Telly.

"HI, HONEY. WHERE are you?" I ask.

"I'm at home getting ready. I'll pick you up in exactly two hours. Eight o'clock sharp, okay?"

"Yeah, I need a bath first, but I'll be ready."

"I'll see ya then." I hang up. I'm getting nervous. We turn on Veterans Parkway about two minutes from home.

"You shouldn't bathe yet, should you?" Mattie asks because of my staples. Then realizing what she said, she starts to apologize. "I'm sorry, Cozy. Where are you all going?"

"He's picking me up for a movie around nine. I'll be sitting on my butt, so I'll be safe." Leaning in I explain to Telly, "I was the one who was shot. I was there when Hilda was taken. I got out of the hospital on Monday, and I haven't been out of the house since. Mattie drug me out, so please, be worth it. Be good to her."

He doesn't know what to say. The car stops in front of my apartment. He gets out and helps me out of the back seat.

"Cosette, I'm so sorry that that happened to you. We knew the eighth victim. We'll find him. We'll find Hilda too, and you'll be safe. Keep praying. God will protect you. Trust Him."

With a hug, I thank him then wave to Mattie as I go inside.

I START MY bath and lay out my clothes on my bed. My most comfortable jeans are worn and holey. But I figure Hilda and I will be walking a long way before we're picked up, and when we are, who cares if I have holes? The sweatshirt is white, so we'll be seen easily, and I think I'll wear my good running shoes. I don't want blisters. I grab my robe and head for the tub.

Scented steam fills the bathroom. I slip in the bubble-filled tub and wash my hair. I smell like a pizza parlor. And just in case I have to go to the hospital with Hilda, I shave my legs and underarms.

"Tonight's the night, Victor. I'm bringing Hilda back, and I'm starting my path to being good. I don't want any more regrets, so I'm going to try hard. I hope up in Heaven, you and God can see that I'm trying. I should get points for effort, right?"

I stand up and turn on the shower to rinse off before I get out. My wound is fully scabbed over, but I'll let it air out a bit before I bandage it. My fluffy robe is warm, giving me comforting hugs. I'm going to need them.

With over an hour before Chris picks me up, I decide to blow-dry my hair. It's too cold to walk around with it wet. But I think I need a new hairdryer. This one smells like it's burning up. I shut it off and sniff it. It wasn't the hairdryer. It was a cigarette, probably my neighbor taking his yappy Maltese out. This reminds me, I need to put Ben's/Tear Tattoo's cigarette butts in the back bushes tonight. And because it's been raining, the ground is soft, perfect for deep footprints. When I walk around in Tear's shoes to drop the butts, I hope I don't sink too deep into the mud.

After my hair's dry, I'll go out there. I'm too cold right now. There's a draft in here or something. Tightening up my robe, I go to my room to grab the baggie.

I flick the light on and scream!

I GRAB MY knife from the dresser and run towards the back door. He chases me down and yanks my hair then holds a cloth over my face. I can't breathe!

Kicking and flailing, I'm not strong enough to get away. He lifts me and slams my legs against the kitchen table, knocking it over and hurting me enough to where I can't kick.

I push against the wall and fall back on him. I want to open Blue up, but I'm so tired, I'm weak. What did he do to me? I can't keep my eyes open. I slide Blue into my robe pocket. I'll have to use it later to free myself from Tear Tattoo.

Chapter ELEVEN

JOLTED AWAKE, I start coming to. I'm being bounced around, but I can't move. My wrists and ankles are tied up. Duct tape keeps me quiet. I'm being kidnapped!

What about our plan? In an hour, Chris is supposed to come get me! He'll see that I'm gone. What's he going to do then? I feel sick. I feel a hollow emptiness creeping over me.

I'm so scared.

I start crying.

Then I hear mumbling. I have to wake up more. As I squirm to roll over, I try to focus on my whereabouts. It seems I'm on the floor of a van, and we've been on a highway for a while. It's hard to see. I blink my eyes, but I'm crying too much. It's very dark out.

"Chris, shut her up!" Tear Tattoo yells.

Chris?

Chris!

He's doing this to me?

Chris is here with Tear?

"Shut up, you stupid bitch!" Chris gets out of his seat and kicks me! I black out again.

Please, please, God, take me. Please let me out of this life!

He betrayed me.

I don't want to stay. Chris betrayed me. Let me die.

"CHRIS, SHE'S AWAKE again," Ben says.

"Let her whine," he responds. He turns and looks down at me. His eyes no longer sparkle. They're evil. Pure evil. My perfect boyfriend glares at me in hate.

"How did you think this would end, Cosette? You killed my uncle! You killed my cousin! Then you come back and don't want to play anymore? Hell no! You're useless to me."

My heart stops. I can't breathe.

I'm going to die.

I hope it's done quickly.

"Don't kill her until I get her," Tear demands.

"No! She's mine first. You can have the blonde all you want. The blonde is payment for the drugs. I told you I would pay you back. You just had to be patient. But this one, this one is mine." He throws a beer bottle at me. It cracks my glasses. "Paybacks are a bitch!"

My body is convulsing. I can't stop. How do I get out of this? If not for me, then for Hilda.

"You stole a shitload of drugs from me, Chris. I want her too. You can have her first, but I want her too."

"You had her stepmom. She wasn't enough for you?"

"What? Who?" Ben asks.

"The blonde bitch behind the pawn shop. Either way, I don't give a shit. You can have her, but she likes pain, so you're going to have to be extra rough. Don't you, Cosette? We'll make sure you like it!"

How can he do this to me? I loved him! Now I see him for the monster that he is, and my heart is crushed. I desperately try to get my hands free.

"What? Are you scared, Cosette? You were so eager to get on Rose the other night. This should be a good time for you. You're nothing but a whore!

"Hey, Ben, you should have seen her the other night. She kissed this tasty redheaded bitch, and she made me kiss her best friend."

"And you want to kill her?"

"I can't trust her. I'll go back for the redhead one way or another. Do you wanna help with her best friend? She's still a virgin. She's pure as snow. We can have a good time with her. Right, Cosette? Mattie will have a lot of fun with us. Here, Ben. Turn in here by the split tree. Then it's four miles."

"I see the tree. It's dark out here," Tear Tattoo says.

"That's the point. You'll see the barn, and just past the barn, there'll be a shed that leads to a cellar. I have the blonde waiting in the back room for you. I gave her a bath earlier today. It was this one's idea. Isn't that nice?"

Chris grabs my hair and pulls me up between the seats. "This one is evil, more evil than you realize. Did you know she killed eight people?" He shakes my head and twists my neck, putting me on display for his uncle. "One of her victims she cut up into... how many pieces was it, Cosette? Fifteen, I think. Fifteen pieces, then we tossed them in the rivers. She's wild I tell you. A feisty thing. I will miss that." He wipes the tears away from my eyes so I can clearly see his hate.

The van stops, and by my hair I'm dragged out. I glance into the back of the van. There's no baseball bat. Chris planned this revenge, playing with me the whole time.

It's cold and rainy. I'm freezing with bare feet, wet hair, and a wet bathrobe.

"Ben, go into the shed and down the steps. Inside, the blonde is there. Don't kill her yet. I want to see this one and her together." He chokes me to get my full attention. "If she doesn't perform, I'll rape and kill her mom."

The duct tape muffles my cries, and then I hear them, the screaming goats. I start to cry harder. There is no hope. No one can hear me, and even if they did, they wouldn't know it. Chris throws me over his shoulder and carries me to the farmhouse while Ben creaks open the shed door.

I can hear Hilda screaming.

I am so sorry, Hilda. I'm so sorry. I betrayed you. I let him take you.

Chris drops me to the kitchen floor. The farmhouse is empty. His cousins are still out spending their inheritance. My last few moments in here will be hell.

He pats my robe down to find Blue. The knife snaps open and he cuts the tape off my ankles. Then he straddles me, holding my legs still. "So, Bonnie, here we are. I know this is not how you planned it. Your idea seemed perfect, but it was flawed. Shh, shh, shh. Just listen. He can't be kept alive. He's our fall guy, and he would talk."

I shake my head no.

"Are you upset? Are you hurt? Don't be. If he was going to be the fall guy, the plan needed to be perfect. He had to be the one to kidnap you."

He wipes the tears from my eyes. "Bonnie, I love you. I need you to be Bonnie again. Shh, shh, shh, shh. It's okay. I love you. Your Clyde loves you. I'm sorry about what I said. I didn't mean any of it." He holds my face and looks into my eyes. "You still don't understand? Bonnie, I needed it to be believable. I needed it to look like a real kidnapping. I love you. You're safe. This is part of the plan. Our plan."

My eyes shift back and forth as I try to comprehend what's going on. All of this was fake? This was part of the setup? I look into Chris's eyes.

They smile at me.

I cry out in relief. He grabs the edge of the duct tape. "Are you ready? You can scream if you want."

I nod my head.

"One, two, three!"

I scream, loud. It feels like my face is being ripped off!

"I am so sorry. I didn't want to hurt you. Bonnie, I'm so sorry." He kisses me and apologizes over and over. "I love you. I will never betray you. I love you so much. I'm so sorry. I never want to see you scared like that again." He hugs me tight.

"You could have warned me." I can't speak very well. I'm still crying.

"I didn't want it to look staged. It had to be believable. You had to really be kidnapped. Now listen. He's about to take Hilda. He will force you two to go at it. Let her know you were kidnapped too but that you have a knife. That way she'll follow along. He doesn't have a weapon, and I've cleaned out the cellar. You do whatever you can to kill him and get back to me. You wanted Hilda, so this is your chance. You only get one shot at this. Here, take Blue."

Adrenaline races as I grab my knife.

"After he's dead, you need to get her and escape. Run to the split tree and turn left towards the highway. Got it? Left."

I nod trying hard to focus.

"I have to leave. I'm supposed to pick you up in an hour for our date. That's when I'll call the cops, when I see your house was broken into. You trashed the place pretty good trying to get away from Ben, so it looks perfect." He stands up and pulls me to my feet. "Okay, Bonnie, I have to move fast. You can take your time." He holds my face, lifts my cracked glasses, and kisses my bruised cheek. The glow of his love is back.

"Enjoy Hilda. In her eyes, you're being forced to do this, so do what you want. She will still be a little high too. Remember that before your long walk. Do not leave Blue behind. You are only in a bathrobe and will be walking a highway. You might need it if a cop doesn't pick you up first."

He gives me a long kiss.

"I love you, Cosette, but I need you to be Bonnie tonight, okay? This will be our last one. I need you to be Bonnie. Can you do that?"

I nod yes.

I can be Bonnie.

WE GET TO the cellar. "You do whatever you need to get back to me." He opens the door and shoves me in. I fall to my knees. Tear Tattoo has his shirt off and his pants down. I can hear Hilda gagging. He turns and smiles at me, the dirtball. He pulls Hilda off and comes to me. I touch my pocket. Blue is secure. He squeezes my cheeks against my braces until my mouth opens.

I yank my head away. "I bite!"

"Fucking bitch!" He punches me. "If you won't suck me, I know you will suck her." He yanks my hair and forces me on Hilda.

She's still high, but she knows it's me. "Cosette?" She starts crying harder. "Cosette, help me. Please. I can't take any more. Please, just kill me. I can't take this. Just kill me."

I straddle her. The asshole took off all her clothes. She's naked and shivering. But I love it. Heat rushes through me. Bonnie is awake and alive and excited. Hilda's tied up, beautiful, and scared, but I have to focus. I need her to stay alive. She's my token. I need to focus to protect my token.

"Kiss her, you bitch! If you do good on her, I'll be easy on you," he yells at me.

I lean in to kiss her. She turns her head.

"Hilda, you have to do this."

She turns back to me. I kiss her then stop. I have to control my personal demons to get us away from this tattooed demon. He kicks my side.

"More, you whore! Touch her!" He strokes himself as he watches us.

I submit. I kiss her more and more as I run my hands down her naked body. I reached my hands down between her legs. She tightens her thighs. Gently I rub her. I need her to trust me. I run the tip of my tongue along the edge of her ear. This pleases him. He closes his eyes and moans. I whisper to Hilda. "I'm going to get you out of this. I promise."

He stomps on her shin. "Open wide for her!"

She screams and obeys.

I graze my lips across her neck and whisper. "Shhh. I have a knife. I am going to hide it down there. When I get up to choke him, you get it out and stab him."

Her eyes open wide. She understands, but this request scares her more. By my hair, he pulls me down between her legs. Gently, I massage her thighs as I kiss. Moving in, I lift her hips to hide Blue under her.

She tightens her legs around my head, panicking. "No, please."

I look up at her and whisper, "You don't want to?"

She shakes her head, and the tears pour out. Poor girl is so weak, even if she could physically, mentally she's broken.

"It's okay." I tuck Blue back in my robe and climb up her. "I'll do it." I kiss her stomach, then up to her breasts. "It's okay. I'll protect you." And with that I press my lips to hers, receiving my hero's reward.

I sit up and wait.

"Go back down! You're not done. You haven't even started!" he yells.

Her body starts shaking. She's petrified at the sound of his voice.

He slaps me. "I said you're not done!"

I look at Hilda and smile then stand up and kiss him. With an approving grunt, he kisses me back, hard. "That's right. You like it rough don't you, bitch? You're my freak tonight!"

I push him against a wall, feverously kissing him. Gagging at the taste of cigarettes, I pull the back of his hair until he lies down on the floor. Then I straddle him. This is my favorite position.

I spread open my robe. He likes what he sees, so I let him touch. Then I lean in and lick his neck. Glancing over at Hilda, I can see she's scared for me. Barely shaking my head no, I tell her to close her eyes. She turns away.

Grasping Blue tight, I suck on his neck and moan loud so he doesn't hear my knife snap open. His hands are everywhere. I should be disgusted, but knowing I'm about to get high, I let him have his way. The adrenaline is kicking in, so everywhere he touches only increases the effects. I take my time and let him work, amazed at how erotic this moment is.

Stripping off my robe, I throw it behind me and spread my naked body across his. Skin on skin, he's warm. His body is calling to Bonnie. She's here and excited to answer. I bite my bottom lip. The time has come. With a firm grip on Blue, I press the tip against Tattoo's neck. His eyes open in surprise.

"There you go. That's what I want to see." I spin the tip of the blade around while I lick his lips. I'm so turned on. The fear in his eyes turns to dread, as well it should. I'm just taking my time, savoring the moment.

"Can you taste us? I want you to remember us." I lick his lips again. "I want you to remember her." I look to Hilda, who has turned back to watch. "Remember what you did to her. That's why I am doing this to you." His stiff body starts to tremble. My naked thighs are so sensitive to it. I kiss him. He stops kissing me back. It's time.

I shove the knife in. He gasps for air. I tighten my lips to his, selfishly stealing his last breath. They tremble then stop. His wide eyes dim.

Bonnie is back. And she is very, very happy!

Chapter TWELVE

I SIT THERE for a bit kissing him, still twisting my knife. His squirting blood brightens the gray floor. It's beautiful.

"Cosette. Cosette? Cosette!" Hilda cries out.

I don't want to look at her. I'm sucking in every moment of pleasure I can.

"Cosette, he's dead."

"I know." I'm disappointed. "It happens so fast." I sit up and wait. When his chest and stomach sink in, I wipe Blue clean on his chest.

I straddle Hilda again, because I can, and cut off the straps that hold her captive. Her arms drop limp. I rub them to circulate the blood. "You need to get dressed. It's raining outside, and we have a long walk home."

"What are we going to do with him?" She shivers.

"We're going to leave him here." I stand up and grab my robe. After I shake it off, I put it back on. "We need to find help and call the police."

"What? Cosette, we can't call the police!"

"Yes, Hilda, we can. I covered up my last murder in case you don't remember. The police will need to find him. We stopped a serial killer. You're safe. We're safe. Let's go."

With her arms wrapped around her knees, she just sits there. "Cosette. You killed someone."

"I know. Can we go?" I grab her clothes.

"I can't believe you killed someone."

"What the hell is wrong with you? You didn't realize we were going to be his next victims? We saw his face. He never leaves anyone alive!" I throw her clothes at her.

She doesn't move.

"If you don't get up and move, I will leave you here."

She cautiously grabs her clothes and puts them on.

"Good girl."

She's moving slow. I guess it doesn't matter. No one will be searching for us just yet. Chris won't lead them up here.

I calm down and kneel by her. "Hilda, I'm sorry."

"For what? Killing someone to save my life?"

"I'm sorry you went through that. Did he hurt you?"

"All week," she whispers.

Good. Chris did his job.

"I'm sorry. Hilda, I'm so sorry."

I go to hug her, but she flinches. "I won't hurt you." She stays back. "You think I'm a monster?"

She looks down.

"I won't hurt you."

"You enjoyed it, didn't you?"

I stand up and start to walk away.

She pulls my robe, and I kneel back down. "What, Hilda? What do you want me to say to that? I saved you. Does it matter the method?"

"I wasn't going to say anything."

"Believe me, I know." I lean in to her ear. She's still trembling. "Because if you do, I will kill you too. And yes, I will thoroughly enjoy it."

This scares her more. She holds her breath. I pull back, brushing my lips across her smooth cheek. She's so beautiful, even in this hell.

83

"Stop shaking, I get off on it. Now let's go. It's dark and cold, and I want to go home."

She quickly follows me out the door. We run up to the van, but it's locked. "Stay here. I'll go find the keys."

She flings herself at me. "No! No, don't leave me! Please, Cosette, don't go. Don't go!"

I didn't expect this. She hugs me so tight I can't move. "Do you want to go back to the cellar to find the keys? I'm sure he has them."

"I don't want to get in that van. I can't be in there. Please don't leave me. Can't we just walk? Please, I just wanna go home. Please?" She hides into me like a scared child.

I hold her. "We'll just stay on this dirt road until we hit another road. Hopefully, we'll find the highway." She's cold and shaking. I stand and pull her up. "Here, hold my hand. I don't want to lose you." She does what I ask. This is good. Control is good.

The full moon peeks in and out of the rain clouds. It helps us in these dark woods.

We walk for about thirty minutes in silence when she stops. "Cosette," she pulls my hand, turning me to face her. "I don't want you to hate me, but…"

"But you were just kissing me to get out of there? I get it. I'm not stupid."

"I would have done anything."

"I know. I hope you enjoyed it while it lasted," I say.

"I did." She slightly smiles.

"Well that's good. Don't tear down my ego any more than it already is. Do you mind if I take a break?" I sit on a small boulder on the side of the road.

"What happened?" She points to my staples.

"I forgot you were out for that. After you found out what I did, I had to go for a run to clear my head. I had decisions to make."

"Like the decision to kill yourself. Again?" Her voice quivers.

"Yeah, pretty much. Anyway, as I was running, I heard a scuffle in the alley. Just like the time before. When I went in, you were already knocked out. I took out my knife that I always carry now, and when he saw it, he shot me." I open my robe to show her the entry and exit wound. "I couldn't help you. I'm sorry. He took you and left. I guess he found out who I was and got me today. It wasn't hard with the story all over the news."

"What? I'm on the news?"

"Hilda, you have been on every newscast for a week now. There is a big search party looking for you. Mattie said you called her, and she went out looking for you. She heard the gunshot and found me. They knew instantly who it was and that you were taken. The FBI is here and everything. That's why we need to find the highway. Your picture has been plastered across every screen. Some driver will recognize you and will pick us up and hopefully call the police."

She sits down next to me. It's overwhelming for her. She breaks down and starts crying. "I thought I wouldn't make it. I was so alone and scared. I didn't think anyone knew that I was missing."

"There has been a search party for you every day. Mattie's parents are hosting the coordinators from their parking lot. Everyone in town has been looking for you. Your dad hasn't slept. Even the mayors have gone out looking for you, but for them, it's political."

She falls on her knees bawling. It's a week's worth of anguish being released. I kneel down and hug her. She hugs me back so tight, so desperate.

It feels strange comforting her, knowing it's half my fault, knowing I sent Chris to torture her every day this week. I wrap my arms around her trembling body. Knowing what happened doesn't make me sad for her. I'm feeling antsy. I'm craving her. I can understand why serial killers keep souvenirs from their victims. I'm enjoying this. She will be my souvenir. I hug her tighter.

"I was so scared, Cozy. I was so scared. I prayed over and over for God to get me out of this. I told him I couldn't take anymore and for him to just kill me."

That sounds familiar. That's what I felt a month ago.

I got better.

"AND JUST WHEN I thought I had had enough, he came in without his mask, and I knew it was time. I knew I was going to be raped for the last time. But then you were there. You saved me. You saved me, Cosette. You were sent by God to save me."

"I think we should go." I stand up and pull her with me.

"God sent you, my angel, to protect me."

"Let's go now!"

"Cosette, you're my guardian angel!"

I slap her. "Enough! I am no angel! I have killed, and I liked it! Don't you get it? Think, Hilda. I am a monster, and I can't help it! The last thing I am is an angel! I am no savior! I was not sent by God!"

She touches her face. Her watering blue eyes look at me in disappointment.

"Oh, Hilda, I am so sorry, I'm so sorry!" I kiss her cheek. "I didn't mean to hurt you. I don't want to hurt you." I kiss her and hold her face. "Are you okay? I promise I won't hurt you. I just need to get moving. Please? I'm so sorry."

"It's okay." She holds my hands against her face. "I guess it's hard on you too. I guess you have to deal with..." She stops, not wanting to bring me down further.

"The guilt. I have to deal with the guilt. I have to deal with the fact that even though it was for protection, I still killed someone." That brings me back down. I'm crashing and crashing hard. I need Chris. "We have to walk. Talk about something else. Anything else."

She stutters. "Uh, okay. I have a personal question."

"Great. Can you wait on asking? I'm trying not to implode here. Let me ask you a question."

"Okay."

"Why do you hate me? I mean, besides the fact that I just slapped you, why were you so mean to me?" I know the answer. I just want to hear her say it.

"Don't freak out. I don't want you to kill me."

"If you tell me the truth, I won't."

"I have been in love with Chris ever since I saw him. And when I found out he was in love with you, I got jealous. I didn't want him to like you, so I tried to make you look bad."

"You know it only made *you* look bad."

"I know. I had no idea it would do that to you. I got carried away, and I couldn't stop. I found myself liking the control, liking hurting you."

Wow, she and I have something in common.

"Do you still like him?"

She answers, "Yes," slowly. But then she quickly speaks. "I know he's yours, and I won't do anything to try to take him. I promise I won't. Don't hurt me."

That's a good answer. Let me see how she reacts to this. "If you want, I'll let you have him for one night."

"What?" She stops.

"If you want, I'll let you have him, but he's still mine." I'm not sure if I'm offering because the idea of him being with her turns me on, or if it's the control I have that I'm allowing her one night with him that turns me on. Either way, my offering throws her into shock.

"You would let me sleep with him?"

It's the control. "Yes, but remember, he's mine. You can't have him anytime you want. You have to ask me. Every time."

"What kind of sick game are you playing?" She steps back in shock. "What's he going to say when he finds this out?"

"He might say no. He might ask me to join." The thought makes me tingle. I step in close to her and stroke her shoulder. "Don't forget, he did catch me kissing you on my bathroom floor."

"Yeah, and he yanked you off!"

"Not because he was jealous."

She swallows hard, starts shaking but doesn't respond. She turns and starts walking. Finally we reach the split tree. I lean against it and brush off my bare feet. How stupid of me not to go into the farmhouse and at least try to find a pair of socks or call the police. Too late now to go back. I doubt Hilda would've wanted to stay and wait anyway. I tighten my robe, and we start walking again.

"You were going to kill me, huh? That night in the bathroom? You laid on me like you did that guy. Holy shit! You were going to kill me that night!"

"Shhh, I think I hear the highway over there. I think we should go this way."

As soon as we turn towards the highway, it starts to rain hard. This is not what I want.

"Cosette, were you going to kill me?"

"Tell me about your mom."

87

Hilda decides not to press the bathroom issue. "My mom is high maintenance. My dad made lots of money, but my mom spent it all."

"Why did she leave?" I overheard it from her dad, John, when he and my mom were talking, but I want to hear Hilda's version of it.

"My mom didn't leave. My dad kicked her out. He found out she was doing Paige's uncle."

"Holy crap! I thought you and Paige had a falling out because of how you treated me." I'm almost laughing.

"Is that what she said? She was sparing her family the shame. A missionary's brother should know better than to be with an adulteress like my mom. Sorry, Cosette, but you were just an excuse."

"I thought it sounded a little too righteous."

"That's Paige. I don't blame her though. She's at the mercy of her parents. We're all at the mercy of our parents."

"Yeah, I get that."

"So, between the affair and her spending sprees, my dad kicked her out. I feel bad for him because he has to raise me on his own."

"I know how you feel. My mom has to raise me because my dad did pretty much the same thing. But he's dead now, so I don't care."

Her eyebrows wrinkle and she shivers. I'm so flippant about my dad's suicide that the lack of humanity bothers her.

It doesn't bother me.

Chapter THIRTEEN

"COSETTE?"

"What?"

"If our parents keep dating and end up getting married, then you kissed your sister."

"And I enjoyed it too." I put my arm around her.

"You're a sicko." She puts her arm around my waist.

"I've been told that before. Look, we're almost there. We'll hit the highway and start walking, I think, right. I'm not sure though. We'll just walk until someone picks us up and can call the police. I'm so tired. If no one gets us, we'll just keep walking till we hit a rest stop."

"That sounds good." She gives me a little hug. I smile.

"Oh crap, Cosette, I'm sorry. Did that hurt you?"

"Oh, my naïve Hilda, I wish I could tell you everything, but no. I'm fine, you didn't hurt me."

"Why can't you tell me everything?"

"Are you seriously going to ask me that? I don't tell Mattie everything, and she's my best friend."

"I won't say anything," she says.

"That's because you know I will kill you."

"Exactly, so what have you got to lose?"

"You tortured me for six months, and now you want to be best friends who share secrets?"

She stops walking, grabs me, and kisses me. How funny that she thinks I can be swayed by her kisses. Maybe it would work, but I'm still on such a high from my kill that I have better control. I take my time kissing her back then I laugh at her. "Now you're getting desperate."

"I'll do whatever you want."

"Yes, I know you will." I hold her hand and we keep walking. "Thanks for the kiss. I won't make you do anything. Ask me what you want, and I might answer."

"Were you going to kill me?" Her hand squeezes mine nervously. "In the bathroom? Is that why Chris yanked you off? Were you going to kill me?"

"Yes."

"Do you want to kill me now?"

"No."

She starts crying.

"I'm not here to torture you, Hilda."

"Why not? After everything I did to you? I deserve it. I'm a horrible person."

"I think you've been tortured enough. I'm not happy about what you did to me, and I'm not happy that this monster came out of me because of it. But I am who I am. And you'll just have to deal with it."

The rain lets up a little, so we sit for a second.

"The TV reporters are going to interview you. Please don't bring me up," I ask her. "Also the politicians are going to use you to get votes. You will be stared at in school, and people are going to assume the worst. Carla and Sarah were on TV sucking up the spotlight. I don't think they're good friends."

"I know. I don't think they are either. Did you know Sarah's dad is a trash man? She tells everyone he's a salesman."

"I like my trash man. He's a hard worker. What's wrong with that? Her brother's law firm helped search for you."

"Her brother's a private investigator for the law firm. He's not a lawyer. He's the guy that spies on cheating husbands. If there's a car accident, he'll take pictures from each driver's point of view. Then he gives both drivers the law firm's number. Whichever one signs with the firm is the one whose pictures they'll use against the other."

"That's illegal, I think. It's almost like blackmail."

"Yup. But Sarah likes her dirtball brother better than her hardworking dad. She's a snobby bitch. And Carla chews her hair. It's a bad habit."

"That's a disgusting habit. Why are you telling me this?"

"I don't know. I've never told anyone that. Now I feel like a shit." Guilt over outing her friends clouds Hilda's face.

"I think Mattie is perfect. She has no faults. She is the same at school as she is at work as she is at church. I have never met a more honest, kind, loving friend than Mattie. I can definitely say she does not deserve me as a friend."

"Does she know about you?"

"About what? That I killed, or that I..." I couldn't list the things I hide from her. I'm ashamed to say them out loud. "I love her, as a friend of course. I love her too much to tell her stuff. I don't want to bring shame to her or her family. I'm more worried about her finding things out than my own mom."

"I think it's called respect."

I agree. "Yeah, I think it's called respect."

She jumps up and hugs me.

"What was that for?"

"We're here!" She points to a highway sign tucked behind a tree.

"You're odd." I look at her. She's acting so giddy. It's a nice side to her. I'm glad she's feels good enough to be like this. She's kind of funny. She drags me to my feet, and we start walking again.

"Cosette, aren't you happy?"

I am, but I'm not. I don't want to face what I'm going to face. Everyone is going to be happy to see her. How are they going to act toward me? She's the victim. I'm the murderer.

"Hilda. I don't blame you for whatever happens when we get home."

"What do you mean by that?" She stops me.

"I killed someone, Hilda. Think about that. My mom and Mattie and Chris and everyone's going to know what I did. However you treat me, I'll understand." I let go of her and walk on.

Then I stop. I can feel it. The ground is starting to pull me down. She comes up and grabs my hand.

"I have to stop for a second."

"Cosette? Are you okay?" She holds me up.

I close my eyes. Here it comes. I imagine the ground glowing fiery red as I fall to my knees, ready for hell to take me. "I don't think I want to keep walking. I don't want to face them with you. You're close to the highway. You go ahead. I'll go alone."

"I'm not going without you." She kneels by me. She can't feel it. How can she? She's done nothing wrong. Hell won't take her tonight.

"Hilda, please go. You'll get a warm welcome. You'll be safe. There is nothing but handcuffs and a cell waiting for me. I just want to stay free for a little bit longer."

"Cosette, you saved me. It was self-defense."

"I kill people."

"You're my savior. You're my hero."

I pop up. "Never! Never call me that!" I start walking.

"Stop! Cosette, stop!" She holds my shoulders and stops me.

I stand there crying. This is the last place I want to be, standing in front of her crying. So much for control. What a coward! "I can't go on. I can't face them."

"Yes, you can! Let's go. Please, Cosette, I need you." She hugs me and holds on.

"You're scared of me. You don't need me. After we get home, then what? Are we going back to hating each other? You said you used me to get out of that situation. How are you going to treat me when we get back? Are you going to tell them how I really killed him? Are you going to tell them what a freak I really am?"

She hugs me and tilts her head to kiss me.

"Don't." I stop her. "You can't make me feel better. Just don't. It's fine. I'll walk back with you. I should expect nothing in return. Tell them what you want. It won't matter anymore."

She kisses my cheek anyway. "I won't tell them about the first one, but I'll tell them what I saw. You were being attacked, and you stabbed his neck. You saved me when I couldn't do anything. Then you walked me back to safety. You're my hero, and I love you."

I glower at her.

"Uh, as a friend, I love you. I'm sorry."

"I am no friend. You don't want me as a friend. Let's walk."

We finally reach the empty highway. Once every five minutes, a car passes. They won't even slow down. A few semi-trucks shift down but only to get in the left lane away from us.

"I'm sorry," Hilda says.

"Now for what? You've done a lot of apologizing on this walk."

"I've had a week to think about why this happened to me, and I realized I deserved everything I was getting."

"Don't say that. You didn't deserve being...uh, being raped."

"I was horrible. Maybe I didn't deserve the pain of the first one, but I didn't learn my lesson, so I deserved this week of um, reflection. So I'm sorry. You are the only one I have to apologize to, and I will do anything to make it right by you."

"That doesn't mean you have to kiss me every minute, although I am starting to enjoy it."

"I'm enjoying it too. Besides, I owe you my life. You saved me. You saved my life."

Guilt for what I allowed her to go through this week is making me sicker than I'm already feeling. "I didn't save your life. I took a life. You owe me nothing. God, you know Hilda, you really piss me off!"

"I know. I'm sorry I..."

"No! Shut up for a second. What I did back there was more for me than you, so stop with this 'I owe you' crap. If you want to be close to me, then great. I'd really like that, but don't do it because you think you owe me."

"No wonder Chris likes you."

"Stop it."

She touches my hand. Shaken, I yank it away. The hurt in her eyes shames me. I grab her hand and give an apologetic smile.

"I guess you're jumpy too. I just, I just, uh." She sighs.

"It's been a long week, and you just need to know you're still here, alive and safe."

"Yeah, I guess that's it. You're kind of like my security blanket." She pulls me closer.

I put my arm around her. "I like that. I can live with being your security blanket." I squint trying to focus on a highway sign. "I can't see with the rain, and since these glasses are cracked, they're altogether useless. Can you read the sign?" I take the glasses off and stick them in my robe pocket with Blue.

"The next rest stop is seven miles away. At least we have a destination."

"My feet are numb, and the cold's creeping up my legs. My hair is so heavy, and this wet robe is weighing me down. I can't wait to get into my warm tub."

"A warm bubble bath and a book. Oh, and pickle chips and a coke. That's what I want." She giggles.

"I think that's doable." I hear a Jake brake from a semi behind us. A dirty white truck with frozen black slush stuck to the trailer slows down a few yards ahead. All I can think about is how he must have come from someplace cold, which means his cab must be warm. Hilda and I run. I jump in and she follows.

His cab is warm but smells like smoke. I don't care. Hilda sits on my lap, which helps warm me up faster. I'm happy and so is she. We don't even stop to look at the guy who just picked us up. We're too exhausted.

"WHERE TO PRETTY ladies?" the gruff southern voice of an older man asks.

"Jeffersonville. Do you know where that is?" I shiver. Hilda wraps her arms around me, trying to keep me warm.

"I'll turn the heat up a bit fer ya. Yeah, I know where Jeffersonville is. I wanted to go to a funeral there today, but with the weather up north, I didn't make it. Y'all a bit far from home, ain't ya?"

He turns up the heat and pats Hilda's leg. "It'll be okay. It'll warm up fast."

"How far away are we?" I ask.

"We're bout a half-hour away."

"Thank you for picking us up. Everyone else drove on past."

Hilda's teeth are chattering.

"Well, I have a few hours before I have to pick up my next load, so I was on my way to a rest stop."

"Thank you. You didn't have to, but thank you," I say.

"It is sure cold out there. What were you girls doing out there, especially dressed like that?"

Hilda quickly answers, "We ran away from home, but we're going back."

"It's a rough world out there." He chuckles loud over the cab noise.

"You have no idea," I say. My body's starting to warm up.

"Are you two girls, uh, together?" The corner of his mouth raises along with his eyebrow.

Shit, I don't like his tone or his question.

"Yes, we are together," Hilda answers again.

"Is that why you two ran away?" His voice rises with delight.

"Yes, sir." Hilda tucks herself into me like we're a couple.

He touches her leg. "I understand it can be a rough world out there," he repeats as he rubs her thigh.

She moves his hand. "I only go one way."

He touches her leg again. "I'm sure you do pretty lady, but this ain't no free ride. You want a ride, you have to slide."

How disgusting!

I'm tired and wet and cold and pissed off, and now this guy wants sex for a ride to Jeff?

"I'll pay. Leave her alone," I say.

She leans in to me and whispers. "Please, Cosette, no. Please."

I kiss her neck and whisper. "You've been tortured enough. I will not let you go through that again."

He runs his hand all the way up her leg.

"Leave her alone! I'll pay!" I slap him off her.

"Stupid bitch! I get both of you!" He grabs her knee hard and squeezes.

She screams and hunches over. Then he grabs her hair and slams her face into the dash twice. I pull her back to me. She's bleeding and crying.

"Fucking asshole!" I slap his arm.

He lifts it, threatening to hit her again.

"Okay! Okay! You can have both. But me first! Me first. Pull into the rest stop." I hold her.

This poor girl. My poor token.

My plan isn't working. My token isn't stopping me from killing. I try to be normal, but when I'm stuck in these situations, I have no choice. I'm going to kill again.

"No, Cozy. Please. Please, no more. Please, no more," she begs.

"Do you want me to let him have you? Do you think I can sit back and watch him hurt you? You want to go through that again? What do you think I'm going to do when it's my turn anyway? I saved you. You're mine now, and I will defend you."

"I don't want you hurt." She kisses me. I don't understand why. Maybe just heat of the moment nerves?

"I'm already damaged. You're mine, and I protect what is mine. When I do it, run into the rest area and find help."

"You all figured out who's first?" He rubs her upper thigh.

"Get in the back." I tell her. She gets off and sits on the bed in the back of the cab. I open my robe as a peace offering. "I'm first."

He reaches over to fondle me. I almost puke. I shut my robe and tell him he'll have to wait.

Furious, he punches me. He hits high on my cheekbone. I hear his knuckles crack. "Fuck!" he yells at me.

He pulls over into the rest area and parks out of sight. "Hold on, Blondie. That pretty little mouth of yours has got to get me warmed up."

I shift in front of her to touch him. "I said I go first."

"Well then, she's gotta get you warmed up." He reaches behind and pushes her against me.

SHE RUBS UP on me as much as she can in the cramped space. Jealous, he yanks me onto his lap. I follow his direction and straddle him. He opens my robe then leans in to lick my naked breast. He pulls Hilda in to do the same, then he unzips his pants and starts to stroke himself.

The look of disgust on my face must be evident because Hilda brushes my hair back and starts kissing me.

He grabs my hand and shows me how to stroke. "You like that, don't you, whor…"

I shove my fingers into his mouth, refusing to allow him to talk to me like that.

"Mmmm, kinky. I like that." He starts sucking on them. "You ready for me now?" He shoves his fingers inside me with such force I scream. He spits my fingers out. "Shut up, or it's going in your mouth."

"Gently," Hilda tells him. Softly she removes his hand and replaces hers. "It's okay, baby. Let's show him how much fun we really are." Cold hard steel accompanies her soft fingers inside me, and I'm so grateful to have her here.

With her other hand she holds his member to free up my hands for Blue. She kisses him, diverting his attention while I take my knife out and warm up the blade to skin temperature.

HE PULLS AWAY from Hilda and licks his fingers. Then he wraps his hands around Hilda's, showing her the proper way to stroke. He moans loudly.

"I wanna watch you," she mouths to me.

"No."

"I'm not leaving until it's done," she whispers in my ear. "Please let me watch."

"Then you become an accomplice."

She smiles.

"You are so hot," I mouth back to her.

"So are you, and right now, I'll do anything for you." She pulls away from him, opens my robe wide, and kisses me all over. Her warm hands massage all the right places. At the moment, I don't want this to end. I'm excited to have her as mine. I'm excited to have another victim. I'm excited about Bonnie coming out for a visit.

I secure Blue and while kissing his neck, I cut him.

It takes a second for him to realize what's happening. I sit back as Hilda keeps petting me.

"Look at me," I tell him. Hilda stops also. "I am the one killing you."

Stunned, he doesn't move until he feels the warm blood flow down his chest. He shoves her away and swings his weakening arms. He gets a few good hits on me and struggles to get me off his lap. Hilda holds him down as I tighten my legs, holding him steady. The blood is flowing nicely.

His eyes are slowly closing. "Hilda, look. Watch the dimming." I open his eyes and stare in them. Fascinated, she stares too.

His body goes limp under me. His eyes close.

"IS HE DEAD?" she asks.

I pause.

"Yes." I smile at her. "Are you scared?"

"Yes."

WE SIT THERE for a second. I kiss him then hang my head. "It happens so fast."

I touch her face, her beautiful cut-up face. I kiss her soft lips, hoping she wasn't using me to get out of another situation. Thankfully, she kisses back. My whole body flames up. We keep kissing until I feel his warm blood drip down to my inner thigh.

"Mmmm, I'm glad you're still here," I tell her.

"I am too."

"Listen carefully, Hilda. You were almost raped again. Our faces will prove it. Run into the rest area and start screaming. You were just attacked. I'll fix things here."

She kisses me again.

"You know I own you now."

She smiles. "I know. I like it. I really like it."

Chapter FOURTEEN

THE HOSPITAL ROOM is warm and bright. I don't remember much after the police-escorted ambulance ride here. My mom is crying while talking to Chief Rickert outside of my room.

"Mom!" I reach out to her, but my arms stop. "What the? Mom!" I yank on the restraints pinning my arms to the bed. She can't hear me. I turn away and cry.

THE NURSE COMES in to check on me. "Hi, Cosette. I'm sorry to wake you. The doctor will be in to check on you, and I…"

My blank stare tells her I'm not listening. Pretty soon, I'll have plenty of people talking to me: a judge, a warden, my cellmate. I don't want to listen to anyone right now.

"And I, I just want to tell you how blessed we are to have you here, Cosette. All the other nurses and I want you to know if you want anything, we're here. The doctor says you can have sweets. You want chocolate?" She goes over to one end of the room and picks something up. It's hard to see without my glasses. "See?" She brings a heart-shaped box of chocolates up close. "Chocolate makes everything better."

"You can have them." I lift my cuffs. "I'm, uh…"

"Oh, okay. Let me get the chief in here for that." She exits.

A few moments later the chief comes in with a stiff, FBI I'm assuming. He shuts the blinds, blocking my crying mother from watching. "Hi, Cosette. How are you feeling? Are you okay? I just want to ask you a few questions while things are still fresh in your mind. What is the first thing you remember?"

"Am I under arrest?"

"Why would you ask that?"

I wiggle my hands.

"You were thrashing when the paramedics tried to put you under. You were screaming at them 'No drugs! No drugs!' But you needed pain killers. In the ambulance, you were warming up. Your feet were regaining feeling. They're in bad shape, but I'll let the doctor tell you about that. Why did you not want drugs? Is it because of Hilda?"

"I don't like not being in control of my body. How is Hilda?"

"She's doing better than you. Please, while it's still fresh, tell me what you can."

"Oh, uh, I got out of the bath. I was getting ready for a date with my boyfriend. When I went into my bedroom, someone was there. I grabbed my knife and ran away. He put something over my face…"

"Chloroform. We found the towel in your kitchen," the stiff says.

"Oh, okay. I woke up in a van, then he took me to a house and then to a cellar." As I tell him the whole chain of events, all I can think about is Hilda. I want her here, but now that we're back and she's had time to think, I wonder if she'll see me as a freak or a hero. "Where is Hilda? Can I see her? I want to see her."

"She's resting. She's safe. Her father is with her. Hilda told us everything that happened from the cellar until we found you two. She told me you're a hero. You saved her from the Poser and a serial rapist."

The stiff approaches my bed. He softens his voice. "Cosette, there's been a nationwide search for that trucker for the past four years. He has been picking up hitchhikers and forcing them… Cosette, you're a hero."

"Don't." I turn away. "Don't ever call me that."

The chief pats my hands. "It will take a while for you to adjust. I have set up appointments for you and Hilda with our psychiatrist. I think he will help you both come to terms with what has happened."

"With what happened? I killed people! That's what happened!" I try to sit up, but I'm still strapped down. I yank at them. "Ugh! My mom knows! My best friend knows! My boyfriend knows! The whole school will know! It's on the news already, isn't it? I'm a murderer!"

"Cosette, please calm down. It will take a while, but we have counselors. Do you want to talk to them?"

"No! No counselors." I lie back and turn my head away from them.

"Alright then, I want you to know we found the farm and the cellar and the man who kidnapped you. From what Hilda told us and the scene itself, it's an open and shut case."

"I agree. We will keep the media away as much as possible, but you must keep quiet also. Don't bring on any unwanted attention," the FBI agent says.

"I just wanna go home. Are we done here?"

"Yes. I'm done," the FBI agent says. "Chief, I'll see you at the station." He leaves and closes the door before my mom can sneak in.

"Cosette, I just want to know... I am going to ask not as a policeman, but as a father. How did he die?"

I can't answer. I stare at the cold hospital floor.

"Cosette, it wasn't a violent scene like I would have expected. How did he die?"

"I used whatever tools I had to get out of the situation." I speak soft and slow, out of shame. "He dragged me in there, and I had to watch him hurt Hilda. He came to me next. I knew what I was there for and how it was going to end. I gave him what he wanted to get the upper hand. I'm not strong enough to fight."

The chief is tearing up. He probably imagines what his daughters, Shelby and Sierra, would do in that situation. Shelby wouldn't do what I did. She would fight hard and maybe not make it out because of it. Sierra, I'm not sure about her.

Disgust of what I'm saying is written all over his face. "Go on."

"I let him touch me. I wouldn't give him everything, and when I started to resist, he got mad. I used my knife when I could before he hit me again. Please don't tell my mom. I don't want her to think I'm a whore. I did what I had to do. Do you think I'm a whore?"

"Oh my god, Cosette! Absolutely not! You were very smart and cautious. Because of that, you both walked away from a man who has killed many women."

"I didn't want to be like this. I'm sorry. I did what I had to."

"Yes, you did what you had to. Remember that."

He unbuckles my straps and stands up. "We'll keep watch over you so you will never have to make that choice again. Remember, in our eyes, you are a hero." He walks to the door and opens it. "There are a few people here to see you."

My mom, Mattie, and Chris run in. My mom frantically kisses my head and hugs me. Her face is swollen from crying.

Chris stands at the end of my bed and carefully touches my feet, which look like footballs they're wrapped up so much. They burn. All that barefoot walking in the forest and on the highway in the freezing rain must have torn them up. I guess they were so numb I didn't register the damage I was doing.

"I'm sorry, Mom. I'm sorry I'm like this. Can I go home? Will you let me come home?"

She doesn't answer. She only continues to cry. I'll take that as a no. "Mattie. I'm sorry. I'm sorry who I've become."

"I'm not," Chris says. "You saved her life. Twice!" He's trying to pick me up in case I start descending into the deep depression.

Mattie knows better. Or does she? She isn't giving me a condemned look. As she leans in for a hug, she whispers, "The first one was training, Cosette. You needed strength to get out of that situation." I start to object, but she stops me. "I prayed for you, and you had the strength." She looks at my mom and puts her finger on her lips shushing me. "The method doesn't matter."

She's lying.

The method does matter. It truly is one thing to kill in self-defense, in the heat of the moment. What I did was...

The method does matter.

My mom takes some deep breaths and wipes her eyes. "Baby, I'm so glad you're safe. I'm proud of you. I'm so sorry I couldn't protect you more."

"It wasn't your fault, Mom. I, I wanna go home. Am I allowed to go home?"

"You'll have to talk to the doctor first," she says.

"Am I allowed to come home?"

She stands up. "Why wouldn't you be?"

"Because of what I am. Don't make me say it, Mom."

"Cosette, your mom loves you." Chris gives me a cautious eye. "We love you. You'll be safe at home. We fixed the locks."

I better stop questioning my mom. I think she wants to stay blissfully unaware . What mother wants to think of her daughter as a murderer?

"Cosette, the house is safe for you. And I want you home. I'll go get the doctor now that you're awake." My mom leaves right as the mayor of Jeffersonville comes in.

"What the hell? I don't want my picture taken! Go away!"

His deep voice slightly chuckles. "Miss Hugo, Jeffersonville wants to thank you...."

"Save it! I don't want to hear it. Go away."

"Cosette!" Mattie thinks I'm rude, but she knows how the mayor used my brother's death for political reasons. She grabs my hands, trying to keep me calm.

"Mayor, sir, I can promise you that you will lose votes if you use me in any way. I am not my brother. I am *not* a hero! I am a murderer, and I will have to live with that the rest of my life. I respectfully ask that you go away."

"I understand. Please know that there are no photographers here. I just want to say thank you. You have done well protecting your friend Hilda and protecting this town."

I don't answer. Mattie squeezes my hand in an attempt to get a polite response out of me. But I refuse. The mayor takes his cue to leave then pauses. "Miss Cosette, not speaking as the mayor, but as a dad, thank you. Thank you."

My body relaxes and I smile. He begins to softly close the door when my mom approaches with Dr. Wigham.

"I am glad to see you awake and alert, Cosette. I just wish I saw you on better circumstances." She stands next to me, inspecting me. "You have fifteen stitches in the right foot and eleven in the left. We had to do a lot of scraping getting them cleaned out. They are very raw. You will stay here tonight, and tomorrow I'll send you home with supplies for your mom to take care of them. Do not get your feet wet. Take a bath with them hanging out of the tub or something, at least for the first few days. Your gunshot wound tore a little but nothing significant. We patched you up, and you should be good to go. You have four stitches on your cheek and a few other little cuts, but I think scarring will be minimal." She continues to talk as she signs my forms, "...should be out of the wheelchair by next week though walking will be slow."

"Wheelchair? Ugh. How's Hilda?"

"She's not as cut up as you. But we'll have to keep her here also."

"Why? Can I see her?"

"I'll see what we can do." She hangs my chart at the end of the bed and leaves.

After a few hours, so does everyone else. Visiting hours are over and things have calmed down, but I still haven't seen Hilda, and I'm not getting any answers on why she has to stay.

Chapter FIFTEEN

"GOOD MORNING." A soft voice wakes me. I turn over to see Hilda in my doorway.

"Good morning." Why am I so timid? I wish I could hug her, but I don't know how she would react to me. This is what I would imagine the morning after a one-night stand would be like. "How are you?"

"Sick. They flushed me out yesterday."

I hold out my hand hoping she'll come in. She doesn't. "Flush? I don't understand."

"All the drugs he gave me. The doctors cleaned me out, but I still feel like crap. They said I'm on the lighter side of an addiction and should be fine since I didn't drug myself up. Since it's associated with pain and not..." She wheels herself up to me and looks at my outstretched hand. "Cosette, I, uh, I'm not sure..."

"You don't have to say it. I guess it was all because you were high and wanted to get home." I'm hurt and disappointed. "I'm just glad you're safe. I hope you feel better." I turn away, cocooning myself in the thin blankets ready to break down crying.

Hilda wheels around my bed. "Please don't turn away from me." She grabs my hands and pulls them into her. "Please, Cosette, I can't be alone."

I break down crying and pull her cold hands up to my lips. I kiss them. She climbs into bed with me, and I hug her as we cry and cry.

THE NURSE OPENS the door. She smiles at us and then closes it, giving us our privacy.

"I need you, Cosette. When the nightmares come, you're the only one who is there to rescue me," she cries.

"I didn't think you'd want to be near me. I thought I would remind you of..."

"The night you saved me, kissed me, and brought me to a new high?"

"I don't think the flushing worked. I think you still have drugs in your system." I wrap my arm around her as she wedges herself into me, putting her head on my shoulder.

"I'm not high. I'm alive. I'm reborn." She looks up at me. Her baby blues are bright this morning.

"Your eyes are still bloodshot." I laugh.

"I feel like crap." She snuggles in, covering herself with my blanket. "I don't want to move."

"They aren't gonna to let you stay here."

"Yeah, they are." She strokes my hair then pulls it up to her face. "I guess the rain washed it away." She sniffs for my scented hair therapy.

"I wouldn't think you'd want to smell that again."

"It was one of the few things that kept me going. Now that I know it belongs to my savior, I want to smell it." She props herself up on her elbows. "I got stitched in three different places, all on my face."

"I beat you. I got stitched on my face, stomach, and feet."

"I went through rapid detox," she sarcastically brags.

"Yeah, well I won't be able to walk for at least a week."

"Yeah, well I was tortured all week." She shifts her head.

"Yeah, well I kill people, and my mom knows." I smile with pomp.

"You beat me there. I would rather be the victim that everyone loves."

"You fit the part. It helps that you're beautiful."

She gives me a puppy dog face. "You think I'm beautiful?" The tears start flowing.

"Yes, and you deserve a better life."

"Okay, ladies." The nurse walks back in. "Sorry, doctor's orders." She shakes a mini paper cup full of pills for me.

Hilda climbs back into her wheelchair. "Can I stay? I need her." Her voice sounds so desperate the nurse almost tears up.

"I'll do whatever I can for you two." She hands me the cup and a glass of water.

"What am I taking? What are these?" I look down at the four horse pills in my cup.

"Antibiotic and painkillers."

"I'll take the antibiotics, but I don't want the painkillers," I state.

"You're taking the painkillers." Mattie opens the door in time to give the nurse reinforcement. "Or I'll suggest they give them to you as an enema."

"You're mean," I tell her.

"Yup," Mattie nods in agreement. "Hilda, how are you? I'm so glad to see you." Mattie, overwhelmed, comes to where Hilda is and reaches out to hug her. Hilda cowers. "Oh, I am so sorry. I should've, I just... I guess since we've been searching and praying so hard to bring you back, I just..."

"Hi, Matilda," Hilda says. "I'm sorry. I'm just a little jumpy. No offense."

"Absolutely none taken. I'm so glad you're home. If you need anything, anything at all..."

"I could use some rice croquettes," I pipe up.

"Really? Really, Cosette? It's nine in the morning."

"And I'm hungry."

The nurse checks my temperature. "Breakfast should be here soon. Hilda, you might miss it if you're not back in your room," the nurse says as she leaves.

"I don't wanna go back. I'm not hungry!" Hilda yells after her. She starts breathing hard, scared they're going to force her to leave me. Poor thing, I think she really needs to stay with me.

"I'll bring you food if you miss breakfast." Mattie smiles at her.

107

Hilda's eyes start to water, and her nose turns red. "Oh, Hilda, it's okay." Mattie goes in to hug but then stops. She kneels down in front of her chair. "We'll take care of you."

"You're just like Cosette said you were. I'm sorry." Hilda drops her head into her hands and cries. Mattie puts her arm around her, comforting her. As soon as she does, Mattie's expression shifts. She glares at me.

She knows.

Mattie knows what Hilda and I did.

She pulls away and with a smile says, "I'm praying for you two. God can fix you guys. You just have to let Him. I have to go. I'll be back with food." She comes over and hugs me. Before she lets go she whispers, "Protect her, Cosette."

As Mattie walks out of the room, I wonder what she saw. Protect her? Maybe she didn't see what we did, but she sees what Hilda's going through. I do need to protect her. I need to protect my token.

"Come back up here," I tell Hilda.

She climbs back into the stiff hospital bed with me. "Better?"

"Better."

Chapter SIXTEEN

"SEE? WE REARRANGED the apartment to fit your wheelchair. It might be difficult, but it's better than that cold hospital."

"Thanks, Mom. Thanks, Chris." I look up and give Chris a kiss as he wheels me into my living room. "After three days, that hospital smell was numbing my brain. It'll be nice to get some sleep."

"You didn't sleep well?" My mom drags herself in.

"Hilda shakes in her sleep."

Chris lifts me to the couch, then grabs a pillow and sits with me. "I'm surprised the hospital allowed her to stay in your room, let alone push the beds together."

"Hilda needed me." I don't like Chris's tone of jealousy.

"With what she's been through this past week, I think she deserves some special treatment." Mom lays down her purse and heads for the bathroom. "Poor girl must have some horrible nightmares. John's going to be dropping her off in a half an hour. I'm assuming you want a bath. I'm starting it now." Mom sits on the edge of the tub and sprinkles bath beads in.

With the water running loudly, I turn to Chris. "I know you don't care about Hilda or what she went through, but you need to act like you feel sorry for her. You're being cold-hearted."

"I'm sorry. I guess I... I don't know."

"She's going to be spending a lot of time here, at least until we go to school next week, so you..."

"Then I'll be here too," Chris says.

"She's not going to pick on me. Believe me, her bullying days are over."

"I'm not worried about that. I know you can handle her."

"That's right. I'm a ninja!" I wiggle my football feet.

"Yes. Yes, you are." He nods in agreement.

Mom yells from the bathroom. "Bath is almost ready. Chris, can you drag her in here?"

Chris grabs a lock of my hair. "Sure, be right there!"

"Oh, you're too funny, mister caveman." I lift my arms, and he carries me to the tub. He sets me down on the edge.

"Chris, help me with her." My mom looks frantic. I don't know why. I'm not an invalid.

"I can get in myself, Mom. You can get ready for work. Chris, you can go to school. I do have knees. I can crawl." I try to shoo them out of the bathroom.

"I'm staying until Hilda comes, and you're out of there. You and bathrooms don't have a safe history." Chris kisses my forehead and leaves the bathroom.

"I'll go get ready." Mom lights a few candles and turns off the lights. "Here ya go, nice and peaceful." She closes the door.

"Thanks, Mom." I pull my lounge dress over my head and slip everything else off. It takes some finagling to get my panties over my wrapped feet, but I do it. As I slip into the hot water. I breathe in a sigh of relief.

I lay my head back to let the water soak in, and the last few days soak in as well. I can't wait until Hilda comes. I've grown closer to her, and she's dependent on me. The way she snuggles into me makes us feel so good, both Bonnie and me. Bonnie because we killed together, and me because, because, I guess I don't know. I just like being with her.

"Honey?" My mom knocks on the door. "Since Chris is here, I'm going to leave for work. Are you going to be okay? You've been in there a while."

"I was just relaxing. Besides, I'm not helpless. I'll be fine," I yell back.

"Alright. If you need me, call. I love you."

"Love you too, Mom." I hold my breath and wait for her to close and lock the front door.

"She's almost out of the driveway," Chris yells. "She's out of the neighborhood. I'm coming in!"

He opens the door while I zip the shower curtain closed as if I'm embarrassed.

"Haha, nice try." He opens it wide, exposing me. "Too bad the tub is small, or I'd get in."

"You'd have to be invited first," I hide behind the curtain.

"You're mine. I will do what I want."

"Oh, you think so, huh? We'll see about that." I pull him down to kiss me.

"I know, Cozy. I know who controls this relationship. Just let me think it's me. I'll feel better about myself." He pouts, giving me a puppy dog look while batting his hazel eyes.

"You make me melt."

"Are you sure?"

"What do you mean by that?" I pull the drain plug and shift up out of the tub. He wraps a towel around me and carries me to my room.

"I mean, I don't know. I guess I'm not happy about you spending every waking hour you had in the hospital with Hilda." He puts me on the bed and lies down beside me.

"I'm yours, Chris. Hilda just needs me. I guess it's a Florence Nightingale sort of thing. I saved her, so now she only feels safe around me. Besides, she's so beautiful and..." there's a knock on the front door. "Well, speaking of Hilda. Be nice please." I send him to answer it while I get dressed.

"Hi, come on in," Chris welcomes her.

"Thanks. I'll be okay, Dad. You go to work. I'll be fine here." Hilda says. Her voice is confident, like she wants to show herself strong.

"I'm leaving to go back to school, but I'll be here this afternoon too," Chris assures John, Hilda's dad.

"Okay. Thank you, Chris. I'll check in on you girls later," John says. "I promise I will never let anything happen to you again."

John sounds like a broken man. He knows he can't keep that promise.

"I'll be fine, Dad. You're just a phone call away. Go, go to work. You've already missed too much, and I have soap operas I'm missing."

I hear the front door lock then, "Whew, I thought he'd never leave. He's very protective."

"He should be. I'll take your coat." Chris is polite, for my sake I'm sure.

"Thanks. Where is she?" Hilda asks.

"Bedroom."

"Am I allowed in?" Hilda asks Chris's permission. It's good she knows her place.

"Don't ask me. Ask her though I doubt she'll say no to you." Chris responds with his heart on his sleeve.

"Come on in you two," I yell. "I'm dressed."

She walks in looking at the floor, desperately clinging to the front pocket of her sweatshirt. She stops at my side. When she brushes across my hand, I get a rise.

"Do I have competition?" Chris asks.

She guiltily looks up at him then back to me.

Securing her hand, I assure her. "It's okay. He won't hurt you."

"Don't count on that," Chris says. "We're a package deal, Hilda. If you want her, you must have me."

"Stop it, Chris. Don't scare her. She's mine. I created her. I own her."

She sits next to me on my bed and grabs my hand. She's freezing and shaking, but I know it has nothing to do with the temperature in here.

"What?" Chris slowly asks, comprehending. "Cosette. What?" He grabs my shoulders, mad. "You did what? What did you say?"

I don't answer.

"Bonnie!" He shakes me hard. Hilda lets go of me.

"We did what we had to," I tell him.

"What the fuck? What did you do?" He turns to her. "What did she make you do?"

"Nothing. I wanted to, I, she didn't." Hilda stands and clings to my bedpost.

"Leave her alone. She's mine! And if you want to share, then you're gonna have to calm down!"

"Shit! Shit! Shit!" He's freaking out. I don't understand why. I would think he'd like it.

"Chris, I... I wanted to stay. Cozy didn't make me. I wanted to. I'll do whatever she wants. It's okay with me." She touches his hand. "Don't you want me?" Her voice turns seductive.

"Good girl," I say.

"You cannot keep her!" Chris yanks his hand away.

"She's my token!"

"Not anymore! Hilda, did you help her?"

She leans over and strokes my hair. As she looks into my eyes, she confesses, "Yes, I helped her."

"Fuck!" he yells.

"You should have been there, Chris. She was perfect."

"We'll have to do it again sometime." She strokes my cheek.

"Holy shit! What did you just say?" He pulls her back and pushes her up against the wall. "What did you just say? You want to do it again? Hell no! Don't you understand what this does to her? You were there! Remember your suicide watch in the bathroom? I will not lose her so you two can get off! It will not happen again!"

She ducks away from him.

"Leave her alone! In case you don't remember, it's not my fault we were in that situation! We did what we had to do. I refuse to feel guilt for that. And I don't know what you're freaking about. I would think you'd be happy. Besides, we won't do anything. Not if we don't have to. Right?" I pull her up to me. She's shaking. It's good she fears him. "Chris. She's ours. Ours."

I grab his hand. "Chris. Relax."

"I can't trust her, not yet."

"I don't expect you to. Just don't reject me. Please." She stands and presses her body against his as the fear of rejection tears her up. "I know Cosette's yours. Just please, don't push me away."

"Hilda, can you give us a second?" Chris shakes her off then holds the bedroom door, inviting her to leave. She wipes her eyes then leaves. He shuts and locks the door.

"You don't have to touch her, Chris, but I own her."

"Did she see you kill?"

"She saw both. But she held the truck driver down for me. She followed my lead and then held him down. It was the sexiest thing I have ever seen."

"Cosette," he whimpers, hurt. "I thought you didn't want to go there. Killing together?"

"She wouldn't leave. She watched the first time and wanted to help the second."

"There cannot be a third." He sits and holds my hand.

"I know. I just wish you were there. You should give her a chance. You might actually enjoy her company."

"I did enjoy her company. All week long." He stands up and grabs the doorknob. He pauses and drops his head. "I'm sorry. That wasn't fair to you."

"No, it wasn't! And it's not fair for you to be upset by what we did. You're the one who forced me into that situation! I didn't want to kill anyone. I was only going to frame him and free my token."

"You're right. I'm sorry. But, Cozy, I had to make it believable. We couldn't leave any loose ends."

"Well, now you're going to have to deal with this loose end. Hilda is mine, and I won't give her up. You better learn to like it since you're the reason she's with me."

He comes and sits on my bed. "I'm sorry. I love you, Cosette."

"And I love you too. Don't be jealous. I'm yours first, but I need her. I need to feed Bonnie, and she's a replacement. She's just, just our..."

"Pet. She's our pet."

"Be nice, Chris."

"If you want her, you need to realize what she is to me. Meat, that's it. She's a pet, not on the same level."

"Will you be good to her?"

"I will, but in order for me to accept this, that's how I have to see it." Chris stands and gives me a kiss. "Meat."

"Be nice." I squint my eyes, warning him. He rolls his eyes and laughs at my futility.

"Come on in." He opens the door.

I hold out my hand and Hilda crawls into bed with me. I put my arm around her, and she cuddles in her rightful place making Bonnie very, very happy.

Chris sits on the other side. "So, now what?"

"Now we paint our nails!" Hilda wiggles her fingers, trying to lighten the tension. It works.

Chapter SEVENTEEN

"COSETTE, WAKE UP!" Mom yells. "You have a visitor coming."

"Hilda's not a visitor anymore. She's my nurse." I swing my football feet off the bed, which shoots a jolt of pain up through my legs.

"Is she helping you? I know you two had your issues before, but I assume..." she yells over the hairdryer. I can hear her fine, but I don't feel like yelling back. I pull my wheelchair over and slide in.

"Hilda needs me just like I need her." I wheel to the bathroom. "It's more than just helping out, Mom. She means more to me. It's hard to explain."

"I think she's afraid to be without you. Whatever you two saw or went through, you're the only one she looks to for comfort. John has been having a hard time getting her to open up," Mom says as she brushes through her hair.

"What girl wants to talk about that with her dad? She was drugged, raped, and beaten. John doesn't need to know anymore. The details will kill him." I wheel up and grab a lock of Mom's hair and the brush. "Do you want me to fishtail it?"

She turns to me and dabs her watering eyes with a tissue. "You are the most perfect daughter."

She leans in to hug me, but I push her away. "Not that perfect. I haven't brushed my teeth yet."

"You're so silly, and I love you. Thanks." Making her laugh prevented her from a total meltdown before work. "And you better get minty because your visitor is not Hilda."

"Please don't tell me..."

"No, don't worry about the news stations. Everyone is keeping your identity a secret. I've seen what those reporters have done to invade Hilda's privacy. Animals." She grabs the brush and tosses it in the drawer then spins her hair up to a bun. "No, your visitor is Melodious. I guess she's back for her mom's incident."

"M&M? She's here?" I bounce with excitement, which causes me to almost pee. "Mom, I gotta go."

She understands and leaves the bathroom. With the door closed she continues. "Anyway, Melodious and Pearl are moving back and I offered them a place to stay until they find an apartment, but they said they already have a home. They wouldn't say with whom, so I'm assuming I don't want to know."

"Ignorance is bliss," I yell.

"I guess. Anyway, I have to leave in five minutes, and Hilda will be here soon, so you better get out of the bathroom."

"HI, IS COOKIE here?" M&M asks Hilda when she answers the door for me.

Hilda looks M&M up and down then tries to close the door on my ghetto friend. "I think you have the wrong house."

"Whatever, Barbie. I know she's here." M&M pushes her way in and sees me on the couch. "Cookie!" She runs to hug me. "Who's the Barbie?"

"I'm her girlfriend." Hilda stands next to me, demanding respect and outing our relationship at the same time.

"Well shit, Cook. I didn't know you spread that way." She ignores Hilda. "Pearl's going that way too. Smudge says it's to make up for lost money now that Mama's gone." M&M turns to Hilda. "No worries, Barbie. Pearl! Hey, Pearl! Ya coming?" she yells out to her sister. Hilda sits down next to me, claiming her territory. It's kinda adorable.

"This is M&M from my grandma's old neighborhood," I tell Hilda.

"I'm going by Mel now," Melodious says.

Pearl comes in and runs up to hug me. "Hey, Cook. You looking good. Kinda. Sorry about your grandma's house burning down."

"Sorry about your mom getting arrested, again," I reply with no guilt in my voice. I'm not too upset that their mom was my scapegoat when I killed her drug dealers, Binge and Bounce.

"I'm not sorry she got arrested," Mel says. She and Pearl sit on the loveseat while Hilda sits a bit closer to me. I slide back and snuggle up to her, easing her mind.

"Yeah, I'm glad Mama's in jail," Pearl says. Hilda shifts uncomfortably. "It's okay, Barbie. We're used to her getting locked up. Who are you anyway?"

"This is Hilda Dyson." I intertwine my fingers with Hilda's.

"Holy shit! That was you?" Mel asks. "I'm so sorry, girl, shit!"

"If you're Hilda, then, Cookie, are you?" Pearl and Mel gasp at the realization that I'm Hilda's savior. The news hasn't released my name yet, but I know my secret's safe with them.

"She's my hero. I owe her my life," Hilda says. "Why do you call her Cookie?"

"We don't have real names in the hood," Pearl says.

I laugh. "But your real name is Pearl."

"Yeah, and I'm black. Someone fucked that up, huh? And that's why we got kicked out when we went to live with grandma's kin. So get this, we gets there, and grandma set it all up for them to get us at the bus station. We wait there for four hours," Pearl says.

"Let me guess. They thought you'd be white?" I ask.

"That's why we're back here. I guess they didn't know Mel was mixed, and they certainly did not want no black ho, that's the daughter of a murdering crack-whore, living in their house. I ain't turnin tricks in their living room or nuthin. White folks be racist." Pearl laughs.

Mel and I laugh with her. Hilda doesn't. This is obviously a whole new world to her, and I was loving it.

"So, you got kicked out. Now where ya staying?"

"With Smudge. I'm working for him," Pearl admits.

"You're kidding me! You're working for Smudge? Why? Isn't he pissed?" I ask.

"We don't think Ma killed Binge and Bounce. She's a fucking bitch, and we're glad she's gone, but she ain't no killer."

My heart starts to beat faster. Not because I think they suspect that I had anything to do with it, but because remembering my fun killing Binge and Bounce is getting me antsy. I hope Hilda can't feel my body heat up.

"You're a killer, Cookie. Do you think she did it?" Mel blurts it out.

"Really? I haven't seen you in a year, and that's what you ask me?" I laugh.

"Yeah. So tell me what happened." Pearl sits on the edge of her seat.

"No, let's not," Hilda says. "If it's all the same to you, I don't want to hear it." Hilda looks out the window, avoiding eye contact.

"Shit, Barbie, you're right. My bad," Pearl says. "So anyway, Cook. Ma would be too high to kill them. She doesn't even know who she's blowing. Besides, she had a thing for Binge. Smudge thinks it's Bounce's supplier who found out his brother started dealing some new Brazilian stuff. Anyway, Smudge needs me, and he's always taken good care of us."

"As long as you're safe." I pull the curtains back at the sound of Chris pulling into the drive. "Have you gone to visit your mom?"

"Hell no," Mel says. "Bitch can rot in there for all I care. All the shit she did to us, fuck her. I want to thank the person who did this to her. She's better off and I'll miss Binge, but Bounce had it coming. I would kiss the guy that off'd Bounce. Hell, I'd even do him, and I won't charge as much as Pearl." Mel laughs, so does Pearl, completely accepting her career choice.

"I am sorry about your grandma's house though. No one is talking, but if ya hear anything, please call me. I wanna thank them," Mel says.

The front door opens suddenly and Chris walks in. "Hey, Cozy, I'm home." He comes over and gives me a kiss then, surprisingly, he kisses Hilda's forehead. "Who are you?" he asks Pearl and Mel.

"Shit, Cookie. You got a Barbie and a Ken?" Pearl shakes her head. We all laugh.

"YOU SURE DO keep interesting company, Cosette. What's with the hoochie-mama clothes?" Chris asks as he watches Pearl and Mel drive away.

"They're prostitutes," Hilda says with distain.

"Pearl is. Mel is not." I sit up and stretch. "So did ya get our homework?"

"I'm not desperate to do schoolwork." Hilda stands and goes to the kitchen.

"I got it," Chris says as he empties out the folders on the coffee table. "I also talked to Mattie."

"I've been texting with her," I say.

"Obviously you haven't mentioned your new friend," Chris whispers.

"I didn't go into details because I'm not clear on details. Besides, I don't have to say anything. Mattie knows everything anyway."

"Well then, that makes this situation odd," Chris says.

"Just for me." I can only imagine what Mattie is seeing in her head. Does she see Hilda as my girlfriend or pet like Chris does?

"I also had a little chat with Rose and Decker. They'll be coming to visit tonight," Chris says.

"Good. How is Rose?" I ask.

"In what capacity are you asking?"

"Oh, you're too cute. Like you could get her without me," I whisper.

"You don't need any more," Chris says, glancing in Hilda's direction.

"I might have to take on a new hobby. Killing is not socially acceptable, and I don't want to do it."

"Yes, you do. You will always want to, and it's big business. Look at all the TV reporters that want to talk to Hilda. Why do you think she hangs out here?"

"I thought it was for me, but I guess this is a good hideout. Hey, Hilda!" I yell. "Are you using me to avoid the reporters?"

"No. I'm using you so I'm not alone." She comes out of the kitchen with apple slices for me. She's like a mother trying to keep me healthy. "I'm using you so I don't freak out when I smell cigarettes. So every time I hear a truck or van drive up the road, I don't cower in a corner."

"I thought it was because you had a thing for me," I joke, trying to ease her mind.

"I do, it's just that, I'm weird about it. I didn't expect to feel this. You're my first uh, girl. Crap, I can't even say it. I know I should stay away, but I'm scared to leave."

Chris pulls her to sit between us. "I'm not thrilled with this, but Cosette needs you too. But I'm warning you, Hilda, I am her first, I will be her last, and I will deny her nothing. Do you understand that? What Cozy wants, Cozy gets. And not me, and certainly not you, will stop that."

"So, what do you want, Cosette?" Hilda asks, confused.

"I want to be satisfied. I want to be normal, but that's not going to happen anytime soon."

"You want a purpose?" Hilda asks.

"Yeah. I guess I do."

"I can understand that. I want one too. I don't want to be labeled 'the last victim'." Hilda puts on her coat and grabs her homework from the coffee table. "My dad's here. I hope you find what you're looking for. Even though it's not me, I'll still be here tomorrow." She gives me a long kiss. "Did that help satisfy anything?"

"No, you made it worse," I laugh.

"Good to know. I'll see you tomorrow morning."

I stare out the window as her dad drives her away.

"WHAT DO YOU want, Cosette?" Chris probes, hoping for what, I'm not sure.

"Right now I want to run. This brain can't think being cooped up in here. I haven't been able to run in almost two weeks.

"Yeah, well running is overrated. Last time you ran, you got shot," Chris jokes.

But it isn't funny to me. I'm stuck in this apartment and when I'm alone my thoughts run wild, my memories toy with me, and Bonnie comes out.

Especially now. I've enjoyed two more kills since I tried to stop. It's only made my craving worse. I should just give in and find somebody. Maybe this is what I really want.

"What time are Decker and Rose getting here?" I ask.

"About an hour, why?"

"Nothing. It's nothing."

"Do you want me to take you somewhere? Can I get you anything?" Chris asks as if he could give me the moon.

"No."

"Are you sure? Because the way you're pinching your arm tells me you're holding something in. Are you nervous about the Reds coming over?"

"No. I'm just... I'm going to the bathroom." I stand up and walk. My walking is off balance only because the bandages are so thick. The pain is excruciating, and I love it. I make it to the bathroom in time to close the door before I collapse on the toilet. Shocks jolt up my legs, telling me that was stupid, but it satisfies me just enough to make it through another day of being cooped up. I take my time washing my face and brushing my teeth.

Chris comes to the bathroom door. "Do you need me to carry you out, or are you planning on torturing yourself more?"

"I just want to feel." I drop my head, sad and frustrated.

Chris comes in, throws me over his shoulder, and carries me to my bedroom. "Just because you're cooped up doesn't mean you can't have fun. I'll make you feel."

Chapter EIGHTEEN

"...AND THEN I woke up in the hospital and now here I am. That's the whole story," I tell Rose and Decker.

Rose has tears in her eyes. "When we heard, we were so scared."

"Yeah, but then when we heard you're a murderer, I thought, yeah, I can see that." Decker, arrogant as always.

"Don't be mean, Decker! She did what she had to do. Look at her face and feet!" Rose yells then gets up to sit by me. She holds my hand to comfort me. "I'm sorry my boyfriend's an ass, Cozy."

"Maybe he's still pissed you kiss Rose better than he does," Chris taunts.

"Fuck you, Chris," Decker says.

Chris laughs. "He's still pissed, or jealous."

"I'm not jealous," Decker announces jealously.

"Then you wouldn't mind if she kisses Rose again?"

"Stop it, Chris," I say. "Be nice. Besides, we share. If I get Rose, I get Decker too. Then who would be jealous?"

Rose giggles and tightens her grip on my hands.

"It's okay, Rose. I won't do that to you. I know it'd kill you to see another girl kiss your man." Personally I don't think it would bother her one single bit, and I'm playing along with this because,

because, I don't know why. Maybe it's satisfying Bonnie. I hope Bonnie appreciates it.

"That would make me jealous, and it would make Chris mad." Rose shifts to get more comfortable on the couch. She's playing along too.

"I don't get mad." Chris stands. "Go ahead, Deck. I bet you're too chickenshit. You can't handle Cosette anyway." He walks to the kitchen, leaving on purpose, I'm sure.

"I'm not chickenshit," Decker quietly defends. He's been called out, and he hates it.

I shift to kneel on the couch. "Come on, Deck. Let's prove him wrong."

Decker doesn't move. Rose is all but jumping up and down.

I softly touch his face. "It's okay. Just one kiss to prove him wrong." Bonnie is stirring inside. She's getting excited. I turn his head. His body is shaking. He's scared.

In one slow fluid movement, I straddle his bouncing knees. "Relax, Deck, it's just me." I skim my lips across his and kiss his neck. Slowly I kiss back towards his lips, and then I kiss him. He can't kiss back.

I like it when they don't kiss back.

I like it when they're too scared to move.

I like the tremors between my thighs, and Decker is terrified.

The darkness floods over me, and I kiss harder. I'm going to enjoy this one. Oh, I'm going to really enjoy this one. I give his cheek a small slap for him to obey me and kiss back.

Rose watches up close. I grab the back of her head and pull her into me. It startles her when I kiss her too. Bonnie's getting high. I let go of Rose and force myself on Decker. My whole body grinds against his. His hands don't move; he's so stunned. My eyes open wide, and I look straight into his. I want to see everything.

I reach around and can't find Blue. No worries. He's starting to kiss back, but it's too late. I rub my hands up his chest up to his neck, and with both hands wrapped around, I start to squeeze.

Chris runs in from the kitchen, grabs my hair, and yanks me to the floor! He straddles me and holds my hands above my head. Then he whispers, "Settle down, Bonnie. I'll find you someone else, not

Decker."

"What the hell, Chris!" Rose jumps up. She's angry he's so rough with me.

"Cozy tends to get a bit violent. I don't want her to hurt Decker," Chris says.

Rose kneels down next to me. "It's okay, Rose. He's right. Decker's a good guy. I would have hurt him. I'm sorry."

Chris gets off me. "Here, Rosy, take my place until she calms down."

Rose's expression questions Chris, but she does it anyway. "Are you okay?" she whispers.

"I'm frustrated now." I pull her down for a kiss. She giggles and gives in to me.

Chris gets up and sits next to Decker. "So, Decker, how ya like her now?"

"What the hell is wrong with her?" he asks quietly.

"Nothing, she's perfect."

"She's a fucking psycho." He tries to wipe me off his lips.

"She's my psycho and I love her. Apparently, Rosy does too. I think Rosy can handle her. Can you?"

Decker doesn't say anything. This is more than he bargained for.

"Go on, Deck. You're a wrestler. See if you can take her." Chris eggs him on. Decker doesn't move. "If you want to have my kind of fun, then you're gonna have to loosen up a little." Chris pats Decker's chest. "Okay, you two, are you done?"

Rose sits up. "Not yet." She rolls off me then erotically crawls up on Decker. He's putty in her arms.

"My sweet Bonnie." Chris pulls me up to the loveseat. "You are so manipulative," he whispers.

"You started it."

"Yeah, I know. It's nice to see you using your powers for good."

"Don't be so sure on that one. I almost lost it. How can I replace one high with another if I can't control it? Chris, I think you will be the only one to handle me from now on. When they leave you have to finish what you started in the bedroom."

"We can go now." He raises an eyebrow.

"Patience is a virtue."

The Reds keep kissing when my phone alarm goes off. "Don't mind me. I just need drugs."

"I'll get you water. What are you taking?" Rose asks.

"I need an antibiotic."

"No painkillers?" Rose asks.

"I stopped taking the painkillers when I got home from the hospital. I don't like them."

"Aren't you hurting?" Decker asks.

"So innocent." Chris laughs. "Decker, she likes pain. That's why you'll never be able to handle her."

"That's funny," Rose giggles "Deck, I guess you're stuck with me."

"I think I'm okay with that."

Chapter
NINETEEN

"WHO'S THE TAIL?" Mattie asks as she walks into my apartment.

"What are you talking about? What tail?" I wheel over to the window.

"That car has been here the last few days." Mattie points to an old green Saturn sedan.

"How do you know? You haven't been here the last few days."

"I drive by, and when I see Chris or your mom's car, I know you're alright. Besides, my mom has me working double-time. Ever since we hosted the search party for Hilda in our parking lot, our business has doubled.

Anyway, I just wanted to see you and pray with you. And I kinda miss you, ya know." Mattie leans down to hug me then drops a bag of breakfast burritos on my lap.

"I really miss you too. You can text all you want, but it's good to see ya. Hilda's been here every day helping me."

"Interesting. So when were you planning on telling me?"

I wheel to the kitchen. "Telling you what?"

"That you and Hilda are going out. You don't think I know? I can feel it walking into this house. I can feel a lot walking in this house. What have you been doing?"

Hoping that she's not referring to Rose, I decide tell her about Hilda. "Hilda and I haven't done anything official. Besides, why should I tell you when you know everything anyway?"

"Oh that's brilliant!"

"Why are you getting mad? I know you're not jealous. I offered to kiss you, Mattie, but you turned me down." My joking doesn't help lighten her mood.

"It's not right, Coz. It's especially not right since you're still with Chris."

"Chris knows." I take a bite of the breakfast burrito.

"Sick, Cosette. That's sick."

"She needs me."

"Then support her, but don't kiss her. When she wakes up from her nightmare and you're still standing there puckering up, she's going to hate that you took advantage of her. I told you to protect her. Now you're just using her."

"What about me? What about how I feel, Mattie? You think I'm doing this just to toy with her? Am I that much of a bitch that you think that's all I'm in it for? I really like her."

"She's not your type. Chris is your type. Hilda is a, a, she's a princess," Mattie says right as Hilda closes the front door.

"Are you talking about me?" Hilda asks, walking into our tension.

"Hi, Hilda. And yes, we were." Mattie admits.

"You think I'm a princess?" she pouts.

"I'm, uh, I'm sorry?" Mattie stumbles.

"I'm just kidding. I know I am. Cosette laughs at me all the time. Are you going to laugh at me too?" She twirls her hair.

"Maybe. No," Mattie stutters. "But I refuse to get a manicure with you two."

"Good." Hilda grabs her hand and inspects her fingers. "Because the condition these cuticles are in, they'd charge double."

Mattie can see the hurt through Hilda's humorous façade. She gives her a long hug. "I'm praying for you, Hilda. I'm so, so sorry."

A knock at the door prevents Hilda from letting her guard down. She lets go of Mattie and answers the door.

"HILDA? WHAT ARE you doing here?"

I know that voice, and I hate it. I wheel myself to the front door. "What are you doing here, Sarah?"

"Holy crap, Hilda! This is Cosette's place? You sure are slumming it now that you're back." Sarah steps in and smirks at my bland apartment.

"Don't be a bitch, Sarah. They've been through a lot," Mattie says.

"They?" Sarah closes the front door. "They? You mean Cosette was with her, which means... Crap! Cosette's the one the news has been trying to find? Cosette's the hero who killed those two guys? Holy shit! Wow." She huffs, turns her back on Mattie and me, and focuses on Hilda. "So why are you here? I went to your house yesterday, and you weren't home. Only a crowd of news vans was sitting there. I had to tell them you didn't want to be disturbed."

"How nice of you to do an interview on Hilda's behalf. Did they pay you for that?" I ask.

"Of course not. I'm not like that. But they did wanna know who her hero was. And now I know. Wow, I can't believe it's you." Sarah glares at me with disdain.

"You're pathetic, Sarah. By the way, how's the lip? Kissed any good tables lately?" Mattie refers to the face slam she gave her and Carla a few weeks ago.

"I think that was Sarah's nose and Carla's lip, Mattie," I joke.

Sarah ignores us and stands closer to Hilda. "Why haven't you called or come to school? Why are you hanging out in this dump?"

"Why haven't *I* called?" Hilda growls. "Do you have any clue what happened to me? Why haven't you called me? Yesterday was the first day you thought to come see me? Are you kidding? Look at my house! I have to sneak out every morning to get here. And how did you find me anyway?"

"Shark drove me."

"How did your brother know I was here? Never mind, I already know. If you had called me, you wouldn't've had to have your snooping brother tail me."

"Yeah, well, we were busy. So why are you here? Now that you're home, why are *you - here*?"

"I'm helping Cosette. Our parents are dating, and my dad said she needs help. I'll go to school on Monday."

"Fine. Then I'll see you on Monday." She looks at me then my wrapped up feet. "I do hate you, Cosette, but I guess I'm glad you're okay." She leaves. Her brother Shark's green Saturn putters out of the neighborhood.

"Well, now we know who your tail is," Mattie says. "I'm leaving too. Gotta get to school. Love you guys. And I'm praying for you two. With friends like that, you need all the love you can get." She hugs us then leaves.

I lock the door, wheel back to the bedroom, then text Chris.

"So what do you want to do today?" Hilda follows me.

"Me? I'm going to school. I don't care what you do." I shift to my bed.

"You can't go to school."

"I can't be here." I rewrap my feet furiously.

"Why are you leaving? Are you mad?" Hilda stands in the doorway.

"Why should I be mad? Not like you outed me in front of Mel and Pearl, but couldn't even tell Sarah we were friends? No, you told her you were helping because your dad makes you, not because you actually wanna be here with me. No, why should I be mad?" I put on my long skirt and sweater and roll out to brush my teeth.

Stopping in the bathroom doorway, I pause. "Hilda, are we even friends?"

Chapter TWENTY

"I KNOW YOU'RE mad at her, but school is not where you should be right now," Chris says as he pushes my chair from English into the lunchroom.

"She couldn't even claim me as a friend."

"How much do you want that token now?" he whispers.

"She's mine, and she will change. But I just couldn't stay there and be near her. I feel betrayed. And after all I've done for her."

"You mean like keeping her captive and letting your boyfriend have his way with her?" he snarks with a crooked smile.

"Don't put it that way. That makes us sound cruel. We did what we had to do."

"And she did what she had to do. Just remember that when..." We turn the corner to a sea of glaring eyes. The bustle of the lunchroom ceases, and Chris stops.

Hilda's here.

Her table is full. Sarah and Carla smile at me.

"Shit. No wonder nobody talked to me my last two classes. Sarah must've told everyone I was Hilda's..." I turn my chair and wheel into the hall. "Oh my god, Chris, everyone knows. Everyone knows! Everyone knows I'm a killer. I think I'm going to be sick.

Chris, I can't stay here."

"Well we can't go home."

"Everyone knows. I'm a murderer, and everyone knows." My heart starts racing, and I want to run. I want to get out of this chair, this school... this body.

"It might not be that bad." He comes around and kneels in front of me. His hands cool mine as he comforts me. My blood is boiling, and it's hard to focus.

"It's okay, baby, breathe. Think about it. Cozy, you don't have to hide. I mean you need to hide the details, but you don't have to hide. Who's gonna mess with you? No one! Holy shit! Think about it. You got it made. Everyone knows, and now you can be yourself. You are exactly who you were meant to be. You're a killer and you don't have to hide it. You are so hot to me right now!" He plants a huge kiss on me. He sits and waits for me to calm down. "It'll be okay. You can finally become Bonnie. You're free. Come on, let's go back."

PAIGE, SHELBY, SIERRA, Rose, Decker, and Mattie are already at our table waiting quietly. Hilda's at her table, but she's not happy sitting with Sarah and Carla. Apparently, they have added a few new acquaintances who want to share in the temporary popularity.

She gives me a remorseful look. And with it my heart weakens. I am such a bitch. I forced her to come here. It's too soon for her to be out, and I should've been more understanding. Now she followed me here, and she's in the spotlight. She's not ready for this. I'm a horrible person.

"Hey, slugger!" Decker welcomes me in a way only Decker can. Rose hits him.

Chris sticks me at the head of the table next to Mattie. "Hi, guys." I smile at Mattie. She looks at Chris and gives me a cautious smile back.

"Are you feeling okay?" Paige cautiously asks.

"Physically, I'm fine. Wasn't expecting the stares though."

"Sarah came in and spread the news that you were the one who killed those two guys. The whole school knew before second period," Paige says.

My stomach is still churning, and I want to puke. "What a bitch. The police were protecting me from the reporters."

"I guess now the cat's out of the bag," Decker says. "But we like you, no matter how many people you kill."

"You're only saying that because you're scared of me." I smile at him. My body relaxes. It does feel kinda good to be open. Maybe Chris is right.

"I am scared of you, and that's exactly why I'm saying it. See, Chris? I told you she was a psycho."

"Yeah, but she's my psycho." He kisses me.

SHELBY'S STARING AT me. "Yes, Shelby?"

"My dad likes you. He says you played it smart. I don't think I could handle that." She looks scared.

"I used what tools I had to work with." I look to Chris and then to Mattie. She's not saying anything. She's seeing how this is going to play out.

"How are you and Hilda doing?" Rose asks, staring at Hilda. "She looks miserable."

Hilda does look miserable. She stares at our table, embarrassed to sit at hers. I wonder what she'll do if I bring her over.

She looks at me with bloodshot, watery eyes and mouths 'I'm sorry'. My stomach aches for her. My poor token.

"Hilda and I have an understanding," I tell Decker.

"You mean she thinks you're psycho, and she's scared of you too?"

"She owes you big time. She owes you her life. Twice." Rose perks up.

Mattie huffs.

Chris grabs my hand. "She does owe Cozy. She'll do whatever Cozy says."

"Stop it, Chris." I squeeze his fingers, warning him.

"Her and Cozy have a love-hate relationship. It was hate; it turned to love." Chris smiles at Rose, who turns red in mixed company. "Cozy owns Hilda."

I crunch his knuckles as I turn and whisper, "Stop it."

Mattie watches us closely. She can see where this is going, and it's not the way she wants for me. I want to be normal. I want to feel like a regular teenager. I really do. But the more Chris talks about Hilda and the more she stares over at our table, the more the butterflies in my stomach flutter.

I do own her.

She should be here with me.

She's mine!

Carla and Sarah are just using her, and she knows it. I'd rather her sit here as my pet than there as a popularity excuse. They don't deserve her. I do!

I earned her!

I killed for her!

"WELL, CHRIS, IF Cozy does own Hilda, then why is she sitting with those media whores?" Decker turns to me. "Or is Hilda the only person you're still afraid of?"

I look to Mattie. "I am afraid of a lot."

"I doubt that. Prove you own her. If you do, then she'll do whatever you say." Decker's baiting me.

I agree with him. She is mine. The girls surrounding her are making her feel ashamed. They're wide-eyed and waiting for her to give details of her weeklong rape. She wants to escape.

"Sorry, Deck. With great power comes great responsibility."

"You have no power," he says coldly.

"Hilda, come here," I call out.

"Cosette, don't do this," Mattie warns.

"That's my girl," Chris encourages me.

Hilda stands up. I didn't notice back at home, but she looks good today. Her blue button-down shirt is open enough to show some cleavage but closed enough to hide fading bruises. Her normally tight jeans are loose. I guess she didn't eat much in captivity.

She cautiously walks over to me then looks back towards her table. Everyone seated there is intensely watching her. The whole lunchroom is, except for the teacher who is relishing what little spare time he has.

Hilda stands by my chair. Her nervous eyes scan those at my

table.

"Coward," Decker whispers to me.

I grab her shirt at the cleavage and pull her down to me. I have control, and I'm getting high. She can tell. She's scared and shaking.

"Not here, Cosette." she begs me in a whisper.

"Why are you here?" I ask.

"I can't be alone. I'm sorry." She can hardly speak.

"You're mine, not theirs."

She nods, knowing her place. I pull her down to a kiss. I kiss her long. She barely kisses back.

Mattie gets up and leaves, disgusted. The whole lunchroom is silent. The teacher clears his throat. I let Hilda go and tell her to sit. She does. She has to. Where else would she go? I hold her hand while she looks down, ashamed.

"IN CASE YOU all haven't met, Hilda, this is Rose, Decker, Shelby, Sierra, and you already know Paige."

Paige looks away.

"Hi, Hilda. Welcome to our table." Rose smiles big at her then gets up and hugs her across the table.

"She's fucking psycho," Decker whispers to Chris.

"She's my fucking psycho." Chris smiles at me and holds my hand. He reaches across and holds Hilda's too.

The rest of my group greet her and smile. They're welcoming. They'd better be.

EVERYONE VACATES THE lunchroom as the bell rings. Hilda gets up quickly and darts to her class. Chris gives me a kiss. "I'm proud of you." He wheels me towards my locker.

We pass the commons. Mattie's sitting alone.

"I have to go talk to her. I'll see you later," I say.

"MATTIE?" I WHEEL up to her knowing she's pissed. Time to face the fury.

"Is this what you do with your second chance? You humiliate Hilda to show you have control?" Mattie's calm but furious inside. "You own her now?"

"She's mine."

"No, she's not. And she's going to turn on you, Cosette. Not because that's who she is, but because you will force her to."

"She won't turn on me."

"You can't control her by fear."

"She controlled me by fear!" I yell a little too loud.

"So this is revenge? You come back to life to get revenge?"

"I never wanted to come back, Mattie! I wanted to be gone! I left that night hoping to stay gone!"

"Suicide? That's what you wanted? That's why you went out?"

I start to wheel away. She yanks my chair back.

"Cosette, no. Please tell me no." Her eyes start to water, and her nose turns red. She's so hurt. "Suicides go to hell."

"I know, Mattie! Which makes this life the only heaven I'll ever see. Pretty fucked up, huh? Not really worth it, is it?" I wheel away. "You shouldn't have brought me back, Mattie. You brought back a monster!"

Chapter TWENTY-ONE

"WILL HILDA DYSON and Cosette Hugo please report to the front office? Hilda Dyson and Cosette Hugo."

Crap. I close my calculus book and wheel myself to the front office.

Mrs. Hurley opens the door and greets me. Hilda is already waiting. "Mr. Peeler heard that you two kissed in the lunchroom. Just wanted to give you a heads up."

"Thanks, Mrs. Hurley. Hilda, let me talk, okay? I don't care what happens to me." I hope to save what little dignity she has left. "Principal Peeler, you wanted to see us?"

"Yes, please close the door. I heard from your fellow students that you two showed a PDA in the lunchroom."

PDA is a politically correct way of saying we kissed. Public Display of Affection could really mean anything from holding hands to groping.

"Yes, I wanted to comfort my friend. We've had it rough the last couple of days. Besides, you were the one who said we would become great friends through your tutoring program. So now here we are, great friends." I love being a smartass though I don't know how I'm going to get away with this.

"I don't think you two need to be a part of the tutoring program. And I think your presence in this school is disturbing the students. Wouldn't you two feel better at home?" He strokes his beard. Condescending asshole.

"Are you kicking us out?" Hilda's appalled.

"I just think it would be wise to not have you all tramping around school, balking at the rules. Kissing is not permitted, especially..." He stops before he says anything that could get him labeled a homophobe. "I just feel you all are taking away from the other students' learning. Why don't you two stay at home until things calm down?"

He glances out his window. His eyes widen, and his bushy eyebrows curve to worrisome. More news teams have gathered, now aware that both Hilda and her rescuer are inside.

"We want to be here," Hilda says. "Besides, we see others kissing all the time and..." her voice rises, but she stops to calm down. She grabs my hand and squeezes it for support. Then, accepting his suggestion, she turns to leave. "Never mind."

Turning my chair to roll out, Hilda gasps when she opens the office door and sees the news teams. She tightens her grip on my wheelchair handles, and her body starts shaking. She's mad the reporters are now here instead of her front lawn.

"Listen up, you asshole!" She turns back to Peeler, her face bright red. "I was raped! Raped! I thought I was going to die every time that bastard unlocked my cage! I was beaten and humiliated! So I don't need to come here and get this shit from you! If you call me down here again, you better have a damn good reason. I don't care if I'm making out with my girlfriend in the lunchroom or blowing the entire football team in the locker room. We're staying at school! Actually, I might decide to do an interview about your unfair treatment of rape victims to the media frenzy that's outside!"

"No!" he protests, running to the front of his desk. "No, it's fine. You two can stay. Just watch yourselves. That will be all."

She slams Mr. Peeler's door. Mrs. Hurly hides her smile with pursed lips. She pumps her fist at us in solidarity. The rest of the office workers stare in shock. Hilda walks upright and proudly wheels me out.

"HILDA, I'M SORRY. I am so, so sorry. I shouldn't have done that to you. I was selfish, and it was horrible. Mattie was right; I shouldn't have embarrassed you like that."

She rolls me to an empty lunchroom. We sit in a corner.

"Don't worry about it. We were already the talk of the school. This is nothing. Besides, I like your table. They're much better than the new popularity whores Carla invited to my table. Why? What did Mattie say?"

"Mattie is perfect. She was mad I did that to you, and she's right. She knew we were together. I didn't have to say anything. She gets these messages from God. He protects her, and she uses that to do whatever she can to help others. I'm her latest case.

"I wish I could be good, especially for her. I want to be good, but I'm having a hard time with it. Normally I'm fine when I'm near just her and her family. There's like a bubble she's in, but when I'm not around her, things happen, and the bubble pops."

"That's kinda odd," Hilda says.

"No, it's nice to know there are good people out there. I just wish I was one."

"So try harder."

I smile at her. It sounds easy, but it's not. Not after you've already dug yourself into a deep hole.

Correction, not after you've already dug a hole and shoved ten souls into it. I try to hide my thoughts, but I have the worst poker face.

"You don't trust me?" She looks straight at me.

"Why do you ask that?" I don't know if I trust her or not.

"I don't blame you. I'll prove myself to you."

"I just want you to be yourself, Hilda. Please don't prove anything."

"Chris doesn't trust me."

"Chris has a lot of reasons, none of which involve you. He's protecting me."

"You've done a lot of bad things, huh?"

"Yes. Please don't ask me anything else."

"I don't know what it is about you, but I need you. I want to be near you no matter what you tell me or hide from me. It's as strong as the feeling was to hate you, but this is even stronger. And I don't swing that way at all. Maybe you have your own bubble too."

Shit! That's not what I wanted to hear. I know the source of my bubble is not the source of Mattie's.

"Maybe it's just temporary," I say. "Maybe it's a Florence Nightingale thing. Just be careful around me. Please be strong around me."

"I can't." She scoots next to me and grabs my hand. "Let me take you home."

"Let *me* take her home."

"Chris! You scared me." She moves away from me, startled.

"Have I become obsolete?" He stands behind me.

"N-n-no," she stutters, not knowing what to do.

"Remember we're a package deal, Hilda. Otherwise I will assume you're trying to steal her away from me, and you don't want to be on my bad side."

That threat is so sexy coming from my clean-cut all-American boy.

"I'm sorry, Chris. I don't want to steal her." She stands, and changing her tactic, she presses him against the wall. "And I'm a package deal too. You want her? You get me too." She kisses him hard. She's shaking, trying to hide her anxiety.

I guess she's so afraid of being alone that she's willing to take this to the next level, even only a week after her captivity. They take me home.

TWO HOURS. THAT'S all I can think of. Two hours of pure pleasure. With these two around, I have no chance of being good.

The shower shuts off.

"Chris is done. It's our turn." Hilda rolls off me.

"How are you feeling?" I ask.

She lies on her back, and I snuggle into her. "I feel good. I thought I would freak out when it was my turn with Chris, but I guess with you here, it was perfect. I hope I did okay."

"We're not experts, so I'm not critiquing, but on a scale of one to ten, I think you were an eleven." I run my fingers between her breasts, giving her the chills.

She giggles. "Eleven? You guys were at least an eight, so I guess I did good."

"Oh, you're funny!" I get on her, and we start kissing again.

"No more fooling around ladies. I'm taking you two out to dinner." He lifts me off her and takes me to the tub. The water is warm, and bubbles fill the air with a fresh ocean scent.

Hilda ponytails her hair then gets in in front of me.

"I didn't notice this before. What is this?" I gently hold up her arms. She has patches of raw skin on her sides, arms, and thighs. In the water, they turn bright red.

She holds her head down. "I can't scrub him off."

"Oh, princess." I hold her, and my eyes start to water. Even though I know it was Chris, and I know he's clean, I feel dirty for her. "You're with us now. We'll make you forget. We'll make you clean."

"I'll never be clean." She leans back on me in the warm bath then changes the subject. "How are your feet?"

I curve my feet around her to see them. "The cuts are healing, and the bruising has faded to a yellow." I grab the body wash and my loofa and softly scrub her back and massage her front. While kissing her neck, I rinse her off. She purrs.

Chris pops in. "Hey, ladies, sorry to rush you but your mom's driving up."

"Oh shit!" Hilda quickly jumps out, dries off, and gets dressed. "We've got to get you out of there." She peeks out of the bathroom as my mom greets Chris. It's muffled, but I think he's keeping her engaged with small talk.

"Don't worry about her. Just help me rinse," I tell Hilda.

My mom taps on the bathroom door then tucks her head in.

Hilda's hovering over me, rinsing my hair. "Hi, Mom. I didn't know when you would come home. I was getting ready. Chris is taking us out to dinner."

"Oh, Hilda, honey, you don't have to do that. I can help."

"I didn't want to wait, Mom. Hilda's already seen me at my worst, so I think we'll be okay."

"I am so proud of you girls sticking together like this. Hilda, your dad was going to stop by to check on you and Cosette. He should be here in a few." She closes the door.

"Are they almost done?" Chris asks her.

"Almost. Chris, thank you for being there for her..." Her voice fades as she walks to the kitchen.

"WHY DID SHE not freak out?" Hilda asks.

"Her daughter is a murderer. What could she say? 'I don't want Hilda to see you naked, knowing what you two went through together'?"

"I guess you're right." She drains the tub and wraps my hair in a towel. "I need help," she announces, cracking open the bathroom door.

Chris comes in. "Your mom was on the phone and signaled me to help you."

"Naked out of the tub?" I ask. "Okay, help me up." He wraps me in some towels and puts me in my chair then goes to sit on the couch before my mom wakes out of her fog of denial.

HILDA WHEELS ME into my room and sits on my bed while I dig out a bra and panties. She flops back on the bed and stares at the Switchfoot posters on my ceiling.

"I've never heard of them," she tells me.

"They're my favorite Christian band. When Victor died, I did nothing but sit on my bed and cry to their music, no matter what the tempo. I love them, but someone like me should not be promoting them."

"You get down on yourself a lot."

"Apparently not enough to do better. I'm not doing you any favors by being with you."

Ignoring me, she flips over and flops her hands on the side of my bed. My diary's there. I forgot I left it tucked out on the night of my suicide attempt. She pulls it out.

"Can I read?" she asks.

"You won't like what is in there," I warn her.

"Is it about me?"

"Yes."

I get my bra and panties on and crawl up into bed with her. I lie on her shoulder and wrap myself around her.

Her body heats up as she's reading. She's hurt. I know she's embarrassed. I hold her tight, letting her know it's okay.

My mom answers the front door, and I hear John's deep voice. Hilda doesn't even notice her dad is here. She keeps on reading as he comes into the room. He's startled to find me half-naked, wrapped around his daughter. He's about to say something but then notices her crying.

"Hildy, baby, it's okay. We're here." He comes up to the edge of the bed and kneels down. She wraps her arms around him and breaks down crying. I crawl back into my chair, get my clothes on, and wheel out. Before I roll away, I pause and stare at them, sad.

I miss my dad, that son of a bitch. He used to hug me like that. There is more security for a daughter in a father's hug than in a mom's. But sometimes there is more understanding in a mother's hug than in a dad's. Both Hilda and I are half-complete.

143

Chapter TWENTY-TWO

SINCE I FORCED our school debut yesterday, Hilda and I decided to come to school today. It's Friday, so if it goes bad, we have the weekend to recover. Fortunately, Sierra told her dad we were at school yesterday. He sent officers to escort us past the news vans.

I wheel into first period art. Mrs. Iris is beaming that I'm in her class today. She gives us instructions and we settle into our sketches. A few minutes before the class ends, she comes over and squats down in front of my chair. Her leather hands hold onto my armrests, most likely to keep her from falling off those hot pink three-inch heels she wore today. Don't know who she's trying to impress now that vice-principal Jarvis is in jail. Maybe she wore them because they match her long fake nails.

"Cosette, if you ever need to talk, then I am always here." She tries to look sincere.

"I needed you to be there for me before Christmas break. I told you the scarf I made was my mom's *only* Christmas gift, and you still took it from me. So, uh, fuck you, Mrs. Iris. I don't trust you," I say with a smile. I figure this is one of the few times I can get away with saying that, so why not? I wheel away from her and start on my sketch.

I hear her sharp intake of breath and notice the rest of the class holding back smiles.

I'm halfway to the door as the bell rings when one of the shyer students jumps up to hold it open for me. "Thanks," I tell him. He just smiles and gulps like he's never talked to a girl before. Cute.

"HILDA!" IT'S LUNCHTIME, and I want her to sit with us. I try to get her attention, but in this wheelchair, I'm losing sight of her as all the kids pour into the hall.

She makes her way towards me, giving me the most desperate saddest look ever. People step aside to allow her to come to me. It's an odd thing to see. I don't think she notices they're doing that.

"Will you sit with me at lunch?" I ask.

"I kinda have to. Where else would I go?" She places her books on my lap and rolls me towards my locker. "So how are you doing today, Cosette?"

"I told Mrs. Iris to fuck off. So I am having a good day."

She cries out a laugh. "I only got stares. Turtle asked me how many stitches I got. She was the only one who talked to me all morning. I have to drop this off at my locker. I'll be right back."

MATTIE'S WAITING FOR me at my locker to wheel me to lunch. I don't know what to expect. It's hard to look at someone who knows everything you do and thinks you're foul because of it.

"Hi, Matilda." I don't know how else to address her.

"Your feet aren't footballs anymore."

"I can walk. They just want me to take it easy. And since I'm slow at walking, I have to wheel around," I say.

"I don't know how to say this, Cozy, but..."

"But you don't want to be my friend? You need a break from me? You feel the filth dripping off of me to you?"

"Everything is permissible, but not everything is beneficial," she says. I had to think about that one. "I'm not leaving you, Cozy. Don't push me out."

"Really? Why not?"

"I'm not here to judge you. I'm here as your friend. And I will stick by you no matter what. There'll be a time when I will be the only one you have left. I will wait for that day. I won't leave you."

"I know you want what's best for me, but I'm fine."

"I'm just letting you know. You can do whoever or whatever you want. I will not change, no matter how much *you* do. You'll come back around to being the normal Cozy. I have faith."

"I'm sorry."

"You are who you are, for now. I'm just glad you're still alive. You're second chance is ongoing." She smiles.

I don't understand her faith. I'm soulless. It'd be easier for her to push me away and write me off as condemned. Instead, she's placing herself in a compromising friendship to save me.

"I love you. Thanks, Mattie."

"Just warn me if you're going to freak out on me, okay?"

"I will." I hug her. She hugs back.

Hilda walks up to us.

"Hi, Hilda," Mattie says.

Hilda looks down. She feels the same shame I do around Mattie. "Hi, Matilda."

"Call me Mattie." She starts wheeling me to lunch. "I'm praying for you two. It hasn't hit you yet, but it will. I'll be here when it does."

"I don't get it." Hilda touches my hand.

"This is what you get from someone who knows everything," I tell Hilda. "I guess when 'it' hits we'll know who to go to."

"Yup." Mattie wheels me up to the table. The regular crowd is there.

"Hi guys." I smile, and with my foot, I push out a chair for Hilda, who sheepishly sits. Carla and Sarah's table is empty. Their fifteen minutes of fame didn't last without Hilda.

"Hey, slugger."

"Funny, Decker. So I should be out of the chair soon. My feet should be good by Monday."

"Until you find another way to mutilate yourself," Hilda says.

"I think I'll take it easy for a while."

"No more killing?" Decker's sarcastic. "You still haven't given us the details."

"About what? All ten or just the last two?" A big grin crosses my face.

Chris chokes on a fry.

"You're a..." Decker stammers.

"I know, a psycho."

AND THERE IT IS. I just clicked: confidence, security, acceptance of who I really am. I'm not excited about it, but I'm accepting it. But accepting it is completely different from acting on it. Just like Pearl accepting that she'll always be a whore, I'll always have Bonnie.

Doesn't mean Bonnie and I are going to run out and paint the town red or anything.

This just means I have control, and I refuse to give it up. *I* decide who I am. *I* decide what I want to be. I accept who I am.

I still want to do all I can not to kill again. But if I have to, then I'll be happy, very happy. But I won't fan Bonnie's flame unnecessarily.

BEFORE DECKER CAN fumble out another quip, I get called to the principal's. The chief of police's car is outside, and my instant shot of confidence is gone.

"Time to go." I wheel away from the table.

"What's going on?" Hilda's confused. "You're kidding about the ten, right?" she whispers to me.

I kiss her and hug Mattie.

"Chris, can you wheel me in?"

"Think I should be there in case they question me about my seventeen?" Chris asks sarcastically.

"Yes, just in case."

HE GETS UP and kisses Hilda too then pushes me out of the

lunchroom. I can hear Hilda questioning the others. "They're kidding, right?"

"Those two are psychos, Hilda. Be careful with them."

"Stop it, Deck. Don't worry, Hilda, they're only kidding," Rose unconvincingly assures her.

THE OFFICE IS dotted with officials: the chief, Officer Crance, and an FBI guy. I feel like I'm in a snake pit. I shift my body to innocent victim mode.

"Cozy, hi." Officer Crance comes to greet me.

"Can Chris stay with me?" I ask.

"It's up to you," says Chief Rickert. "If you feel more comfortable with him here, that'll be fine. We just had a few questions. No need for you to come down to the station. We figured you'd be more comfortable here. Principal Peeler, is there a room where we can meet in private?"

Peeler leads us to a conference room. He's much more accommodating to us with Chief Rickert here.

We close the door, and the chief sits next to me. "Cosette, I know this whole ordeal has been horrible for you. You've been really brave, but I have something to ask you. As you know we have your knife, and..."

"You have my knife? Where is it? I want it back!" I killed three people with Blue. The first one I cut up into fifteen pieces in Chris's uncle's barn. I want my knife back!

"Yes, we took it for evidence at the truck stop when we picked you up. We had to run some tests on it. Can you tell me where you got it?" the FBI agent asks.

They ran tests? That's why I'm here. I'm caught! No wonder the FBI is here! They're waiting to arrest me!

Chris speaks up. "I gave it to her." She was training for the Kentucky Derby Marathon, and she ran a lot. I wanted her safe, so I gave it to her.

"Can you tell me where you got it from?" The chief turns to Chris.

"Uh, no, I don't want to," Chris says.

"It's okay, son. Just tell us the truth. You'll be okay."

"Okay, you're not gonna like it, but I stole it from my Aunt April's fiancé."

"You did what?" I ask Chris. "You never told me it was stolen."

"I'm sorry, I just wanted you safe with all the..."

"And what is his name? Your soon-to-be-uncle?" Officer Crance tries to get Chris to focus.

"Ben Hernandez," Chris tilts his head in shame.

"This is your uncle? Ben Hernandez is your uncle?" The chief shows him the same mug shot that's been blasted on every news station in the country.

Chris pushes it back, nodding. "Yeah, that's him. Not something I go bragging about."

"Well, this clarifies a few things," the chief says.

"Wait a second. I killed his uncle?" I start breathing heavy. "I killed his... Chris, why didn't you tell me? And I did it with his own knife? Are you serious? I think I'm going to be sick." I know who I killed of course, but I start bawling anyway. It's a real cry, that's for sure. It's a release of pent-up anxiety about my situation.

"I'm sorry about asking you this, Chris. Do you know any Tolmans? Can you tell us about the Tolmans, Bradley Richard Tolman and ..."

"Yes, they passed away around Christmas, my Uncle Pen and cousin Dickey."

"Another uncle? How are they related?" the FBI agent asks.

"Uncle Pen was my dad's half-brother. Why?" Chris is starting to get nervous. He's squeezing my hand.

"Have you ever been to your uncle's farm?"

"Of course! He was my favorite uncle. Cozy and I had to go up to feed the goats after the funerals. My other cousins were out of town. But one of them got back a few days ago. She told me she was taking the goats to be sold. Why?"

"We found your hair, Cosette, in the farmhouse and barn."

"Yeah, we were feeding the goats and trying to clean out Chris's aunt and uncle's stuff for donation after his uncle passed away."

"I understand, but we also found blood in the barn," the chief says.

"I bet. My family hunts a lot. My aunt had them process the deer out in the barn." Chris plays naïve well.

"This blood was human blood. It matched the blood from the knife we tested. We've yet to identify a victim." The FBI agent eyes Chris.

I turn around and grab the trashcan then dry heave. Officer Crance comes over to me and holds my hair back. Nothing comes out, so she gives me some water.

I'm caught!

I used Blue to kill the guy from the parking garage before I chopped him up in the barn. I left too much evidence. I left strands of hair, and I didn't clean my knife! My prints were cleaned off the axe and the other tools I used from the barn. But I just didn't clean the inside of my pocketknife. How stupid! I'm still so new at this. How damned stupid of me!

My gut wrenches. They have me. They don't know it, but they have me. And to make it worse, Officer Crance gives me an 'I know something' look. I can't breathe, but I still have to play the innocent victim.

"Wait a second." Chris stands. "Why were the police at my uncle's farm...? Am I missing someth..." Chris asks. The chief doesn't answer. "What are you saying? They were at my uncle's farm? Hilda and Cozy were..."

Leading the police to the cellar on the same property where I dismembered my last victim was not a smart thing to do. Anxiety is taking over, and I feel like puking again.

I'm caught. I'm caught. I'm caught!

"This is the connection we needed. We weren't sure how Ben found that farm. Or how he knew your Uncle Pen and his son Bradley, so thank you." The FBI agent has a satisfied look on his face.

"So, Chris, I'm sorry but this means that your two uncles, Ben and Pen, and cousin Bradley, were the Poser gang." The chief puts his arm around Chris, consoling him.

The agent continues. "And we believe that the death of your

Uncle Pen and cousin Bradley was the reason for Hilda being taken. She was the one who got away, and your Uncle Ben wanted revenge. When Cosette found Ben attacking Hilda in the alley, she interrupted his plans and he shot her. We think Hilda was tortured for a week as payback. And he also needed time to find Cosette since she survived the shooting."

Chris wipes tears from his eyes. "And now you know where the knife came from, which explains how he found Cosette. He found her through me?" Chris's voice is weak.

"Yes, we believe so. I'm sorry, Chris," the chief says.

I start shaking. They still don't have a suspect in Pen and Dickey's death, and they don't have a body for the blood found on the knife. But I'm caught; they just don't know it. The darkness under my feet is starting to pull. "I think I want to leave now."

"I'll walk her out," Officer Crance says. "I didn't expect this, but it all makes sense. All we need is a victim to match the blood."

She helps me back to my wheelchair. "I'll come with you," Chris says. I bet he can see the cold dark depression flooding over me.

"I'd like to ask you a few more questions, Chris," the agent says.

"No! I need him. I can't be alone." It's been a while since I've had this depressed feeling, and I know what it leads to. But this time I'll have to work through it. No suicide for me; too many eyes watching.

"Chris, we have to tell Hilda before she finds out another way," I say.

"We will tell her," the agent is sterile and cold.

"No, she's our friend. You already solved the case. Let us tell her the bad news. It was my family after all," Chris says.

The chief and the agent give each other confirming glances. Then Officer Crance wheels me out to the hall. "Why don't you two let it settle in first? Chris, we'll have to talk to your dad also."

"I'll call him and tell him to go to the police station."

"Do you want me to tell Hilda with you guys?" she asks. "I'll be kinder than the chief and the FBI agent."

"No, thank you. She's ours. We'll take care of it." Chris takes over my chair and wheels me to the lunchroom table.

"Thanks, Officer Crance," I say.

She walks around my chair and kneels in front of me. "You take care of yourself and Hilda. No one will understand what you went through. You two are in a group all your own. You two need to stick together."

She looks up at Chris then back to me. She whispers, "Thank you. Thank you so much. Thank you from my sister. Thank you. You're going to go through a hard time I'm sure, but please understand that so many people have your back. We are so proud of you. Thank you." She gives me a hug then leaves me to Chris.

THE BELL RINGS and students from the lunchroom storm out. Some of our friends move from our table.

Everyone can see our demeanor has drastically changed.

MATTIE LOOKS HARD at me. Softly she says, "You stupid, stupid, stupid girl." She knows we did something, but to what degree? I don't know.

"I can't stay." Paige looks at me with a wary eye. "I'm sorry, Cozy. I need to get to class."

"Hilda, we have to tell you something." Chris sits and holds her hand. She starts shaking.

Shelby stands. "Come on, Sierra, we need to get to class."

"But I wanna hear what happened," Sierra whines.

"Ignorance is bliss, Sierra." Shelby gives her final words. Sierra leaves with her sister.

"You might wanna leave too," Chris tells Rose and Decker.

"I can handle it," Decker boasts.

"No, Decker. You already hate me. I'm not going to... Some things you don't need to know," I say.

"Is it illegal?" Rose perks up. Her eyes sparkle at my bad girl image.

"Yes, and you need deniability," Chris warns her.

"You're gonna tell me eventually, Chris. Might as well get it over with." Decker's curiosity is going to get him in trouble.

Chris waits until the lunchroom is empty, save our table. The lunchroom ladies don't understand much English, so they ignore us. Chris rubs Hilda's hand, preparing her. "Hilda, I come from a very bad family. Lots of drugs, a few criminals, but very bad. A few days after your first attack, Cozy was attacked."

I scoot in closer to her and hold her hand with Chris. Mattie covers her mouth and closes her eyes. Tears are pouring out.

"I didn't know you were attacked. What happened?" Hilda's quivering voice is barely audible.

"Same thing happened to him that happened to your first attacker," I say.

"My first attacker? In December? So you killed him too?" she asks.

"You what?" Decker blurts. Rose hits his leg hard.

Chris continues. "The guy who attacked Cosette was a meth-head. He was my cousin." He pauses and lets her think about it.

"Okay," she says.

"My uncle also died back in December."

"Oh, Chris, I'm so sorry." Hilda's shaking.

"And my Aunt April's fiancée was killed a few days ago. All of them the same way." Chris stops and waits. I'm shaking so bad Rose wraps her arms around me.

"So, do you... who...?" Hilda's trying to comprehend. Her eyes dart back and forth as she figures it out. "All of them the same way? You know who attacked..., you know them? Wait, you're... You're related to them and...? And Cosette killed him? Them? All of them?"

Decker stands up. "Holy shit! She is fucking psycho, Chris! She's wiping out your family!"

"Fuck you, Deck!" Chris stands.

"Decker, stop!" Rose pulls Decker down, trying to calm the situation.

"So, Chris," Hilda's eyes are shifting like she's seeing the pieces and is putting the puzzle together. "Cosette stopped my first attacker who was your uncle? And so the second guy went after her? "DID, DID YOU know who took me? How come you couldn't find me? Why didn't you come get me? Why..." Hilda starts crying.

"No, precious." I hold her tight. "He didn't know what they were doing. He didn't know where you were. The police just told us who his uncle really was." My whole body is burning up. "Hilda, we were at his uncle's farm," I squeak out.

"So, Chris, your two uncles and cousin? They were the Poser gang? And, Cosette, you killed them?" Hilda repeats, trying to get the facts straight. She's crying hard and shaking. Then she stops and stares at me. Bright blue puffy eyes bore into me. "Cozy, you killed four people to protect me? Four people?" Hilda squeaks out.

I nod. Hot tears run down my face. She throws her arms around me and whispers, "I love you, Cozy. Thank you."

"I'm so, so sorry." I hold her tight.

She gasps then whispers in my ear. "So you were serious about the ten?"

I can't answer.

Mattie knows, but I still don't want to admit it. Rose thinks I'm fascinating, like I'm a TV character in a vampire show.

Decker jerks his head back. "Ohhh, that's great. That's fucking great! Four people? What the hell have you done with yourself? You went from being a wet noodle to this in a matter of weeks. This is her fault, isn't it?" Decker points to Hilda. "She turned our Cosette psycho! You did this to her by being a bitch to her all year long. So, Chris, is that why you two are taking turns with her? You fuck her over so you can fuck her over?"

"Shut up, Decker!" Mattie yells.

"Oh, like you're one to talk! Little Miss Self-Righteous. You can't tell me you aren't sleeping with them too. You can't tell me you haven't been all over Cosette like Rosy and me! She'll make you a whore just like she's doing to Hilda. Just like she's doing to Rosy!"

I leap out of my chair and charge across the table, throwing my hands around Decker's neck. He falls backwards, hitting his head on the hard linoleum.

I straddle him and with every punch, I defend Mattie. "Don't you ever talk to her like that! You son of a bitch! She's perfect and pure, and you should consider yourself lucky that she even talks to your sorry ass!" Retribution's swift. He will never speak about Mattie like that again!

Chris yanks me off and holds me down. I growl and yank, but I can't get free.

Decker stands up and shakes himself off. He's bloody. "Fucking psycho bitch!" He kneels down by me. "You better learn to treat your friends better." He leaves without demanding for Rose to join him.

I cover my face and cry. Hilda, Mattie, and Rose surround me.

Chris stays on me, holding my shoulders. "We can't leave her alone for one minute. I'll take her home for the first watch."

Mattie pulls my hands down to look me in the eye. "I can defend myself, Cozy. It's Decker. Decker." She stands up. "I'll be there tonight after the café closes."

"I'll come after school for the second shift," Rose volunteers then leaves.

"I don't need to be on suicide watch," I snap at Chris.

"No, but you do need to be watched. Let's go." He picks me up and whisks me out of school.

"I REALLY FREAKED out on him, didn't I?" I wheel into my apartment.

"It was awesome!" Chris closes the door and carries me to the couch. "Hilda was shocked by what he said. He blamed her for your being psycho. Do you think he's right?"

"I don't know. I don't think so. Wouldn't you have to have this all your life? If everyone turned into psycho from being bullied, then the whole planet would be crazy."

"Did you sleep with Decker?"

"Not yet."

"Yet?" he asks.

"I'm not attracted to him if that's what you're worried about. I'll take Rose before I take him."

"Then why yet...?" He eyes me, thinking, reading into my answer. "You're very manipulative. You would sleep with him to control him? You are so hot right now." He climbs on top of me. "And you already control Rose. I think she finds you dangerously attractive." He starts kissing my neck.

"Speaking of dangerously attractive, Hilda should've come with us. She's a slow driver," I say.

"Hilda smiled."

"When?"

"When you didn't answer about the ten."

"You heard that whisper?"

He nods. "Was it really ten?"

"Yes. It doesn't seem real. I remember each face, but it fades away until the next one. Then the flood of pleasure from the time before comes over me. The highs get higher." I look at him. "Of course, the lows get lower. She smiled, huh?"

"Yeah." He pulls my body closer to his. "I think you and Decker need to make up."

"I bruised his ego. That's harder to make up," I say.

"We'll go out. I'll take Rosy, and you do what you can for Decker. We might need him someday, especially with Hilda joining us. I think you created a monster there."

"I'm trying to behave here, so stop. You're turning me on." I swing my legs off the couch and sit up. "I think I want you to go to church with Mattie and me."

He sits up. "Uh, no."

"I don't want to chop up people and kiss all my friends to have a good time. I need an outlet. So do you. I'm not helping your addictive personality."

"I don't think church would be a good outlet for us. What if it burns down the second we step through the door?"

"I've been there before," I say.

"And a lot of good it did you. You are who you are, Bonnie. It would take a miracle from God to change that. And I doubt He will waste a miracle on us. Believe me, I would like to change too, but it's harder than you think." Chris wraps me in his arms, consoling me.

"I need something else then, a replacement high."

"Then you'll have to resort to sex or killing animals. We can break into someone's house when we need the high. But I don't think God wants us in his church any more than we want Him showing up during one of our sessions."

I nod in agreement. Maybe I'm giving up too easy.

A car door slams, and Chris gets up to let Hilda in. She comes over and sits by me. "Are you okay?" she asks.

"I'm fine. Decker's always been an ass like that. I didn't mean to go off on him that bad."

"Hilda," Chris holds her hands. "I'm sorry for what my family did to you."

"Did you tell them to come after me?" she asks.

"No."

"Did you tell them to attack Cosette?"

"No, but..."

"Did you tell them to kidnap me, hurt me, and then shoot her?"

"No, but I'm still sorry. Trash runs in my family. I'm sorry they got ahold of you."

"Yeah, well, I'm sorry it happened, but now I have you two, and I've changed for the better." She sits up and pulls us in. "I'm sorry all of it happened, but we're here now and I'm happier." She's living in a fantasyland, escaping what's really going on.

She kisses Chris deeply and starts to undress me when we hear a car alarm beep.

"Shit! Is your mom here?" Chris stops Hilda from unbuckling his belt.

"No, my mom has the late shift." I peek out the window. "It's Rose. Holy crap, Rose is actually skipping class."

Chris opens the door. "I thought you were coming after school. Shame on you for skipping, Rosy."

She takes off her coat and hands it to Chris then sits between Hilda and me. She huffs and blinks her tears away. Her knees are shaking.

I grab her hand. "What's wrong?"

"He called me a whore." She's pissed and hurt.

"You know Decker didn't mean it. He's probably hurt too. When has he ever disrespected you?" I ask. "I mean, he does act like a chauvinist pig sometimes..."

"All the time," Rose says.

"Most of the time. But he does have redeeming qualities."

Chris comes back in and sits on the coffee table, facing us. He puts his hands on her knees, calming her down. "He's upset his perfect girlfriend is changing."

"He told you that? That I'm changing?" Rose asks.

"No, but I'd be upset too to have some psycho kissing all over my girlfriend without my permission. No offense, hon."

"None taken," I say. "I don't think he handles change very well. I'm not the quiet, boring wet noodle anymore. Hilda's not the enemy, and Chris, well, Chris hasn't changed much. His skeletons are still in his closet."

"I think Decker's problem is with me." Hilda purses her lips.

"Well he's going to have to get over it," I say. "Because now you're one of us."

"Yeah, you're one of us," Rose agrees.

"And now we're all one happy family." I stand and pull Rose and Hilda up for a group hug. "And we support each other and love each other."

"Well then I wanna hug too!" Chris begs.

"If you hug one, you hug all. We're a package deal, Chris," Hilda jokes.

"I can deal with that." He hugs all three of us. First, he kisses Hilda, then me, then he steps to Rose. Gently he holds her chin and softly pulls her in. She starts quivering then steps back.

"I can't..." Rose turns to me.

"Yes, you can," I press up against her. "Relax. We won't hurt you." I turn her back around, wrap my arm around her waist, then brush her hair back. Gently I kiss her neck. She closes her eyes and tilts her head. I pull Chris in to kiss her. She leans away, but I push her forward. He skims her lips with his. I can feel her body heating up. He kisses her. When she kisses back he goes in deep.

We have her.

She's enjoying this, and so is Bonnie. Chris kisses Rose, then me as I pull Hilda into Rose. Though shaking, Rose is receptive to all three of us.

Chris takes Hilda to the loveseat while I guide Rose to lie down on the couch.

"Just relax. I'll make you feel good." I kneel on the floor next to her.

She lies back, but her body's as stiff as a board. I stroke her hair and give soft little kisses all over. Her hands are wringing, so I separate them by intertwining my fingers with hers. She pulls me on top of her, giving in to my will.

"Why don't we make you a little more comfortable?" I take off her sweater. She has a lace-lined t-shirt on underneath, and I'm surprised by her wardrobe. She has fantastic breasts, yet she keeps them covered. I wonder if that's Decker or her parent's doing.

"These are nice." I cup her; she quickly covers up. "Relax, Rose, it's just me." I hold her wrists above her head and kiss her pouty lips, then on down her neck to her full cleavage.

IT DOESN'T TAKE long before she's acclimated to me touching her. But before I can fully take her, a car door slams and draws my attention away.

I get up to answer the door, throwing a blanket over Chris and Hilda's state of undress.

A COOL BREEZE enters with Decker. He has a black eye, not a big one, but just enough of one to make me proud. "I'm sorry I beat you up," I tease, welcoming him with a kiss.

"You're not getting an apology from me." He turns to sees Rose on the couch, and Chris and Hilda on the loveseat in their underwear. I can feel his heart jump to a faster pace. He's mad and hurt.

I turn his head to face me. "I don't need you to apologize, Decker. Can you handle me this time?"

"Do you think you can handle me?" He touches his eye. "Paybacks are a bitch. Chris says you like pain. Let's see how you like this." He grabs my arm and pulls me to the floor in front of his Rose. He's jealous and angry, and he starts to take it out on me. I love it. He quickly strips off my shirt and yanks down my pants. Rose watches us. She's excited, terrified, and worried.

He's forceful and vengeful.

I can take his pain, but he can't. He looks up at the grip he has on my wrists. Then he looks down at my half-naked body and my bullet wound. Defeat clouds his face. He lets go and pulls me up to a hug. Wrapping his arms around me, he holds me, whispering, "I'm sorry, Cozy. I don't want to hurt you. I can't. I can't be this guy."

"It's okay, Deck." I hold his face and run my fingers through his short soft red hair. "Relax, do what makes you feel good. We're just having fun. It's only for fun." I rock my hips to get him started again. I pull Rose into a kiss. She gets undressed and joins us. Relieved, he kisses me soft then deeper, then deeper until he's relaxed enough to understand I'm not taking Rose away from him. He's not losing anything, only gaining.

Chapter
TWENTY-THREE

"HAVE YOU GIRLS recuperated from this weekend?" Chris walks us into school holding my hand as well as Hilda's. The murmurs begin. Yes, the entire class body thinks we're freaks. And they should.

"I'm doing great. You two are fun." Hilda gives Chris and me a kiss before running off to class.

"How are you doing with all of this?" I ask Chris. "Are you okay with the whole Decker and Rose thing?"

"You ask me that now? Now that we've slept with them?" He pulls me aside. "As long as I know you're mine, and mine first, then I'm fine with it. Actually watching you with them, I like it. Besides any feelings of jealousy fade away when I think of what they are to me."

"Meat?"

"Meat." He holds my wrists, squeezes them to the point of almost bruising. "Just remember you're mine. I earned you."

"Yes, you did." I say.

"So, is this gonna work for you?" Chris moves my braided hair to my back and focuses on my eyes.

"Is what gonna work for me?"

"Meaning, you're trying to replace your first addiction with another. Do you really think it's gonna work?"

"I'm not addicted to the first, and I won't be addicted to sex either." I try to leave for class.

He grips my wrists tighter. "I wasn't talking about sex. I know you, Bonnie. I know you better than you know you. You're addicted to the control, and you've figured out how to get it."

"That's not what I'm..."

"Yes, it is. And as soon as you realize it, the better off you are. You think you can replace one with the other, but you can't. Not as long as you act like you're just having fun. The real fun starts when you open your eyes and embrace the real you."

"I gotta get to art. See you at lunch." I twist out of his hold, give him a kiss, and walk into class.

MRS. IRIS PURSES her lips when I walk into art. I ignore her, pull out my sketchbook, and start my assignment.

My table bumps me out of my concentration. One of the guys from the other side of the class dares to come talk to me.

"What?" I sketch my assignment without making eye contact.

"Did you really kill someone?" he asks quietly. He has light tan skin and jet-black chin length hair parted in the middle and pulled behind his ears. He's very nervous.

"Yes. More than one. Did they dare you?"

"Y-Y-Yes," he stutters. He looks back at his friends, who quickly put their heads down. "You're not going to hurt me for talking to you, are you?"

What a funny question. He's cute and has on a faded shirt with Donkey Kong on it. I can see him owning an array of retro video games. I can also see why he was the one singled out. He seems like the only one brave/dumb enough to come over.

"I have criteria for killing. You don't fit it."

He looks at my assignment and raises his eyebrow acknowledging my talent. "Are you going out with Hilda?"

"And Chris."

"That's so awesome."

I pause my drawing and turn to him. "Let me ask you a question, and I want you to answer truthfully."

"Otherwise you'll kill me?"

"I'm not going to kill you. Just answer me."

"Sure." He sits up like a kid who's happy that a girl wants to talk to him for any length of time.

"What are people around here saying?"

He leans in, trying to get closer. He has minty breath. I'm glad. "Some people are scared of you. Some think you're setting Hilda up to get her back for being a bitch to you. But mostly everyone thinks you're cool. They all want to know details."

"What about Chris?" I ask.

"They think he's doing all three of you."

That surprises me for a moment, "All three of who?" I ask.

"You, Hilda, and Mattie." He gives me a look like he's wondering who else would be on the list.

"Mattie's not involved." I keep my eyes on my paper.

"Sure."

I fist my pencil like I could stab his eye any second.

"Okay, okay. Mattie's not involved." He holds up his hands, backing away.

"Listen closely." I grab his collar and pull his face to mine. "Mattie is perfect and pure and innocent, and if anyone tries to change that or hurt her, I will cut them. I will cut them slow and watch as their eyes go dim. Do you understand that? Mattie is not like me. She is good and perfect, and she will be protected."

"Got it… I'm sorry."

I let go and start sketching again.

"Are you scared of me?" I ask.

His voice cracks. "Yes. But you are so frickin' hot!"

I scoff. "I'm not hot. I'm normal. Just plain old Cosette."

"Which makes you even more hot." He gulps, embarrassed that came out.

"Are they expecting you to ask me something else or do something?" I watch his friends trying not to watch me.

"They're more scared of you than I am. But they think you're hot too."

"You're going to be the cool one now that you had the balls to come to me, huh?"

His eyes smile. "Yeah."

"Here then, take this back with you." I grab his shirt, kiss him, then let him go. He falls back in his seat just as Ms. Iris looks up from her computer. He scurries back to his stunned and impressed friends.

HOW PATHETIC THAT I just made his day. I'm nobody, I killed someone, and now I am somebody. How pathetic.

HILDA AND ROSE are by my locker talking, waiting to walk me to lunch. My pace is slow, but at least I'm not rolling.

"Hi, guys." They each kiss my cheek. I'm surprised Rose did.

"Do you guys want to come over for a sleepover on Friday?" Rose asks. "My parents will be there, so it will have to be a sex-free zone," she whispers.

"Will your parents let us in their home? I do have a reputation," I laugh.

"Yes, of course. Chris and Decker can stay for a movie but have to leave after."

"I think it sounds like fun. It might be nice to be normal," Hilda says.

"Normal from whose point of view?" I joke.

"I asked Mattie and Paige. Paige flat-out told me no. Mattie has a date with some guy."

"His name is Telly, and he's perfect for her. We need to be careful. Mattie needs to stay good. I will never pressure her into anything. You girls have to promise the same."

"I don't understand," Hilda says.

"Mattie is one of the few truly good people in this world. I will protect that fiercely. We can't try to change her. Got it?" My tone's a little dark and forceful. They're naturally scared of me, so it doesn't take much convincing. They nod.

Shelby, Sierra, Paige, and Mattie are already at the lunch table. Chris comes in and pulls out a chair for Hilda and a chair for me. Decker kisses Rose's cheek and pulls out her chair.

Mattie knows something's going on. So does Paige. She looks at the five of us and shivers.

She whispers to Mattie. "I can't be here. I can't sit near this."

"I know, Paige. I see it too. But I can't leave her like this. Pray for me," Mattie whispers back.

"I will." Paige stands. "I'm sorry, you guys. But I can't sit here. You all are doing something wrong. I don't know what, and I don't want to know. I just can't be around this. When you all go back to being normal, then I'll come back. But until then, no hard feelings?"

"We understand, Paige. Bad company corrupts good morals. I'm sorry you have to leave, but we understand." I stand and give her a hug.

"I'm praying for you, Cozy, especially you. You are their ring leader; lead them to a better place."

She leaves. Shelby and her little sister, Sierra, follow.

Everyone's stunned.

"It takes a lot of guts to do that. We need to respect her, okay?" I look at everyone. Rose seems hurt. "We made our choice, Rose. She's standing for what she believes in."

They all look to Mattie. "I do know what it is you all are doing, and I think you guys are disgusting. But I won't leave you. Just don't be insulted when I don't show up to one of your little soireés."

"I love you, Mattie," I say.

"I love you too. You all know the whole school is talking about you three, soon to be five?"

"Yeah, we know," Rose says, disappointed.

"Fuck them," says Decker.

"How so very you to say that. I'm sorry, guys. I didn't mean to bring you all down to my level." I reach across the table to hold their hands.

Hilda wiggles my fingers. "Stop getting down on yourself. I'm actually happy. I'm sorry I was such a bitch before."

"How the tables have turned," Rose says. "Have Carla and Sarah talked to you since the kiss?" she asks Hilda.

"Oh, no. I ruined their status."

"And now that we're out in the open, Sarah's brother has no reason to spy on you," I say.

"I hope not," Hilda says. "Last thing I want is Shark tailing me wherever I go. It's bad enough some reporters are still hanging around."

"I can kill them if you like." I laugh; Mattie doesn't. "I'm kidding, Mattie."

"Well don't. Don't joke like that. Words become reality," Mattie says.

"Then I'll kill them," Chris jokes.

"Talk about bad company corrupts good morals. Look what you've done, Cosette. You've damaged the poor boy, screwed him up big time," Hilda says, trying to look serious.

They still think I'm the worst out of the two of us. Maybe I am. I still don't have as many victims as Chris, and I don't plan on catching up. Despite what Chris says, Bonnie will have to be satisfied with my newfound pleasure.

"I did screw him up, huh? Sorry, honey. I guess you're stuck with me."

"Don't think I'm innocent."

"Oh please, Chris, no one believes your 'seventeen' crap." Rose rolls her eyes. Everyone else agrees with her. This is good. This is very good.

Chapter TWENTY-FOUR

"Welcome to our home, you guys." Rose's mom opens the door to Chris, Hilda, and me. She's average height, light red hair, and a little curvier than Rose. But if I were to bet, I'd say we're looking at Rose in twenty years.

"Thank you. We brought drinks and chips." Hilda holds up the two liters of soda.

"I made cookies," I whine, trying to get attention.

"Thank you all. You girls are going to have so much fun tonight. I used to love slumber parties. We would do each other's hair and paint our toes."

"Mom?" Rose calls her mom back in an attempt to save herself from further embarrassment.

"I better go help. I made pizza for you all. Go on downstairs. Decker is already there, and Sierra and Shelby said they'll be here in a few." She leaves us and grabs a wooden paddle the size of a snow shovel on the way out the back door.

Turns out Rose's mom is a fantastic cook. She's cooking our pizza in an outside wood burning oven. No wonder the neighborhood smells so good.

Walking into the foyer, I can tell the evident age of the house by looking at the creaking dark hardwood floors and wainscoting. It's huge compared to my apartment, and it looks professionally decorated. I would have never thought to put sage green, rusty orange, and plum together, but here it works well.

We're led downstairs to a finished basement. There's a pool table and an enormous TV. Instead of couches, Rose has three beanbag sofas that turn into beds.

We settle in and pick out a movie we know we won't watch. Her mom comes downstairs with pizzas and drinks. We eat and laugh and play around like a normal group of teens having a normal party.

I've never been to a normal party like this, so I'm actually nervous. I know these are my friends, and even after our fivesome earlier this week, I'm not sure how to act.

To make things more uncomfortable, Decker is actually laughing.

"What?" he asks me, noticing I'm staring.

"I've never seen you laugh like that. It's good to see you laugh," I say.

His bright grey eyes roll at me. "I laugh when I have a reason to."

"I guess I have been a little too preoccupied to notice. Soooo sorrry." I slather on the sarcasm.

"So anyway, guys," Chris gets everyone's attention. "In case you don't know, Cozy's birthday is coming up, and I want suggestions."

"It is? Your birthday's coming up? How fun! I have tickets to Paoli Peaks. Do you ski?" Rose asks.

"Ohh, that sounds like fun." Hilda bounces up to her. "Let's ski."

"I suck at skiing. Let's do it!" I agree.

Chris bounces up to Rose, mimicking Hilda. "Yeah, let's do it!"

"See, Cozy, that was funny. I laughed at that." Decker bounces too.

"You two are stupid." I get up to refill my drink.

"We should invite Mattie and her new boyfriend. If that's okay with you guys?" Rose asks.

"Of course," I say.

"I'd like them to come," Chris says. "It'd be nice to meet her boyfriend. What's his name?"

"Telly. It's short for his last name, which I forgot," I say.

"As much as I like our little gang here, I don't want to leave out any of our other friends. By the way, Shelby and Sierra are very late." Rose goes to the other side of the room to call the sisters.

"Good, I didn't want to be the odd girl out," Hilda says.

"You're not the odd one." Decker slides a glance my way.

"Thanks, Deck. By the way, now that it's out in the open, what made you come over the other day?"

"Rose. I didn't want her to hate me. And the fact that I don't trust you."

"What? Why?" I'm insulted. I know there are plenty of reasons, ten actually, for him to not trust me. But other than those, I'm a very honest person.

"I'll screw you, but I don't trust you. I don't think you can control yourself. You're like an animal that once you taste blood, you will always want more." Decker doesn't hold back.

"I won't hurt her." My integrity is still semi-intact, but now he thinks I'm a loose cannon.

"You won't *want* to hurt her, but I doubt when the time comes..."

"All the people I've killed have been people who've attacked me! It was all self-defense. You should be more afraid."

"I am afraid. You're a..." Decker stops his sentence as Rose approaches.

"Shelby and Sierra are on their way. What are we talking about?" Rose tucks her phone back in her pocket.

"We're talking about the ski trip." Chris changes the subject. "Would your parents let you all stay overnight? I'll rent us a cabin."

"My dad will let me stay the night since I have Cozy." Hilda cuddles up to me.

"My parents won't. Deck and I will have to meet you three up there in the morning. I'm assuming Mattie and Telly will drive up that morning too?" Rose asks.

"I'll text them. When do we want to go? The weekend before or the weekend after my birthday?" I ask.

"The weekend after," Chris says. "I have someplace special to take you the weekend before."

"Ooooo," everyone chimes.

Chris rolls his eyes.

My mind's racing, trying to figure out what he would give me for my birthday. I have everything I need.

"Great. It's set!" Rose says.

"Rose, I think you guys should have car trouble and stay up there with us," I suggest.

Rose shakes her head, "I don't know that I could do that."

"Sure you can. You're at the mercy of Decker's car, right? Decker, I think your car'll need a tune-up when we get back."

"Wow, Cozy. Manipulative psycho." Decker says.

He has a barrier I want to break.

I walk over and crawl on top of him. "That's sexy, manipulative psycho to you." I seductively kiss him.

"Yes, it is." Chris comes over and pulls me off. "We have non-members coming. Let's not embarrass them." He kisses my ear and softly reminds me, "You're mine."

Relieved, Decker pulls Rose closer.

The doorbell rings and the ceiling above us creaks. "The sisters are here," Rose announces.

AFTER THREE LAUGH-FILLED hours of playing stupid games and an embarrassing defeat in Pictionary, the guys have to go home.

On the steps up, out of Shelby and Sierra's sight, we all kiss each other bye.

"Be careful, Cosette. You're still green," Chris whispers then leaves. I don't get his warning. I'm anything but naïve.

Rose sits on the steps, waiting and listening. The front door closes and locks, then a set of headlights streak across the basement windows.

"Now the real fun begins," Rose says. "Shelby?"

"I brought them." Shelby pulls out four different kinds of hair irons. Rose claps. She's excited to play. She's such a girly girl. These two and Hilda are good at this sort of thing. I am not. Sierra reluctantly brings out a slew of nail polish. I think she's a bit more like me.

They primp and play at glamour while Sierra and I open up the beanbag beds. Laid out, they cover the floor like two king-size beds with a foot thick of fluff. We spread ourselves out, and each of the girls takes a long lock of my hair and braids it in different ways. "I didn't know there were that many ways to do it."

"We're glad you finally came so we can experiment on you," Shelby says.

"I was never invited before. I didn't think you guys liked me."

"We didn't know you. How could we? You hardly said a word." Rose shows me her braiding skills.

"I like it. You're welcome to come over every morning to fix my hair for school," I tell Rose.

I try to hold still while Sierra's painting my toes. She's tickling me. Sierra's a year younger, and I'm cautious around her.

"Cosette?" Sierra wiggles my big toe to get my attention.

"Yes?"

"Did you like it?" She whispers, but it catches Shelby's attention. Shelby's eyes grow big waiting for my answer.

I want to scream 'Hell, yeah! I loved it!', but I can't. It wouldn't be responsible.

"I did what I had to do," I say.

"I think I would have liked it. Getting revenge. I don't know that I would have stopped at just stabbing his throat. I would've mutilated him for what he did to you two."

Revenge. Pure revenge. I don't get off on the violent part of it. If I did, I might have mutilated Tattoo in twenty different ways after seeing him on Hilda. But, no, I did it slowly, enjoying every moment, every tremor. I have to watch what I say. I refuse to create another monster or stir up the one I already have inside.

"When it happened, I surprised myself. I knew what I was doing was horrible, but I had to. There is a feeling of revenge, which is a high, but there is always a low."

"What do you mean?" Shelby asks. So much for me keeping quiet.

"I killed someone. I'm going to have to live with that for the rest of my life. It's not something you forget like cheating on a test. Let's say you do cheat on a test. You're happy when you get away with it, but then the guilt comes. Well, the guilt with something like this is unbearable."

As I'm talking, the girls are scooting in closer, hanging on every word.

"But you shouldn't feel guilty. They attacked you," Sierra says.

"Those men will never get the chance to do better. They will never get the chance to change. They had family that loved them despite their horrible nastiness. They had family that will miss them. Even without that, there is always guilt. You can't sleep at night. You wake up screaming. I'll look down and feel the floor drop out from under me like Hell is sucking me in. At random times, the guilt will flood over me, and sometimes it's too much. I'll throw up. Or worse."

"What's worse?" Rosy cautiously asks.

Hilda pulls me in. "Suicide," she says.

I start tearing up. "Sometimes the guilt is too much. I used to love being alone. I would run for miles. Now I'm afraid to be alone. I'll be good one minute; I'll want to end it the next. I am not good alone."

"Is that why you have a boyfriend and a girlfriend?" Sierra asks so matter-of-factly.

"Interesting question, I never thought of it that way. No. I just refuse to choose one over the other."

Hilda sighs and puts her head on my shoulder.

"My friends think you're the coolest thing ever," Sierra bubbles.

"I'm not. Please don't put me up there. I never chose this. I wouldn't want anyone to be like this. I'm not stable, and yet I think I'm doing better than most would in my situation. Please don't let them think of me as cool."

"That makes you even more cool." Her eyes twinkle.

Shit. This is not what I want.

"Let's change the subject," I suggest. Just then my phone rings. "Saved by the bell." I answer, "Hey, Mel."

"Who's Mel?" Rose asks Hilda.

Hilda whispers, "They're her prostitute friends. Very ghetto."

I scowl at Hilda. Sierra perks up, her fondness of me doubling. Great.

Mel talks loud. "Pearl has a client, so I thought I'd call. I'm tired of hearing her."

"Anyone you know?" I ask.

"Business man, frequent flyer. Smudge is out dealing with some Brazilians who want answers in Bounce's death."

My gut starts tightening up. "Any new clues?"

"He ain't gonna find shit, and mama don't know nuthin. Whatcha doing?"

"I'm at a slumber party. You're now on speaker. Say hi, Mel."

"Hi. You all curling hair and shit like that?" Mel asks.

"Hi, Mel. This is Hilda."

"Barbie!"

Sierra and Shelby laugh.

"Yeah, I'm here. What are you doing?" Hilda asks.

"Waiting for Pearl to finish. Hey, listen. I'm gonna put the phone up close so you can hear. I'll put you all on mute." Muffled moaning and grunting comes through loud and clear. We all giggle. Mel comes back on the phone. "And that, my friends, is why you should stay in school."

We all bust out laughing.

"Thanks for the public service announcement," I tell her.

"You all have fun. I'll catcha later, Cookie." Mel hangs up.

"You have the coolest life," Sierra says to me. "So, I want to get my ears pierced. Will you do it?" Sierra digs out a cosmetic bag. "Shelby got hers done two years ago at a party, so now it's my turn."

"Who did yours, Shelby?" Hilda asks.

"No clue. I was drunk at a party."

"Look at Shelby, the party animal," Hilda says.

"You have no idea." She smirks at Rose, glancing at the liquor bottles lined up behind the bar.

"Okay!" Rose cheers.

What? This is not what I want! This is not where I need to be. Chris is right; I am naïve. I had no idea this would happen. "I can't drink. I shouldn't drink. You all go ahead. I'll be your lookout."

"Awww, c'mon. I bet you're really fun!" Sierra takes the first shot. She coughs.

"Shhhh. Rose's mom is going to wake up," I warn them.

"My mom takes a sleeping pill. We could play the drums, and she would stay asleep. Shelby, you're next." Rose hands Shelby the bottle.

Shelby takes a swig and passes it back to Rose. Rose takes at least two shots. The expression on my face makes her laugh.

"We don't have cooties, do we, Shelby?" Sierra asks.

Hilda takes the bottle and grabs a glass. "If I drink out of the bottle, Cozy won't kiss me. She's a germaphobe." She pours a shot.

Rose crawls up to me. The alcohol seems to be kicking in. "It would just be like kissing me."

"Yeah, and we already know you don't have a problem with that," Sierra says.

"Cute, Sierra. I can't help it. I don't know why I'm like this," I say.

"You don't have a problem kissing anyone from what I can remember," Hilda blurts out.

I take the bottle from her and give it to Shelby. "And that is why I don't drink," I warn Hilda who's trying to figure out what she said wrong.

No one caught the inside quip, and none of them dared to ask for an explanation. I do enjoy kissing. My last three kills I kissed, sucking in their last.... I have to stop. Focus, Cosette, focus on being normal.

Shelby takes another drink and the rest follow, at least two more shots each. I don't want them to get sick, so I cut them off. They're lightweights; it doesn't take much. They laugh about the stupidest things. I fluff my pillow, sit back, and watch them.

Rose is a giddy drunk. Shelby and Sierra are cuddly with everyone, and each other. It's kind of weird. They play steamroller and roll over all of us. Hilda watches her hands a lot, and she adjusts her bra a lot too.

They each spill numerous secrets. It's wonderful. I'm glad I'm sober for this. I want to remember all of it. I keep thinking about what Chris says. Maybe I do like the control. Even if I drank, I doubt they would remember anything I'd say. Maybe my not drinking is a way to watch over them, to put them in a position where I have the upper hand.

I do have the upper hand. I could take all of them as my own now, and they wouldn't care one bit. Then tomorrow they would have to fall in line.

"...and that's why Sarah and I will never double date." Hilda laughs.

Rose rolls next to Hilda. "Let me try on your bra. I think we wear the same size."

"Okay." Hilda pops her shirt and bra off.

"Please, don't make me jealous. I don't want to compare chest sizes," I tell them.

"Good idea!" Sierra says.

"I don't think so, wild child." I stop Sierra from feeling me up.

Hilda comes over wearing Rose's bra. "I don't care what size you are. I like them." She hugs me.

"I like yours too." I hug her tight.

"Okay, then, how about truth or dare?" Sierra asks.

"What?" I'm shocked. Apparently, Shelby and Sierra aren't as virtuous as I want them to be. If I had come to this party in November, I think I would have left. Chris was right, and I'm a little disappointed I was so naïve. "What happened to my innocent, perfect friends?"

"Don't be a prude." Sierra rolls on me. "And what makes you think we're so innocent?"

"Nothing now." I roll her off.

I UNDERSTAND WHY Mattie said she was busy. I think that even if Telly wasn't taking her out, she would have missed this one. I'm glad she's still pure, still perfect. I pray she stays that way.

First Truth or Dare question comes to me, of course. "I don't think you all are drunk enough for me to play this with you." I ignore the question.

They agree and swig another round of whisky. Hopefully, they won't remember anything in the morning.

Every time it comes to me, I call for dare. I'm ending up doing things that would make Chris blush, but at least I don't have to answer any questions.

"Hilda, truth or dare?" Shelby asks.

"Truth."

"When did you lose your virginity and with who?"

This should be interesting. I know what I don't want to hear. I don't want to hear that it was Tuesday before Christmas break.

She's so drunk and her speech is so slurred they can barely understand what she says. But I understand. It gives great insight.

"It was with my mom's boyfriend. I was eleven." Hilda says.

How sad. The others don't comprehend. But I can feel the rage growing in me. I don't want my Hilda hurt.

They laugh, and she blows it off like it's the norm.

"My turn," Hilda announces. "Cozy, truth or dare, and you've already done the worst dares, so say truth."

"Fine." Not like they'll remember. "Truth."

"How many people did you kill?" Sierra blurts out, taking Hilda's question.

Of course. I look into all their glossed over eyes. I doubt they can spell their name, more or less remember this fact.

"This week? Or this month?" I tease.

"Total. How many?" Rose asks.

"I think we're done playing this game," I say.

"Me too." Shelby stumbles to the bathroom.

Hilda spreads out on top of me. She strokes my hair. "You're so beautiful. I wish you were all mine."

Sierra cuddles next to me. She kisses my cheek. "How many? Is there gonna be a next one? I wanna see the next one. Can I come with you?"

"After you kill him, Coz. I'll have Decker take him and burn him for you." Rose cuddles my other side, kissing my neck.

"Please, Cozy. Let us go with you," Sierra begs.

I can't do this. I can't turn these girls. They may not be innocent as far as sex goes, but I will not do this to them.

"I don't do it for fun."

"Yes, you do," Hilda whispers, stroking her fingers across my lips.

I grab them and kiss them. "Aren't you all afraid of me?"

"Yes, that's what we like about you," Rose says.

"We'll be your assississsitants. You can have your own vig, vigil. Shit, what's that word? Vigilante squad." Sierra slurs. She keeps kissing my cheek and rubbing up against me. I have to remember they're drunk.

They're drunk, and it's not fair for me to manipulate them.

What harm can come from saying okay? They won't remember.

"If I say yes, how do you want to do it?" I ask.

I let them talk. They go on and on with the different methods they would use. Shelby comes out of the bathroom and joins in the brainstorming. I'm enjoying their ideas.

I'm getting antsy.

I'm getting scared.

They talk and talk and talk. Finally they fall asleep.

Innocent, not promised anything, not confessed to.

I made it through the night. I will never ever do this again.

Chapter TWENTY-FIVE

CHRIS PICKS HILDA and me up. She has a bad hangover. They all do. Of course, I am fine.

"How are my beauties?"

"Far from it this morning. I think Hilda needs to go home to sleep this one off."

"Feeling a little rough this morning?" he teases.

She nods. We drive her home, and he carries her in. I guess her dad, John, is out working because the house is quiet.

We open the door to her room, and Chris and I start laughing. "You are a princess, aren't you?" Chris says.

She moans and flops on the white canopy bed then cocoons herself in the pink polka-dot comforter. I close the pink drapes and turn off the pink beaded light.

I hate pink.

"Sleep tight, princess." I kiss her forehead then we leave.

CHRIS DRIVES ME back home. "So how was it after we left?"

"I was disappointed. Those girls were more tainted than I thought."

"I knew that. I told you that you were green. Do you not sit at the same lunch table?"

"I guess I never noticed it. I thought they were all like Mattie and Paige. I thought I was the only whore there."

"First of all you are not a whore! Don't you ever call yourself that! To me you are perfect. Absolutely perfect. All five of us have done all five of us. We're all in the same boat, and we're keeping it in the same boat."

"Not really. You haven't been with Decker," I joke.

"And I never will. And second of all, you think good of everyone. You place everyone outside of your bubble thinking that they're in a perfect world where you're the only screwed up one. Everyone has baggage. Mattie is a rare breed."

"Thank you." I scoot over to sit next to him.

"What were Shelby and Sierra really like?" Chris asks.

"If I had gone to that party in November, I would've had to leave. But my recent experience with y'know, the boatmates, I fit in fine. When they get drunk, there is no holding back."

"Interesting." He smiles. "Did you drink?"

"No. I was afraid to drink."

"Good. You should never drink around anyone who doesn't know you or can't physically handle you. I guess that leaves only me."

"I've never been drunk. But apparently, it makes you tell the truth."

"What do you mean?"

I'm afraid to answer. But I now hide nothing from him.

"Sierra wants to kill someone with me, so does Hilda. Rose said she'll make Decker take care of the body. They kept on asking me how many I've killed. I didn't answer. I let them talk themselves to sleep thinking about it. I tried to give them a dose of my reality and how low I get. But they don't get it."

"Were they drunk enough that they will forget it?"

"I think so, but maybe not Hilda. And unfortunately not me."

He pulls the car over into Ice Cream Willie's empty parking lot. "You wanna explain that?"

My heart screams, "No! I don't!"

I have to tell him, and I hope he still looks at me the same because I need him. I really need him to be here for me, to stop me. I take a deep breath.

"Chris, I think I'm in some serious mental trouble here. I am so scared that I can't even focus to tell you."

"What, baby? Tell me what?" He holds my hand and strokes my cheek, trying to calm me down.

My body starts shaking. My stomach's tying in knots. I'm so scared and so sick.

"They kept on talking about it, giving me ideas. Chris, I am in so much trouble." My mouth feels like it's stuffed with cotton. "I don't want to say it. I don't want to admit it." I look deep into his eyes. When I confess, I want to see help. I need him to rescue me. I want to see hope for me.

Please let me see hope.

"Admit what? My perfect Cozy, it's okay. I love you. What is it?"

"I need more, Chris. I want to do it again. I'm so scared. I crossed that line, and I think I'm stuck. I want to do it again." I start crying. "When I came back from being shot, I had a chance at being good. I could've changed, but then I had to free Hilda, and Bonnie came back. Chris, I don't want to be Bonnie, but she's fusing with me. She's becoming more of me.

"Chris, I need to kill again. I'm craving it. It's no longer me waiting to be attacked. I'm burning for it. I need a victim. I need help, but I'm so scared. What've I done to myself?"

He pulls me in and puts my head on his shoulder. His arms wrap around me tight, trying to hold in my tremors as I sob. "You're perfect. I love you. I love you. I'll help you. Don't worry, baby, we can deal with this."

Hope found.

"We'll find someone, baby. I'll help you. We'll find someone for you to kill." His eyes sparkle. He's so happy.

I'm not. This isn't the help I was hoping for.

"I went there, didn't I? I went to that place I promised I wouldn't go. I am in so much trouble. I thought I had control, but I gave it all away. I gave it all to Bonnie."

"You admitting this gives you more control. Don't you see? You're perfect. I brought you back; you're finally here. I am so in love with you. I have so many things I want to share with you. So many things we can experience together." He cups my face and smiles into my eyes.

Relief, that's what he's feeling.

"Welcome to my world. My beautiful world. We're going to be so happy together. I promise."

He beams.

I cry.

Chapter TWENTY-SIX

"LOOK WHAT I picked up for you, Ms. Murphy." He carries in my sleeping bag while I make sure my eyes are tear free.

"Did you girls have fun?"

"I was stuck at home, so no, I didn't," he answers her.

"Silly boy." She takes the sleeping bag from him. "Do you want to stay for breakfast?"

"No. I'm meeting Carl at the gym. We have a meet in a few days."

I didn't even notice he's wearing his gym clothes. I feel bad for him having to drive me home. I could've walked.

"Oh, by the way, Mom, since my birthday is coming up soon, all of us are going skiing. Can I go with the girls to stay the night? The rest of the gang will drive up in the morning."

"Is Mattie going?"

"She has a new boyfriend, Telly, so she'll drive up in the morning too."

"Is Hilda going?" she asks.

"I hope so. We'll have to ask her dad."

"Let me warn you about that. He's being very protective now that she's back. The only reason she got to go to the sleepover is because you were there."

"I know. We're like sisters now. I don't want to go without her," I say.

"What date is it?" she asks. "I bought us some tickets to a concert."

"Not this Saturday, but the following one."

"Cosette, that's the date of the concert."

"If it's not Switchfoot, Joshua Bell, or YoYo Ma, then I don't care."

"No, it's Barry Manilow," she claps with excitement.

I try not to laugh. I know she likes him, and I like some of his songs too, but if I had a choice...

"I know a man who goes by the name of John, I think, who would love to go to that concert with you. I also happen to know that his daughter will be busy that weekend." I fold my hands, begging.

"Fine, you go. I'll take John, you take his daughter. I don't blame you. Will there be any parents there?"

"Rose's parents have season tickets." It isn't a lie; they do have season tickets. They most likely won't be using them that weekend, but they do have season tickets.

"Alright then. You all have fun. Are you going to the gym with Chris?" she asks.

"I think Cozy needs her sleep, and I need to concentrate. She's very distracting you know." He winks at me.

"Ahh, teenage love." My mom bats her eyes.

"Fine, I'll get some sleep. Will you come back this afternoon?"

"I will always be here for you." He holds me in a hug.

"You two are sappy. Alright, Chris, you have a good morning at the gym. I have to go to work at two, but I'm meeting John for lunch at noon. Maybe he's into Barry Manilow."

"One can only hope." Chris laughs as he walks out.

A KNOCK AT the door wakes me from my nap. I slither out of bed. My eyes can barely focus out the peephole. It's Officer Crance.

The cold air wakes me up as I open the door. "Come on in. I'd say good morning, but I think it's afternoon."

"Late night?" she asks.

"I went to a slumber party." I head to the bathroom to brush my teeth.

"I hope it went well." She plants herself at my kitchen table.

"I'm boring. A little too boring. I didn't want to answer truth or dare questions, so I went to sleep early."

"I'm sorry. That's no fun."

I like Officer Crance. She's only a few years older than me, and rather than acting like I'm a victim or a killer, she's treating me like a friend or sister.

She waits patiently while I do my four-minute brushing routine. I offer to make her coffee, but she declines.

"Cosette, I wanted to ask you about your boyfriend, Chris."

"You're scaring me."

"I just want to watch out for you. When did you two start dating?" she asks.

"We've sat next to each other at lunch since the beginning of school. Please tell me what's wrong. I think he's perfect. Don't break my heart."

"Do you know his family well?"

"Besides the fact that he's related to the Poser gang?"

Her smile tries to assure me. "I just want you to be careful around the rest of his family. I know you think he's a good guy, and maybe he is. But it's his upbringing I'm... I don't want to overstep my boundaries but... Do you have a computer?"

"Uh, sure. Hold on." I bring my laptop to the table. She lifts the lid and opens a website.

"What's the address here?" she asks.

I tell her as she types it in. The site maps out my home and the neighborhoods around me. My apartment is a star, and the screen begins spotting randomly with red dots.

"This website shows you how many sex offenders live around you." She turns the computer to face me. I stare at the page. There are so many of them, I'm sickened. "This guy here," she says as she highlights a dot and opens up his info, "He molested five girls under the age of ten. This guy raped his niece. This guy was dating a fifteen year old when he was eighteen, and her father pressed charges. You don't need to worry about him. This cat lady had a lucrative online child porn business but got off on a technicality. But this guy," she pointed to a house nearby, "was caught attempting to meet a blonde sixteen year old at a bar. It was a sting operation, and he was caught before anything happened."

I lean in to focus on the last dot she highlighted. It's Chris's house. The offender's his father. My heart starts racing.

"I am not saying 'like father like son', but I am saying be careful. Chris has a very colorful family. Chris may be the white sheep out of the whole black flock. He may be the one good one, but please be careful around them."

She can see the angst in my expression.

"Cosette, you are so much like my sister. I was the bad seed growing up," she confesses. "My sister was the talented one. She was the one most likely to succeed. She was a cheerleader and honor society student. I barely graduated; I was the black sheep. I had my reasons though. Here, let me do something."

She turns my laptop to face her, and she enters in a different address. The star was only surrounded by three red dots.

"This guy was caught with child porn. This woman slept with her student. But this one... this red dot created this black sheep."

Her? This one created her?

"Is that your house?" I point to the star.

"Yes, I still live there with my parents. They need me. When my sister went missing, before we found out the Poser got her, the police went straight to him. He was our babysitter for years. I took all the abuse so my sister didn't have to. I gave her a chance at life only to have the Poser take it away."

Tears are running down my cheeks.

"He came from a family with a long history of abusers. He was only five years older than me, and he still lives there. I see him every day, and there is nothing I can do about it."

She hands me a napkin for my tears.

"Cosette, I'm just telling you this because I don't want you to get hurt. You killed his uncle, and his father is a registered offender. Please be very careful. I want to protect you, I guess. This is not protocol for an officer, but I just want you to be strong. His family is being watched, but that doesn't mean you should let your guard down. Do you understand?"

"Officer Crance?"

"Call me Jenny."

"Okay, Jenny. I, I'm sorry that that happened to you. I'm sorry you have to see him every day."

"I see a lot of horrific things, but the ones that stay with me the most are guys like that. I took an oath. Unfortunately that sometimes means I have to serve and protect those I want to kill. But I do it for my sister, the one person I couldn't protect."

"I'm so sorry."

She stands up and heads for the door. "I just wanted to warn you. I'm watching his family and you should too."

I follow her to the door.

"He got the wrong girl, the Poser. It should have been me. I'm the black sheep." She gives me a hug. "Thank you for killing him. I know it must have been hard. I would wipe them all out if I could. You're so brave. Thank you for killing him."

She closes the door behind her. I go back to my laptop. I have some research to do.

"HI, HONEY." CHRIS comes in with a smile and a kiss. He smells so good, fresh from the shower.

"Tell me about your dad," I say, still standing in the doorway. He looks at my open laptop in the kitchen, still on the sex offender website.

"How did you find out?" Shame clouds his face.

"Officer Crance came by to warn me about your family. You could have told me."

"And said what? 'Hey, Cosette, I want you to meet my dad. He's a sex offender, and people think 'like father like son'. Oh, and I'm also in a gang of rapists with my uncle and meth-head cousin. Hope you don't mind. Ya wanna go out?"

"I've been honest with you," I say.

"Yeah, but it took a while. It's not a secret we pass on while playing 'truth or dare'!"

"I said nothing!"

"Because everyone knows already!"

"I'm not mad at you! Stop yelling at me! I would just like to have known."

"I'm sorry. You're right." He wraps his arms around me. "Let me take you out. I'll give you our family history."

"No, I don't want to leave. You can't butter me up with food. Nice try though."

"There's not much more to tell. You've met my hillbilly redneck family. We're mostly criminals. We date back to the Wild West. We've never grown out of it."

"Why did you and your dad move here? Where's your mom?"

"She left when my dad brought home his fifth or tenth girlfriend. I lost count. We had to move because of me."

The excitement that I'm dating a bad boy makes me want to take him straight to my room, but I need to learn control. Talk about hormonal teenager. "Come sit. Tell me."

He sits on the loveseat and pulls me onto his lap.

"When I was ten, my dad caught me with the neighbor girl. I made her do some bad things. Well, bad for a ten year old. When I was twelve, I was caught choking this kid because he wouldn't let me see naked pictures of his older sister. I stalked his sister for about four months. She became my obsession. Her family blew her off saying I was a scrawny twelve year old, and what could I do? They eventually moved away.

"At fourteen, my cousin let me secretly watch him and his girlfriend do it. They became my obsession. I was infatuated with the idea of a perfect girl. Then she broke up with him for another guy. I hated her. I broke her leg and two of her ribs. He had another girlfriend who did the same thing. I caused her to accidentally wreck her car. She's still alive and knows it was me, but she's too scared or embarrassed to say anything.

"None of those girls were good enough. Maybe they were for him, but they weren't to me.

"So I started setting standards for myself, and I had to learn control. We moved here to be near my uncle, and that's when he started me in gymnastics. He made me practice hard because of my addictions.

"I couldn't get rid of them, so he helped me by showing me the right way and wrong way to use them. He taught me how to stalk a girl, a skill which my dad employs often."

"How long had you stalked me?" I ask.

"A very long time. I had to go through Mattie first. She's smart, so it was great. I had a good lab partner and then a way to get to you. But that took a while, so Pen and Dickie decided to take me out with them one night.

"I was so good at helping them and keeping control since I was holding out for you. The girls were not even close to my standards, so I waited. I started basing everything on you."

I liked that. I liked the idea that he was so focused on me that he waited.

"I'm sorry," I say.

"Now what for?"

"You waited and held back, and here I am sleeping around. I didn't start off that way. You know you were my first. Do you want me to stay away from the Reds?" I ask.

"No. We'll need them, and that's how you keep control. You keep them under your wing. You use whatever tools you have."

"Well, today I want to use my tools on you, and only you."

"But I can't be controlled by you," he teases as I climb on him.

"Then maybe you should control me."

He grabs my wrists and forces them by my side. "Too easy."

AN HOUR AND several bruises later, we shower.

"WHAT'S THAT LOOK for?" he asks as he digs through my freezer.

I open the freezer door wider and from it, I pull out the ice pack he was looking for, and I hand it to him. He presses it on my back, trying to hide the physical evidence of our adventurous sex life. "I want to be everything for you. I want to be everything you need."

"You can't, Cosette, and I can't be everything you need. We both have problems that we can support each other in, but there is no cure for this."

"I just want to know there is hope."

"Hope for whom? For you? For me? Yes, but it comes with a price that we don't pay. Others pay it. We have to deal with the side effects. It's an addiction where there is no cure."

"We have to be really careful. Jenny says your house is being watched."

"Who is Jenny?"

"Officer Crance. She told me your family was being watched."

His eyebrow raises. "Did she now? Why would she tell you that? Did you give her something?"

"No. Nothing. She just wanted me to feel safe. You killed her sister, well, the Poser did, and she wants to protect me from your family. She's like an older sister. Speaking of sister, let's get Hilda." I get up to get dressed.

"Not tonight. I need help, and you need training."

"Doing what?"

"Stalking. I'm working for my dad, and I figured you could learn a few things."

"What a perfect date," I tell him.

Chapter TWENTY-SEVEN

"WAKE UP, SLEEPYHEAD." I lean in to kiss Hilda. She slept all through Saturday, and here we are, Sunday morning.

"Wakey wakey, eggs and bac-ey." Chris kisses her too.

"Ughh. Let me go brush my teeth." She rolls out of bed and shuffles to the bathroom. "I'm gonna shower. Give me ten minutes. I'll meet you all downstairs."

Chris and I go to the kitchen and sit with John.

"So how are you all doing? You all aren't getting sick like Hilda, are you?" John asks.

"I don't get sick," Chris says.

"No," I say. "Hopefully it's just a 24-hour thing."

"Yeah, if her hangover isn't gone by now, I don't know what I should do." John smiles.

Our eyes open wide. Hilda's caught.

"I know my daughter. Thank you for bringing her home." He sits, noticeably uncomfortable. "She's scared." John opens up. "She'll wake up screaming. Her nights are violent. I think if she hadn't seen you kill him, it would be much worse."

"I didn't want her to see me do that."

"It was closure for her. I know there are a lot of stages she'll go through. I am glad she has you two to be there when she goes through them. She mentioned something about a ski weekend. She can go, just don't leave her alone for one minute. Stay with her all night."

"We won't leave her," I promise.

She comes downstairs bright and happy to see us. "Hi, guys." She kisses both of us, on the lips, in front of John.

He blows it off like it's part of her healing process. Maybe it is. Either way, I'm stunned. "What are we going to do today?"

"I have no idea. It's freezing out," Chris says.

"Let's stay in and watch movies." Hilda bounces.

"Chris, were you going to practice today?" I ask, inviting Hilda and myself to watch.

"I'll go without you two distractions. I'll go while you're out with Mattie."

"Where are you going with Mattie?" Hilda sounds jealous.

"Church, this evening. Her boyfriend's band has a concert. Do you want to go?"

"Not the church going type," she says.

"Fine. It'll be just me without you two sinners then." I laugh at them.

"Well," John stands up, "I have two homes that I need to prep for inspection tomorrow, so I will see you all later. Here's my card if you want to order pizza or something." John drops his debit card in front of Hilda and leaves for work.

The second his truck is off the driveway Hilda turns to us. "So when are you guys going to take me out for my first real one?"

"Never!" Chris answers.

"We're not doing anything unless we're attacked. And even then I don't like the idea." I sit on the couch and pull her next to me. I have to get through to her. "Hilda, you have no idea what you are asking. It's like trying meth. Once you do it, you want more, but it takes more to make you high. Our last kill was only two weeks ago. Don't you still see him in your nightmares?"

"I still see him." She gets closer. "I see me kissing him and looking into his eyes as they grow dim. I see you on top of him slowly slitting his throat." She rubs her hand up my thigh. "I see you getting high on his body shaking beneath you. And I want that."

My body's heating up, and my heart's racing. Bonnie is awake. Hilda continues to describe our last kill together, and it's making my palms sweat. Chris is just sitting back, watching.

She straddles me and starts unbuttoning my shirt. "I want to feel what you feel. There's something deep in you that I can't get to. And I want it. You seem to feel more."

"Hilda, I do it out of self-defense. Yes I enjoy it, but..." I trail off. I want it so bad it's starting to hurt. After the slumber party, the urge grew strong. And after my stalker-training date with Chris last night, I'm craving my next victim. It's growing inside now, and I can't settle it. Bonnie's clawing to get out.

"Your reds are redder. Your blues are bluer. I want to see things like you do." Hilda kisses my neck. "I want the depth that you have."

"And you think this is the way?" I tighten up my fists; my nails break into my skin. I'm trying to fight it, but I'm having a real hard time here.

"I know what I saw. I want that feeling." She takes off her shirt.

"Hilda, stop. You need to back away." I grit my teeth and swallow hard. I put my fists behind me to hide the fact that I drew blood.

She just flits her eyes and keeps pursuing. "Can you give that to me? I want to feel it all. And I want so much more."

"Hilda, I'm not doing well here. Get away," I squeak out to warn her. My throat is choking up. Bonnie is impossible to control.

She reaches in, opening up my shirt, inspecting the new bruises Chris gave me.

"Please, Hilda. You don't want to be like this. You don't want this." I can't hold it in.

Bonnie won't stay in.

Hilda runs her fingers across my bra. "I want everything you have to give me." She leans in, pressing her lips to my breast, when I attack. I throw her off me and jump on her. I grab her wrists as she fights against me. They slip out of my bloodied hands, but I get a good grip and hold them above her head. She's terrified! I'm thrilled — so turned on. It's like my first time with her on my bathroom floor. Wanting every part of her, I quickly take control of her body fighting against me.

Slamming her legs together between mine helps me control her kicking. A forceful kiss stops her screaming. She doesn't kiss back. I love it when they don't kiss back.

I lick her neck and work my way down, but now I'm stuck. My knife is gone, and I can't control her arms. They need to be tied. Looking around for something to tie them, I see him; Chris is smiling, waiting, watching me.

I suck and kiss her smooth, perfect skin. I'm like a snake ready to eat her whole. My body wraps around hers, controlling her every move.

I lick her then bite her.

She screams! The taste of her blood is erotic to me. I breathe in deep before I go in for more.

"Okay, that's enough for now," Chris says.

A sharp pain starts at the back of my head and travels through my body.

I black out.

Chapter TWENTY-EIGHT

MY EYES HAVE a hard time opening. This room is not mine. It's bright. It's pink. Ugh, pink. I squint adjusting my eyes, trying to figure out where I am. There's a white rocking chair in the corner. It's blurry, and someone's on it.

"Hello?" My mouth is dry. My head is cold.

"Shhhh, it's okay," Chris whispers. He's lying behind me, spooning me, and holding an ice pack to the back of my head. It stings.

"Hilda? Oh my god, Hilda, I am so sorry! Hilda, I'm so, so sorry!" I fall off the bed to crawl to her. She's cowering on the rocking chair, holding a fuzzy purple pillow. I reach out to her. Terrified, she pushes herself back deeper into the chair. Chris pulls me away from her.

"Give her some time, Cozy. You scared her quite a bit."

I get back on the bed and cry in his arms. "I don't want to be like this. I hate being like this." I brush the hair out of my face when I notice my hands. They're still bloody from my fingernails digging in.

"I think we know the lengths you go to to control yourself. You might want to cut your nails shorter. Hilda now knows that 'no' means no. Don't you, Hilda?" Chris asks her.

She doesn't answer.

I taste blood. It's Hilda's. My heart's sinking with regret. "Did I hurt her bad?" I whisper to him.

"You got her pretty good. She might scar. At least it can be covered up with just a tank top."

Disgusted with myself, I get up to find the bathroom to scrub my hands and rinse my mouth.

Splashing cold water on my face, I try to wash off Bonnie but she keeps on looking at me in the mirror. "I hate you," I tell her. She doesn't care.

The knot on my head throbs as I walk back to the room. Carefully, I approach her. "Hilda, baby, that's the last thing I wanted to do to you. I am so sorry."

Her bent knees are up to her chest with her arms wrapping them, protecting. She's hiding her face in them. I get on my knees and touch her toes.

"Hilda, I'm so sorry. I don't want to scare you, but this is my reality. Is this what you want to be like?"

"Don't leave me," she whispers.

"What? You should leave *me*."

"I can't. I'm scared to," she cries.

"I won't hurt you if you leave. It would be better for the both of us."

"I'm scared to be alone without you. I will let you bite me ten times if it means you won't leave me." She turns her head and peeks through her hair falling across her face. "Please. Don't push me away."

"This is sick, Hilda. This is an abusive relationship. It's not normal."

"Don't leave me." She drops her legs down and pulls me in to her. I open her robe to see my bite. Anger takes my breath away. I get up and go downstairs.

AN HOUR LATER, Chris and Hilda come to the living room.

I'm too ashamed to look at either of them. Hilda kneels on the floor in front of me. She spreads my legs and presses in to hug me. I softly touch her. My fingers run through her hair. I am so sorry.

"I promise I won't press you again," she says. Her head rests on my lap.

"That's what the victim of domestic abuse always says." I lift her head to look at me. "Don't you see? Can't you see what this does to me? I can't have you be like this too. It's not fair."

"Hilda and I came to an agreement," Chris says, sitting by me. "We won't let her hunt, but if we just so happen to stumble on someone that has become your prey already, then we'll let her have a piece. This way we'll protect her."

"I am so sorry, Hilda. I tried to tell you all at the slumber party, but you all still wanted to watch. It's sick. It's absolutely sickening."

"Just don't let me go." She brushes my hair back.

"Never." I rub my head. "What did you use?" I ask Chris.

"The coaster holder." Chris holds up a wooden holder for ceramic coasters. Only one coaster broke.

"Thank you. You could have stopped me earlier."

"I think you both learned your lesson."

Chapter TWENTY-NINE

NERVES TINGLE IN my fingers as I open the door to Three J's café. I'm meeting Mattie for church tonight. Her boyfriend Telly's band is playing. I walk in, and Mattie's mom, Lucy, gives me a hug. I miss her, and I miss Mattie's dad, Mike. I break down and cry.

She holds me tight. She's like a warm blanket on a cold night. I just cry and cry in her arms. I'm so ashamed to be here with her, but she doesn't care. She just wants to comfort her lost lamb. Mattie comes in and finds us in the back corner of the café since someone else is sitting in my papasan chair by the fireplace.

I feel like I don't belong. I know it's my own doing. But I also feel the love in here pulling me back. My soul wants a release, to give them control so they can straighten me up, but I can't. I can't put them in that position. It wouldn't be fair to do that to Lucy and Mike, or Mattie.

"I got her, Mom. Thanks." Mattie hugs me. "Are you going to be okay? Rough morning?"

"I can't even begin to tell you. Please tell me Telly is here. You need backup around me. I'm not safe, Mattie."

"I have God to protect me. I'll be okay, but if it makes you feel better, Telly is here," Mattie says.

"Thank you. Your insanely mental friend says 'thank you'."

"Just remember where my strength comes from. He is more powerful than the demons running through you."

I hug her tighter. I don't want to let go. Bonnie's not here when Mattie's holding me.

Telly comes up and sits. "Hey, Cosette. Are you okay?"

I wipe my eyes and straighten up. "I'm fine, just a little off."

He looks to Mattie who shakes her head no, to not ask more. He changes the subject, "Are we convoying it up to Paoli Peaks? What time are you all driving up?" Telly asks.

Grateful for the change, I smile. "Chris and Hilda and I will already be up there. Rosy and Decker will drive up in the morning. We should hit the slopes around 9:30 or 10:00."

Telly gives Mattie a crooked glance. Apparently he doesn't approve of us staying the night.

"Cosette is learning how to be a good girl. It's taking her a bit longer than I expected," Mattie explains.

"Patience is a virtue," I say.

"How many are coming to this ski party?" Telly asks.

"Chris and I, Deck and Rose and Hilda. I think that's it. I'm not sure about Shelby and Sierra. I'm thinking Paige is out. I don't think I'll even ask her."

"No, you should not." Mattie is clear.

"I know. I'm sorry. I am glad you guys will be there," I say.

"Should you be skiing this soon after getting shot and all?"

"Telly, you're cute. I'll be fine." I turn to Mattie. "My mom is taking John to Barry Manilow."

"So that's why we're going! You're using your birthday as an excuse to skip on Manilow." Telly laughs.

"Smart man." I nod. "I think it will be good for John to get back to normal."

"Okay, who's John?" Telly is still learning all of our names, and we're flooding him with more.

"John is Hilda's dad. He's dating my mom," I say.

"And Hilda's the only one on this trip without a date, right? Should I ask one of my friends to go?"

"No!" I shout.

"Something wrong with my friends?" Telly asks, insulted.

"No, I'm sorry. I didn't mean that at all. No, there's something wrong with mine, except for Matilda of course. Mattie is my most perfect of all friends. I don't have any more like her, so your friends'll have to be on their own. Mattie is not a reflection of us. She..."

"Cosette, I like Mattie." Telly stops me. "I like her a lot. She not only wants to make a difference in the world, but she's working on a plan to do just that. She's gonna be somebody. She's a great Christian, and I know how hard it is for her to live like she does when everyone else around her isn't. So you don't need to keep selling her to me. I like her. I like her a lot." His eyes twinkle. My heart melts for her.

"What a great guy you have, Mattie. He described you to a T," I say.

Mattie kisses him.

"Okay, so no date for Hilda. I do have other friends."

"Telly, let's go get a drink." Mattie takes his hand and leads him to the counter. She must have explained Hilda's relationship with us to Telly because he swiftly turns and looks at me.

They come back with drinks.

"Okay." Telly takes a deep breath. "So now that I know what I'll be dealing with, I can handle this. Okay."

It sounds like he's trying to convince himself. Poor guy got hooked on Mattie and is stuck with her friends.

"Well, I need to be there for a soundcheck, so let's get going." Telly holds out his hand to me to help me up. It's chivalrous. He holds out his other for my perfect Mattie. It makes me smile.

TELLY'S CHURCH IS significantly larger than Mattie's. I don't feel as warm and happy here. Maybe it's just my guilt putting me in a protective bubble.

Mattie whispers, "Don't judge God by those who are only here for the T-Shirts."

"I know. You're a rare breed. Don't you feel it? The stares they're giving you because you're next to me?" By the looks I'm getting, some of these people have no problem letting Mattie or me know they don't approve of my killing in self-defense. Even though the news portrayed me as a hero for saving Hilda's life, I still feel more judged here than in Principal Peeler's office. I hate Sarah for letting my name out.

"Love doesn't know when it's being done wrong," Mattie says. She loves people so much that nothing they do affects her.

"Mattie, I love the way you always quote the Bible to me to make me feel better and not to hurt me. You have no idea what that means to me."

"Yes, I do. God stuck you with me. He gave you a second chance, so I have to teach you as much as I can while I still can."

"What do you mean by that?" I ask.

"You don't see it, but I do. I'll be shut out soon. Not only that, but I'll have to leave for the Academy in the fall." Mattie gives me her best Yoda impression: "Much to learn you have."

"I will, master." I bow to her.

"It's gonna start soon. Let's go." She bounces with me up to the front.

Telly's band is excellent! Telly is excellent! I'm so impressed. I also know almost all of the songs they're playing, though I haven't heard them in a while. I guess I stopped listening to the Christian station when I stopped hanging around Mattie. But it's good to hear them again. They flood me with happy memories.

Telly steps up to the mic. "This song is dedicated to a special guest out there. You'll know who you are when you hear it. I don't know why God chose this song for you, but He did, so listen up." Telly steps back and starts in on one of my favorite Switchfoot songs.

"Mess of Me" hits me like a ton of bricks.

THE LEAD SINGER starts. "I am my own affliction.
I am my own disease.
There ain't no drug that they can sell.
There ain't no drug to make me well."

The dedication is for me. I did make a mess of me.

I stand there, unable to move. Everyone around me is jumping and dancing, but I can't breathe. My whole world seems to move in slow motion. The feeling of weightlessness engulfs me. Each word was written for me.

I'm tired. I'm worn out. I'm so sick of my feelings going back and forth.

The song is over, and everyone cheers.

I DON'T KNOW what they played next. I don't know the last ten songs they played before we left. I wasn't aware of the drive home or the conversation we had. I remember Mattie asking if I needed her to spend the night. I said no. I remember her asking if I wanted Hilda or Chris to stay the night. I emphatically said no.

"I need to be alone, Mattie. I am not suicidal. I just want to be alone."

Chapter THIRTY

"HAPPY VALENTINE'S DAY!" Chris hands me a small bouquet of daisies when I climb in his truck.

He's a sight for sore eyes. My night was horrible. After Mattie left, I laid in my bed just staring at the Switchfoot posters on my ceiling listening to "Thrive", "Vice Verses", and "Mess of Me" over and over. I'm so tired of going back and forth between wanting to be good for Mattie or accepting my new life.

Why would God make me like this if He doesn't want me to act on it? Is this even God's doing? Me being in the right place at the right time, isn't that God? If God made me this way, then can't I be both? Or is my dark host the one pulling all the strings? Whose puppet am I?

All I know is I was at the right place. I saved some people, and I'm a hero. Besides, doesn't God put people in our lives to help us, guide us? I have Mattie who doesn't understand because God didn't make her this way. He made me this way.

But He did give me Chris. Chris understands. Chris would never force me one way or another. Chris lets me be myself, and even though I didn't want to kill Hilda with him, he didn't condemn me for that. He let me keep her. And when I killed Tear Tattoo and the trucker, he was okay with that. Chris is okay with me either way. He makes me feel like me. The second I see him, smell him, touch him, I'm home. Mattie makes me feel good. Her family makes me feel love, but Chris makes me feel alive.

"Awww, flowers. I love them." I give him a kiss.

"Now that the real you is back, your real gift is coming this weekend along with your birthday gift. They go together." He starts driving to pick up Hilda.

"Can I guess what it is?" I snuggle up to him and bat my eyes.

"If you do, then you don't get them." He rejects my bribe.

"Okay, well, happy Valentine's Day to you too." I hand him a gift bag. He waits until we pull into Hilda's driveway then opens it.

"Sexy, but I don't think it will fit me." He holds up the purple and black lace teddy.

"I hope it won't fit you. It's not for you to wear. It's like art."

"Look but don't touch?" he asks.

"You can touch, just not now. Hilda's coming."

"Happy Valentine's Day!" She climbs into the truck, kisses both of us, and hands us matching candy boxes.

"I went traditional this year," she says.

"So did I." Chris hands her a small bouquet of flowers.

"Two for one sale?" I ask holding my flowers next to hers.

"Yup," Chris says. He turns the truck towards school.

"Well, me too." I hand Hilda her gift, which is the same lacy outfit as mine, just in pink.

"I love it. We're gonna have to try these on tonight." She wiggles.

"Sounds good to me," he says as we pull into the school parking lot.

THE BELL RINGS just as I walk into art. My brave nerd and his friends are sitting near my table. Their eyes light up as I enter the room. That makes me feel good.

I guess I should learn this guy's name if he's going to be hanging around. But I don't want to be rude and ask. It's good to know someone's name before you kiss them. In this case, it's too late for that.

"Hi." I sit down.

"Ask her, Dave." One of his friends nudges him.

Dave, good, I can remember that.

"Ask me what?"

"We heard that...holy crap! What happened to your hands?" He grabs my hands.

I forgot about them. I guess I could have wrapped them up. My fingernails cut my palms deep.

"I don't ask you about your weekend adventures. Don't ask me about mine," I tell him. I pick up my sketchpad and continue where I left off last week.

He leans in away from his friends' hearing. He lets his hair shield his whisper. "And what happened to your collarbone and neck? Did someone try to choke you?"

I should have worn a different shirt. How stupid of me. I fan my hair out to cover Chris's bruises. "Did you want something, Dave?"

"Are you okay? Is someone trying to hurt you?"

He actually has concern in his voice. It's sweet.

"You're cute. No, no one is trying to hurt me."

"Because if they are, we can tell someone."

"If I tell you a secret, are you going to run to your friends with it?" I ask very softly.

"I wouldn't do that. Besides, wouldn't you kill me if I did?"

"Funny, no. Will you not tell them because it's the right thing to do and not because you fear me?"

He understands and nods. "We all have secrets," he assures me. "I won't say anything. Of course, mine aren't as interesting as yours, but I won't tell them. Is someone trying to hurt you?"

"Pain doesn't bother me. Most of it I enjoy. These mean I had a good weekend. So no, no one is trying to hurt me."

"Okay, I think I understand. Boy, you are hot."

I glare at him.

"I won't say anything."

"How was your weekend?" I ask.

"You're asking me how my weekend was?" He's happy.

"You're obviously not afraid to talk to me, so talk," I say.

"It was good. I went to a concert at church last night. And on

Saturday I was at my grandma's all day."

"I went to a concert too. Who was it?"

"It was a Christian band. They did all cover songs."

"Did they play Switchfoot's "Mess of Me"?" I ask.

"You were there?" He sits back, surprised.

"Shocking, I know. Switchfoot is my favorite."

"I can understand that. A lot of their songs seem appropriate for you."

I grip my pencil out of anxiety.

"In a good way! In a good way!" he backtracks. His dark brown eyes blink. He's scared.

"Relax, I'm not going to hurt you. I'm not insulted. I think you're right." Of course he's right. Me playing "Thrive" twenty times last night tells me he's right.

"Before all of this happened to you, would you have ever considered going out with a nerd like me?"

"I hadn't considered you a true nerd. I think we're in the same league."

Dave laughs. "Not hardly. You're beautiful."

"Not anymore," I say flatly.

"It would have been nice if I had met you earlier. Maybe if you were in different place, say at the movies with some nerd, none of this wouldn't've happened to you."

"That would've been nice. I'd love to be normal now. But I can't. It's too late. So many mistakes. So many regrets. Be careful with yourself. Think twice about everything. Please."

"Thanks, Cosette."

"Cozy, you can call me Cozy."

This makes him happy. In silence, he sits next to me for the rest of the period. It makes me happy.

SHELBY AND SIERRA are already at the lunch table laughing with

Mattie. Chris and Hilda are sitting close, and Rose is pressing up next to Decker.

I come to sit and Hilda scoots away from Chris to fit me in. It's nice she knows her place.

They're talking about the slumber party. Rose and the sisters are nervous because I'm not saying a word. They think they confessed something horrible while drunk. When they mention anything about that night, they look at me for a reaction. I purse my lips.

One, it shows them I can keep a secret. And two, it shows I have something over them I can use at any time. I would never do that, but it's nice to have control.

"Cosette, you aren't talking much," Decker says.

"What happens at Rose's stays at Rose's." I smirk.

She mouths 'thank you'.

"So not this Saturday, but next Saturday is skiing for my baby's birthday. I already booked a cabin online," Chris says.

"We need to pitch in. It's not fair for you to pay for everything," Hilda says.

"How about you all pay for her lift ticket and food, and we'll call it even," Chris says.

He's letting us off easy. He has his uncle's inheritance to foot the bill for almost everything.

"Telly and I will buy you lunch. I don't know that we want to be around you all for your party." Mattie points a fry at us.

"We'll be good. We know how to control ourselves," Rose says.

"Some of us do." Chris looks at me, then whispers under his breath, "But I didn't bring Bonnie back to have her controlled."

I'm not sure how to read this. I don't think he meant for me to hear the latter. Hilda leans in to hug me, reminding me she forgives me for biting her. It's upsetting.

Chris steals one of Mattie's fries. "Don't worry, Mattie, we'll be good. Maybe if we relieve some pressure before we come, say Wednesday at my house, you all?" Chris asks raising his eyebrow.

I choke on my drink. Why would he say that in front of the sisters, or Mattie especially? 'You all'? Did he just invite everyone to his house for a sex party?

"And on that note I lost my appetite. I'll see you guys tomorrow." Mattie gets up and leaves.

"Why is she leaving?" Sierra asks Shelby.

"Never mind," Shelby responds.

"What's going on at Chris's house?" Sierra asks. "I wanna go."

"You don't want to go." Shelby's protective.

It angers me Chris says things like that in mixed company. That will be changing.

"Are you two able to go skiing?" I ask the sisters, changing the subject.

"Are we invited?" Shelby sarcastically, cautiously asks.

I reach across the table to Shelby. "I'm sorry about that. Sometimes my boyfriend should show a bit of *decorum!*" I speak up. "To quote from Mattie's Bible, 'everything is permissible, but not everything is beneficial'. You two are invited, but you definitely should NOT come to everything. Do you understand? Please don't be upset. I'm not shutting you out; I'm protecting you."

"Don't worry, we know our limits. Don't we, Sierra?" It's odd how Shelby phrases the question. Almost as if she's asking Sierra for permission.

Sierra shakes her head yes, but I can tell she doesn't agree. I'm kind of worried about her.

The bell rings, and we all head off to class.

AFTER SCHOOL, I find Chris and Hilda are already in the truck waiting for me. I don't feel like riding home with them. I have to think. "I need to walk. I'll call you guys later." I wave and smile as the policeman who directs school traffic signals them out.

I'm confused about what he said. "I didn't bring Bonnie back to have her controlled? What the hell does that mean?" I say out loud, hoping to stir up some answers. And what happened to him wanting to keep a low profile? Inviting everyone to a sex party? It's like once I was out in the open, then everything was out in the open. I don't like it.

My pace picks up. I haven't been running since I was shot, and I know I shouldn't now, but I need a release. I'm almost up to a jog, but since I still have my backpack on, I keep a slower pace.

Chris and I need to reset some boundaries. I will not put up with this. Taking a right at Ice Cream Willies sends me the long way home. The air is bitter cold. Out here, I feel free.

THE FREEZING WIND whips loose strands of hair into my face. That doesn't bother me, but I am growing more and more angry at my whole life. At the fact that Bonnie is craving after the slumber party and not being fully satisfied with our get-togethers. And, it's been two weeks since Tear Tattoo and the truck driv.... Holy shit!

My knees buckle as I stumble to a dead tree off the side of the road. Thoughts race through my mind, and I have to calm down. Clarify. Think, Cosette. Think.

Everything comes into focus now and I'm pissed! Holy shit! Chris did bring Bonnie back! "That fucking asshole!" I grab a fallen branch and start hitting the tree, venting my anger. "You fucking asshole! Shit!"

Chris forced me to kill! He set it up, making my killing Tear Tattoo the only way to free Hilda. 'I brought you back' he said. He knew killing Ben would wake up Bonnie! Killing the trucker just deepened her need. I scream and hit the tree again. The branch shatters, sending a shard up to slice my chin.

Calm down, Cosette, calm down. I have to arrange my thoughts. My head is spinning.

The cars zooming by slow down to stare, so I start walking again. I'm considerably far from home. A truck pulls up behind me. I know exactly who it is.

"Cozy, please! I'm sorry! Please come in, it's freezing! It's not healthy for you!"

"You're not healthy for me!" I keep walking.

The truck speeds up then parks in front of me. Chris jumps out.

"You need to back off," I warn him.

"I'm sorry," Chris says. "Cosette, you're bleeding." He steps to me. I hold my hand out, blocking him. "I'm sorry."

"What are you sorry for? Do you even know why I'm mad?"

"Please get in the truck. I'm freezing."

"Deal with it! Why am I mad?" I press my chin, hoping the blood will clot.

He relents. "You're mad because I invited everyone to an orgy at my house. I'm sorry. Now that you're out, I just felt more free. I'm sorry."

"In case you don't remember, we still have secrets to keep. And in case you don't remember, we promised to protect our friends. Unlike you protecting me."

"What does that mean?"

I charge at him. "You brought her back, Chris! You betrayed me, brought Bonnie back, and now I'm fucked! You son of a bitch! You betrayed me! What the hell are you trying to do to me?"

He deflects my blows and tries to hug me to quiet me down. "Cosette, you need Bonnie. You are Bonnie!"

I push him away and start walking. "I told you before the kidnapping that I didn't want to do that again!"

"You need it! There is no going back. There never was. You proved that in my uncle's barn." He chases after me, grabs my arm, and whips me around. "When I brought you bags for your fifteen pieces... Cosette, there is no going back from something like that."

"So you decide to make it worse? I was doing better. I didn't have to kill Ben!"

"The kidnapping had to be realistic. You know that! And you trying to get out of it is you denying yourself! You need Bonnie, and you need me." He tries to pull me close, but I push me again.

"But I don't want Bonnie. That's what I have my friends for."

"They will never work! You can't separate it."

"How did you keep your secret for all those months? How did you keep that 'All American Boy' image after you killed all those women? You separated it, and you kept your mouth shut."

"You can't quit cold turkey, Cosette. And you using your friends is only going to make you crave more. Hilda is well on her way to being Bonnie Junior."

"Not by choice!" I step closer. "I didn't know she was going to watch me! Both times I shoved her away. And by the way, I'm not the one who put her in that position either! How was I supposed to know she would like it? Have I not warned her? Have I not done everything to show her what it's like to go through this? The only way she'll really know is by doing it. And if that happens, then it's too late; she's already a monster!" I start to walk around him.

He grabs my arm. I pull away.

"I'm trying to protect my friends, Chris. Bonnie cannot be around them."

He yanks me into him. "If you wanted to protect them, maybe you should have thought about that before you fucked Rosy and Decker!"

Rage burns. I shove him. "Fine then, I'm out! I'm done with them, and I'm done with you!"

"Fine! Thanks to you, I have backup. I bet Hilda's free tonight."

"Fuck you!"

"No, fuck you, Cosette! You need to get over yourself and see that I did it for your own good!" He gets back in his truck.

"Go then! Go have your fun! Might as well call the Reds in too!" I yell as he drives away.

I wait until he's out of view then cut across a golf course, walking further away from my house. There's no noise. No trucks. No cars. Nothing. I sit on the edge of a sand trap and cry.

MY TEARS HAVE all dried up, and it's getting dark. My phone's been buzzing, but it's not my mom, so I've ignored it.

I am a soulless creature.

I thought about my dark host visiting me in the hospital room. I thought about how he told me to do what I wanted up here because my work wasn't done.

Is this what he meant? For me to slowly control my friends? For me to lead Hilda into killing because regular teenage highs aren't good enough? Is this God putting people in my life to mold me? Or is the dark host the one controlling Cosette?

"Victor?" I call to the sky. "He's right, isn't he? Chris is right? There is no going back." I stand up and dust myself off.

"Shit. This is it, isn't it? I no longer have to ask 'what have I become'. I know what I am. I am Bonnie. She's staying, Victor. I've made a mess of me, and there is no going back. I'm accepting her, embracing her. I am Bonnie."

The wind dies down as the darkness falls. I'm a long way from home. Two point four miles according to my phone map. With a deep breath and a stretch, I start moving.

"Y'KNOW, VICTOR, I know I'm Bonnie, but I also know who my friends are. And this isn't it. Rose and Decker should be fine. If I stop with them, then they can have a normal relationship and get back on track.

"But I'm concerned for Hilda. I think I lit a spark in her that will not go away. Maybe I can burn it out fast before she feels the full high.

"Maybe I'll help her kill, but I'll let her deal with all of the consequences. The fear of hiding it, the guilt that someone has lost a loved one and it's your fault. The shame that everyone is looking at you, and you think they know what you did, but they don't.

"If the opportunity arises, and she insists, then I'll let her go there. I've warned her enough. The lows cannot be described. If she's willing to take that chance, I'll let her. I'll go behind and help her not to get caught, but I won't let her know. Then we'll see how fast she crashes. Then I'll have my Hilda back."

Victor doesn't answer me from Heaven. But I do get a text from Hell.

Just got done with Rosy, Deck, and Hilda
Good idea, thanks, BTW Happy Valentine's day
TTYL
Chris

"Fucking asshole! I need a victim. Now!"

Chapter THIRTY-ONE

"HELLO?" THE MIDDLE-AGED woman answers her door. Cat odor floats out to me.

"Hi, I'm Cindy's daughter. She just called asking to borrow some sugar," I say, hoping my crying eyes have stopped swelling.

"I didn't get no call, sweetheart, and I don't know any Cindy." She has a raspy voice, and her temper is short with me.

"I'm sorry. Now I feel stupid. Do you know where Mrs. Mason lives?" I slick my hair back into a ponytail.

"No, you definitely have the wrong house." She looks me up and down then huffs at me. "Y'know, I do have some sugar. Come on in. It's better than you knocking on every damn house on the block." She steps back and lets me in.

"Thank you so much." I put my gloves on. As I cross the threshold, five cats scatter. Three lurk about, watching me.

"Come on in; just kick them out of your way." She walks to her cluttered kitchen.

It's oddly quiet in here. The TV is off, but her laptop is open. The screen is black. I touch the mousepad, waking it up.

What is displayed both disgusts me and pleases me. Two prepubescent girls are blindfolded and tied together side by side. There are several men's hands fondling them.

It means I'm in the right house.

"You can come in here, sweetheart. How much sugar do you need?" she asks.

"My mom's making cookies for my little sister's class tomorrow, so I don't know." Studying my surroundings, I get excited. So many ways to play.

"I'll give you a cup. That should be enough."

"Thank you. I'm sorry to bother you." I approach her.

"I'm not busy," she says. "Just doing some editing."

"Any famous authors?" I ask.

"No, video editing. Here's your sugar." She hands me the baggie. I put it on the counter. Taking an iron skillet off the stovetop, I hit her across the face.

"Thank you for the sugar. That's very nice of you." I put the skillet back. "You're a nice lady."

After dragging her to the bedroom, I tie her to her bed, which strange enough, is a mattress resting on wooden crates and cat towers. Clearly this woman is single. I sit on a chest at the foot of the bed, waiting for her to come to.

"YOUR LAPTOP IS filled with disgusting images. You should be ashamed," I tell her as she moans herself awake. "How much money could you possibly make editing that crap? You have sold your soul, for what? A smelly house and cats that couldn't care less if you live or die?"

"What did you do to me?" she mumbles and tries to touch her head, but she's strapped in well. "Who are you?"

"My name is Bonnie, and I am pleased to meet you. Is there anything you want to say before I kill you?" I crawl on top of her carrying her laptop. "Actually, I don't care what you have to say. Everything that is hidden will be laid bare before the eyes of the Lord," I quote. The Bible verse seems very appropriate for how I'm going to leave her.

"Why are you doing this?" she cries.

I start up the slideshow she was working on. Images of child porn plague the screen. "This is why I'm doing this." I lay the laptop between her outstretched, tied-up legs. "You can enjoy your last moments alive watching the horror you created."

I prop her head up so she can see the screen. She starts yelling for help. Her cats meow with her. It's eerie. I go to her dresser and pull out a sock then shove it in her mouth.

"Did those kids scream like that? Do you even know?"

She shakes her head no as if she has no responsibility.

"Oh, sure, you're innocent, right?" The ringing of a grandfather clock tells me it's ten. I better get moving.

"I would love to sit and chat with you, but I can't stand to be near you. You make me sick." I get off her and go to the kitchen. Shopping around for the perfect knife, it hits me. I won't use my usual killing method of slitting her throat, but how I kill her will give the police a place to start.

Chapter
THIRTY-TWO

TUESDAY MORNING COMES fast. By the time I clean up, it's time for school. I have to take two showers: one with my clothes on to wash off my victim's blood, and one with them off to scrub the rest of me.

I hate cats; they make my eyes itch. They're horrible protectors too, sitting around, watching me as I shoved a knife up into her. At first I didn't mind them watching, but I did mind them seeing me get off on the experience, kissing her, stealing her last breath. It was a little invasive. I would assume it's how porn actresses feel the first time they're filmed. It was debasing and exhilarating at the same time. Either way, I got what I wanted. So sorry those who paid for child porn pictures won't get what they wanted. Happy Valentine's Day to me.

I roll my clothes into the washing machine and turn on the hot water. I know it'll shrink them, but I don't want to burn them on the grill. Maybe they'll fit me better. I haven't been eating well.

IT'S BEEN A while since I've rode the bus, but I don't want anyone to pick me up. All I want to do is sit back and enjoy the high from last night.

My mom buzzes me. "Hey, Mom."

"Cosette, what are you doing? We have your orthodontist appointment today. I came home, and you were gone."

"I can't believe I forgot! I'm at the bus stop. I'll head home."

Mom drives up behind me and beeps.

I get in her car. "Mom, I'm so excited. I totally forgot! How could I forget?" I forgot because I'm still high.

"Well, I have another surprise for you when we're done. Today is going to be a mother-daughter day. Just you and me."

"I love you, Mom. Even without the surprises, I love you."

"COSETTE, YOU'RE BEAUTIFUL." Mom smiles at me smiling at myself in the mirror.

"You're just saying that because you're my mom and you have to. My teeth are smooth and slippery. I look like a new person without the braces."

She parks in front of my eye doctor. "I think with your new smile, you need new eyes. I'm buying you contacts today."

I squeal. I'm so excited!

SHE GIVES ME a full makeover, including my hair. They cut over a foot off and I donate it, but with my length, you can't tell too much.

"It'll be easier for me to curl," I say.

"Which will look great with your new outfits." She turns the car into the mall parking lot.

"Mom, this is too much. You don't have this kind of money."

"I have some. You want to hear a secret?"

"Always," I say.

"Your father didn't change one of his insurance policies. The check came in, and I decided his daughter needed a makeover."

"Nothing for Eponine, Tawny's daughter?" I don't hide my distain for my stepmother, Tawny, despite the fact that she's dead. Despite the fact that Chris, acting as the Poser, killed her.

"Eponine has money from your dad and Tawny's other

insurance policies. Besides, Kevin and Wendy have ignored all my phone calls. I guess they're scared I'll tell them off after they were so rude to you at your father's funeral."

"They were horrible to me. Telling me 'you have no sister'. I only wanted to help take care of Eponine. She is my half-sister after all. They deserve a good telling off."

"And you deserve this!" Mom says.

"Damn straight!"

"Damn straight!" Mom agrees with me and opens my car door "Now, Cozy..."

"I know, we're ladies and we don't talk that way."

She hugs me.

We start walking through the mall, and there are a few stares. I wonder if Mom notices. If she does, she's not saying a word.

She takes me into all the stores, trying to figure out my style. I never really had style before because we couldn't afford one. I bought a few form-fitting jeans, but nothing too tight. I want to be able to breathe. I also found a few skirts, long ones down to my ankles and short flippy ones just above my knees.

I have the body to wear sexy, but I'm not out to prove anything. Just because I slept with all my friends doesn't mean I need to dress like a whore.

"You hungry?" Mom asks.

"Always."

We make our way towards the food court. The subtle glances and sly finger pointing continues. Mom says nothing. There's an elephant in the room, until...

"Are you the one?" An elderly, tearful lady comes up to us. "Did you kill him?"

I don't know what to say. I freeze. So does my mom. Not wanting to make a scene, I nod my head.

The woman whimpers then hugs me. Out of sympathy, I hug her back. We embrace for a long time. Seems like she hasn't been hugged in a long time.

"She was my granddaughter." She sniffles as she pulls away from me. "Her car broke down, and he picked her up. After he raped her, she was never the same. She killed herself. Her funeral was the day you killed him. If she could've held out for a few more days, she would've felt safe. She could've met a hero. Knowing he's not here to hurt anyone else makes her death bittersweet. I'm praying for you, my hero. Thank you. Thank you." She hugs me again and walks away.

WE JUST STAND there, stunned. I don't think my mom's dealt with reality yet.

"Mom, I'm sorry about that," I say.

"Do you get that a lot?"

"Usually I just get stares, both good and bad."

She sits down. "I am having a hard time picturing my little girl going through that."

"Then don't. I'm still your little girl." My heart is breaking for her.

"You will always be. I'm just... it's just that... you grew up so fast. In one day, you were forced to grow up. I wish I could get that innocence back for you, but..."

"Enough. I love you, Mom. Let's get moving. I don't want you to start crying. We look awful when we cry, and then you'll have to get a makeover too." I have to cheer her up. She's not fully ready to deal with this.

"Shoes. I think you need shoes." She stands up, wipes her tears, and marches on.

After an hour, and three pairs of shoes later, we leave the mall.

"I'm proud of you, Cosette. I'm sorry you get dirty looks. If they walked a mile in your shoes, if your roles were reversed..."

"If the roles were reversed, they wouldn't have survived." I regretted that as soon as it left my mouth. I don't want to explain it.

"I am proud of you, honey."

"Thanks, Mom."

THE REST OF the afternoon is filled with texts from Mattie, Chris,

Rose, Hilda, and even the sisters, wondering where I am. I only respond to Mattie, asking her to come by after school.

She knocks on the door. "Hold on, Mattie, I have to pose."

"Please tell me you're dressed. I don't need any more surprises today."

"Okay, come on in!" I open the door then spin around. My black flippy skirt waves at her. My white peasant top stays weighted down with long beaded necklaces.

"Holy cow, Cozy! You are absolutely beautiful!" She starts crying.

"Why are you crying? You said I was beautiful."

"This outside is how I always pictured you on the inside. This is the Cozy I know. And I miss her." She hugs me.

"Stop it. I put on fresh makeup just for you." I dot my eyes.

"Are you going anywhere tonight?" she asks.

"No. I don't want to see anyone. Except you of course."

"Are you gonna tell me what happened?"

"Chris and I broke up..." I shrugged my shoulders.

"I figured that. He looked like he was up all night crying. He was in bad shape at lunch. What else?"

I'm sad because I miss him but glad he's suffering about what he did. "What do you mean what else? Breaking up with Chris ain't enough?"

"Today at lunch, the four of them came in with the same look. The look that says, 'I just betrayed my friend'. Hilda looked like she was ready to go back to Sarah's table. It was so depressing."

"I told Chris he could have his little Wednesday party because I was out. So they did. Did they not say anything?"

"It was a horrible lunch, especially since you never showed up. Is this what you did all day?"

"Yes! And come here." I grab her hand and drag her to my room where all of my new outfits are laid out on my bed. "Aren't they cute?"

"You look good in these long gypsy skirts. I like them. I'm happy for you. You are absolutely beautiful."

"On the outside, thanks. Now if I can straighten up the inside,

I'll be good to go." I press my new leather knee-hi boots up to my nose to smell.

Mattie pulls them away from my face. "God will clean you up, just let Him."

I don't respond to that.

"Telly's band was excellent. You should be proud," I say.

"Yeah, he's cute too. I really like him."

"Tell me more." We sit on my bed and I lay back, enjoying her talk about her cute, normal, non-sadistic love life. We talk and talk. Then she drives me to Three J's, and we talk some more.

I get my papasan chair back, along with a plate of rice croquettes and a bowl of mac-n-cheese. I'm happy. I'm happy on the inside and happy on the outside.

I'm finding myself living in the past here in the café. This is what it was like in the spring and summer of last year. I sit in my chair. Mattie works. Lucy whistles as she makes cappuccinos, and Mike makes fun of her whistling.

Here I don't have a Bonnie problem. I don't have a boyfriend problem. Hell's not lingering around me. I like living in this past. Maybe, just for tonight, I'll stay here.

Chapter
THIRTY-THREE

IT'S WEDNESDAY MORNING, and I'm excited to go back to school. I wake an hour early so I can take my time curling my hair and putting on makeup, which is hard to do with new contacts. I also brush my teeth five minutes longer than I normally do. Now that they are brace free, I want them to be polished and perfect.

Mattie pulls up as I'm walking out. I'm surprised to see her. "With that adorable skirt, you don't need to walk, nor do you need to ride that dirty bus."

"Thanks. I think you just want to see Chris's face when I walk in." I get into Little P.

"Has he called you?" she asks.

"And texted at least a hundred times. I've ignored every one. Not to be a witch or anything. I just want him to apologize face to face."

"I guess you weren't home for him to come visit last night."

"Yeah, I'm glad I was with you. Can never get enough croquettes."

WE WALK INTO school. "Aren't you glad everyone is staring at how pretty you look?"

I laugh. "It's a nice change, huh? I better get to art. I don't want to see anyone else until lunch."

DAVE SITS UP the second I walk into the art room.

"Hi, Dave." I sit in my chair. He scoots his right next to me.

"Uh...hi?" he fumbles.

"Don't get shy on me now. Please, I need you to be normal. Please be normal?"

"I am. This is how a normal guy would act when hotness walks in."

"Thanks." I'm embarrassed.

"Wow. I mean, wow!"

"Alright, that's enough. Did I miss anything yesterday?"

"In art or with your friends?"

"I actually meant art, but if you have anything to say..."

"No, I got nothing." He diverts his eyes.

"Truth."

"Fine. Your table at lunch was like a ghost town. Everyone could tell you were gone. They all kinda looked at each other, afraid to talk. Chris looked tired."

"That's funny. I was busy."

"I can tell." He sighs. "I wish I had had the balls to ask you out before he did."

"You don't want to go out with me. It's good I have Chris. He helps control me. You don't want any part of this."

"Are you sure you're not the one controlling him? From what I saw at lunch yesterday, none of them could function without you, except for Matilda, of course."

"She's strong. I'm glad I have her."

"What about Hilda?" Dave asks.

"I'm glad I have her too."

"You're glad you control her."

'I glare at him.

"Just saying. They can't function without you. You control them whether you like it or not."

"I wish I could go back to when no one noticed me."

"I don't recall that time," he said. He pulls his hair behind his ear. "I always noticed you."

"Thanks."

"I'm sorry," he apologized.

"For what?"

"I'm sorry this happened to you."

"I made it worse, believe me. I'm still making it worse."

"You are your own affliction? You are your own disease?"

"Yes, I made a "Mess of Me." I hug him for quoting my new theme song.

THE BELL RINGS and I sneak away to my next few classes.

Before lunch, I stop in the bathroom to freshen up. I want to look good walking to my table.

Taking a deep breath, I walk to the cafeteria and wait in line for my food.

Everyone at my table stops talking and stares at me.

"Yes!" I yell in my head. I grab my nuggets tray and order extra fries. They'll be my peace offering to Chris for ignoring his calls all day. Just as I place my tray down, a manila envelope is slammed on my food.

It's Officer Crance. I close my eyes as my heart drops.

I pick up the envelope and open it. It's filled with beautiful pictures, souvenirs of my Valentine's Day victim. I bite my lip to hide my smile, and close the envelope.

"Do I need to arrest you here?" she whispers to me. "Come with me." She grabs my arm and the envelope and leads me to a private corner in the lunchroom. My table stares. The whole room stares. So much for making a good impression.

I flip my petticoat skirt back and sit down on the cold stool. Since my body temperature has risen fifty degrees, the seat feels nice.

Officer Crance spreads the pictures out in front of me. I'm not sure how a normal person would act seeing these bloody scenes. All I know is how excited I am, admiring my work.

"I wasn't there," I defend.

She pulls out a clear baggie with a very long strand of hair in it. Shit! Shit! Shit!

Now they really have me. I was sloppy. Chris and his damn text.

I just needed a release!

"Cosette, I thought I would be able to match this hair, but it seems like yours is a bit shorter. I'm glad. Whoever did this," she taps my photos, "did pretty well but still missed a few things. This woman's attacker should have cleaned up better. At least whoever it was wore gloves. Very creative though.

"Police are searching for one of her victims or the parent of a victim. The way she was displayed with the laptop going through a child porn slideshow, and a knife shoved up into her... definitely one of her victims. It's a shame though; I doubt we'll be able to get enough evidence for a good lead in the case. At least the killer gave her what she deserved."

Why is she telling me this?

She pulls out a sheet of paper with a familiar map on it. "Do you recognize this?" She looks directly into my eyes.

"This is the map from the sex offender's website."

She smiles and pulls out a pen. "Yes, that's right. But this one also has drug dealers, thieves, and murderers on it." She circles a few of the red dots and crosses out my victim's dot. "This one has been taken care of as of Valentine's Day. I'm glad I was one of the first ones on the scene." She pushes the baggie with my hair in it over to me. "I came for your help. If you know anything, I would appreciate any insight."

"I know nothing."

"Good. Glad to hear it. That's all I have. By the way, your makeover looks great, but there's a cut on your chin. Will forensics find any DNA?"

"No. I cut myself with a tree branch." This whole conversation confuses me.

She stands up, gathers the pictures, and puts them back in the envelope. "Good. Did you need these? Maybe to help you remember any details?"

"I don't need help remembering. I know nothing," I say.

She smiles, confirming. "Here's the map. Just in case you take a long walk, you'll know where to go," she taps a specific circled red dot, "and you'll know what to avoid." She taps a different dot. "You have a great day, Cosette. I'll see you around. Hopefully not for a few weeks. People will start to talk." She winks at me.

She leaves, and I sit there a bit stunned. I look at the map and the baggie with my hair in it. This I'll have to figure out later. Standing up, I fold the paper and baggie and tuck them in my boot. I let out a sigh, and then walk back to the table.

NO ONE SAYS a word as I sit down.

No one smiles at me either.

"Am I sitting at the right table, or should I leave?" I ask. No one responds. "Fine then, I'll leave." I stand back up.

"No!" Hilda pulls me down. "Please don't leave!"

Good girl. That's more like it.

"Fine, so how are you all today?" I ask nonchalantly.

"You are beautiful." Rose reaches across the table.

"Thanks. I got my braces off."

"And you don't have your glasses anymore. It's nice to see your eyes." Hilda's eyes glisten.

"Okay, that's enough. Thanks, guys. I was glad to be noticed for something other than being a freak."

"You almost being arrested again in the middle of lunch doesn't help you much," Mattie says.

"I wasn't almost arrested. She just had a few questions."

"Psycho," Decker coughs.

"Nice to see you too, Decker."

Mattie can feel the tension in the air. "Cosette, I think you look beautiful, but I have to get going. Have a great day, you guys." She leaves and so do Shelby and Sierra. I think the sisters are torn between hanging out with 'good' Mattie or 'evil' me. Shelby's best friend, Rose, chose me. We'll see what the sisters do.

"So, I heard you all missed me?" I say. Might as well get it out in the open.

"It just isn't the same without you," Rose pouts. Hilda agrees, even Decker nods slightly.

Chris says nothing.

"If there is a next time, it will be scheduled through texts, not announced out in the open. Agreed?" I establish the rules.

"Agreed." Hilda sighs relief. I think she's nervous I'd put her out.

"So, now that that's all cleared up, how are you all?"
"Fine. What did she want?" Decker asks.
"Who?"
"The police officer," Hilda says.
"Oh, nothing special. She... uh... nothing special." I smile.

Chris touches my leg, and butterflies tickle my stomach. Though only away from him one day, I missed him.

"Did you do something?" Rose asks.
"Did you need my help?" Decker asks.
"Where did that come from? Really, Decker? You want to help me? You think I'm psycho, and you want to help? You should stay away," I say.
"We'll always be ready to help you," Rose answers for him.
"You didn't invite me?" Chris whispers.
"You were a little busy, Chris." I huff and show him his text. "Remember this?

Just got done with Hilda, Rosy and Deck
Good idea, thanks, BTW happy Valentine's Day
TTYL
Chris

A guilty shade of green sickens his face. I'm glad.

THEY ALL STARE at me with eager eyes. "Okay, I really love you guys, and I am going to say this as clear as I possibly can. Please, please don't go there. If you don't ask questions, I won't have to lie to you. I will not bring you into my nightmare. I will never tell you what I do. I will never tell you where I go. And if I tell you to leave me, then listen to me the first time and get away from me. Please."

"We know. We saw the bite," Decker says with sympathy, referring to Hilda.

"Damn it!" I stand up and leave.

Chris gets up and follows me outside to the commons.

"Don't come near me!" I tell him as I'm pacing.

"I'm sorry." He shivers in the cold. I'm burning up.

"Stay away, Chris."

"I just want to talk." He slowly approaches me like an animal catcher trying to calm a rabid dog.

"Then stand there and talk." I point away from me.

"I missed you. I am so sorry. I'm so sorry. That was horribly cruel of me to text that to you."

"Ya think?" I keep on pacing, talking myself down. I have a flood of emotions going on. Guilt for biting Hilda, shame that they see how I abuse my girlfriend. Excitement after seeing those pictures, but confusion about my meeting. And most of all, shouldn't I still be mad at Chris? He did bring Bonnie back. Was she ever really gone? Would she have come back eventually? I think so, and because of that, I should forgive him. He *has* been apologizing to me. And the five of us agreed not to be so public about our fun. I need to get over myself.

"COSETTE, I JUST wanted to ..."

"Hold on a second." I pace. "I just need a second to clear my head."

"Can I come closer?"

I relent.

"I think you just need your man to hold you." He wraps his arms around me. "To tell you he loves you. To tell you how so very sorry he is and what a manipulative ass he is."

"Yes, you are. But I was stupid to think I could be something I'm not. You're right, I'm messed up, and there's no going back. I just wish I learned that before you betrayed me."

"Don't think of it as betrayed. Think of it like when Shrek kissed the princess, how she became perfect."

"So I'm an ogre now?" I half laugh.

"You're my ogre." He kisses my forehead. "So are you going to tell me?"

"Nope."

"Was it because of my text? Which I am so sorry about."

"I needed a release, and I had a prospect lined up so, yes. Are you upset?"

"Yes."

"Good. Don't pull crap like that on me again!" I push him away.

"That's my girl. I love it when you talk to me like that."

"Oh stop it."

"You are drop dead gorgeous. I missed you yesterday, but I'm glad this came back." He pulls me back in.

"I've gotten a lot of compliments today, but yours is the one I wanted to hear." I blush.

"Who else has been complimenting you?"

"Are you jealous?" I raise my eyebrow, flirting.

"Of course. Do I have competition? Are you taking on another lover?"

"Not hardly. I can't do that to him. He's a nice, normal guy."

"Is this the guy you kissed in your art class?" Chris asks.

"How did you know?"

"Nerd news travels fast when there's a hot chick involved."

"I just wanted him to be impressive to his friends."

"How do you do it?" he asks.

"Do what?"

"How do you work people like that? I bet you can get that guy to do anything."

"Not even."

"If you asked him out, he would say yes in a heartbeat. If you asked him to steal a car for your date, he would do it, no questions asked."

"You seem to think I have all this control. I don't influence people, Chris. I don't demand anything. I've no redeeming qualities. I don't even have a personality. It's not like someone can say 'she's so funny and great to be around, I'll do anything for her'. I don't have that. I have nothing to manipulate with, yet everyone seems to think I have control. I have nothing."

"And that right there is why you have control."

"I don't get you people." I pull away.

"So, do I have competition?" He holds my hand, not letting me go.

"No, Dave is a good guy, and I will keep him that way by keeping him away."

"Well then, I'm so glad I'm not a good guy. Because I don't want you to keep me away." He kisses me hard. My heart melts.

Chapter THIRTY-FOUR

"SO TELL ME?" Mom rolls down her car window right as Chris and I pull into the driveway.

I pop out of Chris's truck and lean into her car to hug her. "Everyone at school loved the makeover, Mom. The whole school stared at me for a good reason. I love you so much."

Chris leans in. "I'm not sure I should be thanking you. Yes, you made my already perfect girlfriend more beautiful, but now she's out of my league and might need an upgraded boyfriend."

"Chris, you are so sweet. I don't think you'll have a hard time holding on to her. She seems to be stuck on you."

"Thanks, Ms. Murphy."

She waves as she drives away.

"I have to stop by my house. You wanna come?" Chris asks.

"Is your Aunt April there?" I ask.

"Yes, she's packing up to move to Indianapolis to live with some other cousins."

"Then I'll stay here. The last person I want to see is the fiancée of the man I killed."

"Are you sure?" He steps in front of me, blocking my apartment entrance. "It will only take a few minutes. You can wait in the truck.

I have to get my gym clothes. I have a tournament..."

"I know. Tomorrow night you have a tournament. But for now, is there a reason you're not letting me into my own house?"

Chris steps away. I go to unlock my door, but it opens wide.

"So much for stalling her, Chris." Decker is in the living room laying a thick comforter on the floor.

"We understand. She's hard-headed." Rose and Hilda emerge from my bedroom in lace and satin. They pull me in and start undressing me. Turns out, they're here to apologize in a very special way.

CHRIS ORDERS PIZZA as we take turns showering and getting dressed. I emerge from my room in my lounge dress and elephant slippers. Decker rolls his eyes at my footwear then turns on the news. He likes to see who the next client of his uncle's funeral home will be. The story of my latest victim is the main topic. No one dares to look at me or question me. Chris holds my hand and whispers, "That's my girl."

"Decker, if your funeral home gets her, can I come over?" Hilda asks, buttoning her top.

Decker looks to me for an answer. I give him a look that screams 'if you say yes, I will kill you'.

"I'll have to ask my uncle, but I doubt he'll say it's okay. He finds it disrespectful of the dead," Decker says.

"Just thought I'd ask," Hilda says.

I think she wants to condition herself. She's gonna get frustrated and do something stupid. I'll have to figure something out.

"I have homework to do," Rose says as she gathers her things. I walk her to the door. "You really look great, Cozy." She kisses me. I pull her into a corner and kiss her back. I love her pouty lips and voluptuous body, especially now that she's let me play with it. "Do you have to go?" I ask.

"Yes, text me later."

Decker leaves with a kiss also. "You really are pretty. Too bad you're fucked up in the head."

"Thanks, Deck. And thank you," I shift my eyes towards Hilda, grateful for her not being allowed at the funeral home.

Hilda grabs her coat and dresses to leave.

"You can't stay?" I ask.

"I have homework also, and I have to be home on time so I'll be allowed to go skiing next weekend. I don't wanna screw anything up."

"Keep the parental units happy. Good idea." I give her a kiss and lock the door behind all of them.

CHRIS CALLS ME. "Now that your playmates have had their fun and left, come into the kitchen and tell me what's going on. What was in the envelope?"

"Envelope?" I had to jog my short memory. "Oh yeah, at lunch. Jenny had pictures of what I did on Monday."

"I see why you left the lunch table." He pours us some sweat tea.

"She said that she was first on the scene and good thing too because the killer was a bit sloppy." I pull out the baggie with my hair in it. "She said she's glad my hair is too short to match this one. Then she gave me this map for when I go walking, just in case I want to go to a few places and avoid others." I tap the dots on which she had tapped.

Chris smirks then studies the map. The ones Jenny tapped catch his attention. "Let's look those up." He grabs my laptop.

After a bit of research, we find out they are the most vile criminals, released for minor flaws in the court system.

"Holy shit, Cosette! She wants you to off these guys!" Chris stands.

"I got that impression too. She said she didn't want to see me for a few weeks because people will talk."

"She's protecting you. Holy crap! How do you do it?"

"I do nothing. Stop making me out to be something I'm not."

"You better be very careful. If she can clear you of a crime, she can easily pin one on you."

"She's a newbie officer. What can she do? Oh, and this dot here lives across the street from her. He used to babysit her. But she pointed to this one."

Chris sits and types the information in, and a profile pops up. "It's an old man. That's interesting. I wonder why he's next. How did the cop know to come to you?"

"I'm thinking she saw something about me. Like I was numb and could handle it." I push away from the table. "It's been almost three months, Chris, since my life turned in that alley. Look at what I am now. Look at how far I've come. There is no way that back in November that I would have ever considered killing people for a rogue cop."

"We need to be very cautious."

"I know. And, by the way, this is only between you and me. Hilda has to be kept out. We'll figure something out for her. But everyone has to be kept out. I will not warn you again."

His face turns.

He takes the threat seriously; for once, I think he's intimidated.

Standing up, I grab his hand, guiding him to the couch. We lie down and watch TV.

"No matter how many friends we have, Chris, it all comes down to us two. I have to be able to rely on you, and you can always rely on me."

"I got a little relaxed these last few days," he says. "I need to go back to how I was when I first started out."

"Me too, except now we have each other, but only each other."

"It's isolating."

"Yes, it is."

He holds me until the late newscast. He strokes my hair and kisses my neck. It's soft and done with love. There's a huge difference between now and earlier today. Love and sex are so far apart in my world. I think he feels the same way too.

"I love you, Cosette Hugo," he says softly. "You are everything to me. I will never leave you. You are my obsession."

At this moment, life is perfect. Absolutely perfect.

Chapter
THIRTY-FIVE

"HAPPY BIRTHDAY, HONEY!" My mom hands me a huge gift bag. I dig in. "I know it's not that cold outside, but next weekend you'll need it when you're skiing."

"I love it!" I hug the blue and green paisley ski jacket. "It's bright, and kinda obnoxious."

"You're coming out of your shell so I figured I'd help you along. You like it?"

"It's perfect, Mom. Thank you."

"There's more." She hands me a card. "This is a gift your dad wanted me to give you. He made me wait until today. Had I known what he was going to do, I would have given it to you earlier. But just know that despite your differences, he loved you. He just didn't know how much until it was too late."

"Mom, how can I open this after you said that?" We're both crying.

"Just do it. And just to let you know, Tawny had no objections. At least that's what he told me."

"So his last statement to you was a lie?"

She smirks. "Personally, I believe she was already gone when he decided to do this, but it's the thought that counts. Now open it."

I carefully tear the envelope. My mom laughs. It was a joke between her and my dad that if I didn't have help, all my cards would be sitting on a shelf because I couldn't open an envelope that anyone licked.

"Stop laughing at me. I got it open." As I pull out the card, a check falls out. I turn it over until I finish reading. It would be rude otherwise.

Dear Cosette,

You are my precious little girl. I love you so much. From the day you were first placed in my arms I fell in love. When you were a baby, I carried you around like a trophy, showing you off to everyone. I was so proud. On your first day of kindergarten, I was more upset than your mom was. I didn't know what to do with myself. I sat in my car and watched you on the playground, making sure you were alright. You grew up so fast. The family changed, your mom changed, then I changed.

When Victor died, I died. He was my firstborn, my son. Nothing is sadder than outliving your children. That's not how things are supposed to work. Life has thrown me some curveballs, but that one knocked me out.

I'm so so sorry you were the one who took the brunt of our troubles. You were the one tossed back and forth, you were the one caught in the middle, and you don't understand why.

I loved you, I really did. We were just too weak, and you are the one that suffered.

Now that I'm gone, I hope you have a better life. I hope you find happiness, a true and faithful love, and a life worth living.

I want the best for you, my precious. No matter what, please know that I, your daddy, love you and will be watching out for you. Forgive our weakness. We're human, flawed, and ugly, but we love you. I love you.

I hope you take this check and use it to start again.

Build your perfect life now.
I love you,
Your daddy.

As I'm sitting here bawling, my mom waits. She's not even asking to read it. She knows.

A knock at the door tells me it's time for school. I don't move. My mom gets up and tells Chris to wait for a few.

She closes the door, keeping him out. "Finish the card, Cosette. Wipe your tears, and finish the card."

I can't. It's too hard. Mom grabs the card and turns to the back. On it dad wrote, "This is your life. Are you who you want to be? — Switchfoot"

He drew an arrow pointing down which guides my gaze to the check on my lap. He knew I would wait to see the gift last.

I pick up the check and cry out, "Holy shit! Fifty thousand dollars?"

"Ten for a car, used of course, and the other forty for college. He gave me a list of investments to grow the money before you need it."

"A car? And college? Mom, I uh, I..." I stutter. What do you say to that? Who do you thank?

She comes over and gives me a hug and we both sob for a good five minutes.

FROM OUTSIDE, THERE'S a humming. It's the Happy Birthday song. "Oh my goodness, I left Chris out there!" Mom runs to the door. "I am so sorry." She opens the door wide, and he comes in with a bouquet of flowers and mylar balloons.

"Happy birthday, baby." Chris gives me a kiss. "You two look awful." He jokes, lightening the atmosphere. He knows how much we hate our crying faces.

"Not another word from you, Chris. By the way, congrats on your first place in last night's gymnastics thing. Cosette said you were perfect."

"It was a small meet, but thanks." He spins as mom rushes around him.

"I gotta go to work. I'll let Cosette fill you in. I love you, birthday girl." She gives me a hug then darts out the door.

"Honey? Baby? Are you okay?" He comes to me. I fold into his arms as he patiently waits.

"SO WHAT KINDA car you gonna get?" Rose asks. She and the sisters made a birthday cupcake for me. Hilda brought a small bouquet of balloons. Decker acts like he's lighting the candle since the school forbids lighters.

"I don't even have a license. I'll get that first so I can test drive at least a hundred cars." I make a wish and fake blow out the candle. We all get one bite of the cupcake.

"Shelby can teach you how to drive. You can't mess up Betsy." Sierra offers for her sister to teach me.

"A parent has to teach you. I think between my mom and yours, we'll learn ya," Mattie says. "So are you all going anywhere tonight?"

"No, my birthday party is the ski trip," I say.

"Actually, I have something special planned for her. Sorry guys, but none of y'all are invited."

"Just the two of you? That's no party," Sierra says.

"I think it's romantic," Shelby says.

"What about me?" Hilda whines.

Chris is at a loss for words. "I uh, hadn't planned, uh…"

"I'm just kidding, Chris. You two are first, I know. Don't worry about me. I'll stay home and uh, do a puzzle or knit or something." Hilda's lighthearted about it. I'm impressed.

"Come out with us," Rose says.

"What are you guys doing?" Hilda asks.

"Nothing, but we'll plan something. Shelby and Sierra have a hot tub," Rose says. The sisters nod.

Decker stretches out his arms, flexing his wrestler muscles under his thin tight sweater. He drops them around Rose and Sierra. "Sorry, ladies, I have a dead body waiting for my special embalming concoction."

"You mean you're gonna be combing dead people's hair and putting makeup on them while your uncle does the real work." Chris deflates Decker's ego.

"That's exactly what I mean!" Decker steals a fry from Chris. "So you all will have to have fun without me." He stands as the bell rings.

"Have fun tonight. I'll be at the café if you all get done early," Mattie says.

"THIS IS QUAINT," I say as I slide into the booth. The converted house makes a cozy restaurant. "And a little ghetto."

"I'm not too creative," Chris says. "It's just dinner and a movie."

"I love soul food. My grandma learned to cook soul food from her best friend. Of course it had her German flair added, but it was still good." I scan the pictures on the menu.

"German soul, yum. So, what do you want to be when you grow up? Now that you have a chance for college, what do you want to do?" Chris intertwines my ankles with his.

"I don't know. Never thought about it really. I guess lately I never expected to make it out of high school."

"I can understand that," he says.

"I would love to be a painter or do murals like my mom used to do, but since I want to make money, that's out."

"What do you think about farming?"

"Uh, no. Farming what?" I ask.

"Well, my cousins and I are in negotiations over the farmhouse. My uncle left part of it to me, and now my cousins don't want to have anything to do with the place."

"Why not? It's beautiful out there."

"Because of what Ben did to all those women and how he died in their cellar. Also, they had very rough childhoods. My aunt was nuts, and my uncle was strict to the point of being cruel. He lost it when she died of cancer in October."

"That's when the Poser gang's first attack happened. Coincidence?" I ask.

"Actually that's the first public attack. I joined them in September. Anyway, it looks like I'll own the farm soon. I'm selling about sixty of my acres to buy their portion. They're just glad to get rid of it."

"Are the goats gone?"

"A few are, but most of them are still there. We can go up tonight if you wanna skip the movie."

"That makes for a late night for you. Don't you have gymnastics in the morning?"

"I'll be there, butt dragging, but I'll be there."

"No, we can wait on going to the farm. You need to get first place this year, and you said that Carl is getting better."

"Actually, he's way better than me; he just doesn't know it. For someone who acts so cocky, he has no balls."

"I don't know him. Is he cockier than Decker?" I ask.

"I do seem to hang around a few, don't I? He's one of the top gymnasts in the state and the only black guy in the top ten. He can sing and he can dance. He has a reason to be cocky, so I let him. Especially since he is like Decker: all bark, no bite."

"You're all bite with no bark. I like your way better." I lean over the table and give him a peck on the lips. When I sit back down, I look around. The place is mostly empty with a few couples trickling in. They stare at us, not in the 'I know that girl from the news' way, but in the 'why is there a white couple slumming it' way.

"Sorry about the slow service," Chris says. "This place is supposed to be pretty good. Maybe the waitress is new."

"You come here often?" I ask.

"No, never been. I was doing some work for my dad when I saw an acquaintance and she recommended it to..."

"Happy birthday to you..." A familiar voice belts out.

Melodious and Pearl come out of the kitchen with a small cake. They sing to me loud and with flavor. I love it. I stand and hug them both.

"Thanks for bringing her, Ken." Mel tells Chris. "Barbie couldn't make it?"

"Not this time," I say. "Pearl, are you working here?"

"Yeah, and I don't make shit. But Smudge says I need legit since I can't be a hoe forever. I's only here part time, but I've picked up a few new clients." Pearl puts down our silverware then leaves.

"I'm here full time, but at least I'm not at home listening to her work," Mel says.

"That's funny. Can you sit and eat with us?" I ask.

"No, this is your birthday dinner so it's on me. But I have to work to pay for it so you better tip big, Ken," Mel warns Chris.

"I'll take care of you," Chris says with a wink.

"You better or I'll…" Mel trails off. Something outside steals her attention. She stares out the front window and starts shaking. Pearl comes out of the kitchen with a tray of food. She sees Mel immobile then follows her line of sight just in time to witness a black Beamer slow down in front of the restaurant. The tinted driver's window slides down, allowing a two-barrel shotgun room to peek out. The gun slides back into the car, the window rolls up, and the car skids off.

"It's okay, Mel. Smudge is handling it." Pearl delivers our drinks, shaking and spilling. "Shit, Cookie, I'm sorry."

"Who was that, Pearl?" Chris asks.

"No one you need to mess with white boy." Pearl walks back to the kitchen.

I grab Mel's hand. "Tell me everything."

Chapter THIRTY-SIX

"HOW WAS YOUR birthday dinner last night?" Hilda asks as we walk into the Kentucky Convention Center.

"It was fun. Chris took me to the restaurant that Mel and Pearl work at."

"They're not prostitutes anymore?"

"Pearl still is, but Mel never was." I turn to Chris. Our eyes acknowledge our agreement not to mention the problems Mel and Pearl are having with some Brazilian drug dealer. "Why are we here?" I ask Chris.

"I told you; this is another part of your birthday surprise. Just keep walking. We're almost there." He holds my and Hilda's hands, dragging us into one of the shows.

"Anyways, Hilda, it was a cute little converted house out on the West end," I tell her.

"Why would you go there?" Hilda's shocked voice gives away her disdain for the ghetto part of town.

"I had work to do for my dad," Chris says.

"What is it that you do for your dad exactly?" Hilda asks.

"Right now, just stalking. Could be nothing. Could be something. Just stalking for now." He stops and buys tickets into the...

"Knife and Gun Show? I love it!" I jump, hugging him. "How did you know? When Victor came home on leave, the Knife and Gun show was his favorite. We spent hours going through each booth."

"Don't give me that much credit," Chris says. "I just thought since the police took your knife that you needed a new one. And we'll get Hilda one too."

Hilda squeals and kisses him. People stare. Some are starting to whisper.

Great, it's going to be a long day.

"I ALMOST FORGOT we're out in public," I say. "We may want to keep our heads down, and I'm sorry, but no kissing, either of you. I don't want to be noticed."

As we walk into the show more and more people whisper and point. I can't believe it. They're so obvious. I'm humiliated! So much for not being noticed.

Chris holds my hand tight. Hilda holds my elbow.

We step into the convention and don't get ten feet from the first booth when Chris freezes.

"DO YOU ALL want to leave?" he whispers to us.

Hilda wraps herself around my arm.

A large, burly man stands a few feet in front of us, blocking our way. I'm not sure of his intentions. I bite my lip, petrified.

He smiles and then claps. He claps loud again and again. He gets the people to join him. Quickly it spreads until there's a huge crowd staring at the three of us, applauding and cheering.

A lady comes up and hugs me, thanks me. Then she tells Hilda she's been praying for her. A man and his two older sons come and give all three of us bear hugs. "That's how you do it! You girls are heroes!" they yell to everyone.

People pat us on the shoulder or shake our hands. Some are tearful, telling Hilda they were on one of the searches for her. Others just wanted to touch us. Bizarre.

We're rescued by an event coordinator and taken to a rest area.

"I'm so sorry to interrupt your show," I tell her.

"I just wanted to get my girlfriend a birthday gift," Chris says.

She sits us down and we huddle insecurely.

She looks older than my mom and is dressed like a park ranger with a gun and two knives on her thick belt. "You're like our local celebrity. You girls are everything we stand for here. It's because of stories like yours that people are educated on the right to bear arms. We collect for show and sport but also for defense. You're the epitome of that. I'm sorry. You probably had no idea you girls meant that much to us here."

"We just wanted a gift for Cosette," Hilda says. "The police had to take her knife, and it's her birthday."

I don't like this attention. Even though it makes me feel good, I feel like a liar.

"Well then. Let's let the crowd settle a bit so you can shop in peace. Can I get you something to drink?" she asks.

"No, thank you." Hilda tucks her head into my shoulder. I pet her blonde locks, calming her nerves.

"I'm sorry. I guess this is overwhelming. We know you two have been through a lot. Come on. I'll escort you around."

We follow the woman to the back booths but end up shaking hundreds of hands from customers as well as vendors. After a while, we relax and let it flow. Hilda and I are offered sponsorships on everything from knives to handcuffs. At one booth, Hilda is offered everything from pepper spray to a Taser from a very flirty guy. She declines, flirting back with a shy smile.

After going through almost a hundred plus booths, we revisit a booth in the middle of the show. I find a knife I like there. Since this would be Bonnie's main tool, I want to be very picky.

"This is your birthday gift. Pick it well," Chris says.

The vendor pats his shoulder hard. "That's a good man. You take care of these ladies. They're very special to us."

"I will. They take care of me," Chris says.

"I bet they do." The old rugged vendor chokes out a raspy laugh. "I'm sure the other booths offered you sponsorships, but I know you girls are still too young for that. I do however have a little something for you all. Just to say 'thank you'. Hold on." He turns around and pulls out a tray full of various single blade pocketknives. "Let's see. You, Ms. Dyson, you look like, here. Hold this one." He hands her a small black-handled stainless steel blade.

"That looks like 'Blue'," I say.

"Who is 'Blue'?" the dealer asks.

Since I feel like I'm in familiar company, I answer him truthfully. "Blue is what I called my knife. The police are keeping it for evidence."

His eyes light up. He knows what I used it for. It's nice not explaining or hiding. "So Ms. Dyson, do you like it?"

"I like it. I like the red one."

He chuckles. "Alright, Cinderella, red it is. Sorry we don't have it in pink. This one is on the house. I'm glad you're safe. I was searching for you. A lot of us were."

"Thank you. Cosette's the one who rescued me." She turns into my shoulder.

"Which leads me to our hero." He sees my disapproving expression. "Our reluctant hero?"

"Humble hero," Chris tells him. He leans in and whispers to me. "Pick out the one you want. It'll be my treat."

"Which one do you like?" The old man straightens out a few on the tray.

I shift the tray over to look in his display case. One knife in particular has caught my attention. I've seen it in a lot of the booths. "I like that one."

The vendor is a taken back. "That's quite an eye you have there."

He pulls it out and gently hands it to me. It's heavier than Blue. It feels good in my hands. I like it. I claim it.

"This is the Spartan, by Cold Steel. You've picked out a serious blade here."

I smile. "Gorgo, my Spartan queen," I call her.

Hilda pulls out her purse. "She saved me from two people. I think she deserves the best."

"It's too expensive..." I hand Gorgo back.

"We'll take it." Chris pushes Hilda's purse away and hands him his debit card.

Hilda puts her wallet away and whispers to me, "You know it

will be harder to hide that big of a knife?" She glances down to the area that hid Blue from the truck driver.

"I'll work something out," I laugh at her.

"Well, since the gentleman is paying for the Spartan, let me have the honor of giving you this." The man pulls out a necklace with a leaf pendant. He opens the leaf into a small stainless steel knife.

"I love it!"

"Then it's yours." He drapes it around my neck.

I wear it proudly as we walk out.

"THAT WAS A lot of fun," Hilda says as Chris and I escort her up to her room. Her dad's in the shower getting ready for his dinner date.

"That was fun. Let me see your knife, Hilda." I say.

She pulls it out. "I like it. I can handle it well."

"You can hide it well," I say.

She snickers.

"What's going on you two?" Chris asks.

"Oh, nothing. Inside joke." Hilda busts out laughing.

"Very inside," I cough. "Are you going to name it? Like I named mine? It's better than saying 'your knife'."

"True. You called yours Blue; I'll call mine Red. Do you like that name?"

"I like Red," Chris says with a wink to me.

"Let me see yours, Cozy." Hilda holds out her hand.

I pull Gorgo out. My mind's racing, thinking of the smooth lines she will make. So thin and so deadly.

I open up the blade to feel her hard edges. The grip curves my palm like she's tailored to me.

"Can I hold it?" Hilda asks.

I'm jealous. I don't want her to touch. Ignoring my quirks, I give Gorgo to Hilda.

"Too heavy for me. I like Red better." She hands my knife back.

I decide to test the blade. I hold out my arm. Under my small scar from my promise with Chris, I make a thin red slit. The blade is so sharp that I barely feel it.

"Well that sucks," I say.

"What? What's the matter?"

I lick my blood. "I didn't feel it. I would've liked to have felt it."

"Then you picked the wrong knife. You'll have to do a significant amount of cutting before that blade gets remotely dull," Chris says with a wink only meant for me.

"I'm sure you'll have plenty of opportunity to use it," Hilda says in such a nonchalant manner that it throws me for a loop. She starts going through her closet looking for something to wear. She pulls out a green dress. "Whaddya think? It's date night with Dad. He's taking me out for Mexican food."

"I like that he does that for you," I say, jealous that my dad never did anything like that for me. "But you're gonna freeze in that dress."

"It's better to look good than to feel good, daaaling," she quotes in an accent. We look at her funny. "Billy Crystal, Saturday Night Live. My dad and I watch reruns all the time. Where do you think I get my sense of humor?"

"More than just a pretty face," I tell Chris.

"Believe me, I need a sense of humor to put up with my life." She lays the dress on the bed and starts taking off her clothes. "How's your arm?"

"It's fine. I wish it hurt just a bit more." I dab a little more blood off the cut.

She holds up my arm and licks it.

"You are a bad girl. You better stop." I hold her face and lick her lips, tasting my blood. I kiss her hard. "Wow, the effect you just had on me. Hilda, that was awesome."

"I am loving this." Chris leans back on Hilda's bed, watching us.

"My dad will be out of the shower soon. I should show some restraint," Hilda says. "Maybe later?" she flirts.

"Definitely later." Chris stands. "We should go so you can get ready for date night with your dad."

"Yes, you two go have some fun. I have an enchilada calling my name." She pushes us out the front door then locks it, giggling.

We stand on her stoop rolling our eyes. Chris grabs my arm and inspects the cut. "Now it's time for your birthday present, part two. Let's go test out your knife."

Chapter
THIRTY-SEVEN

I SHOWER AT Chris's house. We clean up our bloody knives, make love, and then shower again. It's the most wonderful, passionate night I've ever had. I never thought I could feel this way. My whole body tingles. The high from this kill with Chris is lasting so long I'm afraid the crash will be unbearable.

"CAN I SLEEP here? I don't want to be alone."
    "Is the low coming?" His hazel eyes make me melt.
    "No, I can't feel it. I don't want to be alone if it does."
    "You'll never be alone." He puts one of his super soft, worn-in gymnastic t-shirts on me. "This looks better on you than me."
    I shake my head no. We snuggle in bed, and he strokes my hair till I fall asleep.
    Life is perfect.
    Life is perfect.

I WAKE TO the soft touch of fingers running up and down my body.

I turn to lie on my back so he can have full access. My eyes stay closed. I feel like I'm dreaming. His touch is so light, but after last night, I'm in the mood for more.

"You're gonna have to do better than that if you want your shirt back," I tease.

"She's dangerous, Dad. You might want to back off." Chris's voice comes from a distance.

I open my eyes to see Chris's dad hovering over me. Gagging, I quickly flip the comforter to cover up.

"If you like my son, I'm twice as fun," Chris's dad whispers into my hair.

"Alright, Dad, back off. She'll kill you faster than I will."

"I'm sure. She's very sexy."

"Dad!"

"Your loss," he tells me.

I think I'm going to puke.

Chris comes and sits at the foot of the bed. "Sorry about that. I leave to make breakfast, and look what happens. Are you okay? I know he's gross."

"I kind of liked it until I saw it was him. Your dad is a very good-looking guy though, for a dad and all."

"Are you going to take him up on his offer?" Chris jokes.

"Fearful you'd be replaced?"

"Not hardly. I've seen the type of women he picks up. Some are nicer than others. But you'll need to visit the free clinic after a night with him."

"Gross."

"So, what did my dad do that worked for you?" He pulls the blanket back, exposing me.

"Why don't you close the door and I'll show you."

"Can't. I made you breakfast, and we need to pick up Hilda. I have plans for you two this afternoon."

"SO WHY ARE we at your gym? Do we getta watch you practice?" I ask Chris.

"Uh, no. You remember that guy at the pepper spray and Taser booth yesterday?"

"There were a few of those," I answer.

"This was the black guy, Andre. The one that had the puppy dog eyes for Hilda."

"He was cute," Hilda says. I agree.

"Good. I booked him for a private lesson for you two. I think that if we are going to… If we get stuck… If… crap! How do I say this? Okay. I don't want the three of us out looking for people to hurt, but if we just so happen to get into trouble, I want all of us trained and prepared. This will be more intense than your public class at the YMCA. Is that okay with you girls?"

"Cozy, we're gonna learn to kick ass!" Hilda bounces up and down.

"Oh, I am going to have some fun with this!" I clap.

ANDRE TAKES HILDA first while we watch. I take in as much as I can, learning while I stretch waiting for my turn. He's very flirty with her. I like watching, but I'm a bit jealous since she's flirting back. My heart starts to race.

"Okay, Cosette, you're up." Andre claps me out of my gaze.

I take my stance and wait. He starts out slow.

He does a review of Hilda's lesson. "Do you have all that? Are you ready? I'm going to attack you."

Attack he does. And I fight back hard. I try to use everything he's taught me, but I can't take him down. He can't take me down easy either. I end up getting a jab in the side, then collapse.

"Oh, that was a good one." I hold my side. "How did I do?"

Out of breath, he answers. "I know I didn't teach you all of that."

"I'm a quick learner."

"Did you have to fight that hard when…" he holds back from asking a question he thinks will embarrass me. "Sorry."

"I didn't have to fight."

"She has other weapons. Cozy, are you okay?" Hilda kneels by me.

I lift up my shirt to where I was jabbed. It's a few inches from my entry wound. "I'll be okay. It's fun to go that hard, but I think I need to sit out for a bit. Hilda, you go again."

"Love to." She kisses my stomach. "Kisses will make everything feel better."

She has no problem with us in public anymore. "You're so adorable. Get him good."

They go at it again. He isn't as hard on her as he was on me, but that's okay. I don't want her hurt or her perfect body bruised.

Chris sits next to me. "Do I need to take you to your doctor or anything?"

"No, I just need a rest. It's been what, almost four weeks? You would think I'd be okay, but then again I've never been shot before. I don't know how long it takes. It felt good to go at it without freaking out on him. I feel like I have more control. Like I can separate it."

"I'm proud of you. I thought you did great."

"Thanks. Our little princess is doing well. He likes her," I say.

"Are you jealous?" Chris asks.

"Are you?"

"No. Not like I would be if it was you." He helps me stretch until it's my turn once more. Andre and I start again, this time with a little less sparring and a little more learning.

"THANK YOU, CHRIS." Hilda gives him a kiss as we climb into the truck.

"Did you learn anything?"

"I'll have to practice. Ya wanna go at it when we get home?" she asks me.

"No, I need to rest."

"I'll have to call him again." She holds a business card Andre gave her.

"Do you want him?" I ask her.

"I want you."

"That's not what I'm asking. Do you think I'm preventing you from ...uh... dating?"

"I'm dating you," she says like she doesn't want to offend me.

I don't want her to feel like I'm making her the third wheel just to be possessive. Which I am, I just don't want her to feel that way. She holds my hand with both of hers. Chris snickers at me.

I pat her leg. "I need to go home. I need a bath before church. Do you want to come with us? I'm sure Mattie can make room for one more."

"I'll take the bath, sure, but not the church," Hilda says. "Thanks though. I don't need to feel any more guilt than I already do."

That makes me feel good. I want her to feel guilt. I want her to feel so guilty that she won't want to hurt anyone.

Last night with Chris was perfect. I just want it to be the two of us doing that. I enjoyed what she did for me in the semi-truck, but I'm still uneasy about her doing it again.

Maybe I feel like she'll confess or freak out and leave evidence. I don't know. I need to get over it.

"Sorry, Hilda: no church, no bath. I'll go to church for the three of us.

Chapter
THIRTY-EIGHT

WE GET TO Mattie's church a few minutes early. It makes me nervous. At Telly's church, I get the judgmental stares. At Mattie's church, they hug me and want to help, but I feel like everyone knows what I did because God tells them. I'm used to the judgmental looks. I can deal with humiliation. I can't deal with this.

We enter in just enough time for everyone in the small congregation to hug me and tell me they're praying for me. They're all smiles. They're not like the crowd at the knife show that was proud of me. These people genuinely seem happy to see me. I don't like it. It makes me feel odd, especially after my adventure with Chris testing out my new knife last night. And I can't forget about my solo adventure on Valentine's Day.

MATTIE'S MOM IS on the music team. The four ladies get on stage and sing three songs.

Then the pastor comes in and speaks about the number twelve in the Bible. Apparently, it's a significant number: twelve tribes of Israel, twelve disciples. After about an hour it hits me. Last night's victim was my number 12. I must have the 'deer in the headlights' look because the pastor looks directly at me then quickly turns away.

Suddenly I don't feel so well. I won't break down and cry or anything. It's more like a realization that I no longer feel guilt. I should feel guilt. That's what a normal human would feel, right? Of course, normal I know I'm not, but have I numbed myself so much that even in church I feel no remorse?

I'm trying to figure out what it is exactly that I'm feeling. I guess the best way to describe it is loss. I feel like I lost a huge part of me that I know will never come back.

As soon as I think it, the pastor looks directly at me. "Restoration," he says. "'Though you have made me see troubles, many and bitter, you will restore my life again; from the depths of the earth you will again bring me up'."

I feel like leaving, but I can't. Mattie can feel it, I know. I wonder if it's the same kind of feeling for her. Is she feeling loss like I am?

"Brothers, if someone is caught in a sin, you who are spiritual should restore him gently. But watch yourself, or you also may be tempted."

Why doesn't he just come right out and say it? All of these Bible quotes are slapping me in the face. I'm embarrassed. Not for me, but for Mattie. I feel sorry for her having to sit by me. I know she won't be tempted by what I'm doing, but I think she feels obligated to stay with me until I change. I would love for that to happen, but when I no longer feel remorse, what's left for her to work with?

I can picture it: my dark host on one shoulder and Mattie on the other. And even though Mattie is stronger, I'm still engulfed by the dark host. I know it's all up to me.

Once again, I am failing at this task.

"I do not understand what I do. For what I want to do I do not do, but what I hate I do." The pastor quotes the Bible

Ugh! Stop it! It's creepy how he pulls out the exact verse to match what I'm thinking. I think I need to go home and work this out in my head. I am picking the wrong side, and I know it. My problem is that I'm in full addiction mode now. It's not something you just stop doing. But, do I even want to stop? No, I don't think so.

I just want to leave.

AS WE WALK out the door, the pastor shakes my hand. I wonder if he can feel the filth that Mattie sees. I'm sure he can.

"It's good to see you, Cosette. We are praying for you. You were brought back for a reason. You must overcome evil with good. It's takes a lot of work, but it will be worth it for everyone, including your significant others."

"Thank you, pastor." I shake his hand and leave. How strange it must be to know things like that. And how disciplined would you have to be to be able to restrain from calling it out. He said 'others', knowing I had both Hilda and Chris. I'm sure they don't approve of homosexuality or premarital sex here either. I wonder if the pastor can see this tug of war going on inside of me with the good side letting go of the rope.

Overcoming evil with good? It seems so far from me, pure fantasy.

Mattie gives me a hug. "Thank you, Cozy."

"For what?"

"For coming. You don't have to."

"I think I do. I'm having a hard time here, but I think I still need to come. Thanks for being patient with me."

We get in the car and head home.

"What did you think of the message?"

"You mean the one directed at me?"

"I thought it was directed at me. It's cool how he does that." Mattie is impressed with it. I'm bothered.

"I asked Chris and Hilda if they wanted to come. They obviously said no."

"Let's work on you and pray for them. Maybe if they see you change and see you are happy…"

"But I am happy! I am happier than I was in November. Sure, there's a lot more drama in my life now, but I am happy," I say.

"Is it a real happy, or have you just numbed yourself to the bad and are focusing on the pleasure? It's called 'sin for a season'. But the season will always come to an end. I want you to be really happy. True joy. Free from addictions."

"I'm not on drugs."

"Yet you're still addicted."

"I can handle it."

"That's what all addicts say." She pulls up to my front door. "I love you, Cozy. And it's real love with no reference to lust. There is a huge difference."

She thinks I'm addicted to sex? I guess that's a better option. I'll let her think it.

"Do you need me to pick you up in the morning?" she asks.

"No, Chris will. Thanks for taking me. I'll see you tomorrow."

I step inside and climb into bed. I kick my shoes off and don't bother to shower or change. I'm emotionally exhausted.

Chapter
THIRTY-NINE

"GOOD MORNING, BEAUTIFUL," he greets me at the door. "Good morning to you too, Cozy."

"Nice, Chris," my mom yells from the kitchen. "Thank you, but I know what I look like in the morning."

"Cute. You just made her day." I kiss him. "Bye, Mom. Love you!"

His truck is nice and warm.

"How was church last night?"

"Conflicting."

"I can imagine. People like us don't belong there."

"I want to. I feel good there."

"I can make you feel good." He puts his hand on my knee.

"You make me feel too good." I put his hand back on the steering wheel. "Watch it. I can't skip any more school."

"You just want to see your other boyfriend in art class. What's his name? Dave?"

"Oh yeah, let me make sure my makeup looks good. Do you have a mint?"

"You look beautiful, and no, I don't have a mint, only minty teeth. Here, you can kiss me to see." He leans over while we wait at the light.

"I like that. Thanks."

"Anytime."

"Are we picking up Hilda?"

"Yes. The instructor yesterday asked me about her. Are you willing to let her go?"

"I own her."

"So that's a no?"

"Why are you asking me this? She's mine," I growl out. It even scares me.

"I just thought she would have a normal life without us. Isn't that what you want for her?"

"Is that why you got him to come over? Is that the real reason he was training us? To get close to Hilda? To keep her away from me?"

"Do you love her enough to let her go?"

The thought angers me. I'm not so attached to her that I would choose her over Chris, but, "She's mine and you're being manipulative. Stop it!"

"It's not love. She's your pet."

"Fine. Yes. She's my pet," I snap.

I know it's selfish. I'll let her sleep with anyone, but she's mine.

"And I thought I had issues. What do you see me as?"

"You're different." I look at my promise ring. "I belong to you."

"So you're *my* pet?" he asks.

"I'll let you pet me, sure."

"You're mine, and I will do what I want with you," he demands.

"You make me melt."

"You better figure out what you want with Hilda. Either let her go, or let her kill. You can't string her along."

"Where is this coming from? Don't you want her?"

"I have no feelings for her, Cosette. To me, she's only a victim that survived. I like her. I'll hang out with her. I'll use her, but there's no depth there. I'm bound to you. I can't live without you. I can live without her. Is that how you feel about her?"

"No."

"Then why waste her time?"

"I told her she can date him. She said no, she's dating me," I say.

"There's something strange there."

"Well, Chris, she obsessed over you enough to torture me for months. Maybe she's getting to be like that with me. That instructor was a cute guy, and I know she thought so too, but she won't budge."

"Do you think she'll start bullying me to keep you? Should I watch my back?" Chris jested.

"Funny. She wanted you first. I think you'll be okay. It makes me feel better to have my craziness around her. I'll let her leash out enough to see where she goes."

"HI, GUYS." HILDA crawls into the truck to kiss me then crawls over me to kiss Chris. Her beautiful body is displayed across my lap. I run my hands up and down her back.

"Mine," I whisper to Chris.

"Alright, Hilda, you're making it hard for Cozy to concentrate. She has to get to art class. She has a new boyfriend in there."

She gives me a jealous look.

"Not hardly." I touch her face. "You are so beautiful today."

She gives me little kisses.

"Thanks," she whispers on my lips.

This girl knows how to work me.

"Alright, you two. We're almost there and you haven't even buckled up yet."

"Why bother now?" Her hands stroke my hair down to my lap. She runs her hand up my thigh. "Just remember this when you get to art. We should be enough for you."

It's overwhelming the heat that's running through my body. Chris parks the truck, and we play out there for a few minutes.

The bell rings.

"Great, thanks girls. Now that you got me all turned on, I'm late for class. You go on in. I have to sit out here and think about dead dogs or something."

We giggle. "Okay. Have fun."

FOR LUNCH, I give my fries to Chris, but I still snack off them. I'm hungry for some reason.

"Hey, guys. What's up?" Mattie sits.

"We're laughing about Rose tripping and bumping her cheek on a bathroom stall," Shelby says.

"Now you need blush on the other side to even you out." I laugh at Rose.

"Funny, Cosette. Instead of blush, I think I need...." Rose stops mid-sentence. I feel someone standing behind me.

Three 8x10 photos of a bloody crime scene are dropped in front of me.

"Oh my God!" Mattie covers her mouth, gets up, and walks away. The sisters follow.

"Leave!" Officer Crance snaps at Rose and Decker.

"Fucking psycho, Chris." Decker pulls Rose away.

"Hilda and Chris, would you give us some privacy?" she asks.

"They can stay. I didn't do this," I say calmly.

With one glare from her, they get up and go.

"Come on, Hilda, we'll leave. We know she didn't do this." Chris attests to my innocence even though he was there helping me create the scene.

"I DIDN'T WANT to see you for a few weeks." Officer Crance sits down across from me.

"I guess you missed me?" I stare at the pictures. I'm trying not to smile.

"Don't be a smartass to me," she warns.

"What do you want from me? Did the killer leave any clues? Who is he?" I inspect how clear the photos are. I'm careful not to let the rest of the lunchroom see.

"He was a drug dealer."

"He looks like an ordinary guy."

"Where were you Saturday?"

"I was at the convention center."

"I heard. A few officers from my precinct were there. You're quickly becoming a local celebrity. And with you and Hilda together, you're like a power couple." She slams her hand down, covering the picture. "But don't let it go to your head."

"I never wanted this!" I silently yell.

"Well you got it! And now that you have it, you better watch out. You're putting up red flags everywhere. I said I didn't want to see you for a few weeks."

"What do you want from me?" I snarl at her. "He's dead. You should be happy."

"I'm not happy if I have to start looking for a new serial killer."

"Well, then maybe your killer will visit other towns."

She covers her face and rubs hard in frustration.

With her hands still covering her mouth she whispers. "You know what *I* want. I know what *you* need. If you don't follow the rules, I cannot help you."

I cover up my mouth and whisper, "There is no trace of me in these pictures. And I know there will not be a speck of me at the scene. So what is your excuse for coming here? You're making me out to be a suspect when I'm not even linked to this. And since it's out in the open between us, am I supposed to wait for your signal? I have to be in the mood. And you showing me these pictures is not helping my patience." I nervously shift.

"You better learn to control yourself. Lack of control and cockiness leads to mistakes and prison."

"I won't go to prison," I say.

"Why? Because your friends will lie and cover for you? You better protect them by protecting yourself. They can go to jail for covering for you."

"Fine. I'll visit another town for a while. Then will you tell me who's next?"

She gathers up the photos, frustrated.

"Who's next, Jenny? And what is your excuse for being here and showing my friends your artwork?"

"Just tell them it's an ongoing investigation." Sliding the pictures in an envelope, she sighs. "By the way, congratulations on the hero's welcome at the show on Saturday. I heard you got a few sponsorship offers."

"Yeah, and I secretly got a military offer for after graduation."

"You might want to take them up on that before I have to catch you." She smiles at me.

"So there is no trace of me, huh?" Arrogant, I know Chris and I were careful.

"No. You did very well, but I can tell it was you. Aside from the Valentine's Day woman, you kill them all the same. Always in the throat."

"Not really. My first one I didn't. Actually, it wasn't until my fifth that I started with the throat." I casually fold my hands and wait for a reaction.

She stares at me and squints, trying to read me.

I see fear, disgust, and a twinkle of satisfaction in her eyes. She knows I'm telling her the truth, and I bet she's glad she found me.

"I have to get back to the station." She stands. The lunchroom quiets down. She notices but doesn't react. I hold out my hand to shake hers goodbye. She grabs it and pulls me in. "How about a hug? I'll be like your big sister."

"Smart."

She hands me the envelope. "You protect these, if you want to stay innocent."

"I really want them, but I can't get sloppy." I hand them back to her.

"Good. Don't call me. I'll call you." She walks away and I sit again.

MY TABLE IS noticeably vacant. I don't blame my friends for not wanting to come back, especially Mattie. It's one thing to know what I did. It's another to see it in full color.

Dave from art class comes up to me. "I've never seen this table so empty. Why did the popo come?"

"I have issues, Dave." I start eating my cold nuggets.

"That's obvious. Are you in trouble?" He sits.

"No. She just had some questions. You left art quickly today."

"Doctor's appointment. So, how was your weekend?" he asks.

"Conflicting. How was yours?"

"Mine was uneventful," he says. "Why was yours conflicting?"

"There's that verse in the Bible that says 'I do what I don't want' or something like that."

"Yeah, I know that one."

"That's how I feel. Conflicted." I look around but Chris and Hilda are still out. I'm not happy about them not being here for me.

"Well how bad is your confliction?"

I bite my lip.

"Is this where you say 'I'd tell you but then I'd have to kill you'?" he asks.

I nod my head.

"Wow. Well what about Chris? He seems like a good guy. He can help you. Can't he?"

I don't answer. Because it would be a resounding no!

"You have control over him too, don't you?"

No answer.

"Is there anyone you don't control?"

"You," I say with all honesty.

"You could control me easily. The fact that you haven't kind of impresses me. But that's kind of just as manipulative. Knowing you have the power but choose not to use it."

"You read too many comic books." I roll my eyes at him.

"You don't read enough. Every superhero has their weakness. Everyone has an enemy and is conflicted."

"I'm no superhero, Dave."

"No, you're a murderer."

I drop my chicken. He jumps out of his chair. "I'm sorry!"

"Sit down and shut up. I'm not going to hurt you. It was an accident," I say, picking my food back up.

He sits down, guarded and shaking.

"See? You have control," he says.

"Normal, please." I look around the lunchroom. Everyone is hiding the fact that they're staring at my table, trying to listen to our conversation.

"Sorry," Dave says.

"Relax." I pat his hand. "It's okay. Will it make you feel better if

I swear to you that I won't hurt you?"

His eyebrows raise.

"How about this? You be honest with me, even when it seems like I will hate hearing it, and I promise I won't hurt you. I promise."

"What if you don't like what I have to say?"

"I promise. Do you want to make it a blood covenant?"

His worried eyes look like they're about to water.

"I'm just kidding, Dave."

He grabs my arm and sees my slit from my new knife. "*Are* you kidding? What was this promise for?"

"I was just testing out a new knife. I like them duller. I want to feel the pain," I say, inspecting the razor thin line.

"You scare me, Cosette."

"You of all people shouldn't be scared of me. I feel obligated to keep you safe. I don't know why, but I won't hurt you."

"You still scare me. Okay, I promise to tell you the truth. You promise not to cut or maim me."

"Deal." I can't resist flirting just a little. I look him in the eyes and say, "Should we kiss on it?"

"I would love to, but I'm afraid of Hilda and Chris too. They'll be back any second."

"Good answer." I kiss him anyway. He isn't very good at it, so I take a bit longer. I guess I'll have to train him a little.

"Ms. Hugo." Ms. Lazelle calls me out for the PDA.

"What?" I snap.

She wags her finger 'no'.

"You're controlling, Cozy. Very controlling," Dave whispers. "Now that the cop is gone, do you want me to stay with you?"

"For your reputation's sake, you might want to leave."

"I'm a nerd, Cosette. I have no reputation."

"You're not a nerd."

"Not after a kiss like that." He pats my back and leaves. "I hope you feel better."

I eat the rest of my lunch with everyone staring. Carla and Sarah are staring too. I squint, giving them an evil eye while smiling deviously at them. They quickly turn away.

A few minutes later Hilda and Chris come in.

"Where were you guys?" I ask as I stand to greet them.

"We were in the parking lot relieving some pressure," he says.

I looked at her freshly applied lip gloss.

I was getting the third degree from Jenny while he was outside fooling around? Oh, hell no!

"So, Hilda, how about we get your first one tonight?" I ask her while glaring at Chris.

She squeals. "Thank you, thank you, thank you!" She hugs me, and I kiss her while looking at Chris.

"Hummm. Tastes familiar."

Scared, she looks away.

"You manipulative bitch." He grabs my arm.

"She's mine."

"Cozy..." he warns.

"Five minutes. You couldn't wait five minutes!" I quietly yell at him. "Do you have any idea what I just went through?"

I grab Hilda's arm and pull her out of the lunchroom. "Come on."

He could care less about Hilda. I might've let her go to Andre. But he just tightened her leash.

Chapter FORTY

I SHIFT THE curtain to watch Chris leave, thankful that he drove Hilda and me to my home. I'm still upset at him, and he's mad at me, and now I have to explain to Hilda. As soon as he's out of the neighborhood, I plop on the couch and confess to her.

"Hilda, I have to tell you something."

"Are you breaking up with me?"

"What? No. Not unless you want to go. I don't want to prevent you from having a normal life, and being with me is not normal. It's not fair to you."

"I'm sorry about today." She dips her head.

"That's what I wanted to talk to you about. I was pissed. I was mad that you were out there with him while I was getting the third degree from Jenny. Then I sat there waiting for you guys. When I offered what I did, I did it out of anger. I was using you to get back at Chris.

"And I should be more careful about leading you down this road. Once you go, you can never get back. Sure, you may stop, but the damage you do is permanent. It was wrong for me to use you."

"Why would you tell me that?"

"I could have not told you. But this is a horrific thing you want, and I really don't want you to do it. I shouldn't have offered, but now that I did, I won't go back on my word. I just wanted you to know the reason behind it. I know you two have been together without me, and I shouldn't have gotten so mad."

"Is Chris coming back?"

"I don't know. Hopefully after gymnastics. Why?"

"I think you should apologize to him. If you don't want me to do it tonight, we don't have to."

A rush of relief comes over me. "Oh, Hilda, thank you so much. I am so sorry. I am so sorry. I just want you to fully understand and not be tricked into it."

"I just want to make you happy."

"Why? I don't understand you." I sink low in the couch. "It's not like you were attracted to me before all of this. Why do you care what I feel? I'm cruel and scheming. I chopped someone up into fifteen pieces. Think about that. What redeeming qualities do I have?"

"Holy shit! You did what?"

There's a scared and disgusted look on her face. I'm glad. I want her to look at me the way I deserve to be looked at.

"I told you. It's a horrific thing you want to do. Once it's done, you can *ne-ver* take it back. I don't want you to do it. I can't put you through that. I want you to have a better life."

"I'll wait if you want. But this is what I want," she states.

"I just don't want to bring you down to my level. We should be building each other up. Encouraging each other to do better."

"Is that why you asked if I wanted to go out with the instructor?"

"He really likes you," I say.

"He was hot too." She smiles. "Would you go out with him?"

"If you want him, he's all yours. I'll keep my hands off. Normal couples don't share. Normal couples are jealous when someone stares too long."

"I can't." She presses in close to me. "I just can't let you go. I know what we're doing is not right. I know it's not normal, but I need you."

"Don't you think it's a coping mechanism for you to deal with the rape and capture? What happens when you're over it? When you're healed? Then you're gonna hate me."

"I'm here by choice. And I stopped crying about that a week ago, which doesn't seem right to me. But I don't remember much of it anyway."

"I assume you blanked it out of your mind."

"I was drugged up. He would drug me up then rape me. I don't understand why he would have used the drugs. I was glad to have them. I would pass out then wake up sore and bruised. I don't remember a single event. Has Chris said anything about it?"

My heart sinks. "No, why would he?"

"Because it was his uncle, and his other uncle, and his cousin. Cosette, do you think he's leading you on just to make you fall? You killed three people in his family. I know that if someone did that to me, I would slowly ruin their life. I would work my way deep into their trust just to screw them over. Then I would tell them: It's because you killed my family that I'm doing this to you."

She's scaring me.

I don't want to think of him like that. I already felt his betrayal when I was tied up in the van. Everything he told Tear about me still churns deep inside. It hurts. I hurt. I know why he did it then, but did he do it just to prolong this?

No! No I can't think of him doing that to me. He's perfect. He's my perfect mate, and I love him.

My heart is racing. I need to see him now! I need to call him and make sure he's coming over. "I, uh, I think I need to text him."

She leans over to me and slowly strokes my hair. "No, let him practice. It's okay, Cozy. You have me. You own me. I can never leave you."

She puts my phone on the coffee table and smiles seductively. This girl is so beautiful. She gives me small soft kisses down my neck. I felt better, relaxed.

"Lay back. Let me make you feel good," she says pulling off my shirt.

I close my eyes and enjoy.

6:15 ROLLS AROUND, and Chris is knocking on my door. I'm glad to see him, but I have a slight apprehension. He's not too happy to see us.

"Did you girls make your plans yet? Do you have a victim lined up?" Chris asks.

She hugs him and pulls him inside. "We decided not to do it, at least not yet."

He pulls her into his arms, breathing a sigh of relief. "Oh, thank you so much. Thank you. I was so worried."

I try to apologize. "Chris, I'm sorry. I was wrong for yelling at you."

He says nothing and gives me a kiss. It feels cold. "So what did Officer Jenny say?"

"Cozy, did you do it?" Hilda asks as we make our way back to the couch.

"If you don't ask any questions, I won't have to lie."

"I'll take that as a yes." She smiles.

"I don't want to discuss this. Let's go somewhere and have some fun," I say.

Chris takes us across the river to Louisville to Gattiland for the pizza buffet and games. He takes the long way there and the long way back as if he's on another mission from his dad.

I beat them both at bowling but get slammed in air hockey.

It's a good night, but I can feel the tension from Chris. Hilda keeps on holding and touching me to make me feel better. Chris doesn't.

I need to make this right. Once he takes her home, I need to truly apologize.

WE GIVE HILDA our goodbye kisses and leave her home. He doesn't say a word to me. He drives me to his house.

"Let's go." He demands me to follow him inside.

We get up to his room, and he sits me on his bed. He rolls his desk chair over and sits on it to face me.

"Okay, Cosette. At school today, you bitching and moaning about Hilda and I having fun? What kind of shit was that?" His cold stare drills into me.

"I'm so sorry. That wasn't fair of me."

"No, it wasn't. And if you want her, then you're gonna have to share. Otherwise you're the one cheating on me!"

I never thought of it that way. How selfish I am.

"I just... I'm sorry."

"We weren't doing anything major. We didn't know how long you would be, and..."

"Are you gonna hurt me?" I ask.

He rolls back. "What? Where did that come from?"

"Never mind. I think I should go." I stand up.

"No. You will not leave." He gets up and locks the door. "Now what are you talking about?" He sits me back on the bed.

I can't say anything. What if Hilda is right? What if he is slowly getting back at me for killing his family? Then of course, he'll deny it. Now there's always going be a doubt in my mind. I'm scared. I am really scared to lose him. But if it's the Chris from the van, then I never had him.

I'm scared.

"Cosette. What is this about?" He waves his hands in front of my face, getting my attention.

"I'm sorry. I love you, Chris. I never want to hurt you or be the reason you're upset. My body and everything about me aches for you. I can't live without you. I'm sorry."

"You're talking suicidal. Please tell me what's going on."

"I'm not crazy," I say.

"Yes, you are. But you're my kind of crazy. What's going on?"

"In the van, you..."

"You know I didn't mean any of that. You know why I had to do that," he says.

"There's some truth to it though. You don't trust me."

He sits on the bed next to me. He faces me and holds my hands, his face distraught. The tears are starting to well up. "Baby, I don't know where this is coming from, but I will give up my life for you. I live to be near you. When I am away from you, all I can do is think about you. When I am next to you, I'm fearful of when we're apart."

He holds my ring finger up. "I gave this to you for a reason. Remember when you gave yourself to me? You became my obsession. I will give you everything because I love you. I live to please you. How many other boyfriends would go to the lengths that I have to make you happy? I love you for who you are. I love you for who you will become. I will never try to change you. I will support you in everything. I will protect you. I will kill for you. I will never leave you." He holds my face. "And you will never leave me."

I sit there staring into his watering eyes. To have someone love you so much is more than what most girls dream of. His love is deeper than any doubt I could ever have.

I look at my ring then back to him. "I love you. I give you everything, till death do us part. All that I am and all that I will be belong to you."

"I don't know what more I can do, Cozy. You must believe me," he pleads.

"I was just thinking of the van and how I took Pen and Dickie from you and how I was so selfish with Hilda and not letting you have your way with her. I'm a horrible person and a more horrible girlfriend."

"Pen and Dickie meant a lot to me. I knew they would get killed someday. Just like I know you and I will most likely have a violent end too. It's just our way of life. And with me, that's the kind of life you have to look forward to. I don't care that you killed them."

"I'm so sorry. I just had some doubts."

"Do you doubt yourself? Am I still the one, or are you torn between me and Hilda?"

"What I feel for her is a drop to what I feel for you. I think its lust for her and maybe a bit of possessiveness. Not because I'm jealous, but because I own her. I tried to let her go though. I'm sure she's using me to cope with her rape, even if she doesn't know it. But the girl is beautiful. I don't mind being used. You don't feel the same, do you?"

"She's only a warm body to me. I would kill her just as easy as I would screw her."

"Please don't kill her. I like her."

"I'll let you keep your pets. If you do, you have to share, same with everyone else. That includes Rose and Decker and Mattie, if you want."

"Mattie is off limits. I will kill anyone who tries to touch her. Mattie is completely off limits. I feel as strong about that as I do about you. I will rip someone to shreds in broad daylight if they go after her."

"I won't try, don't worry. I respect her too much. So, now what?"

"We have some making up to do." I stand up and get undressed.

"I don't know... you've been a very bad girl." He takes his belt off.

I like that. It's going to be a good night walking the fine line between pleasure and pain.

Chapter FORTY-ONE

TUESDAY MORNING, I'M slow to move. Chris comes to pick me up. He helps me in the truck. "I think I went a little too far last night." He buckles me in.

"I'm fine. Just get me to school."

"Hold on. Give me your keys." I obey.

He runs inside my apartment and brings out the scarf I made my mom in art. It actually matches my blouse well.

"Here, and you need to cover up a little more. And keep your sleeves down." He points out the strap marks on my wrists.

"How are you?" I ask.

"Not as bad as you. I'm sorry." His eyes are remorseful.

"Don't you dare apologize. If you apologize, then that makes it mean nothing." I raise my eyebrow and bite my lip. "I will deal with these aftereffects every time if that's the type of night I get."

He shakes his head. "That was once in a great while. I can't hurt you like that every time. It will numb you, and we have to prevent that."

I wrap the scarf around my neck and spread it wide. I tuck in the end so that it's secure. It hides every bruise. The artwork on my scarf is perfectly displayed on my neck.

"I'm curious to know what happened to you that made you like this." He drives on to school.

"Some deep-seated need for violence? I don't know. I don't remember much except that my childhood was perfect until Victor died. I mean, my dad loved him more, but I guess that's because Victor's male," I say.

"Maybe you blocked it out. This behavior is not normal."

"Thanks a lot."

"You know what I mean."

"I know, Chris. That's why I'm glad I have you."

"Gives a whole new meaning of 'till death do us part'."

"Funny. If you get carried away and accidentally kill me, you have my permission to take me to Decker and have me cooked," I say.

"Speaking of Decker..."

"I don't like the sound of that."

"He gave me a call earlier. He is really freaked out about those pictures he saw."

"I'm sure. They were beautiful. Mattie hasn't talked to me since. I'm sure they freaked her out too," I say.

"Decker is freaked out, but curious."

"No. Hell no. If we're not going to let Hilda do it, we certainly won't let Decker do it."

"He doesn't want to kill anyone, Cozy. He's just curious."

"He'll get to see our next one when his uncle gets him. And it will have to be soon if we don't stop talking about this. So stop. Jenny says we should lay low," I warn.

"I know. I don't really care what she says, but I think we'll have to follow her orders for now."

"I have to heal anyway." I shift my achy body.

AS I WALK into art, Dave comes to greet me. He can tell I'm walking a bit slower even though I'm trying to hide it.

Quietly he asks, "What happened?"

"If you don't ask the question, I won't have to lie."

"Did you kill someone else?" His eyes widen.

"What makes you think that I would *ever* confess to something like that? You act like it's the equivalent of asking if I swiped a pen from Mrs. Iris."

"I wouldn't tell anyone. Is that why the popo was here?"

"Don't you have a fruit basket to draw?"

"Cosette?"

"Fine. Yes, I killed someone. I've killed two more since I've been back and I killed ten more before them. Is that what you want to hear?" I whisper.

"Uh, no." Dave is stunned.

"I won't tell you anything. I feel obligated to keep you safe. Don't make me change my mind."

"Then what happened?" he prods.

"Sex, that's what happened." I unbutton my top two buttons to give him a glimpse. "If you think you can handle a girl like me then keep asking those questions."

His eyebrows wrinkle in disbelief. "Are you okay?"

"More than okay." I smile, remembering. "Now stop asking!"

He picks up his pad and starts drawing. I button back up in case anyone else tries to sneak a peek. Of course, now most kids stay away completely.

"Dave, I'm sorry," I say.

"For what?"

"I'm sorry for snapping at you. You're kind of getting a crash course on all things Cozy, and it's not fair. Thanks for being one of my normal friends. I really am okay."

"Cosette Hugo!" Mrs. Iris yells from her desk.

"Yes, Mrs. Iris?" I yell from mine.

"Are you wearing the scarf you made for the competition?" She beams.

"I'm wearing my mom's Christmas present that you took and used for the competition without my permission. Yes, this is the scarf," I sarcastically retort.

"Please, may we see it? Nina here would like to do a silk painting."

"I'll help her, sure." I sit and holler back. Nina stands next to Mrs. Iris, not wanting to come to my table. Can't blame her.

"Come here please," Mrs. Iris asks.

I look to Dave.

He coyly shakes his head no.

"I won't take it off," I whisper to him. I walk over to her desk. "See, Nina?"

"Take it off so she can see the whole piece. You did such a good job."

"Don't you have a picture of it somewhere?" I ask kindly, trying not to get upset.

She reaches up at it. "Just take it off, and let her see."

I step back.

She gets mad and reaches up at me again. "Cosette. Take it off!"

"If you try to touch it, I will strangle you with it," I quietly growl.

Nina slithers away from us.

Mrs. Iris picks up her desk phone and calls security. I walk back to my desk to gather my things.

"What happened?" Dave asks.

"I think I'm about to get arrested for threatening a teacher." I sit and wait.

Sure enough, the rental cops show up. For some reason, they decide to get rough and push me across the desk to handcuff me. The shocked expressions on the other students' faces say that they consider it going too far, but I don't mind.

Dave stands in shock. I smile. They pick me up, but before they can walk me out, Mrs. Iris comes and grabs the scarf. "For evidence."

"You're a bitch," I say loud and clear.

"And you're suspen..." She pulls it off threatening suspension but stops when she sees the bruising on my neck. "Oh my god, Cosette, I didn't know. I am so sorry."

I tug on my handcuffs. "Just arrest me. Get me away from her." They walk me out the door.

Dave grabs my book bag and snags my scarf from Mrs. Iris who stands humiliated. He runs out following me.

I sit in Mr. Peeler's waiting chairs next to Dave for over an hour. The principal does this on purpose.

"Why are you still here?" I ask Dave.

"I'm afraid to leave."

I laugh out loud. "I don't think you carrying my stuff should get you in this much trouble."

"My mom's gonna kill me. Oh, sorry." He apologizes for the kill comment.

"I think your biggest issue is being friends with me. You might want to figure out how to explain that to your mom first."

Officer Crance walks in. She stops in front of me and shakes her head.

"This explains the hour wait." I sheepishly smile at her.

"Get these off of her," she snaps at the rental cops.

They obey. She walks me into Peeler's office. "Principal Peeler?"

"Officer Crance, thank you for coming." He signals her to shut the door. "I have seen you talking frequently to Cosette, and I thought you needed to be called."

"I'm not sure why. She is helping me with an ongoing case. I'm not a social worker. And from what I hear, it was your teacher who overstepped her boundaries."

"She threatened that teacher."

"If it was any other student, I wouldn't be here. But you seem to be prejudiced against our town's hero. Is there a reason you need the law here for this?"

"She threatened a teacher."

"A teacher who was out of line. I might have to arrest both. Let me make a call to the captain and...."

"No, that will not be necessary." Peeler backs down.

"I have seen how Cosette is being treated at this school, and I'm concerned. Remember the mayor considers her a hero. And so do we on the force."

"I understand," Peeler says, trying to get a word in.

"You have your code of conduct for these types of instances. I don't see a reason to involve us."

"Fine then. Cosette, for threatening a teacher you are expelled."

"What? What!" I can feel the fury starting to burn. Jenny places her hand on my shoulder, calming me down.

"That's fine, Cosette." She whispers to me loud enough so that Peeler can hear. "You might be able to talk to the school board. You have to follow the rules, but so do the teachers. I just hope this doesn't get on the evening news. Come on, I'll walk you out."

Mr. Peeler calls Mrs. Iris to his office while Officer Crance walks me to my locker.

"OFFICER CRANCE, I'M sorry. I didn't do anything. She wanted me to take off my scarf just to show a student, but I didn't want to," I say.

"I can see why. Do you want to explain those?"

"No." I open my locker. "It's nothing bad. I didn't do anything bad. It's just embarrassing, and I don't want my mom to find out."

"Oh. Oh! I think I get it." She smiles and rolls her eyes. "You are twisted, but it explains a whole lot. Don't worry. You'll be back in school by Monday. Until then, put on some makeup and use your hair to hide those. I'm glad this is the reason I was called in."

"I told you I'd behave. I'll be anxiously waiting for your call. Especially now."

She nods. As we're walking to her cruiser, Peeler calls me back to the office over the school's PA system. Like the student-body needs to hear my name called again.

"Please come with me," I beg Jenny. "I think I need a witness."

As we walk back in, the bell rings and it's passing period. I have no scarf, no makeup on my neck, and I have a police escort to the principal's. It's another embarrassing walk.

Dave is gone. Mrs. Hurley, the secretary, smiles at me, letting me know he's okay.

We step into Mr. Peeler's office and close the door.

"Ms. Hugo, I am only putting you on suspension. You can return to school on Monday. I will have Mrs. Iris apologize before I ask for her resignation."

"What? No! You can't do that! She's a good teacher. I don't like what she did to me at Christmas, but I think you're making a big deal out of this. Suspend me, but don't fire her!"

"I had no idea you felt this way."

"How could you? You never ask or listen when we try to tell you anything." I pause to take a breather. I realize how rude I'm being to him. I need to calm down. "I'm sorry, Mr. Peeler, please don't do anything to Mrs. Iris. She's rude to me, but she's a good teacher. And as much as I hate, hate, hate politics and the media and the mayor, if you fire her, I'll have to call them all. Please, Mr. Peeler, you're making a big deal out of this."

"Do you need to be moved to another class?"

"Ughh! No! I just want to be left alone. Don't you get it? Just let me do my work, and leave me alone. Don't fire her, and don't bother me. Please."

He relents. I sign my suspension papers, and Officer Crance walks me out.

"COSETTE, I'M SORRY it went this way. But I'm impressed you stood up for her."

"Even though I hate her?"

"Even more impressive." She opens the back door of the cruiser to drive me home.

"I have to ride in the back?" I ask, looking at the kids pinned to the school window watching me.

"No, come on up." She closes the door and opens the front.

"Jenny? I think I need a name soon."

"You can't yet. The more you use it to satisfy your anger or whatever it is you have the need of then the more you'll depend on it like a drug. Learn other ways to cope. Don't you have any other outlets? Sports or anything?"

"I used to be a runner until I got shot. Now I have to wait until, I don't know when. I like being outdoors. We're going skiing this weekend at Paoli."

"That's good. Who's we?"

"My boyfriend Chris and girlfriend Hilda. Also Mattie. She's the one with the light brown wavy hair. The two redheads, Rose and Decker. And maybe a guy we met at the knife and gun show. He gave us a self-defense lesson on Sunday. He likes Hilda."

"How old is the guy?"

"Too old to be playing with high school girls, that's for sure!" I laugh, realizing that neither Hilda nor I had considered his age. "Kinda gross now that I think about it. Anyway, skiing is my birthday celebration. Chris rented a cabin."

"You all better behave."

"We're just skiing. I don't drink or do drugs."

"Oh no, you're perfect." She sniggers at me. "Still, happy birthday. I'm glad to hear you have something to look forward to. Please focus on that. I won't be giving you a name for a while. They need to clear out these last two cases before you make any new ones. And since I'm not a detective, I have to go where I'm assigned, so you make sure I know what's going on. Otherwise I can't protect you."

"I don't know why you're doing this, but thanks." We pull up to my home. My mom is there. "Crap. Hold on. I have to cover up."

"I'll go in with you. I suggest if you want to play rough that you invest in turtlenecks."

Jenny walks me in and explains my suspension to my mom, who is running late for a lunch date with John.

I get a hug, and she rushes off.

"She didn't even notice," I say to Jenny. "But not like she's noticing anything these days."

"Good. That's good for you. I'll leave. Please stay unnoticed. I'll call you later. Lay low. Take up yoga or something."

"Thanks." I give her a hug and walk her to her cruiser. The stupid yappy neighbor dog comes barking at us. Jenny pets Lily then drives away.

LILY'S OWNER STEPS outside to watch her. "Hi, Cosette."

"Hi." I forget his name.

"How are you doing? I'm glad you're back," he says.

"Thanks. I'm okay."

"I haven't seen your friend with the blue car around. I have seen the green car. But not the one with the blue car." He makes his way over to me. His red Target shirt is wrinkled like he just woke up from a nap.

"The blue car's Mattie. She has a new boyfriend. He's a high school senior also," I say, letting him know he was too old for Mattie anyway.

"Oh," Target responds, disappointed. "I don't have a chance anyway."

I sigh, debating whether I should give him a few pointers or not. Monty! That's his name! I decide to let him in on a few things. "Do you want some advice from a teenage girl?"

"Okay?" He's apprehensive.

"Stop smoking. It's gross. It makes your breath stink. It makes your clothes and everything stink. When you take a shower every day, scrub your hair super clean. Girls like to run their fingers through clean hair. Find a girl your own age. Otherwise, it's creepy. And get out of the house and do something besides play video games. Girls want guys with ambition.

"I am not saying it to be mean at all. I just think you could be a great guy if you did a few little things."

Monty just stands there. I'm not sure if he's insulted or not. He doesn't move.

"I'm sorry if I upset you. It's just the thoughts of a teenage girl." I try to blow off my cruelty.

He says nothing and turns back to his house.

Chapter FORTY-TWO

I SHUFFLE AROUND doing a bit cleaning and organizing the house. After about an hour, I end up on my hands and knees scrubbing the kitchen floor. I jump at the knock at my back door. It's my neighbor Monty, showered and changed.

I open the door and smile. "You look good. You clean up nice. I'm sorry I insulted you."

"No, it's cool. I just wanted to tell you thanks. Teenage girls are always brutally honest."

"Sorry about that. So are you going out? Do you have a date?"

"No," he responds in a pathetic way. I doubt it was intentional.

"So you got all cleaned up for nothing?"

"I don't have anyone to go out with," he says.

"I have an idea. Take Lily to the pet store and buy her a toy. Get her groomed and everything. Girls like guys who are nice to animals. Use her to pick up a date. It happens in the movies all the time. If that doesn't work, come on back, and I'll try to help."

"Thanks." He starts to walk out.

"Here." I dig in my school bag. "Here's some gum. Chew on this and quit smoking. Second hand smoke is animal cruelty."

"Thanks." He takes the gum and walks out the front door just as Mattie pulls up. He waves at her and heads to his apartment.

SHE JUMPS OUT of her car and runs inside to me. "Please, please tell me you weren't just with him. I will puke more than I ever have before."

"I was and he was awesome!" I press her against the wall. "But he's mine. You can't try him out!"

The look of disgust on Mattie's face is priceless.

"Please, Mattie. I'm not that much of a whore! I have standards." I laugh and walk to the couch.

She breathes a sigh of relief.

She sits on the loveseat. "I heard you got suspended."

"I told Mrs. Iris I would strangle her with my scarf if she tried to take it."

"And she still did. I also heard that you saved her job."

"I'm a murderer, not a bitch."

"Don't be flippant about it, Coz. It's hard for me. Try to respect me."

"I'm so sorry. I know better."

"Telly and I won't be able to go skiing with you guys this weekend."

"You decided I'm too sick to be around? It's going to be a regular old ski trip. No sex, no violence. I promise."

"Do you realize how bad that sounds that you have to promise me that?" She's getting upset. "Do you have any idea what it was like for me to see those pictures? I know you did it! I don't know which ones they were, and I'm glad I don't. It's hard enough knowing what I already know without seeing it in full color." She puts her head in her hands. "Stupid, stupid girl."

My stomach tightens up. "I have nothing to say to you, Mattie. I'm so humiliated about it when I'm around you, but when I'm doing it, it feels so good. Mattie, it felt so good."

She starts crying. I'm hurting her really bad.

"Mattie, I don't want to be like this. Why couldn't you just let me die? He said you have all the power. Why did you use it? Why couldn't you just let me die? Look what I did because of it."

"Who said I have all the power?"

"I think I want you to leave," I say.

"I will never leave you. I will never join you, but I will never leave you." It's crushing her. She tries to hold it in. She bites her lip but then lets it out. "Damn it, Cozy! I hate what you've done! I think it's sick and demonic! I know who you've been with, and there's filth that surrounds you! You're covered, and you don't even see it!"

She drops to her knees in front of my feet. "Oh, Cozy, you've been lied to. You are listening to the wrong people. Is this who you want to be? This is your life. Are you who you want to be?" She quotes Switchfoot. It's a low blow.

"No." I quote them back. "I'm not alright. I know that I'm not right." I stop crying and look directly into her eyes. "Mattie, there's been more."

She stands and slaps my face. "Stop! Think about what you are going to say before you do that to me!"

I shut up.

"I am so mad at you right now, you stupid, stupid girl!" She covers her face, grits her teeth, and screams. She fists her hands so tight her knuckles are white.

She walks away before she swings again. "I love you, Cosette, and I will not abandon you! But don't you dare put me in a position that I have to choose! Don't you tell me any details! I know what goes on! God shows me what I need to know, and He protects me from what I shouldn't!

"I don't want to know how many you've killed! I don't care who you've slept with! I don't care if it's Chris or Rosy or Decker or Hilda or all of them at the same time! You are bringing Hell down on yourself! You are pulling them down with you! Because of you, they will join you in this shameful filth that you say you're humiliated about!

"Do you hate them that much to put them through something like this? Do you hate them so much that you want them to feel your pain, guilt, and humiliation?

"Think about this, Cosette." She stands in front of me, hovering. "Think about how you are right now, shamed and disgraced. This is what your friends have to look forward to because *you* can't help it. Because you think it feels good. I love you, Cosette. I love you enough to tell you that you fucked up."

"Faithful are the wounds of a friend?" I ask, holding my stinging cheek.

"No, this is more than that. You are doing these horrible things, and I stand back and do nothing. I want to help you and get you to stop, but it seems like you're getting away with everything. Several people know, and *I'll* be the bad guy if I say anything!

"Cosette, I promised you I wouldn't turn you in, and I won't. Only because I still hold out hope that you will straighten this shit out! But until then, if you want me around, you need to make an effort. We'll work on the sex stuff later. Let's just keep you from killing. Can we do that? Is it too much to ask that you stop killing for one week? Maybe we can go two, three weeks at a time? Wouldn't that be nice?" Sarcasm oozes out of each question. It's for her own benefit, I'm sure.

"I would like to have my Cosette back. My innocent, naïve, beautiful, sweet little Cosette back. I know she's in there. She was going to sacrifice a call to the mayor to save a teacher's job. So I know my sweetness is still in there."

"I'm still here," I cry.

"Not for long if you keep this up. Just try, for me." She reaches out her hand. I hold it as she sits next to me.

"I want to be normal just like you. I just don't feel things like you do."

"I know," she says. "I blame your dad."

"My dad? Why?"

"You're kidding, right? I don't want to badmouth the dead, but he was a horrible father to you. It's like you barely existed, and when Victor was home, it was like, 'Cozy who?'."

"I know he loved Victor more than me. Victor was his son. I'm a girl."

"That's right. You're *a* girl. He treated you like you weren't even his kid. Especially at Christmas. No father does that to his daughter. I wonder if that's why your victims were mostly males, and why you were afraid of females like Hilda. Of course now that problem is solved."

"I don't know. I don't know. I mean, who cares? Why does it

have to be some deep dark problem?"

"Because every day people don't act like this!" she yells, appalled at my ridiculous question. "I knew you were always off. Remember when we went camping and you accidentally hit that rabbit with the four-wheeler, and its leg broke? You felt more sorry for my dad having to put the rabbit out of its misery than the fact that you hurt the rabbit."

"I felt bad for the rabbit too. It's not like I hunted him down just to hurt him."

Mattie smiles big at me. I guess I'm supposed to get some meaning in that statement, but I don't.

"Cozy, I'm just saying that it was always in you, and once it was triggered, all hell broke loose. It'd be nice to find out where it came from so that maybe we can fix it. Fix it from the bottom up instead of masking the symptom."

I like that idea. Maybe it isn't totally my fault. "I know I have a choice, but it's a hard choice to make. To you it wouldn't be hard, right?"

"No questions about it, it wouldn't be hard. And I think Rosy and Hilda's fascination with you is temporary. If they really had a clue the effects you leave behind, not just with the crime scene, but their families, it would make a difference.

"Anyway, I need to calm down." She goes to the kitchen to get a drink. She grabs an icepack out of the freezer and unapologetically throws it to me. I place it on my cheek. "Speaking of families, the reason Telly and I aren't going skiing with you has nothing to do with what a freak you are."

"Really?" A rush of happiness and relief comes over me.

"I wish it was the reason. Maybe it'd help you, but no. Telly's little sister is having a "No Mo Chemo" party at St. Jude's Children's Hospital on Saturday. We have to drive down to Memphis, Tennessee. She's been there for months."

"Oh my god."

"This is a fifteen-year-old girl fighting for her life, and on Saturday, she gets to celebrate a victory. It might be good for you to see. When she comes home, maybe later on, you'll meet her. So anyway that's the real reason we can't go."

"I'm glad you get to go celebrate with her. That's awesome. Wow, what a strain on the family."

"They're a strong family."

"I'm glad you get to go. I'll be thinking of you guys."

"Okay, so I have to get to work, and I will see you later. Hopefully it will be Cosette I see and not this alter ego I don't know."

"Her name is Bonnie."

"What?"

"I call her Bonnie."

"You have a name for your other personality? You're not..."

"I don't have multiple personalities. I'm not insane."

"Yes, you are. It's too bad. You might have been better off diagnosed. I'm gonna come right after school before anyone else gets here and do some praying with you. We'll pray for a hedge of protection around you. You are gonna need it. We'll find my November Cozy." She stood up and gave me a hug. "I love you, Cozy. Say your prayers."

Chapter Forty-Three

AFTER MATTIE LEAVES, I finish the kitchen and am hot and sticky. This floor was disgusting. It's been two weeks without a mop; I'm grossed out. But now it's clean and smells fresh. Too bad I don't.

I get off my knees when someone knocks on the door. I look like a mess, but it's only Rose and the sisters.

"Hi, girls." I welcome them. "Hold on. Give me ten minutes. I stink and need a shower. When the kitchen floor dries, you all can help yourselves to a drink."

I hop in and out of the shower. I have my hair wrapped in a shower cap with a deep conditioner in it. "At least now I have time to do this," I say as I sit on the loveseat. "What's up?"

"We have to ask you something," Shelby says. She's solemn. They all are. They sit on the couch, quiet.

"You're scaring me." I stare at Shelby, trying to read her face.

"How many people?" she asks.

"Excuse me? You mean have I slept with?" The question takes

me by surprise. "I hope that's what you're asking because that's the only question I'll answer."

"Forget who our dad is. Please answer," Sierra begs.

"Are we counting male and females in this?" I ask sarcastically. "It's kind of a personal issue how many lovers I've had." I'm hoping my sarcasm eases the tension. It doesn't.

"Hilda says it's more than the kidnapper and truck driver," Shelby says.

Shit. What's Hilda doing discussing this with them? I wonder if she admitted to any part of the trucker's death. Rose already knows it was four. I wonder what she's told the sisters about the other two or if she's waiting for me to say.

I just sit there with my mouth shut.

"We aren't upset, Cosette. We just thought..."

"Thought what? That it's a casual topic? Have you two asked your dad any details of what he saw in that cellar? Or the cab of the truck?"

"Uh, no, we don't really talk to him about that stuff."

"Good, because you shouldn't. It's disgusting what I did. So what is it you're asking? Or I should say why? Why do you want to know? Why are you guys here? What did Hilda say exactly?"

"She wouldn't give any details."

That's good. She's too pretty to kill.

"We just asked, I just asked what she knew about those pictures that the officer brought in," Rose admits.

"What did she tell you?"

"That you were helping her with a new crime," Sierra says.

Funny way of putting it. Good job, Hilda.

"I am helping her. Those pictures you shouldn't have seen." I stand up, put my hands on my hips, and demand answers. "Okay, I'm getting a little frustrated dancing around here. So please, bluntly tell me what is going on. What do you all really want with me? If you're going to turn me in for something then tell me and do it. If not, then state your business."

"We want in," Shelby says.

"Hell no! Get out!" I walk to the door.

"We support you. We figured out a few things, and we want to help you." Sierra slides between me and the front door.

"You mean you think you know what's going on, and because of that, you want to volunteer to be accessories to murder."

"We can help you. I know everything my dad says and does. I know what's going on in the police station," Shelby says.

"I have a source. I don't need help." I walk away.

"You need alibis. You need a team. Shelby and I don't want to be there or touch anything gross or slimy, but we will help with planning or get away," Rose says.

I don't like this. I think I'd have rather them tell me that they can't be my friends anymore because of what I've done. But it seems they want to be closer. Like Mattie said, I'm fascinating, like a movie character.

"Nothing's going on. I don't need help. You all shouldn't be here."

"We just... we want..." Sierra's eyes light up.

"You want to stay good. Please be my good friends. Please don't cross this line. The more you all know, the more the black and white fades to gray, and the thinner the line is until you can't see that you've already gone too far past it. Believe me, you all get enough attention just by sticking with me. Imagine what it would be like to be me."

"I have." Sierra smiles.

I knew I'd have a problem with her. Rose is too squeamish. Shelby, I think, has her head on a bit less tilted than the rest of us. Sierra will need a little extra convincing.

"I want to help you." Sierra gets right up on me. She has no boundaries.

I'm pissed. They have no idea. "What the hell is wrong with you guys? Do you all realize what you are saying? This is real life. It isn't a TV mini-series. These are forever decisions here. These are human beings we're talking about. People with families and kids."

"Kids that are abused by their pedophile dads. Or drug addict aunts. Or rapists in alleys," Shelby says.

"Fuck!" I walk into the kitchen. Shelby comes after me.

I turn the water on in the sink and decide to rinse the conditioner out of my hair with the spray nozzle. It'll give me time to think.

"Cosette." She leans up to me.

"Get me a towel please." I send her away.

She runs to the bathroom and runs back with a towel. The hot water burns my scalp, so it gives me clarity. I wrap my head up in the towel and twist it tight, squeezing out the water.

"Cosette, Sierra and I figured it out. The one from Valentine's Day, and maybe the one after your birthday. You didn't flinch when you saw those pictures," Shelby says.

"And you think killing someone is a noble thing to support? Did you know that Mattie won't be skiing with us? She's going to a fifteen year old's No Mo Chemo party. That's a noble cause. The girl's a year younger than us. You should support fighters like her."

Shelby presses me against the cabinets. "Please, we all want to help you. We'll do whatever you want." She's shaking as she strokes my arms.

"Good. Go home." I hold her arms down.

"We won't leave you." She stays there, waiting.

"What did I do to make you act like this? Don't you know it can only turn out bad?"

She holds my hands and nervously leans in to kiss me.

I back away. "No, no, you're not like this, Shelby. What's going on?"

"But I need this." She pulls me in to kiss again.

"Why?" I push her away. "Why are you doing this?"

Rose and Sierra walk in. Shelby bites her lip holding back the truth.

"Why are you all here?" I ask Rose and Sierra.

"Curiosity," Sierra responds.

"Curiosity killed the cat," I snap.

"I want drama." Rose steps into me.

"My beautiful Rose. You think our sex-fests aren't drama enough?"

She smiles and hugs me. "I don't want to do anything. I just want in, and I wanna help you."

"You all act as if this is an ongoing thing. It's not. It's over. It's done."

"Well if it isn't, then we want in." Shelby puts her head on my shoulder. Though uncomfortable, she tries to be affectionate towards me. I think Shelby's reason for this is different from the others.

"How about we just drop this and continue like we have, so I won't have the guilt of dragging my friends into my hell?"

"What guilt?" Rose has no clue. "You're a hero!"

"I'm a murderer! And I will not have you all join me!"

"You need us to back you up." Sierra steps into me, knowing my reaction will be to hug her. Manipulative.

"You sisters haven't even slept with me, and now you want to kill with me?"

"We haven't slept with you yet..." Sierra glares at Shelby. Shelby obeys her little sister and kisses me. She's extremely awkward.

"Chris and I are a package deal." I lean away.

"Did he do that to you?" Shelby touches my bruised neck.

"Yes, but that's only between him and me. No one else gets that privilege. Rose is a package deal also."

"Sierra and I are still virgins." Shelby swallows hard.

"Well, then you sisters picked the wrong girl to kiss," I tease. It scares her a bit. It's good. I want to see fear coming from her. "Speaking of which, I think I hear my package coming." I look to Rose. She and Sierra go to open the front door.

I grab hold of Shelby and start kissing her, testing her to see how far she'll go. She's trying but holding back.

"I knew it." I pull away from her. "So are you going to tell me what's really going on, Shelby? Why are you doing this?"

"We want to help."

"Don't lie to me. They want some twisted adventure. Why are you here? You? I know you don't want me, so what desperation is driving you to kiss me, to want to kill with me?"

Scared stiff, her eyes stare into mine, watering. She says nothing.

"You think about it. I won't let you near me until I know the truth," I say, walking away from her. She stands in the kitchen wiping her eyes.

"Hey, psycho." Decker walks in. Chris and Hilda follow.

"You're late," I say, upset that Chris wasn't here to stop this ambush.

"I had to do something for my dad." Chris comes up and kisses my cheek.

"Do you have any idea what's going on?" I whisper.

"Yup. I know."

"What? You know?"

"They're figuring things out, Cozy. Your officer helped them with that. We were discussing it at lunch. You were busy getting suspended. They appreciate what you did for Mrs. Iris. They know how much you hate her, but you still did right by her. They know you're fair."

"I wasn't fair to my last victim."

"I thought we were." He holds me close. "I told them you're not doing anything, and even if you were, you wouldn't tell them. They said they can change your mind."

I huff. "I told them no. Did *you* tell them yes?"

"I didn't answer. It's all up to you. But think about the benefits we have with them. Just like me and Pen and Dickie." He raises his eyebrow waiting for my response.

I look at the group sitting there waiting for me to lead. Sierra is close to Rose who is being pulled in by a jealous Decker. Shelby's chatting with Hilda. I press in to Chris. "So because I was nice to one teacher, they want to join a serial killer?"

"Perception. It's all about perception. Think about it. It's all up to you."

"We can't do this to our friends, Chris."

"Meat, Bonnie. That's all. Accept their help or don't. I don't care what you do with them. The only one that matters to me out of the group is you. And only you. Take control of them. Let's play."

Chapter FORTY-FOUR

THE SECOND DAY of suspension is busy. I empty out all the closets. Between my stuff and my mom's, we'll have at least two trash bags full of clothes for the shelter. Mom has a lot of shoes. I line them up in front of her bed so she can sort them when she gets home. All of her outdated clothes I spread out on the bed for her to sort. Hopefully she'll get rid of all of them and go shopping.

Cleaning gives me time to think. I didn't say yes to everyone yesterday. I don't want their help. No, sorry, that's a lie. I want their help. I just don't want them to live with the consequences. And really, how bad would those consequences be if we're all together to help each other?

No, I shouldn't do that to them. I'm supposed to protect them and love them. Isn't it bad enough I'm having sex with some of them and they still want more? What happens when Shelby and Sierra lose their virginity to us? Will that satisfy them? It won't Sierra. I'm sure Shelby won't find us gratifying. She's terrified, but of what, I'm not sure.

I keep cleaning out my mom's closet as I clean out my mind. Mom has a few boxes stuffed with pictures and mementos. I find the playbill for the showing of *Les Miserables* she went to with my dad when they were in high school. It makes me cry. I hated him, but I loved him. I wish he had been more to me than what he was. Sure could use a father right now. I stuff it back in with the other junk. There are love letters folded in cute origami shapes with drawn hearts decorating them. I'd love to read them, but I doubt I could fold them back up to where mom wouldn't notice. And, I realize, I don't have a single love letter from Chris. I'll have to talk to him about that.

I RIFFLE THROUGH more of Mom's stuff. I'm totally being nosy. There are a few concert tickets, none of them for Barry Manilow though. One is for a three-day concert the spring before I was born. Wonder if I was conceived in a tent on some lawn somewhere? I laugh at the thought. I close it up and stack her stuff nice and neat. I like order.

Mattie texts me that she's on her way. I hadn't paid any attention to the time, but school is out already. Time flies when you're having fun. I get cleaned up and sit and wait for Mattie. She pulls into the neighborhood slowly. I can't see what she's looking at. As soon as she gets out her car, Target and his dog Lily make their way over to her.

She pets the dog, talks to Target for two minutes, points at something, and then comes to my door. Target cleans up Lily's poop then leaves.

"Ya wanna explain what that's about?" I ask, opening the door.

"He cleaned up nice, your neighbor guy. I still wouldn't touch him, but he cleaned up nice."

"I meant with you slowing down and stuff," I say.

"What have you been doing that you have a stalker?"

"Who's stalking me?"

"I think it's Sarah's brother," Mattie says.

"Shark? Is it a green car you saw?"

"Yeah. It's parked in the next neighborhood, but he's in the bushes. I told your neighbor about him and to come over and tell you if he sees the green car again. Especially since you two are great friends now."

"Oh, you're too funny. But thanks."

Mattie takes out her worn Bible. "Lesson time." She sits at my kitchen table while I start dinner preparations. I work while she teaches.

I like learning this stuff with her. She's so smart. To some it may seem useless, her teaching me, like a heart transplant to a death row inmate. But I know she doesn't see it as wasting time. And I want to learn. If there's a chance this will help me be humane, then I want it.

I know Chris and I are exactly alike in how we feel about certain things. I know Mattie is the complete opposite. I wanna know why.

"SO DID YOU learn anything?" Mattie asks as I spoon-feed her a taste of my lemon filling. "Mmmm, lemon meringue pie."

"I always learn something from you. How's Telly?" I ask.

"He's apprehensively happy. His sister has been going back and forth with chemo for years. I'm happy I get to go to her No Mo Chemo party. And speaking of going: I have to work, but Chris and Hilda said they'll be here this afternoon. I think they're waiting for me to leave."

"They're not much for Sunday school," I say as I separate the egg whites.

"Sunday school? But today's Thursday," she jokes. "Maybe they'll come tomorrow for our next Bible lesson."

"Can't. Friday we leave to go skiing."

SHE SMILES, SAYS nothing about Chris and Hilda and me spending the night in a ski cabin, and stands to leave. "Come here a second."

I meet her by the front door. She opens it and a cool breeze comes in. "Did you feel that?"

"Uh, yeah. Duh."

"That's the type of difference I feel when I come in here. A heaviness looms around you. I felt it at lunch without you there, and now it's here. I personally think it's the evil that surrounds you. It's spreading, like it's recruiting. Be careful, Cozy. Protect your friends. And I'm not sure what you all do when they come to visit. I doubt it's a Bible study, but whatever it is, they are coming to *you*. It's all about you. Don't you lead them down the wrong path. And please use protection if you all are..." she doesn't even want to finish the sentence. I don't blame her.

"I'll be careful," I say, happy that I told everyone that they couldn't join my murderous addiction.

"Good, because everyone is acting funny at lunch. I had to leave early. Just protect them. Their interest in you will fade, and if you lead them down somewhere bad, they will hate you." She starts to walk to her car then stops. She waits, looks up, and then runs back to hug me. "Be careful, Cozy." Her voice cracks.

I hug her back, troubled.

THE VIBRATION IN my pocket makes me jump. I wave at Mattie pulling out of the neighborhood. As I lock the front door, I answer the phone. "Hey, M&M. Whatcha doing?"

"Can I come there this weekend?" Mel's voice is shaky.

"You're always welcome. What's going on?"

"Pearl has to work all weekend, and there's a new client of hers I can't stand. He keeps eyeing me like I'm open for business. But she and Smudge have been fighting too."

"Why? Because of your mom?" I ask.

"Smudge ain't here when he should be. I can't be my sister's bodyguard. Shit goes down, we're fucked." Mel seems very scared, which is unusual for her.

"Are you being threatened?"

"Not really."

"Mel..."

"The dealer who works for the Brazilians keeps riding our ass about some missing rock that Bounce and Binge sa'posed ta sell. But no one knows where it's at since they's dead."

"Crap, alright. I'm going skiing this weekend. Why don't you two take off and come with us? We rented a cabin."

"Who's us? You, Barbie, and Ken?"

"And a few others," I say.

"One big doll house, huh?" Mel jokes.

"Something like that. We have plenty of room."

"I think I'll pass. I'll meet your friends some other time, not when I'll be stuck on a mountain with them," Mel says.

"I get it. Just let me know if you change your mind. Try to be careful. Go find some mace or a Taser or some kind of weapon. Keep it close at all times. If you have any problems, I'll come back and kill them for you."

"Whatever, Cookie. Just 'cause you gots one under your belt don't make you an expert."

"I have more than one. I'm thinking of starting a new career," I joke with her.

"Yeah, sounds good, Cook. I'll talk to ya later." Mel hangs up without any other pleasantries.

When I get back from skiing, I'm going to have to do a little bit of stalking to make sure she and Pearl are safe.

"LOOK AT LITTLE Miss Domestic," Chris says as he and Hilda come in. I'm kinda jumpy after Mattie telling me to be careful and Mel's phone call about the Brazilian threat.

"What have you been doing?" Hilda asks as she takes off her coat.

"I'm making chicken pot pie. What have *you* been doing?" I ask her, glaring at Chris. Hilda has a low cut t-shirt on and a noticeable bruise on her collarbone.

"Don't look at me," he says in his own defense.

"I called him, Andre, the instructor, for an extra lesson. And yeah, it hurt. I can't take pain like you can. But I did learn a cool move. I'll show you after you take off the apron. Although it's a cute new side to you," Hilda teases.

"Are you all are staying for dinner? You have to stay for dessert. I made lemon meringue," I say.

"Sounds great. Sure." Chris says.

"My mom will be home in about twenty minutes, and Hilda, I think your dad'll be here too."

I take off the apron and brace myself. "Okay, blondie. Let's see this new move Andre taught you! How far are you willing to go?"

"Wait. Knives? I don't want anyone totally losing control, Bonnie?" Chris holds out his hands.

Hilda takes out her knife. I take out mine. We give them to Chris.

"We can take this as far as you can. If you can," she taunts me.

"Alright, princess." I wink.

"Hold on. Let's make a wager," she says.

"Uh, okay, whatcha have in mind?"

"How about if I win, we plan my first? And I mean plan. I don't want to wait until attacked. I want my own."

I'm not liking this. "And if I win? You won't get a first, period."

"So technically, this is to the death?" Chris jokes.

"You better watch us closely. Don't let me go too far," I warn him.

"Me neither," Hilda sniggers. "Let's go."

Chris pulls the coffee table out of the way.

Hilda comes at me, and I swap her away. She comes to hit me again. I slap her, grab her hand, and push her back.

"Didn't your new boyfriend teach you anything?" I tease.

"It's coming," she warns.

She lunges at me. As I dodge her, she drops down, swiping my leg out from under me. I fall flat on my back. My breath's knocked out. I roll into her legs, knocking her down.

Then it becomes vicious. I know I'm hurting her, but she's fighting so hard. I don't want to lose the bet, and I'll do everything I can to win. Rage from our previous fights needs to be kept inside of me. I don't want to let it loose and really hurt her. She's pinned, but she jabs me in the stomach near my bullet wound and yanks my hair to where I have to roll off. It's dirty.

Unfortunately, I can play dirty too. I elbow her in her new collarbone bruise then grab her leg and yank it back. I know she's not as flexible as me. She screams and rolls out of it, but isn't fast enough to get out from under me. I have her pinned. She hits me hard several times. I might have a black eye after this.

Finally I hold her down, arms pinned over her head. This is where I usually lose control, but I don't, not today. I work hard on holding back. Then she looks up at me.

She has watery eyes, red and puffy. She's terrified, as if reliving the rape. And I'm the one hovering over her. I don't hit her in the face like Pen did, but I still see it.

"Why, Cozy?" she softly cries.

My heart drops. I hurt her. I hurt my princess. I thought I had myself under control, but I didn't. I loosen my grip on her hands and sit up a little. I'm so sorry. This has gone too far.

She folds her hands together and swings.

I black out.

BEEP. BEEP. BEEP.

The timer on the stove wakes me up. I sit up but fall back down. I'm dizzy. My skin burns over my eye.

"Don't worry, I got it. Let her rest." My mom calls from the kitchen, "Hilda, will you set the table?"

"Yes, ma'am," Hilda yells back. She's by my side. "Just rest a bit, Cozy. Our little self-defense lesson went a bit too far for you. You couldn't handle it." She touches my face.

"You played dirty," I whisper.

"I learned from the best to use the tools I got. I used them, and I won." She leans in, touches her lips to mine then whispers, "I... won."

"Shit," I say under my breath. Hilda giggles then goes to the kitchen to help my mom.

Chris comes over. "She got you good. Are you okay? Stay lying back. Keep the ice over your eye."

"I lost. I can't believe I lost."

"She played your emotions. It was smart. You should be happy that you still have emotions, that you're still human. If you weren't, she would've been wasted. You were right on the edge of turning Bonnie and going psycho on her."

"I lost. Do you know what that means?"

"It was going to happen eventually." Chris is flippant about Hilda's first kill. "At least now we have control over it. We can string her along a bit if you want. Tell her we're planning for the right one."

"No. Let's just find someone next weekend and get it over with. If we string her along, she'll go off on her own and do something stupid." I give in. She's fighting hard for it and if she's going to be with me, I might as well teach her a thing or two.

"We'll go up to Indy to find someone."

"Why Indy?" I ask.

"My state tournament is next Saturday up in Indy."

"And you think that's the best time to do it?" I take the ice off my eye.

He puts it back on. "Sure, I'll already be on cloud nine from winning state," he says puffing out his chest.

"Okay, Mr. Cocky. No humility there." I touch my eyelid. It's cold but not too sore. Hopefully, I won't bruise too bad. "When did John and my mom get home?"

"Right when we put you on the couch. We told her it was a self-defense lesson gone awry. She's fine with it. She's not fine with something you did with her clothes and shoes. I don't know what."

"Dinner!" John calls.

Hilda comes in and helps me sit up. She brushes my hair off my black eye and kisses me.

"Hilda, what are you doing?" I whisper. "Are you 'outing' our relationship? Isn't your dad going to freak?"

"Isn't your mom?" She giggles back.

"I think my mom is in denial."

"I'm not 'outing' us. There is nothing to out. I'm not a full lesbian. I'm just having fun." She pulls me to my feet, and we go to the kitchen.

I'm relieved and a little hurt. I thought our relationship was more. Fun is what I do with Rose. I guess I have to deal with this. And with her calling the instructor for a second lesson, it looks like she might be moving on. I wonder how John feels about his daughter dating older black guys. I know my dad would've freaked if I dated anyone out of high school. Hilda might have an easier time explaining me then Andre.

We all sit down.

I say grace.

"SO, COSETTE. YOU think maybe you girls might want to cool it on the self-defense thing?" John asks as he puts his napkin on his lap.

"Apparently I still need it," I joke.

"Besides, the instructor is cute," Hilda jokes.

"Are you sure you want to take on another boyfriend?" my mom asks her.

Hilda says nothing.

"I think that between Cosette and Chris you have enough, Hilda," John tells her.

"I, uh, we are just..." I mumble.

How can we answer that?

"We know about you girls. We understand, but we don't like it..."

"We don't like it at all," my mom interrupts John.

"But whatever it takes to help you two get through this, then that's..."

"So you're okay with it?" I ask, trying not to smile.

"Hell no! It's sick. It's a sin," my mom snaps.

"So is murder," I coldly say.

"That was self-defense," Hilda defends me.

"I'm sure I could have found a different way," I softly say.

"I'm glad you didn't. When it comes to people like that, there is no other way." John's words encourage me.

My mom agrees with him. "If you could have only punished them more..."

Great. I thought. Why not encourage Hilda by giving her an excuse?

We sit there not talking for a while. It's an odd silence.

CHRIS IS DONE eating. He didn't look up from his plate once.

"So when you three go skiing, are there going to be others with you?" John asks.

"We have a whole group going," I say.

"No drinking I hope. Hilda better not drink." He glares at his daughter.

"I don't drink and neither does Cozy," Chris says in the most polite tone I have ever heard him use. "I think Hilda will be fine with us." How uncomfortable he must feel sitting here. I feel bad for him.

"Good, no drinking. People do really stupid things when they drink," my mom says.

"Are we talking from experience?" John flashes a flirtatious grin.

"How do you think I got my two children?" She winks back.

"Gross, you two." I say.

"Cosette," John changes the conversation. "I see you are a bit OCD? The apartment looks great."

"I'm not OCD. I just can't stand disorder, which by the way, Mom, I took the liberty of cleaning out your closet also."

"OCD." Hilda nods to her dad.

"I saw," Mom snarls. "I'm not giving up those clothes."

"You need new, up-to-date, ones. John doesn't want to date a frumpy old lady," I tell her.

"Thanks a lot."

"I think your mom is beautiful," John says.

"That's because you haven't seen her in those clothes." I start cleaning the table. Everyone stands, stretches, and then helps me.

"That was a wonderful dinner. Thank you," John says.

"I hope you all saved room for pie. Mom, do you get to stay home?" I ask while carrying my perfect pie to the table.

"I'll have some, but I do have to work tonight. I'm covering K's shift so I can get off for Barry Manilow."

"Good trade," John says.

WHILE THE PARENTS sit in the living room, Chris and Hilda help me in the kitchen.

Hilda hugs me from behind. I slice the pie and give her two plates. "Are you okay?" she asks me.

"Besides my eye and ego?"

"Why the ego? I used what tools I had to work with. I used your emotions against you." She takes the slices to our parents in the living room.

"Dirty pool, my love," Chris says.

Hilda comes back and hugs me.

"You don't have to do this." I hold her back.

"Do what?"

"This. You don't have to do this, since there is no 'us'. Since you're just having fun, you don't have to... I don't want to..."

She interrupts me with a kiss. She kisses me passionately, not caring how close our parents are. "I'm still yours, Cosette. Sure we're not exclusive, but I don't want you to leave me."

"You confuse me."

"Are we exclusive? Are the three of us or even the five of us? If you want to define it, then yes, I want to be only yours. You own me." She rests her head on me, holding me close. "But you said you'd let me go. I don't want to leave, but if we're not exclusive, then..."

"Just don't bring anything back to us." Chris warns her. "We don't know this instructor."

"I won't. I don't know him well either. I haven't even touched him. Unless you want him to join?" She pulls away.

"Don't look at me. I don't touch men," Chris emphatically states.

"He's all yours. I'm okay with my man. I'm only with Decker when Chris and Rose are around; otherwise, I consider it cheating. Sounds dumb, huh? The rules I make up for myself."

"I'm glad. It protects us all," Chris says.

"Not doing it protects us all," I reply.

"Okay, Mattie," Hilda sarcastically sounds off. She kisses me and turns me back around. "We have dishes to finish. Besides, you can't tell me that Mattie and Telly haven't yet."

"You don't know her. She's perfect. She's saving herself."

"Sounds like you like her more than a friend." Hilda hands me a few more plates.

"There's nothing there."

"Chris, you should try her." Hilda tries to persuade him.

"No. I do what Cozy tells me to. If she says no, then it's no. Mattie's one person Cozy'll literally kill me over. I know my limits."

Chapter FORTY-FIVE

"HOW WAS YOUR night last night, you guys?" Rose asks as we wait in line to get on the ski lift.

"It was great. We went to the cabin after dinner and soaked in the hot tub since Chris was sore from his gymnastics meet on Thursday. Then we went inside, had fun, and fell asleep early."

"Speaking of early, Shelby knocked on my door at six this morning." Rose yawns.

"I know how long this perfection takes to get ready." Shelby waves her hand over Rose's head. I give a knowing glance to Hilda, who is the same way.

"Then Decker came and had coffee with my mom as they made fun of my outfit," Rose whines.

"Not just Decker," Sierra says. "We all think neon pink is a bit uh, pink."

"What?" Decker holds his hand to his ear. "I can't hear you. Rosy's outfit is too loud."

Rose slaps him as the chair lift scoops them up to the sky.

AFTER A FEW runs on the double diamond slope, Rose and Decker check in on Hilda, Chris, and me. I'm glad the three of us equally suck at skiing. Shelby and Sierra are average, and even though they try to help us, they can't.

"You guys can go off and have fun. You don't have to waste your whole day training us," I say.

"Good. We'll meet you all at lunch. Come on, Rose." Decker grabs her hand and whisks her away. The sisters run off too.

I wipe out several times. So does Hilda. On one run, our skis cross and we tumble together. We're laughing so hard we can't move. We wipe out so often that Chris has to escort us to the pro shop to get our bindings tightened.

At lunchtime, we all meet up. I'm so impressed with Rose and Decker. They're humble about how good they are.

After lunch, they both switch to snowboards. It's the coolest thing watching them. It's almost like a graceful dance the way they play off each other. He would cross her trail, grab her hands, and thrust her forward. Then he'd do a few jumps and rails. I almost don't want to go on any more runs. I just want to watch them. But Sierra and Shelby come to drag Chris, Hilda, and me up a run. Shelby and Hilda ride together on the lift. Chris, Sierra, and I ride way behind them.

Sierra's excited to ride up with Chris and me, but we agreed beforehand to keep it cool with her. She's too young to devastate. Even though she's fooled around with Rose in my kitchen, she's still a virgin, and we want to be careful.

Unfortunately, Sierra has no problem letting us know how she really feels. She sits between Chris and me. Shelby and Hilda are four chairs ahead, too far away to see anything. The lift stops, and we're dangling one hundred feet in the air. I hate when this happens.

"I know you guys think I'm too young," Sierra starts. "But I'll do whatever you say. I'll be fifteen soon. Please let me in."

"I am not here to recruit. And you're still a virgin," I tell her.

"Hopefully not for long, but I want in more." She puts her hand on my leg. "And I know you are a package deal, so" she turns Chris's head, "if you let me in, I'll do whatever you want." She pulls him in to kiss.

I sit there smiling, waiting to see what he'll say or how he'll handle her. He kisses her back.

"That will be the last time you get that. Sorry, Sierra, I'm eighteen. You're jailbait."

"Actually, in Indiana the law states that if the two are consenting, until the age of 18, they can be no more than four years apart."

She turns to me. "See? I am useful."

"I like her!" Chris says.

She puts her hand on his leg. "Well?"

"I follow Cozy's orders. She's the boss."

"What will Shelby say?" I ask.

"She'll do what either me or Rosy says. Neither of them is good with gore." Sierra grabs the seat as the lift starts moving.

"Gore?" I'm taken aback. "I thought we were talking about our get-togethers. I don't want you to go any further."

"Yes, you do. You need to have a plan in place. It's always good to have friends for back up. You need us all."

"I've been fine on my own." I look at Chris, knowing that's a lie. I just don't want to drag my friends into hell.

"You'll need us, and we want to join. We want more. Shelby doesn't want to be in the middle of it like I do. But she knows I…"

She pauses, calculating her words. It's like she's interviewing for a job.

"Shelby knows I am very good with, uh, things. I would be a good cleaner. You do what you want with them. I'll clean up after. I just want in."

"Whose idea is this?" I ask.

"Mine."

"How did you approach that?" Chris laughs. "'Hey, Shelby, I want to have sex with all our friends, and while I'm at it, I wanna kill people with Cosette. Is that okay? Ya wanna come?'"

"No, I have my own way of getting her to do what I want. I have a few secrets of my own."

"Interesting. Do you want to explain?" I ask.

"I will but only to you."

She whispers in my ear all the things she has over her sister. From naked pictures of Shelby, to getting her drunk then fooling around with her on camera, all of it to gain control.

"Holy crap! You are evil! Wow, that's really sinister. What do you have on us?"

Chris's face turns pale.

"Are we in?" she asks.

I'm hesitant. I still don't want anyone else to cross that line. But Sierra's already so far gone to do that to her own sister, I'm sure one way or another she'd find a way to get there. But I don't know that I want to be the one to guide her over.

This explains Shelby's reason for wanting to join. She was forced to by Sierra.

Sierra moves her hand up my leg. "If you want, it only has to be our secret. None of the others have to know. I can keep my mouth shut."

Chris grabs the back of her head. "What do you have on us?"

"I'm not going to blackmail you into letting me in. Am I in or not? I'll pay any price."

"I don't know. First price, you have to give me the pictures and tapes of Shelby. We don't do that to family."

"Done."

"Second price, you tell anyone, if you can't keep a secret, then I will kill you. I have no problem with that," I say as we approach the end of the lift.

"You mean you *both* have no problem with that." She positions herself to get off the lift. "I see things my dad and his cops don't." She stands up and nonchalantly skis forward. Chris and I numbly follow.

We ski out to Hilda and Shelby who are waiting for us.

"Did you guys have a nice trip up?" Hilda asks.

"I don't know, did we?" Sierra smiles at me.

I guess the decision is up to me. I feel like I'm being blackmailed. Although, if she knows all these things, including Chris's involvement, it could be advantageous.

"Yes, it was a good ride up." I say looking at Sierra. "I hate it when it halts in the middle like that, and we're left dangling."

"As long as we make it, I'm happy," Sierra says. "Last one down takes Shelby's virginity." She laughs and takes off.

"My sister can be evil." Shelby stands there embarrassed. I feel bad for her.

"We'll look out for her." I move close. "We'll take care of you both."

I don't know if she understands, but it helps her to relax. Shelby starts down the slope. Chris follows. How horrible for her to be degraded and used by her younger sister.

AFTER A FEW more runs, I'm done. I can't handle any more. It's been a while since I've been jogging, and I'm a bit out of shape. And my side kind of hurts from being jabbed on Wednesday.

I turn in my boots and skis and sit in the lodge, waiting for the others to finish. With a cappuccino and a great view, I enjoy watching the slopes.

"MIND IF I sit?" a familiar voice asks.

"Sure."

Officer Crance sits. I'm happy to see her. "What are you doing up here?"

"I have family in the area. I came to see them earlier. You told me you would be here all weekend. Where are you staying?"

"We rented a cabin. Is this business or personal? Either way, it's good to see you. I kind of feel bad about our last meeting. I don't want to screw things up for you," I apologize.

"I think we'll be okay. We just have to be cautious. And if you move your activities across the river to Kentucky or Ohio, then we'll be fine. I can get you names for over there if you want."

"I want. But I want the worst of the worst. It makes me feel better if I have a reason other than my own pleasure. Does that make sense?"

"I am very, very glad to hear that. Our little friendship will go a long way if you have your standards."

She pulls out a bag of chips for us to sit and snack on. It's nice sitting here talking to her casually. She's like an older sister giving advice. She's apprehensive about Chris though. If she only knew he's my biggest help, but I can't put him in that position. I have to protect him, at least until I know her better.

"So you're not going to ski?" I ask.

"I came here for you."

My belly giggles at the thought. "Really? You have a name?"

"Can you get away from your friends? He's local."

"I can sneak out late tonight. I'll do anything." I wiggle, excited.

"Good. Here you go." She hands me a first name and phone number. "He's a recluse. It might be a while before anyone finds him. So no need to rush. Keep it clean. No mistakes. Got it?"

"What did he do?"

"Altar boys." She gets up. "Have fun, no mistakes." She waves as she leaves.

IT TAKES VERY little research to find him on a local map. From what I can tell, he lives on a fifteen-acre lot out in the woods. I have to think. Who am I going to take? Hilda for sure, but Sierra? I'll wait until Chris is done with his ski runs.

My mind is racing, and I'm so excited. Hilda will be excited too.

One by one the gang trickles in, but I'm calm, don't want anyone to know anything yet. I have to define a few rules and make sure I know who's on board and who isn't.

At the cabin, we take turns in the spa-like showers. Some together, some separate. We decide to go eat at the French Lick Casino where a group this size won't draw as much attention as we would in a mom and pop diner.

Chris sits with his plate piled high with food. "You're not eating much, and you're awfully quiet. Are you going to tell me what's going on?"

I lean over to whisper in his ear. "Jenny came by. I have a local name."

His eyes brighten as he tries to hold in a smile. "It's Hilda's turn."

I nod in agreement. I think the high of going again is stronger than my need to protect Hilda. I get a rise when I think of her with me in that truck. I think about her holding him down, kissing him, kissing me, watching the dimming. I'm ready to take her now.

"What are you two whispering about?" Rose asks.

"About what we do best." I smile without adding an explanation.

Decker sits with two plates full. "You know I just noticed, Chris, there are, one, two, three, four, five girls to us two guys. I hope you're up for the challenge."

"Oh, no," I say. "I won't allow Shelby and Sierra to lose their purity to the likes of you two."

"Why not?" Sierra asks. "I want to. I was hoping to. I didn't get invited to the last one." She stares at Chris.

Shelby says nothing. I guess this is a settled discussion between the two sisters.

"I thought this was going to be a normal, have fun with your friends, ski outing. What happened to that? We don't have to have sex every time we get together," I say, even though I'm desperate to, especially now.

"We don't have to, but, let's see." Decker holds Rose's hand. "No parents for miles, cabin by ourselves, five hot girls to pick from... Hmmmm, what were you planning on doing way out here? Read a book?" He's definitely getting over his jealousy issues.

"Not all of us have gone there yet," I remind him. "I don't want anyone to feel obligated or uncomfortable."

"I can have fun other ways. I won't mind." Shelby surprises me.

"Good. Let's go back to the cabin." Hilda's ready.

So am I. The high is building.

Chapter FORTY-SIX

WE PAD THE living room floor with the blankets, pillows, and comforters from the three bedrooms. It's like one giant bed.

I sit back on the couch to watch for a bit. I want to see who takes care of whom. Who is selfish? Who's domineering? Who's submissive? I'm learning a great deal. And Shelby's right, she does have fun in other ways. She's having a lot of fun with Rose and Decker. Of course, the three shots of tequila she downed as we were setting up helps.

Sierra comes up to me. Her tiny body swims in her oversized t-shirt. She wedges herself between my legs. As she kisses up my thighs, her big light-brown eyes look at me. "I want Chris to be my first. Is that okay? Will you help me?"

I shift my hips forward. If she wants Chris, she has to earn him. She smiles and takes her time. She does well, and I wonder if this is what's on the tape with Shelby. I can tell this isn't new to her.

"THANK YOU. THAT was awesome! Relax now, lie back." I tell her after she finishes. As she lies back, Chris comes over to us and lies next to her. His soft hands stroke Sierra's naturally tan skin.

"Hold on." Shelby comes by and stops him. She kisses his neck down his cut chest then down his abs. He's so sexy, and it's erotic watching Shelby go down on him. "You've got to be perfect for my sister. Don't hurt her."

I take off Sierra's shirt and kiss down her stomach. I work on her like she did me, using my fingers to loosen her up for Chris.

After Shelby gets him ready, she puts Chris's protection on then guides him as he carefully mounts her sister.

He's so gentle with Sierra, taking into account that this is her first time. Shelby kisses Chris while I kiss Sierra.

Sierra's eyes well up. She looks up to me and blinks out the tears. I stroke her hair, wanting it to be perfect. But she doesn't love Chris like I do. It's not the same.

"Shhhh, relax." I kiss her gently.

"I can't, Cozy."

"It's okay, Sierra. Try to relax." I massage her thighs as Chris slowly presses in to her tiny body.

Shelby kisses Sierra's neck and strokes her hair, trying to make her feel better. It's strange how these sisters are acting. Sierra has total control of Shelby.

I hold Shelby's hand and pull her away from Sierra and Chris. Hilda comes and starts massaging Shelby with me.

"Since you're not going all the way, we'll pay extra attention to you." Hilda rubs Shelby's feet kissing up her calves then thighs.

I play with those two for a while then move on to Decker and Rose. After a few minutes, I look over to Chris. He's holding back. I am too. As I crawl over to Chris, my craving grows. We're both pumped up and want each other. And no one else can handle what we need.

Sierra's doing better, but it's still uncomfortable for her. I think she's scared Chris will hurt her.

Chris carefully pulls away.

"Do you want me to run a tub? Sometimes it helps." I ask her.

Sierra nods.

"I'll take care of her." Shelby takes her away.

I grab Chris. "It's my turn. I've been holding back so give me all you got. You better make it good."

"I've been waiting for this." He picks me up and carries me to a different room so we don't scare the others. He's rough, and I'm ready. He knows what comes after this, so it charges us both up.

He's cruel and sadistic. I fight back to make him work harder, loving the pain he uses to enhance the pleasure.

After a while, we notice the others are staring at us, horrified. I guess in their eyes, they're witnessing a violent, sexual assault. Hilda sees a reenactment of her rape. She closes the door and lets us finish.

"OH, MY GOD, Cosette! Is that what I heard?" Shelby asks as I make my way to the bathroom. She's sitting on the other side of the bath holding Sierra's hand.

We don't yell or scream. I guess she heard thumps and bumps.

"Do you want to get in the tub?" Sierra asks, looking at my fresh bruises and welts, evidence of my kind of fun.

I nod.

She scoots forward and runs warm water. I get in behind her.

"Lay back on me, Sierra. It's okay."

"Is it always like that with you and Chris?" she asks. She wraps my legs around her and massages my feet.

"There are a few times I like it gentle. But most of the time, that's what I want."

"Do you mind if I leave? I really need a drink." Shelby closes the bathroom door.

"CHRIS WATCHES OUT for me." I lather the soap then massage Sierra's shoulders. "I have to be careful. With my issues, things get hard on me. Sometimes I can't control it, and I almost killed Hilda, twice. So what you heard is sometimes how it has to be. It's my release."

"Aren't you scared?"

"No, unfortunately not much anymore. How are you?"

"I didn't expect that to feel that way," she says.

"It's nothing like what you see in the movies, soft and beautiful. I tried to help you. I'm sorry if I got in the way."

She reaches her arm behind my head and pulls me around to kiss. "You were perfect, and he was pretty gentle too. I guess he was holding back a lot. Thank you." She shifts to the side so she can see me better. "I have something to tell you, Cozy." She holds my hands.

"Anything."

"I know about Chris. Don't worry, I won't say anything." She pours some shampoo in my hands.

"Why don't you tell me what you think you know?" I lather her up.

"I think he likes to kill like you do. I thought he was the Poser, especially after his uncle and cousin were killed. I did a bit of digging in a direction that my dad's cops didn't. I'm glad they didn't. I erased everything." Her childlike expression would make anyone trust her. I am not that naïve. She continues. "I was surprised that his uncle Ben was the Poser, but that's who kidnapped you, so it had to be him."

"I think you need to forget what you found. Until he comes out on his own, I am the only one who kills. Do you understand?"

"I will do whatever you want. But why don't you want anyone else to know about him? Are you protecting him from the group or the group from him? Who's protecting you?"

"Chris protects me. Here sit up, let me rinse you.".

Instead she slides forward and dips her hair in the water. I run my fingers through, rinsing the shampoo out. "That feels good, thanks. I should be getting out." She stands up and turns around. "Wow, he did a number on you, huh? Strange form of protection."

"This protects you guys from me," I say.

I turn on the hot as soon as she steps out of the tub. Chris, coming in, passes her.

She stops him and kisses him. "Thank you."

He shuts the door behind her.

"What's happening out there?" I ask him.

"They're all done out there, but I think we scared everyone." He frowns.

"Did they say anything to you?"

"No, but…" He turns off the hot. "I don't need you to have third-degree burns along with what I gave you."

"I'm fine." My legs are bright red in the soapy, scalding water. "I have to get out anyway. I'm so excited we have a name. Did you tell them anything?" I stand up and squeeze the water out of my hair.

"No, I figured you might want to tell them. Cosette, I love you so much, and I don't want to push you, but we need them. You will be so much better off having them on your side."

"Yeah, I know. I don't like it, but I know we'd be better off. And guess who definitely knows about you?"

"Sierra's that good?"

"She pegged you as the Poser but dismissed it when I killed Tear Tattoo. Apparently, she follows her dad's work closely. She erased what she found. I'm glad we're letting her in. She could've been dangerous if we hadn't. But Hilda has to be the first."

Chris wraps the towel around me with a big hug. "I want you to tell the group. I don't think they're too happy with me."

"Because of me and this?" I take the towel off to dry my bright red legs and dinged up body.

"Yup. I love you so much. I'll never do anything to hurt you. You know I would never do this out of anger."

"I know. I'm fine. Come on, I need to get dressed."

We step out of the bathroom, and I rummage through my bag for clothes. "What? What are you all looking at? You've all seen me naked. What are you looking at?"

"How can you let him do that to you?" Hilda asks in utter disbelief. She's almost in tears.

"Let him? What Chris and I did is what I want. It's what I need. That's my kind of pleasure. I'm sorry if it bothers you guys. Hilda, this is what I warned you about. You wanted to see how I see? My reds are redder? My blues are bluer? If I didn't get that relief from Chris, then you would have been dead a long time ago."

Hilda slightly rubs her bite scar.

"You're a fucking psycho. Have you ever thought about therapy? Or anything?" Decker actually seems concerned.

"Actually, yeah. I go to church with Mattie. I try to be good. She comes over to pray with me. She gives me Bible lessons and stuff. So far, that's the only thing that has remotely helped me. That and Chris keeping me in control. And, Decker, as you already know, all of you, Mattie is off limits. We will not mention our parties or anything in her presence. Got it? I will not recruit her."

They all nod.

"I'M THIRSTY," I casually announce.

We all gravitate to the kitchen and plant ourselves around the table and the countertops.

"So what now?" Rose asks.

"It's too early for bed," Shelby says.

"Yeah, so, Cozy, what do you do late at night?" Rose asks, looking for drama, baiting me.

I shake my head. Chris leans in to me and whispers. "Now's the time, Bonnie. They're gonna keep bugging you, so you might as well let them in."

I purse my lips. I know he's right. It's time to let them in. It's time to play.

"I'll follow your lead," I whisper to Chris. "I don't want to make this decision. If you want, it's on you."

"You're gonna thank me in the long run. Believe me," Chris assures me. He turns to the group who are holding their breath in anticipation of what I might say. They've been anxiously waiting for a few days now. "We have some important things to discuss." They all sit up. "I love Cosette, and I will do anything to protect her."

"We want to protect her too." Sierra is excited. "We know what she's done, and we're willing to do what it takes to join you guys."

Shelby nudges her to calm down.

"You have no idea what you're asking," I say. "You have no idea the shit that comes with this. I'm not on a mission. I'm sick, and you all want my disease. Don't you understand?"

"We understand the ones you've killed deserve to be killed," Rose adds.

"I was attacked. I fought back. There is nothing to join."

"Yeah, we've heard that before. But you need alibis. You need help hiding things. We know what the police look for. Shelby and I know how to keep secrets." Sierra looks at Shelby.

"Let's say Cosette's willing to let you guys in on her life," Chris says. "Are you willing to go to jail for this? Because that's a never-ending possibility."

"If we help, then you won't even be a suspect," Sierra states. I'm not happy about putting others through this, yet I'm happy at the thought of having help. I'm thrilled to know that I can be myself and that I have support. I have a family.

"Okay, here's the deal. I'll give you guys one more chance to back out. You can stay and play and be safe, or you can live with the consequences. You decide."

Everyone sits silent.

"Crap, that's not what I wanted," I tell Chris.

Chris kisses my forehead, assuring me it's alright. "Okay, then by none of you leaving, you all know what you're agreeing to?"

"Yes, we're excited too," Hilda says. Everyone agrees.

"If you have even the slightest bit of doubt, then you need to leave."

No one moves.

"As of right now, you all are about to be accessories to murder. You do know that, right?" he asks them.

"Enough already. Let us in." Sierra wiggles.

"Accessories to murder? Hello?" I wave my hand in front of their faces.

"About to be? Chris, you said about to be. Do you have someone?" Hilda perks up.

The room is instantly energized.

"I will say nothing until we're all sworn to secrecy."

"I got a better idea." Sierra goes around the room plucking a few strands of hair from everyone. Then she places them in a baggie. She then asks for my knife.

"I give my knife to no one," I firmly say.

"Fine. Chris? Hilda? Surely one of you two?"

Hilda brings out Red. "What are you doing, Sierra?"

"Think of it like a blood promise," Sierra says.

Chris and I look at each other. I glance at my tiny scar on the inside of my forearm from my blood promise to Chris.

317

"Here, I'll do it. I've done it before," Chris says. He slices his wrist, and it starts bleeding. Sierra goes to the cabin closet and takes out seven clean hand towels, one for each of us. On each towel, she dabs blood from each of us. Seven hand towels, seven spots.

"There, we're all sworn to secrecy." Sierra says. "If one of us gets caught or breaks, we all get caught. We'll put on a new spot for each victim. Now we have to trust each other. Does that count?"

"Perfect. Also, no one says a word to anyone, even as a joke, even in passing. We cannot trigger any curiosity. Got it? I didn't get this far by being careless. So now do you all agree?"

They all agree.

"One more thing, afterwards you might get depression, anxiety attacks, guilt that will make you want to commit suicide. I know. I did.

"If you all can't deal then please, please, leave now. I don't want you all going through that. Shelby, Rose, the further you stay away from the scene, the more protected you are from the images that will haunt your nightmares."

They nod in agreement.

I continue. "Speaking of nightmares. We are all going to hell because of this. Eternal hell. This moment of pleasure is condemning us forever. It may not be a big deal to you now, but it will be later. If you want out, go to Mattie. She'll help you. I think I'm too far gone for that."

"Also, remember Mattie's gonna know." Chris says. "She probably knows what's going on now. It's a bit disturbing. Just thought I'd remind you about that. Lunch at school might be very uncomfortable."

I agree. "I call it her God-sense. It's kind of creepy, but remember, she knows. Just be expecting it."

"Yeah, Mattie's perfect," Hilda states. "We can't let our filth infect her." I detect a slight bit of jealousy in what she said, but apparently I'm the only one who caught it.

"So now that you generally know what's going on, who's out? And I hope it's all of you," I beg.

No one leaves.

"I don't want to be anywhere near the grossness. I'll do anything else, but I'm in. How do you pick your victims?" Shelby asks.

"They pick me. They attack me or someone else. Then I know they are bad. Like the skating rink guy. And the New Albany couple with the baby. I just so happened to be at the right place at the right time."

"Holy shit! That was you? You killed the New Albany couple? Her eyes were still open!" Decker's in disbelief. He worked on her in his uncle's funeral home.

"I wanted to be the last thing she saw," I coldly say. "So it's final. You're all in?"

"We're all in," Rose naively announces.

They all nod.

"Fine. Twelve. My body count is twelve," I say.

They gasp.

"Are, are you kidding?" Hilda's breath is taken away.

All of them are speechless. I don't think they expected me to come right out and say it, nor did they expect that high of a number.

"Since mid-December, yes, I have killed twelve people. One of them I cut up into fifteen pieces. Oh, that was a great day. I'm telling you this, letting you know what I am. I have no problem with it. And yes, I was silent, trying to protect you, but now that you're in, you have to know who you're dealing with. I love to kill. I prefer it to sex. It's my addiction. I can't help it. I need it. Oh, I do love it.

"I'll let you all help, watch, whatever. I'll let you all do as little or as much as you want. But I don't want you guys to be like this. So if we do it together, then it will be very controlled. Got it?"

"Shit! Hold on! I'm still trying to comprehend twelve." Decker's in serious unbelief.

"Did you really cut him up into fifteen pieces?" Shelby seems worried.

"Yes, she did. And she's got a thing with order and neatness, so I didn't have a problem cleaning up after her."

"Well fuck! Chris, how long have you been helping her?" Decker asks.

Chris cuddles with me and whispers. "Should I?"

"Don't tell them who you are, just give them a number," I whisper.

"Yes, Decker, I help her. This is who we are together." He gives my cheek an endearing kiss.

"How many have you helped her with, Chris?" Rose timidly asks.

"How many have I helped her with or have I killed?"

"No, no, no fucking way!" Decker's shaking.

"Chris hasn't killed anyone, have you?" Hilda pitifully asks.

"Seventeen." Chris answers her while gazing into my eyes. I am so in love.

"Oh, fuck!" Decker stands up. "Oh, fuck! Oh, fuck!" He's freaking out.

They all are.

Hilda holds the wall to keep from passing out. Her all-American heartthrob is a freak. Shelby holds her hands on her face, trying not to cry. Rose is shaking while trying to get a shot of Shelby's tequila.

Sierra just smiles, confirming something she knew all along.

"You'd think if you were going to have sex with someone, you should get to know them a bit better, huh?" I joke.

Only Chris and I laugh.

Everyone else is trying to recover. Rose runs to the bathroom to throw up.

"It's okay, Rose. I did that the first time too. You'll get numb to it."

"Between the two of you, that's about thirty! You're serial killers! We're in a fucking cabin with two fucking serial killers!" Decker was still freaking. "I thought she was the psycho! Chris, you're my best friend! Fuck!"

"Fifteen pieces? Why? What did he do to deserve that?" Shelby asks.

"I was saving myself for Chris. He tried to take my virginity from me. I killed him before I cut him up. I'm not unnecessarily cruel." I roll my eyes at her.

"You all should have seen her." Chris softly holds my chin. "It was beautiful. She spread out on top of him, kissed him, stared into his eyes."

"You saw all of that? I thought you were out."

"I'm so glad I got to see." He caresses my cheek.

"What about yours, Chris? Who did you kill?" Decker asks, hurt that he didn't know.

"Chris's were boring. He used a gun. I like my knife. That way I can slowly watch the dimming."

Chris kisses me in thanks for taking the focus off him.

"What's the dimming?" Sierra's intrigued.

"Hilda?" I look to her.

"Hilda? Fuck! You too?" Decker snaps.

"Oh relax, she didn't do anything. Yet." I reach my hand out to her. She comes up to the counter and stands between my knees, facing the group. I wrap my arms and legs around her. "That was one of my favorite ones," I whisper to her while kissing her neck.

"I only held him down while Cozy killed him. I got to watch the light leave his eyes as he died. That's the dimming."

"You are sick. You two, three are fucked up! Fuck!" Decker yells.

"We offered you an out! You didn't have to stay!" I defend myself.

Rose comes out of the bathroom. "I'm okay. I think."

"I'm not," Decker says.

"Thirty people. Between both of you? I don't remember that many murders," Shelby says.

"Not all the bodies were found. Fifteen pieces, remember?"

The look on her face is disgust.

Rose's is the same.

I'M GETTING UPSET at their reactions. I expected it. I hoped for it. It means I have normal friends. However, they asked for it, and now I feel like I'm being judged! I move Hilda to the side.

"What the hell did you all think you were volunteering for?" I yell.

They sit, ashamed.

"Did I not tell you to leave? Did I not warn you? How clear does someone have to be? I almost killed Hilda twice because it's hard to control! I warned you all! I mean... shit!" I pop off the counter. "I have someone. I'm going to kill tonight, and I'll be leaving soon. You can either join me, or stay here and keep your damn mouths shut. Either way is fine with me, but this is what I look forward to, and you're not going to spoil it!" I go to the bedroom and slam the door.

AFTER PACING AROUND the bed to calm down, I open my laptop to do some planning.

They stay in the kitchen to talk. I wish I knew what they were saying, but at this point in time it doesn't matter to me. They all know; they know what I'm about to do, and none of them have the balls to stop me.

I check the weather. It's warming up. It says it'll start raining around two or three this morning. That's good since it should melt my footprints out of the snow.

I check the satellite of the guy's house and his property. I think I can make this look like an accident. He has a lot of woods to trip and fall in. If I can mask the knife wound with a tree branch or rock then I can pass it off. Hopefully, the cops out here are too busy to deeply investigate the murder of a pedophile.

I sit on the driftwood-framed bed and face the mirrored closet doors. I start a tight French braid in my hair. Rose knocks on the door, comes in, and sits behind me.

"Here, let me do that." She takes over the braid.

Hilda comes and sits next to me. Shelby gets behind her and works on her long blonde hair. "We need you girls to be completely incognito. Is that the right word?"

My bottom lip starts to quiver.

"Oh, Cozy, it's okay." Rose gives me a hug.

I start to cry. "I thought you guys hated me. I know I have a problem, and when I finally came out, I thought you all…"

"Would leave you? Reject you?" Sierra asks as she crawls onto the bed.

"Apparently you don't know us that well," Shelby answers.

"Yeah, you'd think if you were going to have sex with someone, you should get to know them a bit better, huh?" Rose laughs and hugs me.

"Oh, Cozy, don't cry. I'm here." Hilda holds me too. "We're with you. I know how hard it's been on you just with the few we knew about. I can't imagine the stress of being all alone with that many."

"How did Chris find out?" Shelby asks.

"He figured out the ice rink guy. But he had to pick me up from numbers three and four, and five and six. Five and six beat me up pretty bad. I couldn't walk home."

"Is that what happened to your back when I saw it that day in the principal's?" Hilda recalls. "Oh my gosh, Cozy. I am so sorry."

"Stop apologizing. I'm a stronger person now. I'm happier, as sick as it is. But it drove me to suicide.

"Up until I came back from being shot, that's all I wanted. The guilt and pain was too much. So if you have any doubts, please do not join me."

"Rose and I talked," Shelby says. "And we've decided that we'll stay back and help any way we can. Sierra wants to be right there and help you after the fact. I think the only one who wants to engage is you, Hilda, right?"

"Right. I'm next." Hilda beams.

"I'll watch, and help clean up. I want to see this dimming, but I don't want to kill anyone." Sierra sits between her sister and Rose. We all face the closet mirrors.

"So this is it? This is my gang?" I smile as the tears roll down.

"We're all yours. What do you want to call us?" Sierra asks.

"We're not all here. Where is Decker? Is he out?" I ask.

"He and Chris are having a best-friend's heart to heart," Shelby says.

"I think he's hurt," Rose says.

"Chris didn't want to turn him," I tell her. "Just like I didn't want to turn you girls. I hate doing this to you. I don't want to make your lives miserable like my life has been."

"We're there in one way or another. As a matter of fact, you can call us The Miserables. Cosette Hugo's Miserables," Shelby proudly suggests.

"That is so inappropriate and perfect at the same time," I tell her. I always hated that name. Maybe now I'll break down and read the book or see the musical.

Chris and Decker come in and sit on the bed with us girls. Rose is almost done braiding my hair.

"We can't leave any strands behind," she tells Decker.

He sadly nods his head in agreement.

She ties off the ends and turns to hug him. He closes his eyes and hugs her tight. He presses out a few tears. I feel for him. He's now stuck.

They all are.

It's a sobering moment.

CHRIS KNEELS IN front of me. "Are you okay, baby? No more secrets. You can breathe. Here with your friends, you can breathe." He holds my hands.

"So can you, Chris. How do you feel?"

He sighs. "Free. I finally feel free."

Coming Soon

in the

My Beautiful Suicide Series:

How to Kill a Pedophile
Stupid, Stupid Girl

Turn the page for an excerpt from the third book in the series:

How to Kill a Pedophile

Chapter One

MY HAIR IS slicked and sprayed. Every long dark strand is tucked away. Shelby is pinning Sierra's curls back. Rose ties off Hilda's french braid then sprays down the loose blonde flyaways. Chris and Decker call us into the living room. My family, the Misérables, kneel around the coffee table, the Reds, the sisters, my lovers, and me.

The excitement in the cabin is growing as we plan our adventure. Even after a long day of skiing, a night of sex, and a huge secret revealed that would blow any normal teenager away, my friends still want to go with me.

I have an addiction, and today my supplier, Officer Jenny Crance, gave me my poison. This particular poison is guilty of doing altar boys. But this kill is Hilda's. I promised my princess she could have him.

All of us are in agreement. Even Decker's onboard. I guess his insecurity of not really knowing that his best friend, Chris, is a serial killer, got to him. Glad he still doesn't know Chris is one-third of the Poser gang. That secret needs to stay hidden, especially since it was this gang that kidnapped and raped Hilda, the first time.

Sierra's legs are bouncing she's so excited. Her older sister Shelby is not. Shelby's been blackmailed by Sierra to do whatever Sierra wants. This apparently includes killing with us. When we get back home however, I'm confiscating the blackmail videos young Sierra has of Shelby. These sisters are my girls now, and we don't do that to family.

It's one in the morning, and we're ready. Hilda has her knife tucked away in her cleavage. That's an advantage I wish I had. I tuck my knife, Gorgo, in my snow boots. She's bulky. I like that she is. She has substance and strength.

Shelby rides with the Reds, Rose and Decker, in Decker's car. I ride with Hilda and Sierra in Chris's truck. We pull up to our victim's driveway. It's a long dirt road packed with light snow. This is good. Our tires are quieter in fluffy snow. Since it's out in the middle of nowhere, it's perfect for the Misérable's first outing. We park about fifty yards away from his house.

Decker, Rose, and Shelby stand around the car and truck acting as lookouts. Even though we're out in the middle of the night, in the middle of the woods, things still creep and we need to be alert.

Sierra, Chris, and I get our hats and gloves on and sneak with Hilda up to the house. She points to the shed out back. Since this is her scene, we follow her lead. She opens the shed door, whispers to Sierra, and then lets her in. Chris and Hilda hide on one side of the shed. I hide next to the house.

Sierra starts knocking things over, rattling old gas cans, and banging trash can lids, anything to lure our victim outside.

A light brightens his window, and I bite my lip in excitement. The back door squeaks and out comes a balding, heavyset man wearing sweats and a stained wife-beater t-shirt. This is the outfit he's going to die in. Sad. It almost makes me want to ask him to change.

He opens the shed door, grumbling and cursing the damn raccoons that got in again. With a dim flashlight, he lights the corners of the old rickety structure. When he gets to the last corner, Chris pops out and hits the back of his head with a paving stone. He falls backwards onto the snowy path.

Slightly dizzy, he yells at the critter in his shed. We run out to hold him down. Sierra takes one arm; I take the other. Chris sits on his legs.

Brutal awareness wakes him, making him fight hard. Since we don't want to leave marks on his arms that would cause an investigation, Sierra and I wedge his forearms between our legs and use our weight to hold them still. He starts to scream. I shove snow in his mouth to shut him up.

I slide my body up to talk to him, careful to keep my distance from the hair growing from his ear. Has this pedophile no hygiene routine?

"Relax. Shhh, it's okay. You don't have to struggle anymore. I know how hard it is to be an addict. The shame of what you've done, the guilt of hurting people, it'll be over soon. You'll be free from your addiction."

"Come on, princess. Showtime!" Chris calls Hilda to action. She straddles him like I do my victims. She doesn't spread her body out over him though. I guess everyone has their own methods.

"What are you doing?" The victim half-spits half-swallows the snow. "I said I was sorry. Those boys were lying!"

"Lying, huh? I don't think so." Hilda presses her knife up against his cheek. "I want you to think back on them and remember them as I kill you."

By his thinning hair, she lifts his head and places the paving stone Chris used under it. "Open your eyes and stop crying. Now's the time to make your peace with God. Start praying. I'll give you a minute."

She lays her knife on his chest and waits patiently while he mumbles out a prayer. I stroke his gray hair, shushing him, calming him down. I can't help but think of Mattie. Mattie would find it nice that Hilda is giving him time to pray.

"Have you made your peace?" Hilda asks.

He turns his head to me. "Why are you doing this?"

"Because, this is my addiction. I'll make my peace later."

Hilda leaves her knife on his chest then lifts up his head by his ears.

"Here it goes," I say. "I hope you're right with God."

Hilda slams his head down on the stone. His eyes blink. She lifts it again and slams it down a bit softer. "Sierra, look." Hilda shines his flashlight on his face. His eyes slowly close. "That's the dimming."

"Cozy, is that his soul leaving?" Sierra asks me.

"I don't know." I'm taken back. "I never thought of it as that. Interesting."

His body jolts. I guess that'll be the only shaking I'll get from this kill. The red blood melts the snow as it spreads. We all stand up except for Sierra who pulls out our hand towels. She dips her finger in his blood then dots each towel, binding our group together. She rolls them up then stands.

"Hold on; don't move. Stay where you are," she says. "Let me look this over." Sierra shines the light on us, inspecting us and the scene. "Shuffle your feet side to side as we walk back to the cars. We don't want deep prints in the snow. The rain should melt it away." The police chief's daughter shows her upbringing.

We head towards the cars and Hilda stops to look back. "Thanks, you guys!" She leaps up to Chris to kiss him, then to me, then to Sierra. She's so animated. It makes me happy. Even if I didn't get the high I wanted, Hilda's excitement is enough to satisfy me for a bit.

"Is it what you expected, Sierra?" I ask.

"It happens so fast," she says.

"I know. But you can't make it last too long; it's cruel. Now you understand my need for fifteen pieces."

"I get that, yes. I can do that. I'd like that better than this. I'll be the cleaner. I'd like that job. I don't wanna kill anyone." Sierra's eyes smile at the prospect.

WE GET BACK to the cabin, and even as we're warming up, Hilda's starting to shake. I don't know if she's cold or crashing. "Baby, are you okay?" I ask.

"I'm freezing. A warm fire would be nice." She holds my hand and walks me over to the fireplace to turn it on. "Thank you." She pets my long braid. "It wasn't as good as our first time, but I loved it." She kisses me, giggles, and then kisses me again. Excited, she goes around the room hugging and kissing everyone.

"Not enough excitement? You're starting up again?" Rose asks Hilda.

"I'm in!" Chris strips off his sweatshirt. He grabs my braid and pulls me into a hard kiss.

"Shit, Chris!" I yell and push him away.

The red and blue lights of a police car halt our fun. "In the bedrooms, now! You all say a word and I'll kill you myself!"

They scatter into the bedrooms.

Acknowledgements

I WANT TO give special thanks to; Lisa Binion for all her hard work trying to make this book error-free, to Heather Adkins from CyberWitch Press for her formatting making it readable, to Laura at LLPix Designs for the fantastic cover, and to my beautiful cover model, Madison Middleton, for being my perfect Cosette.

And special thanks to my beta readers: Pamela Sims, Beth Swinning, John Harper, Jennifer Klaehn, and Amy Swift. Thank you all for telling me when it sucked and when it didn't.

For more information on Atty Eve and the My Beautiful Suicide series, visit her website at AttyEve.com.

Made in the USA
Monee, IL
10 October 2022